Praise for Sister Souljah's unforgettable novels

MIDNIGHT, A Gangster Love Story

"A tour de force. . . . As finely tuned to its heroine's voice as Alice Walker's *The Color Purple*. . . . Riveting stuff, with language so frank it curls your hair."

—*Kirkus Reviews*

"Winter is nasty, spoiled, and almost unbelievably libidinous, and it's ample evidence of the author's talent that she is also deeply sympathetic."

—*The New Yorker*

"Intriguing. . . . Sister Souljah exhibits a raw and true voice in this cautionary tale. . . . A realistic coming-of-age story."

—*Publishers Weekly*

"Real and raw. . . . If a rap song could be a novel, it might resemble Sister Souljah's book. . . . The message is solid and one that we can never stop preaching to our youth—anything that comes too easy or too fast is also too risky."

—*Booklist*

"Sometimes the stuggle has to be repackaged to get a point across. Sister Souljah, one of hip-hop's perennial forces and a self-described 'raptivist,' does this with her first novel. . . . *The Coldest Winter Ever* is a platform for this resourceful young activist to spread messages that are clear, concise, and true to the game."

—*The Source*

"Souljah has an engaging style that makes the novel a fast, fun read."

—*The Plain Dealer* (Cleveland)

"Hip-hop sage and activist Sister Souljah has taken her talents from the stage to the page."

—*Essence*

"This is a ghetto fairy tale with a surprise ending. . . . There's a lesson to be learned from *The Coldest Winter Ever*."
—*Tennessean* (Nashville)

"Compelling. . . . Tugs at the emotions."
—*Chicago Sun-Times*

"Winter is . . . as tough as a hollow-point bullet. . . . Her voice is the book's greatest strength."
—Salon.com

"This is a wild tale. . . . Sister Souljah has painted a vivid portrait of a girl you'd rather have as a friend than an enemy."
—*Seventeen*

"The power of Sister Souljah's writing enthralled me from the first page. I hope she will continue making young men and women think, letting them know they have choices and that they can change their world."
—Fictionforest.com

"Souljah, an Émile Zola of the hip-hop generation, has written a naturalist novel of a world without redemption. Her story, like the cultures it exposes, is an unflinching eye at the truth."
—*New York Times* bestselling author Walter Mosley

Also by Sister Souljah

No Disrespect

The Coldest Winter Ever

MIDNIGHT

A GANGSTER LOVE STORY

SISTER SOULJAH

POCKET **STAR** BOOKS

New York   London   Toronto   Sydney

Pocket Star Books
A Division of Simon & Schuster, Inc.
1230 Avenue of the Americas
New York, NY 10020

This book is a work of fiction. Names, characters, places, and incidents either are products of the author's imagination or are used fictitiously. Any resemblance to actual events or locales or persons, living or dead, is entirely coincidental.

First Pocket Star Books paperback edition September 2010

POCKET STAR and colophon are registered trademarks of Simon & Schuster, Inc.

For information about special discounts for bulk purchases, please contact Simon & Schuster Special Sales at 1-866-506-1949 or business@simonandschuster.com.

The Simon & Schuster Speakers Bureau can bring authors to your live event. For more information or to book an event, contact the Simon & Schuster Speakers Bureau at 1-866-248-3049 or visit our website at www.simonspeakers.com.

Cover design by John Vairo Jr.
Photograph by Keith Major.

Manufactured in the United States of America

10 9 8 7 6 5 4 3 2 1

ISBN 978-1-4516-1256-1
ISBN 978-1-4165-5626-8 (ebook)

DEDICATION

To powerful minds, deep voices, and long legs.

To committed hearts, fierce fighters, and passionate lovers.

To men who bow their heads, read their books, raise their fists, handle their business, and never abandon their families.

To beautiful men who still have the glow of God in their eyes.

By Sister Souljah

ACKNOWLEDGMENTS

A special thanks to every brother worldwide, who ever had a meaningful conversation with me.

A heartfelt thanks to every brother who ever taught me a lesson or shared a perspective that I did not already know or consider.

A warm thanks to all the brothers who show me both love and respect at the same time.

A resounding thanks to every brother who ever considered my words, thoughts, and feelings and used them to make a positive and powerful change in their own lives.

A revolutionary thanks to every brother who ever stood by my side, back and front in difficult times. The ones who did not run and hide when my voice hit the target, or my words seared the soul, or my truth made things too damn clear.

Warm appreciation to the more than one million females who have read, digested, understood, and reflected on my words. Thank you for buying all my books, passing them around, and using them to become better than what we are expected to be!

Peace.

Cornell, Ozman, Saadi, Esau, Kerry, Mahmoud, Glenn, Guiffrey, Tim, Devashis, Shameen, Bilal, Eric, Steve, David, Haqq, Dru, Jeffrey, Malechi, Maurice, Tony, Jeff, Sam, Byrd, Mr. Miles, John DeSane, and Charlie Mack.

Special thanks to Bill Stephney, Linsay Williams, Vernon Rudd, Kenny Gamble, Ras Baraka, Mandla Kayise, Doug

E. Fresh, Chuck D, Will Smith, Craig Hodges, Chris Webber, Bill Perkins, Esq., C. Vernon Mason, Esq., Alton Maddox, Esq., Michael Warren, Esq., Lennox Hinds, Esq., Dr. Leonard Jeffries, Reverend Dr. Calvin Butts, Reverend Dr. Ben Chavis, Reverend Dr. William Howard, Minister Louis Farrakhan, Bob Law, Gil Noble, Reverend Jesse Louis Jackson, Governor David Patterson, Tupac Shakur, KRS 1, LL Cool J, Ice Cube, Wise Intelligent, Tragedy, Kane.

To the one of a kind: Sean Puffy Puff Daddy Diddy P. Diddy Combs.

A professional thanks to Emily Bestler who welcomed me in, treated me properly and worked through the awesome process. Also to the publishing boss, Judith Curr.

A very special thanks to: Yuki Morita, Sensei Mariko, and Moo.

Thanks to Steve Wasserman and Bob Scheer.

Big up to Brooklyn.

Thank you to Mitsuwa, Edgewater, New Jersey, and Pimaan Thai, Emerson, New Jersey.

Sisterly thanks to: Dr. Monica Martin, Gervonne Rice, Lisa Sweet, Waafa Abdalla, and Kenya Woods.

A loving thank-you to my husband and son as always and forever.

All praise is due to God.
I thank God for my life
and breath, my purpose and
for inspiration, imagination,
protection, and prosperity.
Peace.

MIDNIGHT

1

WORD TO LIFE

I am not who you think I am. If you love me, you love me for the wrong reasons.

Females tell me they love me because I'm tall. They love when I stand over them and look down. They love when I lay them down and my height and body weight dominates them.

Females tell me they love me because I'm pure black. They say they never seen a black man so masculine, so pretty, so beautiful before.

Females say they love my eyes. They're jet black too. Women claim they find a passion in them so forceful that they'll do anything I say.

Females tell me they love my body. They beg me for a hug even when there's nothing between me and them. They want to be captured in my embrace, and press their breasts against my chest.

Some females ask if they can just touch me. Some tremble when my hands touch them. They say they love the muscles in my arms. They surrender when I lift them up. They whine and moan in rapture. Some cry their pleasure. Some shake. Some pee.

Some of 'em even say they love the way my teeth look in my mouth and how my feet look in my kicks.

Females tell me they love the way I walk, like I'm soon to own the world.

Most females say they love that I'm quiet. Then shiver when I finally talk.

All of the women show me that they love my guns, the fact that I walk with two of them at times. Even the ones who get scared fall in love with their fear of me. Then they come at me even harder.

Some females say I'm too serious, then shield their eyes to hide their feelings from the shine when I finally smile.

I can't lie, I enjoy the good times that some of these women offer me. But I don't take them to heart. I know that they don't really even know me. All the shit that they are in love with is just my style and my looks, all window dressing.

I know that a man is his own beliefs, his own ideas and actions. If you knew me, you would know what I believe. If you knew what I believe, then you would understand how I think. You would understand my ideas and actions. Only then should you decide. Either you believe what I believe, or you admire what I believe and want to get with those beliefs. If not, in the long run, we got nothing in common. I can't take you seriously. I gotta go. You got nothing that makes me want to stay.

I don't come from where you come from. I don't think like you do. My whole situation is different. I come from a country of real men who take real life, real serious.

I wouldn't trade places with an American-born man for any amount of cash.

Where I'm from, a son has a first name and three last names. The three last names are the names of his father, grandfather, and great-grandfather. Any male who cannot identify his father, grandfather, and great-grandfather is already lost.

These three names are what *makes* a boy who he is. There is no talk of role models and celebrities. A son is raised under his father's wing, with a grandfather to guide and a great-grandfather as a blueprint, plus an army of uncles nearby.

Where I'm from, a man does not bow to any other man. A man bows down only to Allah. Only Allah created the heavens, the galaxies, the universe, and all of the millions of creatures within.

My father had three wives. Not one wife, one wifey, and a bunch of random bitches on the side.

Where I am from, a man *wants* to marry a woman and establish a strong family. A man can have more than one wife as long as he can treat them all fairly and provide them with love, separate homes, food, guidance, and presence.

There is no such thing as domestic drama. A woman feels fortunate to be selected by a quality husband, a family man, who will be by her side for her entire lifetime. Families are permanent.

When a man is ready to build his family, he selects a woman who he likes, who is from a family who raised her right, a woman who knows how to love and live. She has to be good for him, his beliefs and plans for life. Someone who brings him peace, progress, and pleasure. Then he is down for her for real.

She is down for him too because she feels his strength, craves his love and attention, feels safe tucked at his side, and is confident that every day he is making the right moves for her, his family, and himself.

Our women don't argue with their man. A man knows what he is supposed to do and not do. It is the same thing he watched his own father do and not do. So he does it. Even if a man selects the wrong path, his punishment is between himself and Allah. His woman cannot punish him, judge him, or nag him to death.

In my country, a wife is not a whore or ex-whore. Every move a woman makes matters. She can bring dishonor to her man and family even with a simple glance at another man, if it is held for too long.

Even where I am from, there are whores. They know their place too. They stay within the walls of the illegal whorehouse, never to be glorified, honored, claimed, or married. A whore, where I am from, is the opposite of arrogant. She is used but never celebrated by decent men or women. She knows that she can never enjoy the lifestyle and contentment of a respected sister, daughter, mother, or wife.

The punishment for a good woman who comes from a good family and suddenly behaves whorish is severe. She will be isolated by her parents, family, and friends. Her father and mother may lock her away and confine her to one room in the house. In some cases, she is even murdered by her own husband, father, or brother for bringing shame and dishonor to her family and the people who raised, guided, loved, and provided for her.

The family member who commits the murder is not arrested. The whole country acknowledges that a woman is sacred. Every move she makes is either building her family up or breaking it down. Every thought she has is felt and considered by her children. Every word she speaks either teaches or misleads. She must remain honorable, pure, and righteous, otherwise there will be no happiness, no family, and no reason to exist.

Mouthing off; fucking her man's friends, brothers, and cousins; running away with the children; aborting the babies; lying about who is the father of her children; not knowing who the father is; yelling and disrespecting; doing drugs; drinking; parading around mostly naked; acting crazy; our men don't stand for that. We have not experienced that. We never will.

Our women know their place. They stay in it and live and thrive there. They remain there happily. Our women give love and are loved even more. She is respected, protected, and provided for. She lives proud and at peace.

Where I am from, liquor is illegal and forbidden. We believe that it makes a man behave with ignorance. After drinking liquor, the next step, we believe, is to betray God, and destroy yourself and your family.

In my country, homosexuality is nonexistent. For the absolute majority it is unknown and undone. There have been one or two of those who have traveled out to other places in Europe or America and come back with this bizarre behavior. However, they could never remain with us. Their homosexuality resulted in suicides, or they just turned up missing.

There are no tears for the man who enters into the exit, and builds a life where there can be no balance, reproduction, or family.

Where I am from, adultery is a crime for a man or a woman. Even to fuck someone else's sister or daughter just because you feel like it or like the way she looks, without approaching her family for marriage, means that you have brought about a battle between dishonored families, yours and hers. The man who commits adultery will be punished by his family. The woman who commits adultery will be considered ruined.

Where I am from, men work. Whether he works his own land and is paid in the foods the Earth produces; whether he works someone else's land; whether he is paid in cash, cattle, or otherwise; he works. Hard work is a man's way of providing for and demonstrating that he loves his family.

Each man must have a business of products or services. His product might be fish, meats, vegetables, fruits, jewelry, clothing, crafts, furniture, vehicles, parts and supplies, or other items. Or he may provide services as a doctor, carpenter, construction worker, engineer, lawyer, driver, educator, or performer. But no man can sit doing nothing. His family, backed up by the entire community, would never allow it.

When I talk about where I am from, which is almost never, both males and females feel uneasy. Some look at me in disbelief, like I'm a fucking liar. Others stare off in complete boredom, like it is not a life they would ever want to live. But I feel fine. People where I am from are happy, while almost everybody I know in America feels fucked up, empty, and dissatisfied, especially the Black people.

At fourteen years young, I became a citizen of the United States. It was supposed to be a great day, to be remembered for a lifetime. There we were, becoming a part of what is known as the best country in the world, America, after having been born and living inside of what Americans consider the worst place in the world, the continent of Africa.

We got dressed up and took the A train to City Hall in New York City. We recited some things that we had already memorized. Then it became official.

I should say it became legal. I was an American on paper. I never became one in my heart or mind.

The year I became an American was the same year I got locked up. I went from the projects, to juvenile detention, to prison. Each year I became more and more familiar with the American Blacks. The ones who look just like me. They range from very light skin to my rich dark color, as it is back home. When I first arrived, they were Afro-Americans, then Blacks, then African Americans, and eventually niggas.

They talked like they were the most powerful, clever motherfuckers on the planet. They looked down on other Blacks arriving from any other country in the world. They hated every accent besides their own. They was quick to catch an attitude and say some shit that I could tell they really knew nothing about.

There was no real way for me to separate myself from them. We all looked the same, wore the same clothes, spoke the same slang. All united by our Air Jordan kicks.

I don't talk a lot. Where I'm from, the boys and men are trained to leave the blabbering to young girls.

It wasn't too long before I realized that if I said nothing for the rest of my life, shit would only get worse. I'm telling my story so Black people worldwide will know that we wasn't always fucked up. Also, that a good life takes great effort and sacrifice, but feels so much better than what we all got now. Besides, if the authentic men don't say shit, there will be no evidence that *real* men *really* do exist.

Living side by side with niggas, and watching them play themselves every second of every day, the broke ones all the way up to the rich ones, is killing me.

I'm not a preacher, politician, pimp, or celebrity. Most of them couldn't go to hell quick enough for me. A man who doesn't say what he means or do what he says, craves attention and misuses it when he gets it, doesn't share what he knows and earns, deserves death.

I am not who you think I am. My people are not who you think they are. Our culture and traditions are unknown to you. Sometimes it takes someone from the outside to show you how you look and do. If you're American born and raised, you're bound to get it twisted. You can't see yourselves or don't know yourselves. You're too accustomed to looking at life from only one fucked-up angle.

Everything you have ever seen or heard about Africa is wrong. My African grandfather taught me that the story-teller is the most powerful person in the world after God.

My grandfather said be careful who you listen to and what they are saying. The storyteller is clever and masterful and has already decided exactly what he wants you to think and believe.

The storyteller has the power to make people feel good or bad about themselves. The storyteller has the power to make people feel strong or weak, ugly or beautiful, confident or defeated.

Unfortunately, all of the stories being told to Blacks in America, Europe, Africa, and the Caribbean have made Blacks worldwide feel low, weak, crazy, backward, and powerless. So low that the storyteller has set the conditions for Blacks to be robbed of all of their stuff and too stupid to recognize it.

So put your brews and blunts on pause. Rock with me for a few.

2

BEFORE MIDNIGHT

African born. My father was not a king, but he was a phenomenon. The things he taught and showed me were more valuable than the three sparkling, three-carat diamonds he placed in the palm of my hand.

My father said not every man is qualified to be king. Not every man should want to be king. When unqualified men become king, they destroy everyone one way or another because of their ignorance, greed, or anger. Every day they live with the fear that it will be exposed that they do not deserve their wealth and do not really know how to rule.

My father was the advisor to the prime minister of the Sudan, the most powerful man in our country. He was also the advisor to an extremely popular and influential Southern Sudanese king. My father was a great thinker, the man with the ideas that the king and prime minister pretended they'd thought of themselves. This placed my father in a position of power, quiet power. But it also put him in the position of working to bring two deeply separated parts of one nation together. He was constantly being studied and watched and eventually hated by a handful of men who could not compare. These same men, who couldn't think or see straight on their own, had no vision of the power that would come through unity. They envied my father, rejected his thoughts and ideas, yet imitated his style and finesse.

When crooked men feel threatened, and have no chance

of competing with or matching the intelligence and maneuvers of a man who they see as their rival, they begin to use their insecurity to set that man up and bear false witness against him. They don't stop until they bring him down, drive him out, and eliminate him from holding on to something *they* could never have achieved fair and square.

My father taught me to lay low. Don't be the asshole who wants to be seen and celebrated all day, every day. Be cool. Take it easy. Carry out your plans in life, slow and steady. Push hard.

My father pushed hard, loved hard, lived hard, making great use of every minute and moment. A scientist, he graduated from the University of Khartoum at age twenty. He earned his master's degree at the Sorbonne University in Paris, France. He completed his Ph.D. at Columbia University in the United States of America.

At age twenty-six he returned home a doctor of science. He reminded everyone that Africa was the best place in the world. He didn't just say it. He meant it. He moved back in and worked the land and built businesses from scratch to empire status.

My father was six foot eight and pure black from head to toe—a blessing, not a curse.

An international man, he saw the whole world as his backyard. He made our home in Northern Sudan, the place where my mother was born and raised, the place where I was born also. We lived on his estate; seventy-five acres of land, four houses, eight buildings, and all of the property I could see in every direction was ours.

He named our estate Beit El Rahim, which means "The Womb." He said he chose this name for many reasons. One, he said, because Africa is the birthplace of the world, of human beings, of intelligence, and of all of the Prophets. Two, he said, because women are the key to life. Three, he said, because children born of a healthy womb become the guardians of traditions.

And children born of an unhealthy womb become the curse. So the womb itself is sacred.

If we chose, we never had to leave our property. Most of my family lived there. My father's closest friends' and coworkers' children went to our school on our property and prayed at the mosque on our property. My mother's business was located there in a fully equipped building, exclusively used, managed, and populated by women. Our food was grown on our land. We drew our water from our fresh water wells. Our place was filled with love, laughter, prayer, and music.

My father purchased the finest clothes, most handmade in the Sudan, the rest imported from Italy, France, and America and customized to his size and fit. His shoes were imported from Milan, Lisbon, Gweru, Seoul, and Canberra. But his favorite pair was made by his own father, my southern grandfather, who made the shoes from scratch right before my father's eyes. He gave them to him as a parting gift when my father went off to college, explaining that the handmade pair of shoes were the sturdiest and most reliable, the same as his southern village. My grandfather said those shoes would bring his son home to him where Southern Grandfather believed he belonged.

My father loved and collected music from around the world. Some evenings we grooved and listened to the thoughtful and melodic voice of Bob Marley. Stevie Wonder's lyrics painted pictures in our minds; Miriam Makeba sang us messages from the people of South Africa; Fela rocked us from Nigeria. The young voice of Michael Jackson amazed and excited us. Our homegrown Sudanese singers like Abdalla

Amiago sang us familiar songs framed by familiar sounds, waking and reawakening our love of life and Allah.

In one of the buildings on our property reserved for men, my father sometimes practiced playing his trumpet. Once a month he performed with his just-for-fun band before an audience of family and close friends. He taught me that hardworking men must always find ways to relax and enjoy life without destroying their family relationships.

He spoke seven languages and had acquaintances throughout the world. My father taught me that language should never separate one good person from another. Any man can learn another man's language if he can shut up long enough to listen and sit still long enough to study. We spoke Arabic at home, but he made sure I could speak at least the greetings of several African tongues and I also studied English in school and practiced speaking it along with my schoolmates.

My mother only spoke Arabic. My father loved her so much that she was the exception to many of his rules. He laid the world at her feet. When he hugged and kissed her anyone could tell there was nothing realer than that. Even I could tell he wanted her only to himself. I'd move out of their way and disappear into one of the many rooms of our home. He surrounded her in his love, but still allowed her to have her friends, business, and life within the places built exclusively for her behind the walls of The Womb. He was never shy about expressing himself to her. I saw it all the time. About her, I felt the same way.

When my father did business in the surrounding suburbs and villages, he mostly drove his truck. For big-city and government business he rode in his silver Mercedes-Benz 600, driven by his trusted Southern Sudanese homeboy, the only person allowed to privately transport him. Parked in our garage area was his custom-made cobalt blue Rolls-Royce that rarely left the grounds where we lived; still it was always kept clean and polished.

We also had a small collection of miniature cars used by our staff to move around our property, and to drive outside of our estate to run errands and complete tasks.

Our diamonds, gold, ivory, copper, and silver we got from home. It was automatic, part of our property, our history, our heritage, our assets. We also had oil, homegrown fruits and vegetables, and livestock. Guess you could say despite having to work hard in a hot climate, we invented chilling.

My father had guns galore, real ones, from twenty-twos to forty-fives, to three-five-sevens, to nines, to Glocks, to G-3 rifles, to semi-automatics, Uzis, and AK-47s. There were so many weapons that he had a small brick fort built on our property just to store them. On my fifth birthday, he gave me a key to his fort. It was one of the many tests he gave me to prepare me for life. He often would challenge me, asking, "Where is your key?" I had better have it on me, not in the pocket of the pants I wore last week or yesterday, not somewhere that I couldn't remember or in the possession of one of the house cleaners or my mother even. He taught me that I had to be responsible for my stuff instead of shifting my weight on to any other person.

He taught me how to hold each of the weapons. I felt that most of them weighed more than me. He assured me that they didn't. He taught me how to take them apart, put them back together, and how to clean and load them.

The first time he took me to target practice, I was five years old. The kickback from the gun in my hand lifted me off my feet and threw me to the ground. Within seconds, he had me stand back up on my feet and begin firing once again. "If you fear the gun," he said, "you will never be calm enough to hit your target."

My father was not a military man, but when I got the

chance to travel outside of our estate with him on business or pleasure, he made sure he pointed out Egyptian-made aircraft flying through our skies, German-made watercraft sailing on our waters, Soviet T-54 tanks, and MiG-17 surface-to-air missiles, and more.

Slowly and carefully, he would say so seriously, this one was designed by Germany, this one was designed by Britain, this one was designed by Israel, this one was designed by Italy, this one was designed by Pakistan. "All of these weapons in this section were manufactured by the Americans," he would say, pointing.

"Do you know why they designed and provided these weapons for us?" he would ask me. "Do you know what they want you to do with them?" he would ask. Then he would answer himself. "They designed these weapons so that we could make *their* lives easier. So that you and I would wipe out our *own* family, friends, and countrymen, allowing *them*, the foreigners, to come in and raid and rule *our* land, seize *our* gold, export *our* diamonds, and siphon *our* oils."

"Take a look around," he would say. "Everything we have, some which I acquired through birthright, the rest from hard work, education, blood, sweat, and tears, could be gone in an instant, because it is everything that every man in the world dreams of possessing. *You must fight to keep it.*"

My father said every son is entitled to inherit what his father earned, but *still* must plan to fight for it. Admire your father but *still* become a man who stands on his own feet and works his own accomplishments and miracles.

My father said *every* man *will* be pushed to kill something or someone, either to feed himself and his family, or to keep from being disrespected and dominated. "But don't be eager to kill, son, because when you kill you lose something too.

"It is better to give life than to give death. It is harder to maintain life than it is to wipe it out. There are unreasonable men on this earth who are determined not to let you be as you are, live as you are, love as you are, work as you are. They will bring war to your doorstep, like it or not.

"If you win, good for you and your family, praise Allah. Enjoy the peace.

"If you lose, lay low, go underground, go slow, rebuild and regroup and come again.

"If they take your land, gold, diamonds, and oils, let them have it for the moment while you think, reposition yourself, regain your strength, plan, and purpose. But never allow them to take your women, your children, or your family or you will be defeated forever."

My father said and did a whole lot of incredible things. His voice is louder in my ear than my own.

He taught me that women are one hundred percent emotion. Love them, but don't obey them. A man must go into the world without fear and do what is right, required, and necessary.

The last thing he told me the last time I saw him was "Son, no matter what, take care of your mother and your sister. Guard them and their honor. Protect them with your life."

My family came to America not because we loved it and thought it was a better place and the land of opportunity.

We came to America without our influence and abundant riches, to lay low, to go underground, to go slow, to rebuild, to regroup, to regain our strength, position, plan, and purpose, to come again.

3

THE THREE PIGS

My beautiful mother and I arrived in the U.S. on October 31, 1979. I was seven years young.

We were greeted by three American customs officers who were all wearing pink pig snouts and pink pig ears. We had never heard of Halloween. We don't celebrate the devil in our country. I gripped my mother's hand and heard my father's voice in my mind. "Son, there are unreasonable men on this earth."

I watched closely as the officers searched through our few things. I was confident that they would not discover my three three-carat diamonds in the hollowed-out sole of my right shoe.

"Three wishes," my father called the diamonds when he dropped them into my palm. "Three wishes when everything and everyone else around you fails or when you feel trapped. If you never have the need to use them, then don't. Pass them along to your son, and him to his son."

One of the officers seemed to have a problem with me watching him. He asked me, "What's a matter, kid? No one ever told you the story of the three pigs?"

My twenty-six-years-young mother, a five foot seven, golden-skinned, Arabic speaking, lean, shapely, and beautiful African woman with big dark eyes and a dimple in her chin, was wrapped up from head to toe as Islamic women do. She peeked through her veil and looked down at me for an understanding, a translation of the customs officer's English. I looked back up to her and said in Arabic, "It is a silly game they are playing."

"How old is the boy?" one officer asked my mother. I answered, "Seven." The three of them shot looks at each other and snickered. "Hey, Johnny, have you ever seen a seven-year-old kid this size in your son's second-grade class? What the hell were they feeding ya?" he asked, looking toward me with coffee-stained teeth and a crooked smile.

I didn't say nothing in response to his stupid comments. I was more than half of his short size. I figured that was his problem.

"Remove the veil and head scarf," the American customs officers demanded.

This order was considered an offense and insult to us. Where we come from, a woman is never asked to reveal herself in the presence of any man who is not her father, husband, brother, or son.

I looked at their weapons hanging on their hips. One officer's eyes followed mine as I checked out the mirrors in the corners of the ceiling, the cameras aimed down at us. So I translated to my mother.

She removed her *hijab* and *niqab*, very reluctantly, hearing the authority in the tone of their foreign voices and feeling the threat of the moment. The customs men watched every move of her hands, scanning and admiring the unfamiliar and beautifully drawn henna designs she wore on each of her fingers and on the palms of her hands.

Her thick, long and pretty brown hair now uncovered dropped down to her back. Immediately, they reacted to her revealed beauty with gasps, long lusty stares, and three dirty smirks.

She kept her gaze on the floor and asked me in Arabic if they were finished.

I asked them in English, "Are you finished?"

Still smiling, one of the officers nodded.

The other waved his hand and said, "Yeah, head to the next line over there." I checked them watching her so closely as she wrapped back into her *hijab* and reattached her *niqab* to cover her face, all but her eyes. We walked away.

I heard one of them say to the other, "Wow! I'd like to get my hands on something exotic like that." They laughed. The other officer said, "Funny, I wasn't thinking about my fucking hands, man!"

I thought to myself, *First thing I'm getting is a gun.*

4

DEQUAN

There was nothing wrong with the building, the block, or the sky above. It was the motherfuckers living in there who had to be closely watched.

When we moved in, the first thing on me that got attacked was my clothes. An older guy named DeQuan, who seemed to be in charge of the bench outside of the building door, called me over to his office. I had to walk by the bench to get off the block anyway. I was seven. This cat was about sixteen.

Instead of gold fronts, DeQuan had two sterling silver teeth. I saw him rocking his clothes with the price tags still hanging on 'em, dangling from his fitted hat or hanging from his kicks or plastered across his pants pockets. Most of his shit was labeled Polo, Ralph Lauren, or Nike. His kicks kept changing up daily.

"You can't come outside like that no more. You fucking up the whole look of the building," he told me with a screw face. I just stood there looking back at him for some seconds. I was just learning how to translate the Black version of English and their slang.

"What is it that you are talking about?" I asked him. Immediately he started laughing at my accent, my way of talking.

"All this shit got to go," he said, using his dutch to point out everything I was wearing, from the kufi on my head down to my shoes.

"Around here we wear fitted. Put a brim on your hat, my man. And throw them joints in the trash right now, you're insulting me," he said, looking down at my feet. He got off his bench and pulled the metal trash can, which was chained to the bottom of his bench, closer to me. I didn't move.

He tried to grab my shoes right off my feet. I jumped back and pulled out my knife. He laughed and said, "What the fuck you gonna do with that?" I walked away, past him and the bench and off the block to do what I was doing.

The next day he was on the bench with two other boys when I came walking by.

"Lil' Man, let me build with you for a minute," he said.

I had no choice but to pass by him.

"I'm a big man so I won't fight you. I'll give you one last warning about this fucked-up shit you keep wearing. Get rid of it. If you need work, I'll put you on. But if you come outside one more time with this fucked-up fashion, I'mma put my young brother DeSean on your ass. No knives. Just a fair one, fist to fist, every day until you get it right."

His brother DeSean had on Levi's jeans, no shirt, and the matching jean jacket with some new kicks. He grimaced at me, something I guess his brother taught him to do. I looked straight back at him.

"I got five brothers. DeSean here is nine. DeRon is ten. You can take your pick. I'll bring 'em all downstairs and line them up for you. But every day you gonna have to fight one of 'em either way."

I could tell he couldn't tell, or maybe he didn't care, that I was only seven.

"We can fight," I answered him with no emotion. He tried to stay straight-faced but I could tell he was surprised.

I fought one of his brothers every day for two weeks.

Whoever was on the block at the time took it as entertainment. But DeQuan could see that I took it seriously. Slowly, he learned to show me a little respect. Everybody noticed how I never tried to duck out the side or the back of the building. I showed up ready, with no fear.

I fought the nine-year-old for the first few days. Everybody could see I had more skill. He would start out strong in the beginning but couldn't make it through to the finish. But DeQuan would have him right out there the next day to try again.

Next I took on DeRon, the ten-year-old, who had more weight than me, but my father once taught me a way to fight someone who is bigger and stronger. While we was battling, their big brother DeQuan would stand over us yelling at his brother to do this or that, to move this way or that way. When he would see that one of his brothers was losing, he would start threatening him right there on the spot. "You better whoop his ass or I'm a whoop your ass. Get your fist up. Take him down. Take him down or you're gonna have to fight me next," he would threaten them.

On my last fight with the ten-year-old, DeQuan screamed on him so hard I actually felt sorry for him. When it became clear that I had defeated him too, DeQuan made him strip out of his clothes and snatched off his new sneakers. I gave the kid credit for standing out there in broad daylight in his boxers. He gave in to his brother's orders, but he kept his head up and didn't cry at his humiliation.

Always there would be a small crowd watching. Day by day it increased in size. DeQuan did not know he was doing me a favor. He introduced me to the hood as a fighter, a young one with exceptional stamina who never backed down. It helped my reputation a lot and put some of the young wannabees around our way on pause.

The eleven-year-old named DeLeon posed a problem for me, I thought. The first time I faced him to fight, I figured he must be feeling real powerful surrounded by his two younger brothers seated right there on the bench, and his older brother DeQuan standing right next to him and on point. Aside from the three of them, his thirteen-year-old brother who never sat down was always leaned up against the bench, never saying one word or ever cracking a smile. He stared me in my eyes the entire time. He seemed more foul than the other five and was a threat to me of what was coming up next if I dared to take his eleven-year-old brother down. He was six years older than me and too big. He looked like a fucking cheater, a dirty fighter. So my strategy was to go hard at the eleven-year-old, forcing DeQuan to give me my props, declare me the winner, and to call it all off.

Instead of getting right down to it, we walked around in circles first, staring each other down. He was slightly taller than me. The crowd was shouting out random shit. Somebody said something funny. In the split second that he looked away to chase the joke, I smashed his face with my right fist. His nose started bleeding. He was in a fighting stance now, looking angry and determined. Still he was making the mistake of having his eyes in the wrong place, watching his blood drops splatter in small circles on the cement. "Keep your eyes on his fists," DeQuan yelled at him. The kid got amped up and took a swing at me. I ducked. He missed. I landed a big bare-fisted punch in his stomach and he doubled over. "Stand the fuck up," DeQuan yelled.

I gave him time to straighten up before I punched him in his face again. His eyes turned red and mucus gushed out of one nostril, mixing with his blood. Suddenly his chest started heaving. Tears started to form in his eyes. His two younger brothers were on their feet now, trying to stop the fight. DeQuan pushed them both out of the way, leaned over, and started screaming face-to-face on his eleven-year-old brother.

"Oh, you gonna stand there and catch a fucking asthma attack because you losing the fight? That shit ain't gonna help you win. Cut that shit out!" he hollered at his brother, who could not seem to catch his breath.

"He needs his pump," the nine-year-old screamed.

"He ain't getting no pump," DeQuan silenced him.

"I'll go and get it," his ten-year-old brother said, then ran. But the thirteen-year-old brother caught him by the neck of his jacket and held him right there.

"Now, calm down and take *all* your shit off and give it to him. You don't deserve to have nothing," DeQuan ordered the eleven-year-old. The boy's breathing got worse. His fingers fiddled nervously with his belt.

"I don't want them," I said. "Those are his clothes. He can keep them." I walked away. I had shit to take care of and after fighting today nothing on me was dirty. I wasn't bleeding. My clothes weren't ripped or split. There was no reason for me to go back upstairs.

When I got back home, there was a plastic shopping bag against my apartment door. I looked inside. There was a fresh pair of jeans folded with the tags on, a T-shirt, and a crisp fitted. The kicks gave away the sender. They were the brand-new ones like the pair the eleven-year-old wore for the fight.

I took the delivery three different ways. One, was that DeQuan wanted me to know he didn't have no problem finding out where my apartment was and who my family was and he would come up to our place whether I was at home or not. Two, that DeQuan was admitting the embarrassing defeat of his eleven-year-old brother. Three, that maybe the thirteen-year-old didn't want to fight me next. I took the shopping bag as a message to me, half threat, half reward.

I thought about it for two seconds, grabbed the bag, and shot down the stairs to DeQuan's apartment. I wanted him to understand that I knew he was watching me but I was watching him too. He could come up to my apartment. I could come down to his just as easy.

Before I could bang on the door, DeQuan pulled it open. He had on new jeans and sneakers as usual. But this time he wasn't wearing a shirt and his nine millimeter was gleaming, tucked at his waist.

"What do you want?" DeQuan asked. I handed him back his shopping bag, but couldn't take my gaze off of his gun.

"One of those," I answered, with a nod toward his piece. DeQuan smiled. "Come on in, kid," he said.

All five of DeQuan's brothers were in one back room. There was DeSean, DeRon, DeLeon, and the thirteen-year-old. I didn't know his name.

This was my first time seeing the fifteen-year-old, who was almost as tall as DeQuan. I found out his name was DeMon. Each of them was sitting on one of two beds. Only the eleven-year-old with the asthma was sitting on top of his hands and had his head hanging down.

"Get your fucking head up," DeQuan barked on him. "And keep it the fuck up," he added. Meanwhile, the thirteen-year-old, still standing, stared me down with hatred. I was wrong for thinking that he didn't want to fight me next. Even though he was almost twice my age, he looked like he wanted a crack at crashing my skull.

DeSean, the ten-year-old brother, turned away when he noticed it was me, and looked out the window instead.

"Look this man in his eyes," DeQuan bossed him. Now all six of them were staring, focused on me.

DeQuan had a wall no one could see because from the ceiling to the floor, it was covered by crisp sneaker boxes of all kinds. They were perfectly stacked like in a small store.

"DeMon, give me box number seventy-seven," he told his fifteen-year-old brother. The brother hesitated at first, then he sped up and pulled the box out for him. DeQuan took the box from his brother and told me to follow him down the hall.

In a dark corridor of their apartment, DeQuan squatted down to speak confidentially. He opened the top of the sneaker box, revealing two guns sparkling on top of white tissue paper. I could see one was a twenty-two, the other was a nine.

"A'ight, little man, from now on you're gonna work for me," he said but I cut him off.

"No!"

When I saw the anger moving into his face, I corrected myself. "No thanks," I said. "How much is it?"

"These cannons are big-boy toys," he said, raising up from his squat like he was reluctant or now refusing to sell it to me.

I waited silently for him to quote the price. He's a businessman, I thought to myself. If he was any good at it, it was his job to move his product. He felt my point.

"It's three-fifty for the nine, two hundred for the twenty-two. Bullets included," he told me, cool and confident that he had out-priced me and trapped me in his employ.

I put my hand in my pockets and peeled off five hundred and fifty dollars. "I'll take both of them," I said, pointing toward the weapons. For the first time ever, I saw him actually hesitate. His eyes stayed on my small money stack.

"A'ight, little man, but you gonna have to learn to work with other people for real. I can sell you the pieces. That's what I do. But I *cannot* let you walk around in those fucked-up clothes. I'll sell to you if you change into the clothes in this shopping bag. It's a compromise," he said, staring at me in the form of a threat. I looked at him and thought to myself, this fashion shit must be their American religion. Then I thought again. Protecting my mother, Umma, is my religion. So I accepted. "Deal."

He took the money. I took the bag and the sneaker box and started to leave.

"Show and prove." DeQuan demanded, but I didn't understand.

"Put 'em on now," he ordered. He seemed used to giving orders and having them followed. "And let me tell you this, little man. This is Brooklyn. No matter if it turns two hundred degrees in the summertime, we don't rock sandals. No 'man sandals,' you got it?" he said. "If I ever see you wearing these sandals again, you're finished," he threatened with his most serious tone yet and pointed his trigger finger to the head.

That was my official introduction to NYC. That's how I came up on my first two guns. That's how I got introduced to New York fashion and styles.

"Leave all that fucked-up shit you had on right there." He stood over me.

I laid my kufi, my linen pants, my white silk Islamic shirt, and my sandals to rest. These were all high-quality, respectable clothes made of the finest materials. Where I am from, jeans are considered casual clothes used when laboring, doing construction, working on the land, repairing the house, or maintaining the vehicles. But in Brooklyn, my African dress clothes made me a target and I was prepared to turn my situation around and do what I needed to do to protect my family.

I never rocked another pair of sandals.

Word of mouth in Brooklyn was as powerful as the call to prayer back home. Word of mouth in Brooklyn was even more influential than the talking drum beat in my southern grandfather's village. So in less than twenty-four hours, the whole building knew I, the young fearless one, was packing.

A few days after I copped, I saw my old sandals dangling from the telephone wires that ran from pole to pole way up high throughout the hood. I didn't flinch. It was a symbol, a reminder to me of where I was and who I had to be to hold my position.

5

THE LOST BOYS

There is no place for fear in a man. There is no place for fear in the ghetto.

I considered myself to be at war with every single nigga I ran into, the big ones and the small ones. So I stay fit and strapped. It was no either-or situation for me. In my room I pushed my bed up against the wall and into the corner. I needed the floor space. I did my pushups, situps, and pullups like it was part of my religion.

In the hood, I noticed a lot of out-of-shape types, either too damn skinny or too damn fat. Instead they hid behind the barrels of their guns.

My father taught me that it is always better to have a choice of weapons. So I trained my body, my hands, and my feet to be my weapons too.

Seven days a week in our apartment, I did my unofficial training.

In a Brooklyn Ninjitsu school I did my official training. My teacher, who students called Sensei, was a thirty-something-year-old Japanese man who owned a nice-sized space that we called the dojo. It wasn't a cramped storefront that had different kids dropping in and out all the time. It was a large, spacious four-room facility.

We were trained to fight in the largest room. We had lockers in the locker room. Private lessons were offered in the smaller back room. Sensei had his own office to chill in. The walls were lined with photographs of real fighters in wicked stances, some even flying in the air. The expressions on their faces revealed their killer instinct as though the photos had just been snapped seconds before their opponents' defeat.

The students were all handpicked and selected to train by Sensei. Some people's money he turned away easily. He wanted youth who were serious about fighting and defending something based on a real principle, and not just for the hell of it. He kept sharp rules on attendance and honor. He never screamed and never joked either.

Sensei told us stories of ancient men who constantly had to fight to defend themselves and their families against individuals, corrupt armies and governments. He demonstrated how they used everything they had to make weapons, and went up against their enemies even though they were completely outnumbered and favored to lose. I considered my situation to be just like that. Coming from a foreign land, I did not trust the United States' authorities. I didn't even trust the American people.

Even when I came across those born and raised in the U.S. who introduced themselves as Muslims, I took them for jokers. They lived openly and carefree against the laws of Islam.

I could not trust my new neighbors. We looked alike but I didn't understand the way they talked, lived, and acted. Now I was mastering an ancient martial art form and converting myself into an urban ninja warrior.

My Brooklyn education came quick. The hood ate slow cats. I made it my job to learn the faces of every boy and man in my Brooklyn building. I learned from meeting DeQuan that I needed to know who was related to who, brothers, cousins, and uncles. I ranked each one of them in my mind based on the angle and position they played. I learned quickly that every man in the hood got an angle.

The lowest were the drug fiends. Yet they were the easiest to spot. They were broken men, women, and children worse off than beggars and willing to do anything for anybody for a hit of their addiction. They were going nowhere fast, aging right before my eyes, bent over, scratching, and thoughtless. I'd seen a few of them when we moved in. At first I thought they were poor people. Even back in the Sudan there are poor people. I soon found out and understood their condition. It wasn't that they were poor. A poor man can fight and have a chance of winning. A poor man can earn and build and become victorious. A fiend is a just a fucked-up, zombie, half-dead loser.

Close to the bottom were the schoolboys. They got up every morning and went to school just like they were told. They came home from school every afternoon, just like they were told. They was no real threat to me or anybody else. I kept my eye on them anyway. It wasn't long before I peeped their style. Most of them were a bunch of cowards. When I would see one of them alone, I could smell their fear. They would give a quick, nervous "Hi," and avoid eye contact. Then when I saw them grouped up with their friends, on the stairwell or on the train, or just playing the curb, they acted powerful. In a group they liked to bum rush and knock people over just for the fun of it.

One schoolboy punk named Manny tried to intimidate me once with his crew. About fifteen of them walked close behind me from the train station to my building. They would step up their pace, come up close on my heels, then bust out laughing. I knew they was waiting for me to turn around. So I didn't.

Later on when I caught Manny alone, I pushed my twenty-two into his ribs and he shitted all over himself. I changed his name to Doo-Doo. He never tried that shit with me again. Now every time I see his schoolboy crew, they act like they don't see me and just walk on by.

Keeping everybody on edge was the robbery boys. They didn't go to school or work. They hung around waiting for everybody else to do that. Once the people were out of the building, they ran up and broke into their apartments and spots, stealing toasters, televisions, VCRs, and whatever they could sell. Their team was known as the Smash Brothers. It was led by two brothers, one was named Ronald, the other named Rolland, last name Smash. This team of geniuses would steal from the fifth floor, and sell the goods to the people living on the sixth floor! After one big smash and grab, they fucked around and sold a girl from my building's new red leather jacket before she ever got a chance to rock it. When the girl from the next building over who bought the jacket from the Smash Brothers wore it outside, it tipped off "Girl War One."

A bunch of fourteen- and fifteen-year-old chicks were out front beating the shit out of each other. The real owner of the jacket and the new owner of the jacket were fighting for the coat they'd both paid for. The rest of them girls were fighting 'cause they lived in different buildings and were always beefing anyhow. The boys and a few men from both buildings cheered when the shirts got ripped open and the bras and panties started flying. The fight ended when a girl from the other building bit off the finger of a girl from my building. The cops, who had been standing still watching the fight and enjoying the view, swooped down on all of them. Ronald Smash located the bloody finger and handed it over to the police like he was an innocent bystander and a concerned youth.

I don't go to school. I study at home. Sometimes during the day, I let them robbery boys see my face around the building, so they know if they come running up into my spot, they'll never get back out.

Anyway, the Smash Brothers ain't half as bold as the stick-up kids. They don't wait till you go to work or school to steal your shit. The Cash Crew rolls right up to your face. They'll let you see their faces too and still take your shit. Matter of fact, everybody in the building knows who they are. They wave their guns around, bust shots in the air, or randomly shoot off rooftops. In a tight situation they even bust off at the popo.

Terrorized youth and mothers bend to them. Old ladies gamble with their lives and dime them out to the cops, unaware that the officers they're calling for help are just as crooked as the crooks.

The leader of the Cash Crew, named Mighty Dollar, Mighty for short, didn't deal with stolen toasters, televisions, VCRs, or furniture. His crew stole shit that was either cash or easy to liquidate into cash, like jewels and welfare checks. Mighty was notorious for controlling the mailboxes in the lobby of our building, where people received their checks; the coin boxes from the pay phones; the parking meters; and for hitting up the local arcades.

They was on the prowl every day. But I noticed they did their biggest capers on vacations and holidays. On Christmas Day, they went on a "shopping spree." I know because my family doesn't celebrate Christmas. It is just another day for us. The Cash Crew caught a group of schoolboy suckers running their mouths and showing off their presents, styling and shining in their new gifts. Mighty made all of them run their valuables. They took their new jewels right off their necks and wrists and put it right onto theirs.

Afterward, Mighty and his boys just chilled right there

outside the building, sporting the stolen shit and confident nobody could do nothing about it.

I was on the block when Lavidicus came downstairs with his momma. She had a black extension cord in one hand following behind her teenage son. She stood about twenty feet away as her son went to beg his watch back. The boy seemed so scared his hands and legs were shaking and his bottom lip had dried up and turned ashy gray.

It was as if Mighty had eyes behind his head and saw Lavidicus coming. He started laughing before the kid even got close on his back. Even his boys thought it was mad funny. The kid stood behind Mighty mumbling about "Can I talk to you for a minute." Mighty stayed calm, kept conversating with his boys and wouldn't bother to respond. I understood that. My father always said, "Men don't mumble. Either shut up or speak up."

Afraid and defeated, the boy walked back toward his mother, who spanked his ass with her black cord right outside in front of everybody. He jumped around like he was dancing on hot rocks.

Afterward his mother approached Mighty, with part of the cord still wrapped around her hand and the heaviest part dangling. She started talking loud about how he better give her son back his watch. Mighty said, "How do you know this is your son's watch?" She answered, " 'Cause it's a Tag Heuer and I brought it for him and it cost too much damn money to be playing around with."

Mighty said, "You right, it's a nice watch. That's why I bought it." He laughed.

"You didn't buy that one. I bought it. Take it off and I'll prove it to you," she said with her free hand on her hip.

"If I take this watch off, you gonna have to take something off too," Mighty warned her. "Are your feet as pretty as your face?" he asked the boy's mother. And, in what had to be the worst day of the boy's life, his mother's whole stance switched. She cracked a wide smile of delight at Mighty's twisted compliment and answered, "I do have nice feet."

Mighty showed the mother the watch. She flipped it over and pointed out that she had Lavidicus' name engraved on the back of it. And that "Ain't nobody else around here named Lavidicus."

Mighty gave her the watch. She gave Mighty herself. They became the rowdiest couple on the block, famous for fighting and fucking indoors and outdoors. Mighty even shot at her once as she ran out the back of the building.

The last time I seen Lavidicus, we rode down in the elevator together. I handed him a flyer for the dojo, figuring he might want to start training his mind and his body. As a teenager, he would be starting out late in learning fighting techniques. Still, I couldn't see him surviving in the hood without a whole new outlook, understanding, and stance. We didn't speak no words that day in the elevator. In fact, I never even saw him on the block again although his moms was still living there disgracing herself.

I had one run-in with Mighty and them. I saw their crew out in the dumps, a place where garbage is piled up on top of garbage. They seemed surprised to see me rolling for self, out there where they be plotting at. They watched me as I set up empty cans for target practice. I stayed focused and started blasting the cans rapid-fire quick, letting them see how I hit my target when I take aim the first time. Before the gun smoke cleared, I disappeared.

They were tight that my firing caused the cops to come racing to their meet-up spot. They had to switch up their hideout after that. Still, I knew they was impressed. They couldn't do that shit. I saw once when they got into a shoot-out with this kid named Scooter around our way. I counted twenty or more bullets, let off by three different shooters. Shell casings dropped all over the sidewalk. They never hit nothing or nobody. Meanwhile, their live target is just running at top speed, dipping, zig-zagging, slipping away from them easily.

By watching Mighty and them I learned that a small reckless crew of cats can rule over a whole building off of fear alone. They had guns but no shooting skills. They had easy targets as their victims but no goal, no plans other than dressing up, styling, and playing C-low outside the building with other people's money.

Around our way we got pimps and rapists, same thing. Stupid girls and desperate women are their prey, product, and cargo. Their business is steady and heavy. One day you see a young slimmy walking to the store with her butt poked out. A few nights later you see her going in and out of the side entrance of a little hole-in-the-wall strip club called Squeeze. All courtesy of Larry from apartment 3B, the runner for the main pimp in our area, named Trinidad.

Larry lingers around the building with a pocket filled with Jolly Ranchers, Now and Laters, and Blow Pops. He got an eye for the extra young ones whose bodies are just starting to fill out. The ones who like to cut class, lean on the wall when they walk, look lonely, and ain't got no fathers, brothers, or brains.

Me and him bumped heads once when I went up on the rooftop to clear my mind, think, and watch. I caught him conducting a lollipop licking contest between three little girls, ages maybe ten or eleven, or twelve tops. The little girls were all eager-faced, their tongues dark grape, dark cherry, and dark watermelon. They were licking really fast and hard, really trying to beat each other to the promised "prize," while dirty thirty-something-year-old Larry watched with his long fingers and dirty, long fingernails gripping his crotch.

I snapped, then cracked that motherfucker over the head with an empty Colt 45 forty-ounce bottle. I told them little girls to go home as Larry folded and fell out cold like Thomas "Hitman" Hearns after "Marvelous" Marvin Hagler hit him with that right. Two of the little girls looked shocked. The other one started talking about, "You messed up my prize money. Now you owe me five dollars." I told her, "Shut up and slow down." After that I figured I was wasting my time talking to her, trying to defend an honor that none of them had based on an idea that none of them knew and a belief that none of them understood or shared.

Later Larry and his apprentice, a big seventeen-year-old named Lance, jumped me. I didn't use my burner. It wasn't on that level. Larry backed off when he felt how hard the blows was swinging. He wasn't no real fighter. He was only a conqueror of young girls. He said for me and Lance to shoot a fair one. I went straight to it. I was thirteen years young. I caught more than a few bruises. I didn't care. I thought it was worth it. In my mind pimps are lower than thieves.

I don't know where Larry moved his stripper training camp to. I just knew it wasn't happening on the rooftop of my building no more. It was big news when Lance got arrested for molesting some little girl from the block who wasn't even old enough to strip at the illegal strip joint Squeeze.

Now them same three little girls who I looked out for on the rooftop be wandering around the hood giving me the eye as though they want to get with me and got something that I want. I brush them off, send them home, and remind them to stay off the roof and the stairs and out of everybody's face. I guess they just destined to be fast. I look at them as being exactly how I would never allow my little sister to be. I would rather my sister be dead than to turn out like one of them. In fact, someone would have to either call the coroner to haul off the guy who tried to get at my little sister, or step over my dead body to get my little sister into that low, ran-through position.

Every now and then, the young ones who ain't robbing and stealing or pimping get the bright idea to form themselves a gang. A few of them approached me to see if I wanted to get down with their team. I said, "Nah."

Only some Black American fools could stop and think and then come up with the idea that being in a gang means wearing the same colors, dressing up the same like a bunch of fucking cheerleaders, beating each other down, and running wild scaring the shit out of their own neighbors. These gang types were hilarious to me with their secret handshakes and bullshit nickel-and-dime schemes.

Because they all dressed the same and did the same dumb shit, the cops could easily identify them and had an easy excuse to keep sweeping and locking them up. Every day some of them got picked up and a handful got let out. They snitched on one another so much, there was no way for them to really know who was in or out of the gang at any given time.

I felt sorry for the young gang fools. Some of them had heart but none of them had brains. I figured someone ought to tell them little motherfuckers that America is a country of businesses. If they wanted to be able to buy anything in this country, they had to have something to sell, a product. And everything you eat, wear, do, or watch is a product you could be manufacturing and selling for the right price. But these boys were knuckleheads. Instead of getting a product or building up a skill or talent, they would turn around and sell their own sisters and mama. The way I looked at them was if you don't have no real business, no real money, no real plan, no real power, why should I join you? Should we get together and split nothing nine ways? I mean, I come from a country where men fight over gold, oil, diamonds, and land. Now I live in a country where niggas fight over nothing.

The drug dealers got something though—cars and cash and a constant flow of ass. But individually and together, they seem like disorganized, gullible dudes.

The real hustlers in Midtown Manhattan's diamond and gold district, and the jewelers down on Canal Street, always get excited when they see them coming. They take them for their money and play them for fools. They get them dripping and draped in ten-karat gold, one- two- and four-finger rings, and cloudy-ass diamonds.

The hustlers who think they a cut above the rest insist on fourteen- or eighteen-karat gold. Where I am from, even this kind of jewelry is known as junk.

Around my way, at the time, the dealer's car of choice was the BMW. They also chilled in Maximas, Saabs, Jaguars, and baby Benzes, the 190. Somehow each of them would find some way to fuck up a decent new ride. Either they would put bright-yellow fog lights on, or skirts, or an additional bumper made of plastic or some big fucking letters pasted on the windows, which I thought could only draw even more attention to themselves when it seemed to me like common sense that their line of work required them to hang back and camouflage.

Around the hood they be flossing their money knots, shaking their dice, shooting their C-low, smoking their weed, hugging their forties, making an unnecessary scene in the sunlight when everybody's watching. Any one of them would pull a stack of bills out, line a bunch of boys up, and pay for all of them to get cuts at the barbershop or ice cream at the ice cream truck. I turned down their offers. It wasn't no real money in it for me. Besides, I have a father. I wasn't out looking for none of these cats to play daddy.

All of their deals were loaded anyway. They got almost

everything. You got next to nothing. The police stay on your ass, not the boss'. They stayed styling while you became nothing but a scrambler, a runner, you running all the risk all the time.

One of them, known on the streets by the name Superior, offered me a package to sell for him, with promises of me blowing up over time. I told him, "Nah," I had no time for that bullshit.

Of course there were working people where I lived who had regular jobs. Their work was legit, but their mentality was just as foreign to me. We had janitors, waiters, garbagemen, and postal workers. They were grown men. They did what they thought they had to do on the weekdays and got high or drunk on the weekends to forget it all. They tricked part of their earnings watching and paying young girls to peel their clothes off at Squeeze and paid them a little more to bounce in their laps. Compared to all the other men in the hood, they swore they were doing it. They had legit jobs with benefits and crowned themselves kings because of it. For entertainment they juggled the hearts of the husbandless mothers who outnumbered them ten to one. Their constant lying and creeping made for tight, uncomfortable, volatile rides down on the elevator in the morning where these various women faced off.

We also had a couple of shiny shoe U.S. Army cats living in our hood. They were shipped, deployed, and flown in and out. They were respected for their assumed military skills. On top of that, cats admired that they had permission and orders to kill without penalty.

Envious young niggas got their get back on the military men by making trampolines out of their girlfriends and wives while they were away on active duty.

One cat named Arthur fucked around and caught feelings for one of the army wives, and blasted her husband on the first hour of his first day on leave back home. The army guy had survived the blood, roar, bullets, and bombs of America's unjust wars. He managed to stay alive in the alleys and corridors of Beirut, Lebanon, but got clapped up and gunned down easily on the ghetto-hot streets of BK.

Luther Mathews was a big-time corrections officer, who still lived in our building along with the same motherfuckers who kept getting locked up. He walked around like he was a supercop *and* a deteck. The older females sweated him because he had a job, benefits, and a uniform. I looked at him like he couldn't be too smart, a grown-ass man still stuck in the projects with the wild wolves.

I once saw him behind the building beefing with some young strays like they was his own children. Quick-tempered, he started screaming, "Wait till I get y'all asses up at Rikers," like he was so sure every teen would end up in lockup eventually.

The real cops were like germs no antibiotic could kill. They watched us. We watched them. They were all over the place. So were we. The only difference was, we lived there and they didn't. Still, they acted like they lived there and we didn't. They had beef with everybody who wasn't one of their bitches or snitches.

No matter what a guy's angle is, legit or illegit, around my way you gonna encounter the police. There are random stops, random searches, random beatdowns, random arrests, random police shootings and murders of unarmed teens, and none of it random. So I moved calm yet swift through the streets and I got more than a few hidden places to stash my heat.

The notorious cop around our way was Officer Brandon Huff. Black and built like a bodybuilder, he was known for pulling over pretty young thangs on a routine survey and head count of single mothers. He would entice them with his promises to straighten out their teenage sons who wouldn't "act right" or respect them. He was big on beatdowns and more prejudiced against black youth than a white man. Everybody around my way called Officer Huff by his street name, Stress.

I like math and I am good and quick with numbers. I figured out the smaller percentage of time I spent in the hot spot known as my block, the less of a chance of me getting harassed and bagged by the cops for standing still.

I avoided my block, treated it like one big walk-through. I was looking for something or someplace entirely different. I set up my adventures elsewhere. But since everybody else, including the heroin fiends, stood on the block every day in the same spot doing the same things, it was impossible for them not to notice me moving around.

Over time people thought they knew me. The streets stay watching. But I didn't take none of them for friends or acquaintances or bless 'em with any kind of real conversation. From time to time it would just be one of them doing the telling and me doing the listening and nodding. I had to keep track of the happenings one way or another as a form of defense of my fam.

It was only DeQuan who kept coming for me, trying to pull me into the fold of his fucked-up "community." He kept track of all of the boys on the block, made them fight shit out, even hung a punching bag on a chain from the lamppost. He set up races and games, gave kids new names based on how they battled and competed and where they fit in because everything for him was about muscle, strength, competition, and dominance. He believed in "each one, teach one."

He was a supplier. That's how I saw him. I knew for now I needed him to reup on bullets, plus you never know. So I cooperated with him from time to time. I saw he took a liking to me, maybe because he bet on me a few times and won.

As far as I was concerned, I was at war with every boy, every teen, every man living or working on my block. I was either at war with them with my mind, my ideas and my beliefs, or my fists, my feet and my weapons.

I was sure about one thing. Our hoods were fucked up. Nobody could think or live straight. Everybody everywhere got guns cocked and loaded and one thousand reasons to shoot. I got my guns too. I don't love them. But I need them.

6

UMMA

Umma is my heartbeat. I love her more than I love myself.

I care about what she thinks and has to say. Easily I would give my life to save hers. Yet every day I strive to stay alive because losing my life would kill her.

As Umma's firstborn, and a son, we are closer than skin is to flesh. Without exchanging any words I know many of her thoughts. Her feelings are extremely intense. So sometimes I have to leave her presence to avoid being swallowed by them.

From age seven until now at fourteen, I've held her hand in mine and led her into America. I have translated everything she saw and heard. I've spoken for her in the offices of immigration, at the lawyer's office, at the bank and realtors. Every day I had to pay close attention to everyone, what they were saying and doing in regards to my mother, and had to read and interpret documents they wanted her to sign that were even difficult for me to understand. Ours is a closeness that only a foreigner in a foreign land who cannot speak the common language might really understand. Still, our closeness is more.

Clearly I know the difference between a father, a husband, and a son. I wanted to be the best son possible, not only because my father said to do it; not only because I am her only son; but also because she deserved it and I love and respect her beyond anyone else.

Umma is the opposite of every female that I saw or knew

so far in America. She doesn't change her mind every few seconds, minutes, or months. She is steady. Her love and loyalty are forever. Her friendship is something you can count on. She is an amazing talent, while being so modest and down to earth. She is a young wife and mother, and an extremely attractive woman without conceit. She doesn't need or want everyone to look at her or to give her compliments all day to feel all right about herself. She is an incredible cook, who fills every one of her dishes and pots at every meal, with love. After eating, you could feel the love growing in your belly and strengthening your body.

She is a hard worker but always pleasant. She is so smart, yet so unselfish. Even when she criticizes she is accurate but soft and always sweet. The best thing about her is her certainty. Her belief in and dedication to Allah is unshakable. You could see it in her every action every day, without her preaching a word of it. Her family is her life.

Umma's love for my father is like radiation, something active and extreme that's in each speck of the atmosphere every day. Since leaving the North Sudan, where Umma was born, raised, married, and gave birth, I do not mention her husband, my father, because mentioning missing him would set off a tidal wave of her emotions and desires and a typhoon of her tears that could only drown everyone and everything in its path. We live life like he is right here beside us in the United States.

We bow down and pray to Allah together at the same time each and every day.

When we first touched down at John F. Kennedy Airport in America, we were supposed to be received, cared for, and guided by one of my father's American friends, his former roommate while studying at Columbia University. We were both surprised when he never showed up and never responded to our many phone calls. Especially after my father phoned him from the Sudan and told him, "I am sending my heart overseas. She is with my young son and carrying also my daughter in her womb."

The roommate became permanently pressed in Umma's mind as the symbol of an "American welcome," and the measure of "American friendship."

On our first day in New York, once we made it outside of JFK Airport in Queens, we took a taxi to New York City. We checked into a Midtown Manhattan hotel recommended by the cab driver. At the Parker Meridien, instantly we became familiar with the weight of the American dollar, as each night's stay in our hotel room equaled a month of Sudanese dinars and high living.

At the concierge's desk in the hotel lobby, I collected information and got a few answers to our questions, as well as a map of the city of New York, including all of its five boroughs and a subway guide.

For a month Umma and I lived in our hotel room trying to figure things out. We walked the streets and learned to ride the train together, making and carrying out our plans. It wasn't long before Umma revealed that the shock of this new place, and the weird people and things we saw every day, were making her sicker than she was supposed to be in her third month of pregnancy.

On the train she would comment to me that the women in this country must all be in mourning, because they wore no henna on their hands. Back home women with undecorated hands and feet were either unmarried, uncelebrated, or widowed. Henna was a sign of happiness, good fortune, good health, good life, and beauty.

The train rides were a source of shock for her: singing beggars with either no legs or no arms or both, foul-mouthed youth who wouldn't stand up and make room for elderly ladies or women traveling with babies and young children.

Once there was this man in his thirties, drenched in the smell of cheap wine, who attempted to stand directly in front of where Umma sat before I moved him out of her way. The last straw was when a homeless man seated beside us turned out to be dead. Two young transit workers got onto the train, then stood around arguing over who was gonna clean up the pool of watery shit that filled his seat after his body was removed.

While shopping in the random fruit stores, Umma would say that the fruits here looked abnormal and strangely large. So many of the fresh tropical fruits she craved were missing from the midtown stores, like dates, guava, tamarind, and apricots.

In the supermarkets we checked out, she would say that the raw chicken looked bloated and swollen and unusually yellow, as if someone had intentionally painted them with an unnatural color. In the fish market she would recoil at the stinking smell, saying fresh fish has a distinctive scent but did not have a foul odor. Even the coffee served in the coffee shops was an insult to her. I guess this was not surprising since Sudanese coffee ranks as one of the best-tasting coffees prepared in the world.

Umma spit up even the New York drinking water, saying it was awful and tasted impure. I never doubted her words. On our estate, our water was drawn from our fresh water wells. Back home she picked fruits off our trees, plucked and pulled vegetables from our gardens and fields, crushed fresh coffee beans, fried them, and brewed everyone's coffee. She cooked incredible stews and baked fresh breads and was so accurate in her mixture and blend of spices that an invitation for dinner at our place was never turned down, but instead was met with great excitement and anticipation.

I knew and Umma impressed upon me that we had to find affordable housing and a comfortable living space before our monies dwindled down to nothing. So far we had spoken with many professionals who were all clear and specific about the money they wanted from us as payment. Yet they were cloudy and vague about what they would actually do to earn the money they were requesting and quick to add that they could not guarantee us any results. Umma sensed they were liars and cheaters under the banner of business. Most things we were left to figure out for ourselves.

The urgency pushed me to ask Umma to relax in the hotel room and venture out on my own. I listened as she recited a list of things she wanted and we needed. I put some of our money into my pocket. Then I left to go make it happen. In the evenings I would return and give her the items I had purchased. Also I gave her an update on some of the things that happened in my day, careful not to mention anything that would disturb or upset her or cause her to know how people here tried to boss and cheat a young kid as if I couldn't count or think straight.

Brooklyn is where I discovered a row of Arab-owned stores, where the spices Umma cooked with back home were available for sale: cardamom, ginger, turmeric, coriander, cumin, cayenne, mustard seeds, fennel, and a host of hot peppers. There were dates, tamarinds, apricots, eggplant, okra, lentils, and chickpeas. There was an assortment of Middle Eastern and African flours, which she would use to prepare our breads. They even had a barrel of pumpkin seeds. I picked up a bag as a treat for Umma, who ate and enjoyed them back home from time to time.

When I brought my info and a few treats back to the hotel and spoke of the row of Arab-owned stores, a supermarket, a take-out falafel shop, a jewelry store, and the mosque, Umma wanted to see the places for herself.

She chose to explore the Brooklyn mosque first.

When we entered, an Arab man greeted me and ignored

her. When I asked if we could make prayer, he welcomed me and pointed Umma toward a closed door, which led to a dark, damp basement area where women were designated to pray separately from the men. We were used to men and women praying separately in one space, women behind the men. We were not accustomed to males praying on one level, leaving the women down below. It was the cold winter season outside and colder in the dungeon. It was unsuitable for any woman, especially a pregnant one. He expected Umma to go down there alone. I grabbed her hand to escort her out of there.

Umma turned to the Arab man and, speaking in Arabic, stated, "Do you think that because you are in America that Allah cannot see you and what you are doing?" He seemed surprised that we spoke his language. He never answered her question though. As we left Umma said, "America, where Muslims play and do what they would never do back home." Now she was content to keep our prayers privately. She never asked about the local mosques again.

Brooklyn was also the place where I discovered a bookstore that let me order books printed in Arabic. It was a rainy day. I was amazed at the unfamiliar combination of cold temperature and the freezing downpour of ice water onto my shoulders and back. I stepped under the canopy of one of the stores and stood shivering and facing a bookstore named The Open Mind, built on the triangular tip of two intersecting blocks. I shot across the street and entered a place with thousands of books for sale neatly arranged in a tight maze of tall shelves. Aside from the books, the place appeared to be empty.

As I looked around at the headings—Mysteries, Biographies, Hobbies, Adults Only, Entrepreneurs, Magazines, and Children's—I was interrupted by a short Jewish man wearing wire-framed glasses and a mustache. He folded his arms across his chest like some adults do when they are trying to establish authority over a child. I didn't respond to it because I didn't look at him as a parent or guardian over me.

"No school today?" he asked. I ignored his question and treated him like a bookseller because that is what he was. If he was a good one, I was planning to be a book buyer.

"Do you have a book series called *The Amazing Adventures of Akbar*?" I asked. He repeated the name of the series aloud and scrunched up his face like he was trying to solve a difficult math problem. "I have a children's section over there to the left. But I don't believe I have ever heard of this series," he admitted. "Thanks anyway." I turned to leave. "Wait," he said, calling behind me. "I can order the books for you if you'd like."

I must have looked skeptical because he continued to try to convince me. "Ten days to two weeks. I'll have them right here in my store for you," he said. "Do you know the name of the author?"

"Yes, it's Bashir Hussein. The series is written in Arabic," I told him.

His face lit up. "Where are you from?" he asked.

"Where are you from?" I turned the question around on him.

"No, really," he asked me again.

"I just came from the number two train," I answered him.

He smiled, unfolded his arms, and threw up his hands saying, "Bravo! Okay, kid, you win. I see you're a tough one. But you like books, so I like you. Come back in two weeks and I will have your series for you. If not, then I'm not Marty Bookbinder!" He held out his hand to me. I shook it.

Two weeks later when I returned to The Open Mind, I entered the store and walked around quietly, wondering how this guy survived in this business when I had yet to see him with a customer besides myself. I saw him shoot past me in the maze of shelves without acknowledging that I was standing there. I took that to mean he did not get the books I ordered and didn't feel like facing me. I turned to walk out.

He shouted after me, "Hey, I have your series."

Surprised, I turned back around and followed him to the section where he kept the new books shelved. Naturally I smiled as I saw volumes one through twenty-one of the series my father first chose for me right there in front of my face in this foreign land. "I'll take volumes fifteen through twenty-one," I told Marty.

"That's seven books," he said to me. I thought it was a dumb comment that implied I either did not know that already or could not count for myself. "Each book is seven-fifty," he said.

I put my fifty-two dollars and fifty cents on the counter plus eight percent sales tax. "Put them in a bag, please," I said.

"What about the other volumes?" he asked.

I picked up my bag and answered, "I read them already." I left the store thinking of how much I hate to be underestimated.

"Wait a minute." He followed me. "What's your name?" he asked.

"Maybe next time," I told him.

"That's an interesting name." He laughed. "Listen, please come again. I'll teach you how to play chess. Do you play chess?" he asked.

"Chess? Maybe next time," I said again.

Down that same block, I found a friendly Jewish realtor. I explained to her that my mother didn't speak any English, but we were looking for a place to stay. She was the one who eventually led Umma and me to the Brooklyn projects, into a three-bedroom apartment on the sixth floor. She showed it to us like it was the ideal place for the ideal price.

She charged us three months' rent in advance. Somehow,

only two months' worth of the money we gave her counted. The third month's rent, she said, was her fee for locating the apartment for us.

The bottom line was we were never suspicious that the realtor had led us into a hell reserved for poor Blacks. We didn't know about the crime rate, the condition of African Americans, hostile policing, illegal drugs, welfare, food stamps, or Medicaid. All we knew was the monthly rental price was an amount that we could afford to pay without Umma having to work for the first year while she gave birth to and began breast-feeding and raising the baby, who my father assured us was a daughter.

With the keys to our new apartment in my hands, I went in and scrubbed the walls, toilet, and tub with Dettol. I swept, washed, and waxed the floors in every room. I cleaned all of the windows. I taught myself how to use the stove and oven. I cleaned it out as well as the refrigerator. The job took so long to complete that I never made it back to the hotel where Umma was hand-washing and hang-drying her favorite cloths and packing our few belongings. She did not trust the hotel laundress to do the job.

I spent my first night alone in the apartment with the windows slightly open so the cold breeze would clear out the antiseptic smell of all of the detergents. On the hard, newly sparkling floor, I lay down and listened to the sounds and noises of elevator doors opening and closing, my neighbors walking, and children running through the hallways and even more milling in the streets.

Lying there with a view of a starless sky as black as ink, I thought about my Southern Sudanese grandfather. I had learned not to fear the darkness and the unknown spending summers side by side with the boys of his village. Learning and playing and training with more than twenty or so boys my same age gave me crazy confidence. When we would hear the sounds of the creatures of the night, we did not fear. They had a crew and we had a crew. We knew from watching the boys who were older than us that if we worked together, we would rule over the animals instead of them ruling over us. I felt extra secure in this village. After all, my own father was born and raised there, and my grandfather was the only man greater than him.

My grandfather taught me to see in the dark. Not just to look, but to see. He would sit so still in the dark of the African night. He was so black that only a trained eye could distinguish him from the atmosphere. So he would play on it. I would walk into his large hut. He would have the lamps off on purpose. I would move around feeling as though I was completely alone in there. Suddenly he would grab me with his rough hands. His deep voice would fill the room. When he would laugh at my foolishness in not being able to see him, only his white sparkling teeth would reveal his actual location. "What if I were the King Cobra?" he would ask with the threat animated in his voice. He played these games with me until I learned to pay attention, to see in the dark, to not bump into anything in my surroundings because I needed to form a mental picture of it.

Since Umma was asleep alone in the hotel, I made sure I was back in Manhattan by the time she opened her eyes and in time for prayer.

Dialing the combination that unlocked the hotel safe, I took Umma's jewels, the few we managed to bring from back home, and wrapped them in one of her colorful silk scarves. I carried them on my back secured in my backpack. She folded the remaining cloths, which had now dried, and packed our few pieces of luggage. We checked out of the hotel once and for all, paying a large amount of American dollars.

Inside of seven days Umma transformed our small Brooklyn apartment into a very modest Sudanese home.

The first thing she did was fill each room with the powerful scent of sandalwood from back home. From the ceiling to the floor she hung newly purchased lavender curtains to cover the living room windows and even the clean but bland off-white walls. She handmade huge, colorful, bejeweled suede purple pillows and placed them onto the sparkling floors. Aside from a beautiful dark-brown walnut table that we purchased from an antique shop on the other end of Brooklyn, we had only a few selected pieces of furniture. I admit that when we would return from the outdoor coldness, Umma's fragrances and the color scheme she selected would warm us right up.

Buying a music system for the living room, a special grill and hot plate for Umma to cook breads and Sudanese food the way she wanted to, plus a serving tray and coffee and tea sets, as well as ten-pound bags of long-grain rice and an array of beans, olives, grains and vegetables, honey, yogurt, fruits, fresh-cut flowers, and Halal meats brought the cost of moving in way beyond what we had projected.

We also ended up having to hire movers to pick up our furniture and bed sets because most of the stores wouldn't deliver to our neighborhood. "We don't go over there," various store owners insisted. It was our first hint that something wasn't right.

Even though our new surroundings inside our apartment looked great and were soothing, an unspoken sadness weighed heavy on our hearts. More than anything, we knew not to speak on any of it. It was as if just a simple mention of what was actually happening in our lives would bring the ceiling crashing down onto our heads.

After our telephone was installed, I would see Umma pick up the receiver and, one by one, dial several long-distance phone numbers. The only thing was, there would never be a conversation, only her gripping the telephone and sitting silently and waiting and eventually hanging up and saying nothing to me of what was going on. In her room she would be writing furiously. She would stop the instant I appeared. She would put her papers to the side or in a drawer and not speak on it. I was not concerned about the content of her writings. It was only her I was concerned about, her feelings and exactly how to make a true smile spread across her face again as it always had back home.

Very soon Umma confided to me that she would have to find a job. At the same time, she wanted to sign me up to start in an American school. But she also realized that she could not do both. She needed me to help her search for a job. She needed me to speak English to them and translate their English back to her.

I was against the idea of her working while carrying my sister. I felt my father would not like it either. But if she was going to be traveling outside to meet potential employers, I was definitely going along with her. So when she was six and a half months pregnant, I found a job for Umma working at a fabric factory, a building located inside a group of warehouses where women, most of them foreign, worked on industrial machines lined up in rows.

I spoke to the manager there who offered Umma parttime work due to her pregnancy, at three dollars per hour. He said if Umma was good, she could be bumped up to full time after she gave birth. I liked that there were mostly women working there on the floor where all the sewing was being done. I did not like that all the bosses were men. Back home, Umma's clothing business was run, from top to bottom, exclusively by African women.

The best part about the Russian-born Israelis who ran the factory was that they didn't make a big deal about Umma's Islamic attire. And when I explained that Umma couldn't speak English, one of the bosses asked, "Does this look like a talking place to you?" "Show up on time, work fast and work hard, that's it," the second boss chimed in.

So I escorted Umma to the factory each time she went, and picked her up at the end of every workday. We rode the trains together. At work and in public, she remained covered from head to toe, beneath a *hijab* and behind a *niqab* veil. No one could see her, except me. Her modest clothing gave me a chance to grow up without having to fight grown men all day, every day. Her modest clothing kept me from having to hurt anybody, especially on my Brooklyn block.

My sister Naja was born in a Brooklyn hospital that some fool had the good mind to name The Kings County Hospital, a place where no one was treated royal. Umma was left alone in a room lying down with impatient and unprofessional health-care workers, angry that she could not speak English and bent on keeping me, her translator, in a separate area. As I pressed them at the front desk to call the doctor, one nasty lady in a colorful medical jacket pointed her fat crooked finger at me and said, "Do you see all these people out here?" I did see them, tens of them lying on tables, some in rooms, others pushed against the walls and lined up in the hallways.

"Some of these people have been shot. Has your mother been shot?" she asked me with a monster mug face.

"No, *alhamdulillah*," I answered, meaning, "No, Umma has not been shot, thank Allah." Living in Brooklyn I had seen guns being aimed and triggers being pulled, and shots being fired, and gangsters and thieves and pimps and shootouts, but nothing was scarier than this woman's hatred and disregard for human life. Why couldn't she understand what Umma was going through? She was a woman too. Then I decided that she was really nothing but an empty shell with a booming voice and hole where the heart is supposed to be. I could not imagine that she had ever been anybody's mother or friend.

"So she has to wait, then! The doctor will see the most important cases first."

My sister didn't wait. Umma was drenched in sweat when she burst out. Umma jumped off the table and caught her before her eight-pound body could hit the floor.

Later I found out that the monster lady was not even a nurse. Somehow someone in America had given out colorful medical jackets to the most uneducated, untrained people in the world and left them there to care for the sick and newborn.

A real nurse showed up eventually and said that Umma should have been under a doctor's care throughout her entire pregnancy. She blamed Umma and covered for the crazy lady who yelled at us, explaining that we showed up at the wrong door of the hospital.

Umma said we would have to take good care of ourselves and my newly born sister Naja, to make sure that we all remained healthy. Otherwise, Umma explained, we would fall victim to "the American hospital, which should be called 'the American morgue.'"

The first day we carried Naja to the apartment was the first day we received a real visit from a neighbor. She was named Ms. Marcy. We already knew her because she was an elderly lady who I once helped to carry her groceries inside the building.

Umma said that old people are always attracted to babies. Through me, Ms. Marcy asked about Naja often. Sometimes she invited Umma over for small talks and hot drinks. Since Umma could not really communicate with Ms. Marcy, we knew she really wanted to spend time with the baby. Umma accepted Ms. Marcy as her only neighborhood acquaintance. She said she missed the wisdom, warmth, and love of the elders that she once had back home. Eventually, Ms. Marcy became the only person in our hood allowed to see, touch, and care for my infant sister Naja.

At home I assisted in every way possible. I thought it was amazing, this newborn life. Since all we had was each other, I learned more about infants than I ever would have back home. In the Sudan, our newborns are surrounded by aunties and a host of women of every age who handle everything. Where I am from, a male would usually never interfere in the areas that the women control and are better suited for.

When Umma was breast-feeding Naja once, I asked her what was she thinking when she was in the hospital lying on her back and felt Naja come flying out?

She said "I didn't think at all. It was a mother's instinct and catching Naja was the same as catching myself."

Umma and I grew closer every day and depended on each other and no one else. We made up certain rules between us and even had an emergency plan if anything seemed to have happened to one of us. In our rooms, both of us always kept one piece of packed luggage in case we suddenly had to make a move. We weren't expecting anything bad to happen, but we both learned that things do happen even when you don't expect it.

When Umma, Naja, and I were inside our Brooklyn apartment, we were inside our own little Sudanese world. We adjusted and trusted and believed only in us three. There was only love in there. What went on outside our door we tolerated, dealt with, and handled. I kept my fury for the streets. Inside we were determined to maintain our traditions, ways of being and doing. And we were steadfast in our Islam.

7

QUIET MONEY

Getting money and getting killed seemed like one and the same around my way. Every male I saw getting money ran the risk of losing his life and freedom, and many of them did.

The way I saw it, if you lost your freedom, you lost your life anyhow, *'cause then you really can't get no money.* In two years' time I counted twenty male teens dead. Twelve had actually lost their lives. The remaining eight were hauled off in police cars, heads pushed down by the palm of some questionable cop's hand, cuffed and carted away for a long, long time. And this was only in my building. I didn't count the dead from the other side of my block.

It was crazy how they left the yellow tape on the walkway, tracing out the body of DeQuan's dead little brother DeLeon, the asthmatic one. He got popped on the block at age fifteen. Somebody spray painted the outline of his corpse and drew a mural on the ground in his name that read: ONLY THE STRONG SURVIVE.

I looked down at it one day as I walked by and figured his brothers blamed him for not being gangster enough to stay alive.

Another time, two teens had lost their lives throwing a party around our way in the tiny rec center. They was tryna make some money. One was an emcee. The other was his deejay. Now they just dead. They brought my building body count to twenty-two in two years. In four years the count exploded to forty-six. Getting money was usually the reason, or somebody jealous that somebody was getting money, or somebody stealing money. Or the cops shutting people down 'cause they don't want nobody around here making money or just 'cause they felt like it.

We made quiet money, Umma and me.

It was strange to us how an American salary was so much more than a Sudanese salary, yet American workers remained poor. It was strange remembering how Umma's employees back home earned so much less money but had so much more. Swiftly we realized that a salary here meant next to nothing. We needed to have a business of our own.

Together we decided to build the business most familiar to Umma, modeled on the one she built and operated back home, but on a much smaller, start-up level. I had faith it would work. I knew that there are very few people who can do what Umma does the way she does it. Once people found out about her products, there would be a demand, I thought.

Every day after work, Umma would be telling me her ideas for improving her workplace, including introducing new methods and products. She pointed out that the factory had more advanced machinery and a larger operating budget than she ever had back home, but they worked with a simple and lower-quality fabric and cranked out garments with limited, unexciting patterns and designs.

On the flip side, Umma was an expert in textiles and designs, and could make everything beautiful. She knew all that a person could know about fabrics—cotton, linens, silk, wool, seersucker, jute, leather, suede; their grain, grade, and quality. She also knew about coloring, blends, and dyes. She was so nice with her fingers that she could stitch elegant patterns and pictures on brocades and do embroidery of intricate original designs on cloth, clothing, and upholstery. When she was bored she crocheted and knitted beautiful blankets, sweaters, scarves, gloves, hats, and clothing. All of our beds at home were draped in her work. She told me she began sewing and stitching at age five. She loved creating designs and clothing but said that her greatest accomplishment was a Sudanese carpet she made from an elaborate design she saw in her mind. It was the only carpet she had ever designed and woven in her lifetime.

I recommended that instead of her trying to get me to translate her suggestions to management in an effort to move up in their company, she should keep her ideas to herself and we should start our own hustle on American soil.

At first Umma was skeptical. To earn her factory pennies, she already worked long, hard hours, sometimes randomly being required to do double shifts. She knew the possibility existed of making money in a private business. Yet after she received the huge hospital bills for the birth of Naja, which she had to pay on her own, she really valued the limited health insurance we were now receiving from what became her full-time factory job. It offered a financial cushion and she was afraid to lose it. Also, back home she had a huge family and friends and community to draw her customers and contacts from. In the U.S. she felt anonymous and iso-lated. But I was confident and certain about Umma. Besides, I was right there to help out in every way.

To encourage her, I had one hundred Umma Designs business cards printed up at a local print shop. After dinner one night when I pushed the cardboard box over to her side of the table, she opened it up and read the card, smiled, then cried.

"Umma Makes Everything Beautiful," was the slogan I had embossed in gold script beneath the company name. She could not even read the English words printed on the cards. But she saw and recognized her name on the card and under-stood my intent, which meant even more.

We learned fast that just having the business cards did not guarantee us any business.

Our breakthrough happened when one of Umma's coworkers, a pregnant Black woman with a British accent, approached me as I waited one day outside of the factory for Umma to come out.

"Your Sana's son, isn't it?" she asked. "It's great how I see you waiting here for her each day. I wish my son were so good. Anyhow, I'd like to invite your mum to my baby shower. Here's the invite. You make sure she understands. Good enough?" She looked tired but she was smiling.

"What is a baby shower?" I asked, unfamiliar with this kind of event. She laughed and answered, "It's for the ladies to get together and celebrate the baby that's coming." She rubbed her belly. "Your mum doesn't have to, but most gals bring gifts for the baby. Okay, thanks," she said, waddling off.

I'm sure I seemed calm and cool to the woman but really I was excited. I convinced Umma to attend the shower even though there was a language barrier. I explained to her that this was her perfect chance to show her work. She should look her best and design and sew the most beautiful gifts for the unborn baby. Maybe even for the baby's mother. It was a women's event, so she could get comfortable, unveil, and display everything.

I was positive the women would all admire Umma and everything she wore and made. Meanwhile, as the women exited the shower, I would be seated right outside with the business cards, pen and paper in hand, ready to catch our first customers' orders.

On the way to the shower, packed tightly in the backseat of the Brooklyn taxi cab, I pulled out seven of my mother's gold bangles, her exquisite jewelry that we usually kept stored away. I placed each one on her right wrist as she caressed

Naja with her free hand. The driver jammed on both the gas pedal and then his brakes, dodging traffic.

Instead of Umma speaking to me, she was thinking to herself. I knew an emotion stirred in her because she had not worn jewelry since we lived in America. She no longer saw the need to decorate herself since she was out of the presence of my father.

Today, however, underneath the beautiful cloth of her thobe, she wore a handmade dress with amazing embroidery stitched from the neckline to the hemline. She carried Naja in a handmade satchel with embroidery that complemented her dress. Before stepping out of the cab, I helped her slip out of her flat walking shoes into a pair of gold leather heels. She had not worn these either while living in America, but I selected them especially for this day.

I carried the gifts in one shopping bag, and her samples in the other. We ended up walking up eight flights of stairs because the elevator in the woman's building was broken. I got worried that maybe these women wouldn't have the money to order anything. Then I pushed the thought out of my head because in my building all the broke people dress the best.

I handed the woman the shopping bag stuffed with gifts. She screamed in delight, "Bloody God! You shouldn't have!" I didn't understand her comment. I handed Umma the other shopping bag and said in Arabic, "I'll be waiting outside here until you're finished." The woman invited me to stay as she saw me leaving. I thanked her and left anyway.

Four or five hours later, the women one by one slowly exited the shower. They were all smiling and upbeat. I handed each of them our business card, explaining that Umma made everything by hand and if they wanted to place an order, they could call the telephone number on the card. About eight of the women must have been the British lady's friends and relatives because I did not recognize them from the factory. Meanwhile I told Umma's coworkers they could also speak their order to me any weekday after work when I came to meet Umma.

When Umma finally came out, the British hostess and a small group of ladies were each thanking and hugging her and showering Naja with compliments and attention. It was the first time there wasn't the formalities and distance between them that there was at the factory, where Umma stayed covered and veiled and unusual because of the male presence. Now they had all seen Umma the elegant woman, her face kissed by Allah, her beautiful hands that made beautiful clothing, her authentic jewels, and her very calm and lovable baby girl.

The bottom line was the coworkers were all used to seeing one another. Seeing Umma, really seeing her today for the first time, was a highlight. I could tell that they had all been affected, especially by her genuine, warm, pretty smile.

I carried Umma's first American Singer sewing machine to our apartment from a used appliance shop. I took her shopping in Manhattan's garment district, and carried her newly purchased supplies.

I received our first customer orders that same week. There were women who ordered, "That exact same blanket that your mother crocheted for the baby . . ." "The same beautiful dress your mother wore to the shower, but in my size . . ." "Ten of those baby satchels but in a variety of solid colors so I can sell them to my friends . . ." "Something unique for my niece. I liked the way your mother designed the clothes for the baby. It was so personal."

Now Umma realized that most of her coworkers could work the machinery at the factory, but really did not have magical fingers like she did. If they did, would they get so pumped up on the items she made that they were willing to part with their hard-earned bucks?

Everyone communicated their orders to me. I established the rates, and requested and collected the deposits. I even hooked some ladies up once they explained their concept of "layaway." When their items were completed, I delivered them and collected the balance. I became known for my good manners, nice way of talking, for being on time, honest, and reliable. All of the customers were women, although some were ordering items for men. They expressed their gratitude to me by offering tips. Tips were small but they added up. On the American holidays, my tips doubled because customers tended to spend like crazy.

Eventually, customers began phoning who were friends of friends of coworkers. I brought an answering machine to keep all the orders organized. I put my voice on the greeting and sometimes bugged out on the various accents, requests, and types of messages when I played them back at night in my room. I also ordered a second phone line to be installed for Umma's personal use.

We never told anyone our home address. It was not on the business card. If special measurements had to be taken, which was unusual, we would make an appointment and show up to the customer's place.

We purposely never advertised or solicited any customers in our own neighborhood or building. We kept our money quiet. Nobody knew we got it or how we got it.

My part in the business may sound easy. Yet there were risks involved. I delivered anywhere that a customer lived. I never said no to any address or location. Some of the places were dangerous and fucked up. America, or at least the state of New York, was divided into separate areas. A lot of people were tribal and territorial. Some fools seemed to believe that if you weren't from a certain area, you couldn't enter or walk through that area. Some people thought their buildings were off limits. Some people believed that kids were easy targets, like the two guys who hid in the corners down in the subway then came at me from two sides, surprising me then jamming me in the turnstile. They didn't get nothing. I dropped down and rolled out.

In just the borough of Brooklyn you could get hemmed up by Black American youth or angry mobs of young whites and sometimes even their parents! You could get chased out by territorial and suspicious Jews, who sometimes had their own private patrols and community rules. Even some of the real religious ones considered their neighborhoods exclusive. I handled all of that and the other boroughs as well.

I had to keep the product nice, neat, and in the same condition that Umma packaged it in. I purchased a high-end North Face backpack from Paragon, a sporting goods and mountain gear boutique in Manhattan. I also brought garment bags in bulk from the Garment District to use when the orders were large. I made sure I expressed our appreciation to each customer and even provided handwritten receipts.

I kept my twenty-two on me to defend our profits. Umma sewed deep pockets into my jeans and khakis, jackets, and coats. She did it because I asked her to. I asked her to so I could carefully conceal my joint plus my knives.

She knew I had weapons. Where we are from, a man is supposed to be armed to defend his family.

She never tried to be an obstacle to my manhood. Even when I showed up with wounds, cuts, or bruises, she just cleaned them up and asked no questions, the same way she related to my father.

Umma opened her first bank account with my translation assistance. We placed half of her cash in the bank. We hid one fourth of the cash in a secret location just in case. I kept one fourth of the cash in my room for business operating costs, like extra supplies and transportation fees or the phone bill and such.

My tips were a separate matter. I started storing them in tin cans that used to hold tea leaves. After filling eight of them, I had to upgrade to huge coin jars, which I filled and placed in the back of my clothing closet—pennies, nickels, dimes, quarters, all in their own jars. I marked each jar as it filled up, to keep the count. Small tips were adding up. Inside of each of my volumes of *The Amazing Adventures of Akbar*, I kept my clean double digit paper dollars neatly arranged and pressed.

As time pushed on, Umma upgraded our business in several ways. We developed a much bigger client list of paying customers who had nothing to do with the factory where she worked. Through word of mouth, or should I say the precision of her skills in making women dress and feel better, she received a big order from one woman who wanted Umma to design everything she wore. The woman had deep pockets and never haggled about our mushrooming prices. She attracted a few wealthy friends of hers to our business but never allowed us to meet them. She made their orders run through her.

With more money to invest back into the business, I improved our packaging to make the products more appealing. Umma introduced colorful tissue papers for wrapping each item, some solids, some fluorescent, some paisley, all interesting and different. She added a line of "scented clothing," using a tradition from back home in the Sudan where women draped their cloths in a closed-in room where homemade incense was burning, making everything they wore smell delicious and leaving an alluring trail wherever they went.

Slowly and carefully, Umma began making her secret homemade perfume potions and placing them in small crystal bottles for sale to exclusive customers and as a gift to returning customers who spent more than three hundred dollars with each order.

I was impressed with her and completely dedicated. Everything that she did naturally as a woman was saving our family. She was my father's private treasure and wife and people were willing to pay to get even a small item that she touched up, or an ounce of her everyday aroma, or a duplicate of her personal style, or anything that resembled her elegance.

8

UPSTATE NEW YORK

Funny thing is, when people support you in business, even though you have given them a great product in exchange for their money, they want you and your business to support them in other ways too.

So, when one of my mother's clients organized a bus trip to an upstate New York farm for apple picking and purchasing fresh plucked vegetables and fresh squeezed juices, Umma decided that our family would attend.

It was the fall season. Although we had come to the United States years before, it was our first trip outside of our hood and our five-borough business area.

Two and a half hours into the trip we exited the highways and the rural countryside appeared on the other side of our bus window, presenting me with a picture completely different than my Brooklyn urban view. There were enormous trees with multicolored leaves that were part green, red, orange, and yellow. They floated down from the tree branches and danced to the ground where they formed waist-high piles on some narrow roads. We were surrounded by the colors of autumn.

There were houses, none of them masterpieces of architecture, but sitting on land with large spaces between them. There were broken-down barns and cows and sheep and goats and horses.

Four-year-old Naja was fascinated with these animals,

which she was seeing for the first time in her life. Her little face and hands were pressed against the glass. Umma was excited and relaxed, speaking softly and explaining everything to Naja in Arabic. Naja would speak Arabic to Umma and then turn to ask questions in English to me.

As the bus bumped up a long rocky dirt road and onto the farm, the women put away their snacks and sandwiches, cleaned their children's hands and faces, and walked off the bus and onto the farm together. I told Umma I would meet them back on the farm in an hour. One of the few males on the trip, I preferred to take a look around this completely new area.

On a paved black road with no sidewalks or curbs, I kicked through a pile of leaves. Walking alone on the road, seeing no one nowhere, I stopped, then stood still. I wasn't losing my mind. On my Brooklyn block standing still was a luxury I couldn't afford.

I looked up through the trees and into the skies. The sun was beaming through the colored leaves and small open spaces, creating a kaleidoscope. I listened to the sounds of nature, the way we used to back home in my grandfather's village. I could hear the subtle sounds of the mosquitoes, knowing they were dying out for the season. I could hear the music of the birds flying south. I could hear the wind breezing through the grass. I could hear the deep moan of the cows and stutter of the goats.

A mile down the road I came upon a horse farm. About eight of them were grazing on some grass behind a rusted barbed-wire fence. I stopped to take a good look at one of them that stood about fifteen feet from me. Horses are big and imposing creatures. I couldn't even imagine what Allah was thinking when He created them. Allah is the ultimate designer, I thought. How amazing to think up and then bring into existence thousands of different kinds of creatures, each one unique and awesome on its own. Look at the difference between a horse and a camel, I thought to myself. The horse's skin was more smooth and tight, its body more streamlined. Allah filled the horse's eyes with mystery. It seemed like they knew something that humans did not know. Yet there was no real way for a human to decipher what a horse was thinking and feeling.

I laughed at myself. Ten minutes in the countryside, and my thoughts were filled with Allah. Back home in my building, I can only feel Allah in my prayers, but not in my surroundings and never outside of our apartment.

When I looked down at the plants, I thought of my father, a scientist. He would know something about each of these plants, not just about their beauty but their use.

He could also look at a field that others would describe as being empty, and create a vision in his mind of what it could be, then make it happen. I saw him do that before, back home. He brought me with him to areas that his business developed.

Soon I arrived at a plot of land that had a house for sale. There were no curtains, shades, or blinds in any of the windows. From where I was it appeared to be empty. I wondered if I could stand to live out here. I had spent summers in my grandfather's village. But it was not only the nature that made it great. It was the people, the brothers and sisters, the cousins, friends, relatives that made it incredible. It was the music, the gatherings, the talks, the sports, and even the work that made it a life.

I pulled my pen and pad out from my army-green jacket and jotted down the telephone number of the realtor. If anything, I just wanted to call and find out how much a piece of property out here would actually cost.

Umma and I already knew that we had to move off our Brooklyn block. We talked about it often and had a plan. We were saving up to buy a house with our cash. We agreed that until we had enough money to pay for the house in full we would remain on our Brooklyn block working hard and saving our profit. No tricky realtor with tricky fees. No mortgage bankers or bloodsuckers who a person had to pay for thirty years of their life. No astronomical interest rates and shit that switched up in the blink of an eye and after the shake of two hands. No more monkeys in the middle, loans, leases, or debts.

To the right, I came upon a pebbled path. I could hear some people talking for the first time in four miles. They were inside a graying building with a weathered sign the read "Blacks." Somehow that meant me so I walked up the path and pushed through the antique door with the WE'RE OPEN sign hanging from one rusty tack. It had been cool outside but was mad hot in here. It was a blacksmith shop with one big older white man covered in black grease, banging what looked like a heavy all-metal hammer on a piece of iron, then poking the iron into an open oven shimmering with intense heat and orange flames.

"You need horse shoes?" the teenage boy who emerged from the corner asked me.

"Nah," I answered.

"Then what'd ya come here fer?" he asked me in an unfamiliar accent.

"Just looking," I told him, my eyes taking in all of the iron and steel, the intense fire and heavy tools.

I wondered to myself, why horse shoes? This place seemed like it had the right equipment and tools and was the perfect place to make weapons.

"Where you from?" the youth asked me. His father or boss kept working.

"Just visiting the apple farm four miles down," I answered without giving up no real info.

"Yeah, I know the place," he said casually.

"Let me show you something," I said as I reached into my left pocket and pulled out a small book I had been reading. He stepped up closer to take a look. I went to page sixty-six, which had an illustration of a Japanese *shuriken*, a wicked-ass knife that I wanted.

"Do you think you could make one of these?" I asked him. He took my book into his hands and got a spot of black grease on the page and answered, "Yep, we could. What you want it for?"

I ignored his question.

"If I ordered a set, how much would it cost me?" He looked back at the older man, who aside from a quick glance didn't seem interested at all.

"I could do it for you, a set of four for a hundred." But I knew that the older guy would be a better craftsman. I was concerned about the quality and the dynamics of the knives. I wanted them to be exact.

"Nah. I'd rather him do it." I nodded to point out the older guy. The boy laughed, a little insulted.

"He'll double the price," he warned. I creased the page and tore it from my book. I handed him the page, with a one-hundred-dollar bill as a fifty-percent deposit on "double the price."

"How long before he can have it ready?" I asked.

"A couple of days," he answered.

"I'll be back to pick them up. Hold 'em for me," I told him firmly.

"You better come back. Once my father works the iron you gotta pay up in full. You can't get no deposit money back if you change your mind," he threatened.

I seen he needed to feel like a boss over me, the customer. I wanted the product so I played along with it.

"Here's fifty more. Just let him do a good job on it," I said calmly. Now that more money was changing hands, I saw the youth's father paying attention.

Umma, Naja, and I made the Zuhr prayer on the farm right before sunset with the violet sky as our ceiling and the trees as our walls. It felt completely peaceful. The passengers on the bus waited eight extra minutes for us. When we raised from our prayers we could see them watching us through their windows. When we boarded, they all had odd looking expressions on their faces as we walked down the aisle. Maybe they had never seen a family pray before. I don't know. Thirty minutes into the ride, they loosened up and were back to acting normal, eating apples, playing cards, kids clapping, and an older lady passing around a hat to take up a collection to tip the bus driver. I thought to myself, maybe these people thought that we were strange. It didn't matter though, because after the prayer, they definitely showed us respect.

What started out as a bother and an obligation turned out to be a great trip. At first Umma and I worried about losing an entire Saturday, which was the biggest workday for her side business. Now we not only got some fresh vegetables and fruits that grew up from the ground and hung down from the trees and were picked by Umma's hand the way she liked it, I also had a lead on a house for sale.

When I gave the realtor a call that same week, at first he didn't want to talk to "a kid," on the telephone. I was twelve. I told him my parents didn't speak English and that I was translating for them. He switched from being angered to only being a bit impatient. He priced the house at sixty-two thousand dollars. He also offered to sell us the empty plot of land beside it for twenty thousand.

Through Umma Designs, in two years we'd banked twenty-four thousand dollars. We agreed that when we had enough money to walk in and buy a whole house and the land it sat on, we would disappear from our Brooklyn block quietly. No one would know where we had gone, why, or most important, how.

The *shuriken* turned out sweet. They were curved knives with a fist grip. One graceful swipe at a neck at the right angle and the head comes off.

9

GOLD

A problem did come like I knew it would. I didn't know what it would be or who it would be, but based on my father's words and lessons, it would happen. His name was Gold Star Tafari. He showed up in the parking lot outside the factory where Umma worked.

A dark cat like me, he seemed about twenty-nine, thirty years old. He had a rough face that you could tell was etched by experience. A medium build, he was about two inches taller than me at thirteen. He had two cuts on his left cheek that looked mean. I always liked scars. They belong on men as a reminder. If you ask a male about his wounds, usually he'll tell a good, crazy, original, and action-packed story. Once a youth starts collecting scars, it makes him a better fighter, smarter with his moves in his next encounter.

He had locks, long, wild, black ones that he made sure not to organize, just wore naturally. He was the first cat I noticed rocking the Star of David piece on his chain, and clenching a gold toothpick holder between the top and bottom rows of his teeth.

He showed up at the factory suddenly. It was a Monday, a cold winter evening, five P.M. to be exact. Already I could see the gray sky that comes before the black. You know how the sun rises late and sets real early in the midwinter season? There was a steady flow of nine-to-five workers getting off and walking through the parking area like they did at the end of each workday. Most of them didn't have cars.

He drove up, parked, got out, stood and began looking in my direction. I was checking out the fact that he was wearing a hat made by Umma Designs. It was crocheted with Umma's special stitching using iced green, black, and gold yarn.

It didn't even take me ten seconds to run through the orders in my head. It was easy since all Umma's orders ran through me anyway. I recalled that I sold that hat to a thick Jamaican girl named Shirley. She was easy enough to remember. The first time I met her was on the day of the baby shower. For a long time she never placed an order with Umma Designs. But she would always wave and smile when she saw me.

When I grew some more, she would stop and speak to me while I waited for Umma to come downstairs. She had a thick Jamaican accent, which I had to strain to understand, and a bold style. She wore her clothes real tight, revealing how her legs swung back and gave her an unusual stance.

Finally one day she ordered some hats from me. We went back and forth on the price and the exact shade of green she wanted Umma to stitch. I showed her about seven different variations of the color before she agreed. She said the hats were for her fiancé and described him as being "real choosy." She claimed if she got the color wrong by even a little bit, he wouldn't wear the hats at all. She joked that she liked my quiet, easygoing style better than his loud demands and wanting everything his way. She shot me a sly look and said she would marry me if my age would just catch up with my body. Her eyes lingered on me to check if I caught her compliment. I just laughed at the time, thought it was funny, a female choosing me and then telling me she would marry me like I had no say-so in it.

The last time I delivered Shirley some hats that she had ordered was the last time I saw her. Umma said she quit the job all of a sudden, a few months before her scheduled wedding. Her coworkers speculated on what happened with her because no one got a chance to say their good-byes or had received a wedding invite or even a friendly call.

I waited and watched the cat as he looked around the parking lot. He never made a move that night. None of the workers stepped up to meet him, to say hi or to catch a ride in his car. He stayed at a distance, just leaning against his car and watching me watching him. When Umma came down we left. He chilled right there.

The next evening he rolled up again at five. It was impossible to miss that pale-yellow Fairmount station wagon that leaned heavier on one side than the other and oddly had wood paneling on the outside of the car. If he was supposed to be incognito, that shit wasn't working out too well.

The third night he showed up he was still focused in my direction. When Umma came downstairs and joined me, he stopped leaning on his car, stood up straight, and for some reason removed his hat, his locks falling down around his face like a lion's mane. He shook them one good time and struck a pose like an animal after a mating dance.

"What are you staring at?" Umma asked me.

"Nothing," I responded, placing my hand behind her elbow and moving us away from his view and on our way.

In my mind I was thinking that this man must be thinking that one day he would show up and I wouldn't be there. Then he would seize his opportunity to swoop down on my mother. Then I told myself, nah. Why would he be here for Umma? I mean, there were all these women walking through with either really tight or revealing clothing. Why would he be checking out the one woman wearing loose-fitting Islamic dress whose face and body he could not see at all?

On Friday, the fifth day of his strange appearances, he sat in his station wagon and waited for Umma to come downstairs to meet me. He exited his car dressed in a rust Wrangler corduroy suit; brown Clark weavers; a red, yellow, and green belt; and a hat that looked like a beaver tilted sideways. He walked over toward us, his steps sideways like his hat. Purposely I waited eager to find out his intent. I stepped in front of Umma so that she was directly behind me. "Wait one minute, Umma." I opened my coat so he could see I was holding.

"I-man respect dat," he said. "Overstand?" he added, smiling ear to ear.

"What you need?" I asked him, unfamiliar with whatever he was saying.

"I-man need fa chat wit she fa a minute," he said, leaning to the side to try to catch Umma's eyes and attract her attention. But I was taller than her and she didn't step out from behind me.

"Talk to me," I told him. He reached his hand behind him into his back pocket.

I pulled out my joint and held it at my side where no one but him could see it.

"Hold on, wait, mon. I-man a paying customer," he said, calmly opening the paper he just pulled out from his back pocket. "Why com it always haf a com down to fire power between bretherns?" he asked, but I didn't flinch.

"I want fer she ta put the Lion of Judah on I-man shirt. I-man know only she can do what I-man want. I-man checks Umma styles mon, wicked!" he said, his smile revealing his slow, sly manner and smoker's teeth.

"Whatever I-man wants from Umma Designs, I-man needs to talk only to me," I told him, believing by now his name was I-man. He corrected me, telling me that his name was Gold Star Tafari. He pushed each of his names out like he was pronouncing something sacred or announcing the arrival of a king. I later figured out that I-man was his way of saying "me," referring to himself.

Umma embroidered a gold Lion of Judah on the back of his deep-blue denim shirt, with all of the detail and power presented on the picture that he had handed to me that night outside the factory.

When I called him to let him know his shirt was ready, he offered to meet Umma at her job. I told him forcefully that he should not return there since his business was only with me. He chuckled.

We met. I gave him the shirt wrapped in our packaging. He paid. I gave him a receipt. After I thanked him for his business I turned to leave.

"Hold on," he said. He tore open the package right in front of me. He held the denim shirt up, then laid it down on the wrapping paper and ran his thick, rough, ashy hands over the hand-embroidered designs and shouted, "Wicked! Selassie-I." I could tell that was some kind of vote of approval. I nodded and asked him, "You good?"

He answered, "Umma is good!" I started feeling tight. So I left.

Less than twenty-four hours later his deep voice and strange talk cut through on our voice mail. "I-man wants . . ."

Umma embroidered a Lion of Judah on the pant leg of his jeans. I charged him double what he paid for the embroidery on his shirt. We met at a vegetarian spot called The Green Onion on Nostrand Avenue in Brooklyn. He paid for the package. I gave him the receipt, thanked him, and left.

His next voice mail was directed at Umma. It was crazy hearing his voice saying her name, "Umma." Umma was the name that only our family called her. Even though her business was named Umma Designs, her first name is actually

Sana. "I-man wanna thank you personally, Umma. I-man has a special project jus fa you, Umma," he said.

I played his message three times. I never allowed Umma to hear it, of course. But now I was thinking of this cat as some real threat, a nutcase who knew where my mother worked and didn't mind taking the time to come up to her job looking around and waiting for her. I waited to return his call. I had to let my anger pass.

When I called Gold Star Tafari back, he said he needed to have Umma come over personally to do some measurements for some custom-designed curtains for his apartment.

He was pushing it. I knew he wanted to get my mother inside his apartment, within his reach and control. By now I could tell that he would try anything. He was always calm, though, which fucked with me even more.

So I played his game. I made an appointment for Umma to take the measurements and took his home address. I was glad to know where he lived. Even though he did not know where we lived, he already knew too much about my family, I thought. He lived in Brooklyn, in the corner building at the end of the block directly across the street from Prospect Park on Ocean Avenue and Parkside, over there down by the playgrounds.

When I knocked he pulled his door open slowly. I could hear the metal pole dragging against a metal slide as the door opened. It was an old-school police lock where a metal pole leans against the closed door making it impossible for anyone to enter without the pole being removed. Even if someone was successful in breaking into an apartment with one of these locks, the noise that the metal made would expose the intruder instantly.

When I stepped inside the dim living room, I could see his huge candles burning. I heard his soft music playing reggae sounds, Bob Marley's voice. "I don't want to wait in vain for your love . . ."

I could tell that this was a typical approach for him. His thick cylinder candles were burnt down more than halfway. There was already three inches' worth of hardened wax stuck around their bottoms.

His big fucking welcome smile evaporated when he realized it was me, not Umma, and that she wasn't even with me. I acted like he did, calm and casual. I walked in with the tape measure draped around my neck. I had disregarded his instructions the way he disregarded mine.

"Turn on the lights so I can get your measurements right," I told him.

After taking the measurements and ignoring his screw face I quoted a price for the curtains that I thought would permanently end his relationship with Umma Designs.

"Three thousand dollars," I quoted him for the white burlap drapes he wanted with the brocade borders and the Lion of Judah embroidered on each section.

"I-rie," he said. But I didn't know what that meant. So I started explaining and breaking down to him why my price was so high.

"Five hundred covers only the material and supplies. It's handmade. The material you want is heavy and expensive. The embroidery process will take much longer than usual."

"No problem, my youth," he said. "I-rie." Which I now knew meant something like "Okay," or "That's cool."

He left his living room space and walked into some back room. I was standing there in disbelief that he was gonna pay out the ridiculous price I only came up with to get rid of him for good.

I looked around his little bachelor pad. Behind where I was standing, on the wall, was a five-foot-long horizontal fluorescent poster of the silhouette of a naked black woman lying down on her side. She had wide hips, a small waist, and titties the size of honeydew melons. It was just the outline of a female body. She had no skin, no eyes or nose or mouth even. But she did have two afros, one big and one small. He had ashtrays everywhere, filled with cigarette butts and reefer seeds and roaches. Gold beads hung in each doorway dividing one room from the other. His lamps sat on top of old Guinness stout crates instead of tables. His extensive hat collection lined one of the walls, each hanging on its own nail. There were no family photos or even a sign of a woman's scent or touch. There were no heels or dresses or bangles or perfumes or fresh-cut flowers. I thought to myself that he probably erases every trace of each woman after he uses her.

I imagined that this was his second apartment. Somehow I felt he had a bunch of random girls and random babies, people who he had abandoned. But I did not know for sure. I decided maybe I should stop being so tight and talk to this cat for a minute. At least I could be smart enough to collect some more information on him.

He came back holding a machete. He was using it to cut slices off an apple he began eating. The blade was long and sharp enough to sever his entire hand with one wrong motion.

I seen everything he did was slick and subtle.

There was no fear in my heart. I was holding enough weapons on me to slice him up in pieces smaller than that apple he was eating.

He watched to see if I would react in any way to his blade. I didn't blink.

"One thousand five hundred dollars for the deposit," I told him dryly and calmly. He laughed a little, placed his knife and apple on his heavy wooden table right next to two decks of playing cards, a pile of chew sticks, and a half-empty bottle of white rum. He kept his eyes on me as he slid his hand into his right pocket, pulling out a wad of dirty bills. He counted out loud in his version of the English language.

Seemed like he had a dramatic and different way of pronouncing every English word, *tree* instead of *three* and so on. I took the cash deposit he handed over to me.

"Thank you. I'll give you a call as soon as your curtains are ready."

"Ya want fa sit don ere? Ya look tense, mon, seckle ya self. You want fa blow some trees?" he asked.

"What?" I said.

"Hold on." Barefooted, he left again. He came back with two big spliffs burning, both of them in his mouth.

"Try and com down, na." He offered me one, which he now held pinched between his thumb and index finger, smiling at me like I was his new friend.

"Nah, I'm good," I told him, rejecting his weed.

"When I-man curtains complete we celebrate seen." He laughed. As he began smoking both spliffs, I left.

I didn't know what his occupation or business was. But I was starting to form a picture in my mind.

Umma was excited about earning the money for the curtains and moving closer to our financial goals. I should have been happy too, but I was heated.

"Do you know this man?" I asked her with an even and respectful tone.

"No."

"You never met him before?" I double checked.

"No. Is there some problem? If there is a problem we don't have to do business with him," she answered.

"No problem, Umma. I just want to make sure he talks business with me and doesn't talk to you at all," I said. "I don't want him going anywhere near your job."

"Of course," she said gently.

One late night on the basketball court alone, I thought about how uneasy I felt about this guy because he knew where my mother worked. Whether I dropped him as a client or not, he would still always know exactly where to go to get at her. I also knew that what he really wanted was hidden behind his constant requests for sewing services.

Weeks later when I spoke to Gold on the phone to set up the curtain delivery, his intensity toward my mother had only increased. He requested that I bring her with me to his place because the curtains had to get hung. He tried to keep me from hanging the curtains myself by insulting my manhood. "Ya know dat's woman's work . . ."

I fired back, "Umma Designs is only contracted to make your drapes. The product is ready and in perfect condition. You or your woman can hang the drapes."

He chuckled. "I-rie," he said.

Gold Star Tafari didn't have my money ready when I knocked at his door at the agreed-upon time. That was the first indication that this transaction wasn't about to flow right.

"Come in, na," he said, releasing the doorknob from his grip so that the heavy door pressed against me and the iron bar dragged against the metal as I carried in the well-packaged drapes.

"Where do you want these?" I asked. He gave no response and left the room, disappearing behind the gold beads. I sat the package down on his couch and remained standing.

Instantly I noticed three piles of neatly stacked cash on his heavy wooden table. I stayed where I was standing because I sensed a setup and didn't want to be accused of touching his paper. There was a bag of weed beside his money stacks, at least a pound of it. And there was a weed cloud hanging over the wooden table.

He returned barefooted with his jeans on and his shirt open. He had a scar running down from his chest to his stomach as though somebody tried to split him open once. Not a doctor. It was a raggedy scar ripped with vengeance and passion.

"What good is da curtains dem, witout da couch ta match. I-man need a new covering for me chairs dem. Same material. Lion of Judah on each one of dem, overstand?" he said, pointing toward his couch and chairs.

"Nah. She can't do it," I said, tired of the game he was playing and not giving a fuck about the extra money a new deal with him could bring.

"Be reasonable, na cha!" he said, lighting a cigarette. He took a long pull. Releasing the smoke he asked, "Ya hava girlfriend?"

I didn't respond 'cause it wasn't about business. He continued, "Woman is a good ting, my youth. Like a sweet potato."

"Fifteen hundred is what you owe me right now. We can discuss the upholstery some other time," I told him, fighting to remain calm and professional.

"Lookova de so," he said, pointing at a crate on the floor next to the couch. I looked with my eyes but didn't break my stance.

"Your money is dere, chek-n-see," he said. Then he sat down at his table across the room. I walked over and looked down into the crate. There was an envelope inside.

"You want me to take that envelope?" I asked him to double check that there was no trap, no mistake.

"Go on, na," he said.

So I picked up the envelope. I could tell there was more than money in it. So I opened it up right there in his face. There was cash, a heap of ones, fives, tens, and twenties. His bills were crumpled and dirty as usual. There were also some photos.

I pulled the photos out. "You must've made a mistake. You got some pictures in here," I told him, extending my arm to return them.

"I-man neva make no mistakes," he said. "Look pon da pictures," he said.

I flipped them over and took a look. There were five pictures, all of them of Umma. Each one prettier than the last. She was dressed up and beautiful. Her smile was radiant. Her hair was exposed, as well as her shapely body and elegant face, natural and just incredible.

An anger so strong built up in me, from my toes to my head. It was like a wave from the ocean, gaining a deadly and unstoppable momentum. A wave with a powerful undercurrent and dangerous riptides. It kept me from thinking straight, like I normally would do.

I was trained to control my anger. Yet my training seemed to be failing me now. I stood, boiling yet frozen in that same spot, remembering a line from a book my Sensei once gave me called *The Art of War*. The line was "War is deception."

I kept saying the line over and over again in my head to calm myself down.

"I-man wanna make Umma, I-man's wife. Dis ting is a serious ting, mon. What I-man hafta do to make ya see I-man serious? Whatcha need star? Is it money, eh? I-man has good 'n plenty money." He pushed a stack of bills forward on the wooden table. I was still calming myself down. I didn't say nothing.

"Cha! Ya want mora?" he asked and pushed the second stack of bills forward.

"It's not possible," I said politely.

"Noting is impossible. Everyting have a price seen," he said, pushing the third stack forward. "Look around. Me trade fa any ting ya see ina ere." Then he threw his bag of weed over at me like it wasn't nothing. It fell to the floor by my feet.

"Mr. Tafari, I have the fifteen hundred here in the envelope. That's the balance. That makes three thousand. Now we're straight. Umma is not for sale. Do you need a receipt?" I asked him without exposing any emotions.

He banged the table with his fist, finally losing his cool.

"Me naw want no blood-clot receipt. Give I and I back feme pictures dem and go."

"How much do you want for the pictures?" I asked him calmly, throwing his style back the same way he threw it out there.

He gave me a deadly look. For the first time he had no smile and no chuckle and his temper was brewing. He wouldn't answer me.

Evil looks didn't mean shit to me, so I left with the fifteen hundred and the photos. There was nothing chasing me but a chorus of his curses. I left him throwing a tantrum that could have been recorded on top of some rough-ass Jamaican sound system beats.

He left some recordings of his own on my voice mail. Again he sounded as though he was speaking directly to Umma. He left twelve messages to be exact, over a one-week period of time.

He showed up at Umma's job one Friday at four P.M., one hour earlier than she usually got off work. But I anticipated his plan and had been waiting for Umma each day of that week beginning at three P.M. and sitting until five, just in case.

I realized that I was the one who had influenced Umma to attend her coworker's baby shower. I was the one who had encouraged her to dress up in her most elegant way. I was the one who made her feel like it was all right for her to shine, to let down her hair, to relax and enjoy herself and show the potential female clients the true secret of Sudanese beauty. I was the one who slipped the expensive heels on her feet. I was the one who pushed her to reveal her incredible talents. I now realized that this was the only way that Gold Star Tafari got his hands on the photographs of Umma's exquisiteness.

Putting the pieces together, I remembered Shirley was at the baby shower that day. She must have snapped those photos. Gold was wearing one of the hats I sold to Shirley. That's probably how he got his hands on those photos. He probably glanced at the photos casually and never revealed the depth of his lust to Shirley, his fiancée. That's when he began to put together his plan to bypass and deceive Shirley and capture my Umma.

Setting up in the woods of Prospect Park seven nights later was easy. In the bushes, wearing all black on a black night, no one could see my black face, my black gloves over my black hands, or my black gun. I screwed on my black silencer, paid for with a portion of the cash from Gold's envelope.

I waited three hours in the cold. Only my thoughts kept me heated. When Gold Star Tafari walked around the corner at 1:06 A.M. after parking his yellow station wagon, I clapped him up nice. The Lion of Judah got took down by the Leopard of Sudan.

War is deception, I thought to myself. No sense in being sloppy. Think through shit, control your anger, make a tight plan, and execute it.

10

HEAVENLY PARADISE

"You seem so serious. How come?" It was a female from around my way breaking my concentration when I paused for five seconds on the block to organize my thoughts. It wasn't just any female. Her name was Heavenly Paradise, aka Heaven On Earth. She was famous for her light-brown eyes and mean-ass walk. Boys battled one another for her with their fists and their finances. She always ended up with either the strongest or richest. You could always tell who was getting it by the gold pendant she wore around her neck. They all gave her either their gold nameplate or their pendant to rock. I heard that even when she broke up with them, she never gave it back. Dudes knew they had to pay to play, try to cut their losses, and charge the rest to the game.

In the streets everybody knew she was Conflict's woman these days. He sported her like her pussy was brand new and kept her real close. She was wearing his pendant, a fourteen-karat gold dagger. Everybody knew Conflict was Superior's younger brother. Superior was the most infamous hustler in my area by now. Conflict was his blood brother and right-hand man.

I didn't call this girl over. So I didn't know what she was tryna do by approaching me on the block in front of everybody. I did know that all the males out here sweated her hard. But Conflict had her on lock.

I didn't sweat her at all. She was somebody else's piece and

I respected that. Besides I never messed with another man's women, money, or property.

Ever since I won the pull-up contest that DeQuan sponsored on the block, Heavenly Paradise set her eyes on me and she wasn't used to getting turned down.

Now that I'm fourteen, my voice is deep, accent long gone. I chill every day in the most wanted styles. My kicks are fresh. I keep money in my pocket. I'm closing in on six feet one. My body is cut like what. Girls think I did it for them. I did it for war.

Now I can't keep these females off of me. The more I show them nothing—no interest at all, the harder they come for me. Shit got crazy.

What could I tell them seriously? Could I tell them, "I was born Muslim and we don't believe in dating or sex before marriage"? I was not the kind of Muslim they were used to seeing or being or hearing about. Like the ones who were born Christian in America who suddenly change their name to something Islamic sounding, and other than playing Islamic dress-up, they don't do anything that a Muslim is supposed to do. Or the ones just make believing that they're Muslims, who fuck all the women, never marry them, abandon all the babies, and talk a lot of shit that don't add up to nothing.

Could I tell them, "Yeah, you look good to me," which was the truth, but "You're a ran-through whore and my moms will never accept you," which was the truth also. Nah, I couldn't tell them nothing. So I didn't. I was known for being quiet and serious and silent.

"I see you always got a book in your pocket. Do you read them or just carry them around?" she asked, smiling, and very confident in herself. Now she had one hand on her hip gripping her little waistline, twisting her little body to make sure I could see the curve of her famous ass, which poked out even when she rocked long skirts.

The fact of the matter was, if I was back home in my grandfather's African village, at age fourteen I could rightfully be planning to marry, own a piece of land, and start a family. To some people this might sound crazy. I understood it one hundred percent.

I could feel the difference in myself from when I was twelve or even thirteen. At fourteen, I feel stronger. My observations are sharper. I looked at things a bit differently than I did before. In my body I felt a force, a yearning, a hunger.

In my grandfather's village, they must have understood the human body and mind. They built a village that could stay in step with reality. If at fourteen the natural thing was to feel and become sexual, then at fourteen you could marry and start a family and become responsible and respectable.

In the USA the society was out of pace with the natural development of its young. They made it a shame for a youth to feel and be sexual at fourteen, and looked away while they knew it was happening randomly anyway.

Adults acted surprised and disgusted when teens got pregnant. Then they pressed them to kill their seeds. The laws made it premature and illegal for teens to marry or to even get working papers and become responsible and earn.

I knew because around my way a young teenage girl named Raven got pregnant by a mild-mannered cat named Thomas. Her mother dragged her in tears to the abortion clinic. Three days later Thomas shot and killed his girlfriend's mother for killing his unborn.

I considered myself a disciplined cat. But under plan USA, even when a youth graduates from high school his parent is still hollering, "Finish your education first." Next he does four or five years of undergraduate school at some college. Still the adults are hollering, "Secure a good job first then start a family." No matter how disciplined a youth is, could he really hold off completely? Could he resist his sexual nature until he's twenty-three years old? Or is it the American way for the young to abort all the babies they create up until the time they are eligible to marry, have completed their studies, and are qualified to work?

Reality says no. So the block was bursting with chaos. Everybody's fucking everybody. Nobody's married. Nobody claims responsibility. Nobody's respected.

"I gotta go," I told Heavenly Paradise and pushed off. I could hear her sucking her teeth at me. Even though I knew she would not give up, I just kept it moving. There was more than enough business for me to handle.

11

MIDNIGHT

Monday through Thursday I play basketball at night after my sister and my moms, along with the majority of people in the hood who don't want no problems, were in a deep sleep. I like the court better when it's empty.

Dribbling the ball always releases my tension. Sinking the ball in the hoop makes me feel good about my possibilities.

I dreamed of playing ball blindfolded, getting so familiar with the dimensions of the court and becoming so aware and comfortable that I could just sense the position of the basket and sink the ball, all net. I figured once I could start hitting those three-pointers blindfolded, I could do any fucking thing. But it was just a dream. I'm too smart to close or cover my eyes while I'm out on the Brooklyn streets, even in the neighborhood playground.

After a while, there was an old wino cat who started leaning on the fence watching me play. He used to call me Midnight since I only played late at night. Every now and then he'd bring a drinking partner. They'd stand on the side, drink, and talk shit. It wasn't long before the name Midnight stuck to me.

One night out, the court was all dark and foggy. Either somebody had busted the street lamp, or it just blew out. Since I could barely see anything, I figured this was my chance to test my senses without having to close my eyes.

This was the same night I met a young cat who stepped right out of the darkness and started speaking to me.

"Peace, God," he hollered out. Right off I knew he was a Five Percenter, like DeQuan, Superior, Conflict, Heavenly, and a bunch of people living and dying around my way. They believed that "the Black man is God." So they addressed black boys and men as "God," and the Black girls and women were called "Earth." Some of them claimed to have something to do with Islam. Some of them didn't. It didn't matter to me what they said or called themselves. I kept my eyes on them. It doesn't matter what anyone says, just give them a little bit of time and they'll prove who they are and what they really believe by how they're living day to day. Over time I learned to deal with them like they was just another group of people who were not all the way true or serious. I didn't lock horns with them though. I didn't waste my time tryna knock them. I moved around them and kept my own beliefs, pace, and flow.

"Yeah, you nice with it," he added. "You should come play on the team."

Now, I could see the outline of his body, but not the details of his face. Yet I could tell from his voice that he wasn't from my block. I checked the distance between him and my guns that I had stashed on the side. I told myself I messed up. This guy caught me slipping. If he wanted to do me something, it would be my bad all the way. But it wasn't his angle.

"I'm Tyriq. And you?" he asked. Instinctively, I told him, "Midnight."

He wanted me to come up to the school and play on his team. I told him I couldn't because I was busy and didn't have time for everyday after-school practices and a coach running my life.

"Nah, God," he said. "This is not the school team. We just rent their court and sometimes their gym. You know, like intramural." I didn't know what *intramural* meant so I just stayed quiet. He explained that this team was just "the best young ballers in Brooklyn, competing against one another in a tournament." He said it didn't matter if I wasn't a "schoolboy." He gave me the info on the meeting spot, time, and place and went on his way. I dribbled the ball while I watched him walking away.

My side hustles kept me moving in and out of all types of situations.

We ride together, Umma and I, still. After I get Umma to her workplace, I am free to handle business, homeschool work, or whatever is necessary.

On early Friday and Saturday mornings, I always head to Chinatown, located in lower Manhattan, where I have a part-time job in a fish market owned by a Chinaman named Cho. I caught the job one day while shopping for fresh fish for my mother to cook. She didn't care how far I had to go to find fresh food that she would feel good about cooking. She often said that the local markets were selling Brooklyn Blacks old, expired, and sometimes even rotten food. While searching for a proper fish market, she taught me how to pull the fish gills back and check for the dark-red color to be sure that a fish is fresh. A fading pink meant it was not fresh. If the gills were cut out and the fish was cut into pieces or filleted and flaking, it meant it was old fish and the grocer was trying to get over. If the eyeballs of the fish were bloated or expanded in any way or cloudy, this meant the fish was old. "Flip it over," my mother would say to me in Arabic. "You must check both sides and both fish eyes for freshness."

The Chinaman had fish so fresh that some of them were still alive. He'd stick his hand in a huge tank and yank it out. On the scale the snapper would still be breathing.

When I discovered this particular fish shop, I noticed the Chinaman had a picture on a side wall of himself at the helm of a real pretty red, thirty-six-foot, Reinell fishing boat out on the deep waters of the ocean. I asked him if the boat was his. He pretended not to hear me or understand. They were good at ignoring. I followed up and asked him if he was hiring. He told me the price of my seafood order, accepted my money, and moved right on to his next customer.

I was still interested. I had a thing for boats, ever since I accompanied my father on a business trip in a bad-ass yacht named *Al Salamah*, cruising across the Red Sea on the invite of a Saudi Arabian prince.

In the Sudan, even traveling up the Nile on a felucca was an adventure. It was just the feeling and the freedom that moving across the waters created within me.

Besides, the Chinaman had a crazy knife collection. I liked the way he wielded them, slicing the fish so precisely and easily.

My father taught me that language should never be the thing that separates one group of people from another. It's easy to pick up a language if you just learn how to listen. He also taught me that people will treat you better when you take time to learn their greetings and customs.

Soon enough, I picked up a Chinese language book for a few dollars from a used bookstore. Easily I learned how to introduce myself in Chinese, and of course the Chinese word for boat, *chuan*.

I headed back to the fish store the next week, took my time introducing myself in Chinese, and asked if he had work. I did get a smile, but nothing else from the quiet, hardworking Chinaman, who seemed to only talk and only understand the language of numbers. I placed my order, paid, and bounced.

The following week I showed up in my flannel work shirt, jeans, and Tims, with my fish scaler in my hand. I told him in English that I would work the first day for free. Somehow he understood that! I caught the job.

Every Friday and Saturday from 7 A.M. until 3 P.M. I worked doing everything: unloading fish from the truck, dropping the live ones into tanks, placing fresh and frozen fish on ice, or scaling then chopping off fish heads and splitting fish bellies open and gutting them.

Chinatown for me was an amazing place that sometimes reminded me of my capital city of Khartoum back home in the Sudan, where my father had an executive business apartment separate from our estate. Chinatown was all about buying and selling any- and everything from Chinese herbs to dried-out chicken feet and snake tails, snake oil, clothing, jewels, or restaurant equipment. Every inch of space and property was fully used, nothing wasted, including fish eyeballs and fish heads. I observed short and slim Chinamen making a business out of only two feet of space. For ten hours they would stand on that small spot they had rented and sell whatever they had to offer.

A lot of Chinatown was about language and letters and codes. They spoke a different language, used a different system of letters, and sometimes hung up signs and prices that no one else but the Chinese people could read and understand. On the low they even had separate prices for the Chinese. I watched Cho switch up the numbers when his own kind came around. I wasn't mad at it though. I thought it was cool and the same thing any group of people would do for theirselves and their people if they had any sense.

Cho warmed up to me, I believe, because I always showed up on time, made no excuses, and worked hard at anything he asked me to do. This was how it was supposed to be, I thought to myself. He asked no questions about who gave me permission to work, my age, or schooling. He didn't request working papers or social security numbers or nothing. We just got down to getting what needed to be done, done.

It turned out he knew a lot more English than he originally let on. He paid me in cash at the end of each day, as if that was all he could be sure of. Maybe I wouldn't show up the next day or I'd just completely disappear. He paid me a different amount each time. I guessed he was basing it on how he felt about whatever he earned for the day. He never cheated me so his system worked out fine. I knew that in time he would stop doubting me and I might even get a crack at chilling in the Atlantic Ocean on his big-ass boat.

Eventually he took me on a tour of the world in Chinatown that existed beneath the dark-brown metal doors in the cement ground. These doors, when unlocked, led to a network of basements.

Downstairs from Cho's, there were tanks and cages filled with live long, black eels, lobsters, crabs, chickens, pigeons, and even cats. A narrow cement underground pathway connected each business on the block to the other. Once we walked past his underground property, we entered the next man's underground space, where he was storing unmarked boxed merchandise. Cho said, "Stay on my side." He explained that the merchants on this strip had an honor system not to tamper with each other's products, and a surefire method of dealing with anyone who violated it. I knew what that meant.

I had already peeped the short, bald, Chinese strongman, his body built like a rhinoceros. In the thick of the winter he came around wearing only a T-shirt as though weather had no effect on him. He entered the shop every Friday surrounded by his deadly silence and collected an envelope from Cho. I didn't need to see any more than that to know there was some kind of army behind all of these Asian businesses and that the businesses were forced to pay out protection money.

On the way back through the underground tour, Cho

pointed out a cement shower stall, located on his property, with a high-powered water hose and adjustable showerhead. He held up a big black bar of soap and said it was the only soap that gets every trace of the fish scent off your hands and body. He said, "My wife hates to smell the fish, but love to eat the fish!" He laughed a rare laugh at his own joke. His laughter evaporated. Then he told me, "This is your locker. Bring your own lock."

He introduced me to the only cat in the underground who didn't have a price on her head. She was a black cat with gray eyes named Pussy. I asked him why only this one cat was roaming around freely. He said, "Pussy good."

I checked it all out. I would bring my own lock. I was big on having a locker, a new stash spot. But I didn't plan on showering down there. After work every Friday and Saturday, I would just wash up in the upstairs bathroom to keep my face and my hands clean. Then I would shower each time when I got home.

It wasn't long before an incredibly unique-looking, young, dark-eyed Chinese girl started eyeballing me. She worked on the same side of the block as me, four stores down. I had seen her a couple times on my way in, selling their merchandise: handbags, hats, and umbrellas. She was very pretty, with big pear-shaped dark eyes, high cheekbones, and very long jet-black hair. Sometimes she wore it straight and sleek. Other times she wore it thick and wild. She was always fashionable with a crazy original clothing style. The things she wore were completely different from the items they were selling in her store.

With the Asians in Chinatown, there was a big difference between the parents and their children. The youth were hip-hop style like us. She rocked Nike sneakers, and always had a girls' style in colors I never seen for sale before. I suspected she was buying from the kids' sizes because her feet were really small.

She seemed sneaky. I figured she was spending her whole lunch break walking back and forth checking me out. She never came inside the store or bought any fish from Chö. I didn't know what her interest in me was about. I'd be there in my work boots or work kicks, loading and unloading trucks, sometimes wearing a rubber apron covered with fish scales.

I liked her subtle mannerisms, like the slow way her eyes moved around trying to take a quick look. The way she once bit her lip when she caught me catching her staring. The swift way she walked away and disappeared like one of my two green-eyed Egyptian cats from back home named Kush and Kemet.

Once she held her pretty hand against the store glass, the tips of her fingernails glistening with the thin streak of silver glitter she had painted on.

I liked the crazy color combinations she wore sometimes; shit that everybody knows don't go together, but she wore them with such style and ease that she made it look like it was the thing to do.

On a snow-filled winter afternoon, she was cashmere down in a cashmere tam, scarf, sweater dress, and even cashmere sweater stockings. Her dark-brown leather boots wrapped tight around her calves and climbed high up her leg, stopping just above her knee. She looked high quality, soft, and warm. I could tell that she got at least some of her clothes from the Benetton shop in the Village. I had seen a few pieces she wore on display in their window. No matter what she wore though, she was always styling unlike anyone else, very original with her clever accessories, sometimes strange hats, selected scarves, driving gloves, or a rough leather belt with an unusual buckle, or just a wicked, odd-shaped handbag looking fresh and clean and chilling no matter what the weather or season.

On a fog-filled rainy day once, she still showed up to

check me. She was beneath a beautiful wooden, crimson Chinese umbrella. She was wearing assorted shades of red beautifully woven and crocheted into a wicked patterned poncho. Her colors were so brilliant that day that they cut through the cloudiness and made her light up and stand out from everyone else who, because of the weather, all looked like black or gray globs no matter who they were or what they had on.

She didn't say nothing when she came around peeking. I could tell she was older than me and I wondered if she ever considered that I was just fourteen.

One afternoon when business was slow, I pointed her out to Cho. She was wearing burlap Gucci shorts in the freezing winter, with heavy wool tights covering her legs, a rough-ass leather belt with the Gucci interlocking g's, butter Tims, and a wool Apple Jack hat that matched her stockings. Cho quickly informed me that she was Japanese, not Chinese. He said there was a big difference between the two. He said he had only seen her around the block for less than six months. He said he didn't know her or her people. "They're renters," he said. From the way he said it, his tone, I sensed that he had a problem with whichever Chinaman took it upon himself to rent a store in Chinatown to the "Japs." I didn't ask him about her again.

It was early December the first time I saw her looking. By the time the New Year and then February rolled around, I had never heard her speak even one word. But by that time, at home I caught myself picturing her in my mind. I wondered if she spoke English or only Japanese. I already knew how to introduce myself in Japanese. I learned it at the dojo from my Sensei. I told myself I would walk over and meet her one of these days.

She beat me to it and showed up along with her Japanese girlfriend, lounging outside Cho's store five minutes before I was scheduled to get off. I had washed up in the bathroom and came out and found the two of them standing there. I gave Cho a pound. He shot me a look. I walked right out past the two girls. They followed me.

Out of Cho's sight, I stopped walking and turned toward them. The girlfriend giggled. The pretty one stared. I said calmly, *"Hajime mashite."* The one who liked me covered her mouth with her hand in shock at my using a Japanese greeting. The other one started speaking fast, fluent Japanese to me.

"Nah, chill, that's all I know. Speak English," I told them.

"Sorry," her friend said. "Her name is Akemi." She pointed at the pretty one.

"Can't she tell me that?" I asked.

"She speaks no English," her friend answered. "She's only been here for a few months. Her first time to America."

"Oh," I said.

Akemi spoke in Japanese to her friend.

"She wants to know if she can touch your skin," her friend translated.

I stood there smiling about how bugged out her first request and this scenario was. I was definitely not the only Black guy in Chinatown. In fact, there were Black people shopping and passing through all day every day. Akemi spoke again in Japanese.

"She said you are so beautiful." The other girl giggled. Akemi blushed.

"How old is she?" I asked her friend.

"She is sixteen," her friend answered. Then she asked, "How old are you?"

"Fourteen," I said, clocking their reactions. They spoke to each other. Akemi looked a little disappointed.

"She says you are *so* tall for fourteen," her friend translated.

"Tell her I said it's easy for me to be taller than her."

Akemi's smile returned. They stood there glancing at each other like they were trying to read each other's mind, then glancing back at me. I didn't know where to move with this. I was telling myself, I'm good at getting money, fighting, and guns, but virgin with the girls.

I don't know if she saw my age as an opportunity to switch things around and take control over me. She stepped in and touched my hand. Her off-white skin and clean unpainted fingernails today stroked me until an unfamiliar sensation ran up my arm and into my chest.

She moved her fingertips into my palms and that felt even better. She said some words to me in Japanese. Her soft, musical tone of voice got me hard. My mind was steady telling my body to calm down.

She whispered something to her friend. Then her friend said to me, "She hopes maybe sometimes you and her could go out for a walk and talk together, like friends."

I nodded yes and said, "Okay." I was thinking the three of us must be going out together. Otherwise me and Akemi couldn't talk about shit.

"Are you coming?" I asked her friend.

"I can only come if you guys go tomorrow. I'm just here visiting Akemi. I don't live in New York. On Sunday I'm going back home," she said.

"Okay, tomorrow. I'll come by the umbrella stand around four," I told her friend. She looked surprised that I knew where Akemi worked, as though she'd thought this whole thing just started when she showed up. I knew then that she had no idea how long Akemi had been checking me out.

"Oh, then you know where Akemi works." She laughed.

"I've seen her around," I said coolly. Then they spoke their language to each other.

"Don't come by the shop. Meet us at the bakery on Doyer. Do you know it?" her friend asked.

"Yeah, it's across from the movie theatre. Cool." I watched as they turned and walked away.

Walking to the subway, I thought about Akemi's powerful dark eyes. The curve and structure of her face was so striking. Seeing her up close for the first time, I realized she was even more beautiful, with her small nose and thick, pretty, Black-girl lips.

I guess it was the unknown that drew out my interest in her. The fact that she had staked me out for three months without ever speaking one word was sweet to me. The fact that each time I saw her, she was either alone or working. I couldn't just look at her and feel like I instantly knew everything about her the way I could with the females who lived on my block. They were either very loud and pushy, or quiet but completely predictable either way. Everyone around our way knew which guys had already ran through 'em. They all had copycat styles, crazy attitudes, and ways of talking.

Akemi's style was vibrant and unique, especially compared to some of the very plain-looking Asian females I seen coming and going in Chinatown. After one face-to-face meeting, she already had me feeling like I was on some type of adventure.

After replaying our encounter in my head, I realized her friend never asked me my name. That works out better for me, I told myself. Since I've been living here, I discovered that Americans are either too impatient or too stupid to pronounce a name if it isn't common to them like Bob, Dave, or Jack.

When my mother first took me up to school to get me registered, the people escorted us to meet my new teacher and classmates. When we got to the right room number, I handed the teacher my registration card. My name was clearly printed across the top of the paper. The teacher looked at it and announced, "Welcome. Please introduce yourself to the class." I told them my full name—my first name, my father's first name, and my grandfather's first name, which is customary in my home country. They all started roaring with laughter. One fat boy even spilled out of his chair and onto the floor. One girl, black-skinned like me, started shouting, "Unga Bunga!" My mother tapped my shoulder and we both turned and left.

At the time my mother could not speak anything except Arabic. When we got away from the school, she asked me to tell her exactly what happened back there in that classroom without leaving one word out. I told her the short simple story, which really had nothing to it. On the train she sat silently for some seconds. Then she said, "America, the land of the fatherless children."

We never returned to any public school. My mother said nothing good could come out of a school where praying is forbidden. She had me keep up my studies at home. This included math, science, English, Arabic, and the Quran. At first I was on a tight at-home study schedule. Over the years my mother rewarded my discipline by allowing me to free-style. I read all kinds of books, some from the public library, some purchased at The Open Mind bookstore. I even used to watch people on the buses and trains reading. I would check the title of the book a person was holding and if they looked really into it, I would check out that same title for myself.

So when anyone in this country asks me my name, I tell them whatever comes to mind. Sometimes it's a short version of one of my five true names. Sometimes it's a name that has the same letters as one of my names but all mixed up to spell something else. Sometimes it's a nickname or just the name I want a certain person to call me.

At our Brooklyn apartment that evening, I showered and got fresh dressed. My mother had her merchandise wrapped. She and my sister and I all ate dinner together. Afterward, I packed my backpack and left to do the Umma Designs product deliveries.

As soon as I finished, I headed straight over to the dojo to meet my mans Ameer and Chris. Ameer lives in the East New York projects. Chris is from Flatbush and lives in a brownstone. We all the same age. We all first met each other at the dojo on tryout day seven years back. I was surprised. They was the only boys who showed up with their fathers. I showed up for self.

While most students had class once weekly, the three of us trained side by side, three nights a week in Ninjitsu. Despite being from completely separate neighborhoods, we became best friends.

I think we all chose this martial arts school for similar reasons. It was authentic. Our teacher was actually from Japan, where the art form originated. He taught us things that were important to our survival and didn't feed us a lot of bullshit. I admired that Sensei was a quiet man but very deadly. He made it clear to each of us who survived his try-outs that he trained level-headed boys to become killers in the name of self defense and, at the highest level, to become ninjas. He told us in his presentation that "the difference between a samurai warrior and a ninja, is a samurai is trained to carry out orders, while a ninja is trained to think for himself, master flexibility, execute, and finish off his enemy."

When I went to join up, there were about thirty-five kids who showed up and were interested in trying out. After Sensei gave his no-nonsense introduction and the explanation of Ninjitsu, some of their mothers grabbed their sons' little hands, rushed out the door, and never returned.

He had my full attention when he explained that unlike karate and other martial arts forms, his students did not compete in tournaments. He said fighters who train for tournaments become comfortable with predictable boundaries, limiting rules, particular styles, and planned scenarios. "In the streets," he said, "there is no courtesy or choreography. An enemy will do any- and everything and a ninja must not be locked into one particular style. He must always be flexible and prepared for the unexpected."

He assured the students who took the training seriously that if we practiced hard and advanced, we would even be afforded the elite opportunity to learn weaponry. He told us to forget about belts—white belts, yellow belts, orange belts, red belts, black belts. They had no real meaning. When you become a master, the Sensei and the student will both know and acknowledge. He said that only a fool would advertise his skills. It is much better to move quietly and be unrecognized by your opponent.

Sensei promised we would learn the points on the human body that were easy to attack and difficult to defend. He told us that to finish off your opponent, there were several tidy techniques beyond the barrel of a gun.

Sensei's students traveled from throughout the five boroughs to get his training. We were all drawn to Asian culture, the weapons, and fighting skills.

Up until this point, Chris and Ameer, who were always talking about girls, had never mentioned Asian women. I'm sure they would be surprised if I told them I would meet up with two Asian girls tomorrow. Usually, the three of us could speak about anything. But I already knew I would not tell them about Akemi.

Deliveries completed, I was walking up the busy Brooklyn block on Friday night headed for the dojo. I was checking my left side, my right side, and even using the eyes in back of my head. But I was looking in the wrong direction when Ameer leaped out from where he was crouched down in between two beat-up old cars. He attacked me. He used the handles from my own backpack to choke me. I ran my moves on him, using an elbow to the head causing him to loosen his grip. I took advantage and made him fall backward. He broke his fall and charged forward. I was already in my stance ready for his next attack.

This young kid rolled up talking about, "Oh shit, oh shit!" He appointed himself fight promoter and a small crowd gathered around, charged up to watch me and Ameer kill each other. That time I struck first. There was a series of blows, strikes, and kicks. I got in a few and blocked some. He got in one real good shot to my chin. As abruptly as it all started, we stopped. Ameer came down from mid-air and we just started walking. The crowd booed. They didn't know this is how we normally do. We had them all psyched. As usual, we argued all the way to the dojo about which one of us actually won this encounter.

Soon as we reached the place, we saw Chris getting out of the back of his father's car. Friday nights were reserved for beginners, so we stayed out of the way in the dojo. After seven years of training there, on our nights off we used it as a meet-up spot for us three, like a community center. Meanwhile, Sensei was patiently instructing a class of beginners. I wondered if we looked that out of balance and hopeless when we first began.

"Check this out, I met this cat Tyriq who asked me about joining some basketball team that's jumping off over at Boys' and Girls' High School next Friday night," I told them. "What y'all think about it?"

"What about it?" Chris asked.

"It's some games leading up to a tournament. Y'all want to get down with it?"

"What's the stakes?" Ameer asked.

"I don't know, man. I didn't ask."

"We could hustle up more cash on our own unless they got some kind of real-type prizes," Chris said.

"Yeah, we can't just put in all that work for just one big-ass trophy and some bullshit ribbons and T-shirts," Ameer added.

"You remember what happened before when we won that pee-wee tournament? They only had one brass trophy for the whole team to share," Chris said. We all laughed.

"Yeah, I had to beat all y'all down for that one. That's why that piece of junk is still at my house," Ameer bragged.

"Nah, it's at your house, 'cause I didn't want it," I reminded Ameer. We pushed through the dojo door laughing and cracking jokes, following behind Chris, who had his basketball.

On the basketball court a couple of blocks over from the dojo, we three was known as the Shake and Take Boys, because of how we put it down. At first the Shake and Bake Boys used to run the court over that way, but we beat them enough times that we took their spot, their title, and their money. We wasn't the type of ball hustlers who pretended not to know one another then beat other unsuspecting players out of their paper. We made it known that we worked together. We never let no other players come in and divide us up or pick us onto their squad. If somebody wanted to battle us, they had to bring their three 'cause our three stayed the same. We three had balled on the same team at local parks for so long that our styles flowed together. I never had to worry about passing the ball and Chris not being on point. Chris had what the girls called a baby face. It must've been true 'cause other players used to underestimate him all the time, double team me and leave him wide open. He could sink it way out from the deep wings of the court. So me and Ameer used to feed him unpredictable and slick-ass passes. He stayed alert, played great defense, got good looks, and didn't panic under pressure.

Ameer was nice and smooth with his three-pointers, plus

mad nice with the layups also. He was a showman who was dedicated to making any of his moves look good. He liked to humiliate his opponents, which he did often. He hated punks who called fouls, 'cause he loved knocking players over and respected them more when they tried to knock him over too. If they wanted to fight about it, Ameer used it as a chance to practice our fighting skills with untrained street fighters.

Known for being completely silent on the court, the most swift, and for the way I handled the ball—anything the two of them couldn't do—I picked up the slack.

Whenever a few dudes seen us running the court at the park, they came up with a challenge. Ameer always sets up a bet. We always win.

Niggas can't handle loss, even when it's fair and square. And the older the cats, the more they tend to bitch and moan. Most of the time we three gotta fight. We didn't hesitate. We battled like Brooklyn. We held our own and collected our money. Chris was like our treasurer. He held on to the bulk of our winnings, minus a couple of slices of pizza and drink. We agreed that we was gonna save up to buy a car when we all turned old enough to get our licenses. Chris wanted a Pontiac Sunbird. Ameer wanted the Fiero GT. I had my eye on this mean-ass, pretty Porsche I saw at the dealer. Seriously though, we all knew that chances were we would end up dropping a few g's on a used bomb and all taking turns driving or riding together.

This night the teens who showed up to challenge us didn't have *no* money. They rejected Ameer's bet and wanted to "play for fun." Ameer laughed at their broke asses and told them to step off. They got tight about it 'cause they had four girlies on the side holding their radio and waiting on them. These cats would not move off the middle of the court.

Chris knew shit was about to heat up, so he waved me and Ameer over talking about, "Fuck it, let's bounce. There's no money here." Chris was like that. He would fight when pushed. But he tried to keep fists down and profits up.

Determined, Ameer stepped up to them and said, "We'll play you for your girls. I'm checking for the redbone anyway. If we win, they hang out with us for the night. If you win we'll let you walk with fifty more dollars than you got right now." Ameer smiled waiting for their response.

Chris took a good look at the girls and picked one for himself. Them other dudes was standing there with their screw faces on, mumbling secrets back and forth to one another, vexed at the girls who were looking more and more like they were liking Ameer's bold style. I took a couple of steps back so I could get a good look at them niggas to see where their hands was at and what they was carrying in dem pockets. The shortest dude among them threw up his hands and said, "Fuck it, let's run it! Matter of fact, make it a hundred dollars," the teen said. Ameer hollered, "Deal!"

I had money in my pockets. Umma Design's money, which I had just collected, was in my front pants pocket. My tips were in my inside jacket pocket. I also always kept five hundred dollars of my own in my right leg pocket in case of emergency. I didn't know if Ameer and Chris had enough money on them. I knew Ameer was the type who would place a big bet whether he could pay it off or not. That's how sure he always was.

As Ameer took the ball back and checked it, the girls turned the volume up on LL Cool J's joint, "Rock the Bells." Ameer passed me the ball. Soon as I started bouncing the ball, Ameer started talking shit to fuck with their minds. "It's good y'all took the deal. Them girls was gonna leave y'all asses anyway 'cause you niggas ain't got no money." While the kid checking Ameer let Ameer's words take effect on him, I passed the ball back to Ameer, who laughed in their faces as he shook them and laid it up.

They played hard and sweated a lot, but seemed more focused on their anger than the hoops. Sensei always said, "Anger cancels good judgment."

Soon as one of them reached in for the ball I made it disappear. They didn't see it again until it was swishing through the net. That night, Chris was the high score. Ameer was the showman, who purposely messed with their minds. They couldn't fuck with us.

We ran a full court three on three. In less than an hour, we took them down. Curse words hung over their heads like cartoon characters. Steam blew out their ears. The short one threw the ball against the fence way on the other side of the court. Then they made their move. Two of them went and threw their arms around their girls, the other grabbed his radio and tried to walk off.

"Shorty!" Ameer called out to the light-skinned one. "Come here." She yanked herself from out of the other one's grip and turned back to look at Ameer. Easily, she began walking over to our side.

"Get your ass over here," the other guy screamed on her. She didn't listen to him. Now she was all up on Ameer and all three of her girls had followed her over too.

The three niggas charged us. Ameer pushed the girls to the side and we all started brawling on the cement court. The girls started screaming and jumping up and down like excited cheerleaders, their titties bouncing up and their asses pulling them back down to the ground.

Them boys got tired before we did. We could've fought all night. We left them on the ground and walked away with the four girls.

The short motherfucker stood up, holding his head from the pain we put on 'em. He started hollering about the girl in the blue jacket was his sister. I figured he had to be lying because what would his sister be doing over here walking away with us? Quickly, I looked in her eyes. She didn't say she *wasn't* his sister. Matter of fact, she didn't say nothing.

"Go back over there," I told her. She sucked her teeth, stomped her foot, and went.

Chris' lip was busted. We got a cup of ice from Mickey Dees and kept it moving.

"Where we going?" Ameer's girl asked.

"Where y'all want to go?" Chris answered.

"I don't know," Chris' girl responded.

"We can go to my house," the girl walking beside me said to everybody.

"You think we want to hang out with your mother at your house?" Chris asked her sarcastically.

"She ain't home," the girl said in a bold voice.

"How can you be sure?" Chris asked.

" 'Cause she works all night in the toll booth at the bridge. She on her way to work right now," she said with complete confidence.

"All right, let's do it, then," Ameer said.

"Is your father home?" I asked her.

Everybody started cracking up, a bending-over type of cracking up, and laughing. No one bothered to answer my question.

"Don't worry," the girl said. We all kept walking, now following her lead to the subway. I felt I had to ask at least one more question.

"What about them niggas from back there? Do they live around your way?" I asked. All of my boys stopped walking. They were getting focused now and waiting on her answer. I could see that Ameer now understood where I was headed with my questioning. I wasn't one to walk right into a setup. Why should we give them boys time to get locked and loaded? I didn't want to catch a case on some bullshit.

"Them niggas?" the redbone asked, as if she wasn't just associated with them five minutes ago.

"We don't know them niggas," Chris' girl added then laughed.

"We met them on the train ride up here," the girl walking beside me said.

Chris and Ameer were cool with their answers. They all started walking together again.

"I gotta work early tomorrow morning. I'll ride over with y'all. But then I gotta step," I told them.

"What about me?" the girl walking beside me asked.

"What about you?" I answered her, straight-faced.

"Forget it. You ain't right," she said back.

On the train ride me and her didn't say nothing to each other. The other two couples was all hugged up. The redbone and Ameer were lapped up.

She lived up in Harlem in the Lincoln projects, known to us Brooklyn cats as "Stinking Lincoln." That night, as we rolled up outside her building, we had to get by fifteen or so dudes in bubble jackets and hoods. They were watching us. We were clocking them. I kept my hand in my pocket on my heat. In any projects, even when it's dark outside you can still see and feel the hatred.

On the noisy streets, when niggas confront niggas there's usually a loud silence before somebody starts busting shots. The silence was already there.

The girl walking with me broke it. "What's up, Petey, Brian, Ramel, Mook . . ." She rattled off more than ten of their names like they was a bunch of fucking kindergartners. They spoke back to her. We didn't break our stride.

Somehow, her calling out their names lightened up the tension. With the cease-fire in place, we made it to the building lobby without having to let off.

We elevated to the fourth floor. In the upstairs hallway, in front of apartment 4G, she moved her hands in and out of her back pants pockets and then her front pockets, searching for her keys. Chris and his girl and the other two was laying up against the wall waiting. I pulled out my four-five and handed it to Ameer. "Let me let you hold something," I told him. He took it. "Good looking out, brother," he said.

All the girls' eyes followed my gun. The one fumbling with her keys started staring into my eyes so hard she was melting my pupils.

"Come on, bitch," her girlfriend nudged her jokingly. She found her keys lost through a hole inside her jacket pocket. As she opened her door, they all pushed inside. She stood holding the door open for me. I turned my back to her and pushed through the metal exit door leading to the stairs. I took the four flights down. I left out the side of the building, switched up my path.

12

AKEMI

At Cho's the next morning I was prepared. Saturdays always brought in a heavy flow of customers. Some people realized that fresh seafood is always delivered on Friday. So on Fridays I spent a lot of time unloading and moving boxes and barrels and buckets, and Saturdays I spent a lot of time scaling, cutting, clipping, and gutting fish. Routinely, on those kind of days I covered my head with a bandanna. I put on some welding glasses that I used to keep fish scales and particles from flying into my eyes. I had on my work clothes, a raincoat, and an apron on top of that. I'm sure I was looking crazy and exaggerated. But I was quick and thorough at my job.

Around three o'clock I washed down my counter. I headed down to the basement. I had brought and stored a change of clothes and some other items in the locker. Since I was going to meet the girls, I was gonna take advantage of the convenience of the basement shower stall for the first time. The water was good and hot but the air underground and the floor was both freezing. I guess Cho never had to worry about anybody trying to live down there since it was more freezing than outside.

Fresh, I spotted Akemi even when I was halfway down the block from the bakery. It was the way she stood in those heels. For the first time, I noticed that Nikes on a female's feet don't have the same magic as heels do.

As I came up close I saw she was wearing a black pleated miniskirt. Her shapely thighs were covered with wool tights that hid her flesh but revealed the curve of her legs. She was wrapped tight in a black butter-leather jacket well tailored to fit her shoulders exactly and ride down the curve of her waistline, hugging her hips gently. Her black leather gloves were tucked inside the belt that held her jacket closed. Her black epi-leather handbag was dangling on the tips of her pretty fingers.

"Konichiwa." I calmly gave them their greeting. Akemi smiled and the other one giggled.

"Um. Yesturday, we forgot to ask you your name," the other girl said. I looked at Akemi who was looking at me as though her dark eyes could see beyond my face and into my soul.

"Midnight," I answered. I figured that was the name to give. I had seen some Chinese movie where every character had a hot-ass name. And I knew a lot of Asian names were rooted in the weather, seasons, and the elements.

"Mayonaka," the other girl translated.

"Mayonaka," Akemi said, serious-faced, with a curl of smoke swirling around her pretty lips from when her breath mingled with the cold air.

Now I understood that *mayonaka* meant "midnight" in Japanese. For some reason, the way Akemi pushed out this one word warmed me up like crazy.

"Are you two hungry?" I asked them. Her girl translated my question.

"No, she's nervous," her friend translated.

"Ask her what she's so nervous about. She's the one who wanted to kick it. Tell her I would never hurt her." I was looking directly at Akemi when I spoke my words. She was looking right back at me with those big dark eyes. She didn't seem nervous to me. And I could feel the pull I had on her.

"Akemi says you look so handsome."

"Tell her to tell me that herself," I responded. The girl gave her my message. Akemi lowered her eyes then lifted them again slowly and spoke to me in her language. Her voice was so soft. The flow of her words sounded like the seductive whispers of Sade on her *Diamond Life* album. The soft way she spoke, I had to listen carefully and focus on her hard and block out the regular noises of the New York City streets, with the buses, taxis, horns, and hordes of people moving in every which direction.

A thought came over me real quick. I wanted to take Akemi out, just me and her. The extra girl was helpful, but she had a different feel to her. She interrupted the strong silent signals moving back and forth between me and Akemi.

"Ask Akemi if she can hang out with me on her own." The girl looked disappointed but she translated my question anyway. Akemi answered with a bright-ass smile.

"What time does she have to be back?" I asked her friend.

"Our aunt and uncle will close the gate on their store at 7 P.M. If she wants to ride back with us, she should be back by then. If it's later than 7 P.M., she has to go straight to Jackson Heights, Queens, where they live. She should be back no later than ten. I'll tell them she went shopping. If she goes past 10:30 P.M., it will be a lot of trouble for her," she said. Now I realized that the two of them were related.

Then they began talking Japanese to each other. I watched Akemi's mouth moving as well as her facial expressions to gauge her reactions. I could tell she was with it.

"Okay. I'll go back to the store, then. Are you sure you two will be okay?" Akemi's cousin asked reluctantly.

"Everything is cool. She'll be home on time, don't worry," I told her.

"Oh, and she's an art student. That's what she likes," her cousin said as she turned to walk away.

I knew I could have asked her cousin all these questions about who Akemi is and what she liked. She would give me quick responses in her clear American accent. But I wanted to find out for myself what Akemi was all about. Besides, I was attracted to Akemi's Japanese accent, which sounded so much sweeter in my ear.

I figured she knew all about Chinatown and Asian things. And I could tell that she liked me and wanted to get to know me better. So, I decided not to stick around down there. I would just bring her into my world to see how she reacts and handles that.

It was the end of February. The cold air made us move more swiftly. I saw the bright-orange powerful sun overpowering the light-blue sky, but throwing its heat to the other side of the world. I could see the cold air lingering around Akemi's lips as she breathed in and out as if she was actually smoking a cigarette. But she wasn't. I slowed down a bit and watched the way she moved. She turned to see what I was doing behind her, and smiled when she thought she knew. I picked up my step and she walked behind me from that afternoon into the night.

We hopped on the number six train from Chinatown to 125th Street in Harlem. From the look on her face, it seemed like everything she saw uptown was brand new.

First stop was the record store. I wanted to pick up a couple of joints. The owner of the shop was from South Africa. He had a cool vibe. So whenever I was in the area, I threw some business his way. When we walked in he was playing "Mbube" by Miriam Makeba. Akemi seemed to like it. Her head was rocking to the beat. Her little foot was tapping on the floor.

"Look around," I told her and gestured with my arm.

The store owner switched the vibe and threw on Salt-N-Pepa, "The Show Stopper."

When I was ready to go she had one record in her hand. It was Eric B. and Rakim, their first joint, "Eric B. Is President." I flipped the album around in my hand, checking out the cover. Recently, I had heard that hot-ass joint rocking around my way on a tape. The beats were crazy and the rhymes just reminded me of my Brooklyn block and all of the characters, situations, and everyday happenings. I could understand how somebody who never lived around my way might buy this joint to make themselves feel like they was walking in my hood. But then again, really walking through my hood would be a reality check for anybody who didn't live there.

I bought her *Hot, Cool & Vicious*, the Salt-N-Pepa album, and paid for everything else and we stepped.

I needed a line up. I took her to a barbershop where I had only got a cut two or three times before. I told her to sit down. She did, but within seconds she stood right back up. She preferred to look around. She might as well walk around staring at everything 'cause everybody in the shop was definitely staring at her!

As I'm getting my cut she's watching me watching her through the mirror. Sometimes she would disappear from my sight because I had to hold my head still for the cut. The barber, with his back to her, asked me, "That's you, man?" referring to Akemi. "That's me," I answered. "She's different. But she's baad," the barber acknowledged.

That was something I had to get used to in this country— men commenting on the next man's woman. Back home, this was a wrong move, unheard of. Out here in the U.S. this was common.

After he hit me up with a fresh cut, the brush, and the talcum powder, I paid and tipped the barber. When I turned around, Akemi was holding a handful of my hair in her palm.

"What are you doing?" I asked her, also gesturing with my

hands. She just smiled. She opened her purse and dumped my hair inside a small, nicely crafted, embossed tin box she had with her for some reason. She closed the top on the box and dropped it into her purse.

She held up her finger as if to say, "Wait one minute." She went into the bathroom and washed her hands with the door wide open.

In the Foot Locker she stood staring at the kids' rack. Just like I thought. She purchased a kid-sized pair of white Nike Uptowns. I bought some dunks too.

It was bugged out being with her. There was almost no talking but a whole lot of eye contact and signaling.

On the street she grabbed my hand from behind to stop me from walking farther. She wanted to turn into the Mart, an indoor Black version of some of the outdoor flea markets in Chinatown.

She walked into each stall one by one, starting with the art stores, which were up front. There were several paintings of and by African Americans for sale. She flipped through each painting quickly then paused on a particular one. I watched her run her fingers slowly across the surface of one picture, feeling the texture the same way I would imagine a blind person would do.

In the jewelry stall she wanted her ears pierced. She bunched her hair up and held it with her hands so the woman could see her ears clearly. What captured me were her fingers. I noticed how on each of her natural fingernails she had one Japanese letter painted on in black. Each fingernail glistened as each letter was coated with a layer of clear polish.

The woman placed a dot on each of Akemi's ears with a marker. Akemi gave me a glance. I knew she wanted me to hold her hair for her, so I did. It was soft and very long and felt good in my hands. Her face looked even prettier, her profile now not hidden by her hair. I stood looking at her neck.

She squinted when the jewelry gun pinched her piercings into place. Her eyes filled up with water but no tears fell down.

I tied her hair into a slipknot and left it that way. She seemed to like it. She rocked it that way for the rest of the night.

In the airbrush booth, she pulled her new Uptowns out of the Foot Locker bag and cracked open the box. She wanted her joints spray painted. She looked through the vendor's art book for a sample of what kind of design she wanted him to put on her sneakers. After a while she couldn't find one she liked. She pulled out her wallet and laid her cash on the counter. She picked up the airbrush gun to gesture that she wanted to paint them herself.

"Nah, she can't do that," the cat told me.

"Take your money. Let her try," I said. "She's an artist."

She adjusted the nozzles and started painting her own sneakers. The designs she was making had thinner lines than the design samples the guy showed us. She got intricate with it. It only took seconds to see she was real nice with her hands. She used only one color, black. When she was through with one sneaker, the guy was asking me if she wanted a job. When she finished her second sneaker, the next customer was trying to get her to stay and do hers next.

Outside, the orange sun was replaced by the white moon. The blue sky gave in to the black night. There were very few stars shining in Harlem, yet there were a few trying to break through. It was clear and cold. The sidewalk vendors lined the whole of 125th Street. The people were still out walking, talking, dancing, and keeping it moving.

I was feeling hungry. We walked across Seventh Avenue. Akemi's eyes searched the buildings, into the windows, empty lots, churches, and alleys. We ended up at a spot named The Jamaican Hot Pot. We sat down at a table in the small dining area there. I ordered chicken curry for her and stewed chicken for me.

In the men's room I washed my hands and face. They didn't look or seem dirty, but every New Yorker knows when you ride the trains and walk the New York City blocks, the dirt just accumulates. I brought a wet napkin back to our table and cleaned Akemi's hands. Her fingers were slim and soft and relaxed into mine. She just sat watching me intensely.

When she first tasted the curry sauce, the scotch bonnet peppers made her eyes fill with water again. She ate some of the chicken and all of the cabbage and carrots.

While sipping on some carrot juice, she began to draw a picture on a white cloth napkin, using an unusual marker with a long point shaped like a paintbrush. After some strokes I was surprised how I could really see my own resemblance in her drawing.

She held the cloth up and drew a smile out of me. Then she laid the cloth out flat, went into her purse, and pulled out a thin-tipped red marker. In quick artistic strokes, she wrote in Japanese letters down the right side of the cloth.

"Mayonaka Hansamu," she said, looking me dead in my eyes. I could feel her admiration pouring down all over me. It felt good. It relaxed me a bit and drew me in further.

The red Japanese letters against the white napkin looked wicked to me. I wanted to keep the drawing, but she folded the cloth up and put it in her purse. By now I figured that's where she kept most of her secrets.

I paid our bill. Yvonne, the Jamaican owner of the restaurant, gave me the mean look. I gave her an extra tip for the cloth Akemi took.

I'll admit the whole while we were walking back down Seventh Avenue, I was thinking about myself. Here it was Saturday night and for the first time ever, I was on a date for self with a female. I knew it wasn't supposed to be happening, but I made myself feel all right by staying in public places with her, not doing anything I or anyone could consider improper.

On 116th Street in Harlem, on the steps of Columbia University, I sat her down. It was a nice spot, especially at night. They kept bright white holiday lights on their maple and oak trees all year around. The bright lights lit up the inside courtyard. Students from all around the country and all around the world and New Yorkers moved back and forth and sideways, across the campus from building to building, some of them chilling on top of statues, some of them chilling behind statues, some of them seated to the side on the steps with their books piled up next to them. Others were gripping hot cups of coffee or buying hot cocoa or tea.

This was a place I came every now and then, because this was a place where my father had been and spent a lot of time studying and socializing. I would sit here alone sometimes, thinking of answers to my own questions first. Then I would think of what my father's answers and suggestions would be. Sometimes I would wonder if I was standing in the same space where he had actually stood several years ago.

Akemi did not seem to mind our silent date. But now I really did have things I wanted to ask her. So I just started talking aloud to her as if she could understand me.

"How are you feeling right now and what are you thinking?" I asked her in English. She watched my lips. There was a pause. Then she started speaking to me in Japanese. Of course I couldn't understand one word. I realized she didn't understand my question either.

"So why did you watch me for three months before you finally said something?" I asked her. When I finished speaking, she began speaking Japanese again.

"What were you looking at anyway and why do you like me?" I asked her. Then she spoke Japanese again.

"Do you have a boyfriend? Have you ever been touched by a man?" I asked, feeling comfortable speaking this way to her only because I knew she couldn't understand me. She said something else back to me in her language.

"What do you want anyway?" I asked her. She began laughing a little. Then she kept laughing a lot. Her shoulders were shaking. I started laughing too. I don't know when I last laughed so hard. This shit is crazy, I thought to myself. But I like her. I like her a lot.

"Damn, I wish you could speak English," I said, laughing and frustrated. She stood up and smiled deviously, put her hands on her hips, and said, "Speak Japanese!"

I stood up and pulled her by her hand. Her palms were soft like butter and warm.

Over at the vendor's I brought her a Columbia University hooded sweatshirt. When I gave it to her she smiled like I had given her a brick of gold.

She went into her purse once more and came out with a folded shopping bag. As she opened up each square of the bag, I could see that it was made with beautiful decorated heavy paper, with gold twine for handles. I thought to myself how she seemed to be a female who plans and thinks ahead. Everything she wore and possessed, down to the smallest items, seemed to be carefully chosen. She paid close attention to details and preferred everything she wore, used, and surrounded herself with to be unique. It added to her elegance.

She placed the Columbia hoodie into her shopping bag.

At five minutes to ten, on a Queens corner, in a tree-lined residential neighborhood of medium-sized houses, we stood still in the dark. She was looking up at me. I was looking down at her. She stepped inside my leather jacket, standing close to my body but not touching.

I didn't need my jacket no more, because in the cold air my body was consumed with heat. She reached up and touched my face like I was one of the African paintings whose texture she wanted to feel. Her fingers settled on my lips. I didn't move. She pulled her hand back and stepped back a little.

I got mad at myself for hesitating. I picked up her bags, ready to carry them to her house for her. She held up her hand to gesture "no." Gently, she took her bags back and started walking away.

I followed her instinctively. She turned back toward me and said, "Sayonara." I knew that this word meant "good-bye." I turned and headed back to catch my train to Brooklyn.

My body was hot in Queens, cold in Brooklyn, and warm inside my Umma's apartment.

When I walked through the door my mother took one look at me and said, "You met a girl."

I tried to play it off. It was crazy how she always just calmly stated the truth. She didn't even bother to put it in the form of a question. It was like she already knew and didn't need me to confirm or deny.

Stalling, I took off my jacket and loosened my laces, stepping out of my Nikes. No matter how long I delayed, I knew I could never escape Umma's intuition. My seven-years-young sister laughed at how easily I was exposed.

"I met two girls," I said, telling the truth but trying to throw her off.

"Which one of them made your face light up this way?" she asked.

"What about my face?" I dodged.

Umma smiled and stood staring. I knew no matter what I said, this conversation would end up meaning the world to her. She was clear and strong in her Islam, a Muslim woman of the highest degree. Umma never lowered her standards.

She considered America "the land of women with no honor."

So, I chose my words carefully.

"She just came to this country six months ago. She does not speak any English. I met her at work. We are friends," I said to Umma, speaking only in Arabic. My sister Naja hung on every syllable, fully aware of Arabic and English.

"You are leaving some things out on purpose," Umma said coolly and confidently.

"What things?" I dodged again.

"She is not a Muslim or you would have said that she was. She is *very* beautiful to you and that's why the light is spilling out of your eyes. You three are friends for now, but you already know that one of the two girls is very special."

I just hugged Umma instead of offering her my words. My sister wiggled her way in between us and that was okay too. It was late Saturday night. In our family embrace I said to Umma, "Akemi, her name is Akemi." Umma repeated softly, "Akemi."

Alone in my warm bedroom I dashed my window open to bring in a stream of cold air. As I did my pushups, voices from the streets below also came rushing through. My thoughts spanned from Umma to Akemi, from New York to the Sudan, from Islam to the unbelievers.

Surely I know who I am. Yet the reality is that I am living here. I am young. The niggas on the streets consider religion a trick and a weakness. The believers are seen as the duped and the hustled. The Holy Quran, which is the absolute law where I was born, is *nothing* more than unknown or useless poetry in the eyes and ears of American youth.

I already knew from listening to and observing these American chicks, they didn't give a fuck about female honor. They fucked any random stranger who looked good to them and switched boyfriends like they changed their hairstyles. They definitely gave less than a fuck about marriage. It wasn't even a consideration.

In the Quran I read an *ayat*[1] in a *sura*[2] that said, "Allah knows the count on your womb." In Islam it mattered a lot if a woman laid down for a man, her relationship to him and under what circumstances. In the Quran it was forbidden for an unmarried female to lay with an unmarried male and vice versa. In the Quran every detail was written clear and simple for true believers to follow and limit themselves.

On the other hand, here in the United States, a man gets no respect unless he bangs and twists these females out, right away.

I consoled myself, the difficult position I was in being from there, living here, remembering and believing, and over the years, seeing nothing outside of my little family that reflected my memories or beliefs.

---

1. *ayat* = sentence/line
2. *sura* = chapter

13

GIRLS, GUNS, & FRIENDS

Guns and girls—I keep them separate. Ameer showed up to the dojo Monday night with Redbone on his arm. Me and Chris was looking at him sideways because as a rule, we didn't bring spectators during our training. Even though every now and then there were times when I had no choice but to bring my little sister, Naja, I thought, or I should say me and Chris thought, Ameer's move was a mistake. First off, since he turned twelve, Ameer been girl crazy. Me and Chris watched him act like he had fallen in forever love with about eighteen different females. The girls were all crazy about him too. So it was cool. But we knew from experience that he shouldn't bring girls who we knew he was gonna break up with to any of our permanent hangouts. He already had a female named Sophia turn stalker on his ass. Shit with her got so serious, even Sensei had to step in.

Over the years, when any one of the three of us did anything wrong, we all got the pressure from Sensei the same as if we all had done the wrong thing together. Sensei told us in private that it wasn't enough for us to master the fighting technique. We had to master our desires for women "before the women master you."

I looked at Ameer all wrapped up with Redbone.

"Long weekend?" I joked. Me and Chris both laughed.

Our training takes a lot of concentration. Out on the floor we stretched and worked on katas and rollouts.

Later we sparred at Sensei's demand. He kept the fight scenarios flipping like a quarterback calling out complicated plays. He never allowed us to get used to one sparring partner. I would be out on the floor sparring one opponent, next thing I knew I was surrounded by three more attackers. For half an hour I would be in the defending position. The next half hour I would be one of the attackers. Some of the fighters and students in our dojo were our age. Others were full-grown men. The challenge kept my blood pumping.

Through it all, I kept feeling Redbone's eyes moving on me. I wanted to believe I had her wrong. But I knew I had her right.

Toward the end of the session, me and Chris sparred each other, while Ameer and a next student sparred also. When our class finished up, I pulled Ameer and Chris to the side.

"You got my piece?" I asked Ameer.

"Nah, but we can go pick it up now," he answered.

"Nah, bring it here Wednesday night when you come. But don't bring her," I told him.

"She's cool," Ameer said nonchalantly about Redbone.

"Yeah, she's cool at anyplace except the dojo, alright?" I asked, but it wasn't really a question.

"She wants to get your phone number anyway," Ameer stated casually.

"What?" Chris jumped in before I could even make sense out of what Ameer was asking me. Then Ameer started laughing.

"Don't be stupid. She wants your telephone number so she can give it to Homegirl from the other night. The three of them are used to doing everything together. Anyway, Homegirl gotta thing for you, for real. She asked me for your number so many times yesterday, I almost fucked around and gave it to her. I stopped myself when I thought about how you be running your life like you some kind of a secret agent.

Nobody can come to your house or call your crib at certain times and all that bullshit." Him and Chris laughed.

"Homegirl is kind of cute," Chris said. "She got a pretty face and a tight little waist."

"And thick thighs," Ameer added. "I was gonna take her at first. But there's something so sexy about Redbone. She had them other two beat hands down," Ameer joked and bragged.

"If I wanted her to know my phone number, I'd a gave it to her that same night. Just bring my shit here on Wednesday. You didn't leave it at *her* house, did you?" I asked, growing tight about Ameer not being on point when all it takes is one little fuckup.

"Come on, man. Stop tryna play me," Ameer answered, getting vexed.

Chris jumped in to cut up the unusual tension. He always had a way of calming things down whenever he thought it was necessary.

"Look, you ain't gotta be serious with this girl. Just hang out with her while me and Ameer keep the other two busy. That's how these girls want it, three on three. Make it easy on us." He smiled, trying to get me to lighten up. I looked at both of them, considering the way they was begging me to get with some girl.

All of a sudden, Ameer's facial expression changed. He busted out laughing, a complete switch in his mood.

"I got you, nigga! You *already* got a girl. That's what's up." Ameer called it out. "You got a girl for the first time and now she got you open. You just ain't saying shit about her! So now you don't want to fuck with Homegirl. I should've figured it out before. That *is* the type of brother you are." He laughed some more. There was a short pause before he offered more of his take on the situation.

"That's how you do it, man, one at a time, huh?" Ameer leaned in and teased, while Redbone, who we'd told to stay over there, was slowly creeping closer and closer to the area where we was standing.

"Well—let me tell you something," Ameer said to me. "You got two eyes, two ears, two hands, two legs, two feet, ten motherfucking fingers, and ten motherfucking toes . . ." Now Chris was relieved too and laughing again.

I never answered Ameer or Chris. My smile at Ameer's words just cut through naturally.

"See you Wednesday night," I told them.

Realistically I didn't consider Akemi my girl. But in between the hundreds of things I had to do, I found her popping up in my thoughts and remaining there. I planned to see her at the end of the week again when I went back to my weekend job at Cho's on Friday. But now my thoughts of her were turning into an unfamiliar craving. I was feeling like a week was too long.

On Wednesday, I made two Manhattan Umma Designs deliveries. So afterward, I decided to stop by Akemi's family's shop and check her. I was not sure if she even worked on Wednesdays but I was about to find out. I wanted a chance to see what was up with her family. I got curious why her cousin said for me *not* to show up there at their family store.

I found myself catching feelings for Akemi. I had to be sure she wasn't tryna dis me by keeping me away from her relatives, her job, and her home.

As I came up the subway steps onto the sidewalk in Chinatown, I joined the heavy New York crowds of walkers. One block down, as I turned the corner, I saw Akemi walking in a crowd headed in my direction. It was a gray day. She was wearing a designer scarf on her head, with the rest of her long hair falling onto her back. The pretty pastel colors made her glow. She had on a cobalt-blue, patent leather, trench-style jacket today. It was close fitting, hugged her shoulders and laid across her breasts, with a belt drawn tight against her small waist. Jeans and another new pair of Nikes with dark-blue soles helped her to step lively through the dirty New York streets. She didn't see me approaching and seemed lost somewhere in her own thoughts. I wondered if I walked right past her, would she notice?

Tucked underneath her arm secured in her pit was a large portfolio. In her other hand was a small purse. It matched her jacket and dangled from her fingers on a short handle.

Within seconds, I walked right by her in an uneven crowd of nine or so people who just happened to be moving in my same direction. I didn't look back. Three seconds later, she grabbed my wrist. When I turned she had a penetrating look and a warm welcoming smile on her face. She pointed to her watch. She gave me the "come on" sign with her hand. I didn't know where she was going. Yet, I followed.

Back down in the subway, we were on the downtown platform waiting for the trains headed to Brooklyn. This worked out for me. I had almost two hours left before I needed to be at the dojo.

As the train jerked, she loosened up her jacket and pointed to her T-shirt. It had the words PRATT INSTITUTE written across it in bold letters. I didn't know where or what that was. I knew enough to know she was trying to say that's where she was going.

Staring into her dark eyes, I thought about how I had to teach my mother English, word by word. It's been years now, and Umma can listen and understand more English than she can actually speak. She still only speaks a few words and sentences in English. I thought to myself that Akemi could probably learn the English language faster than my mother, because my mother didn't really care for English. Akemi seemed eager to learn. She definitely was not allowing not

knowing the English language to keep her from learning
how to travel around the city and go exploring.

I touched her hands. Now her fingernails were painted all
of the pastel colors of her scarf. She looked me in my eyes.
I said, "Hand." I held up my hand and repeated the word
hand one more time. She caught on easily, smiled, and said,
"Hand." For the rest of the ride, we learned each other this
way, me touching her hand, fingers, arm, hair, ears, eyes, nose,
and even lips, then teaching her the right words to repeat
and remember. She would touch me back and recite the
right words out loud. I don't know if she was really learning
English. But I knew we were learning each other.

We got off in downtown Brooklyn. It was crazy how in
the winter you could go down in the subway in the light of
day, and in less than a half an hour, walk up into the dark
of night. We ended up over on Willoughby Avenue at Pratt
Institute.

There was a bunch of people there, all in a hurry. They
were young but seemed older than both me and Akemi.

I noticed a lot of females dressed in varying styles it
seemed like they'd made up themselves. Some of that shit
worked and some of it looked a fucking mess.

As she led her way to her classroom, I stopped right outside the door. She grabbed my hand and pulled it toward
herself as if to say, "Come in."

I didn't come. I pulled back and said, "Sayonara," the word
she used the other night in Queens to separate herself from
me. She reached out for my hand again, and bowed to me.
Her head was down. Then she lifted her eyes up and fixed
them on my face. To see her bow to me gave me a crazy
heated feeling. I followed her in, knowing I could only stay
for a little while.

On one side of the huge class there were chairs with desks
attached to them, and a blackboard. On the other side were

a bunch of easels, paints, brushes, and pencils and papers of various sizes and types. I sat at the desk next to hers.

At six o'clock sharp, a young woman who walked with the authority of a teacher entered and stood at the front of the class. She talked some. I wasn't really listening to her. Instead I was inside my head thinking about how I could go to a school like this, with grown-up people who minded their business and just showed up to learn. I liked the way the class was taking place in the evening and people seemed like they came because they wanted to and not because they were being forced.

I noticed her moving toward me, this slim white woman with brown hair, the teacher. "Are you our model for today?" she asked. "I know I've seen your face before," she said, focusing everyone's attention on me. I didn't know what she was talking about or what she even wanted.

"I'm just here for a minute. I'm a friend of Akemi's. Matter of fact, I'm about to leave right now." I stood up. Akemi stood up.

The teacher faced Akemi. "It's okay, Akemi. I understand. He's a friend of yours. We won't undress him, then." The class laughed. Akemi didn't.

"But I'm sure I've seen that face before. It's a fantastic face, not to mention your body. You should consider modeling." The teacher reached out to touch my chin. Akemi stepped in between the teacher's hand and myself. Everybody in the classroom knew what that meant. Some of the students laughed. One of the males said, "Oooh," and the teacher moved on.

A female rushed through the door, out of breath. "I'm your model for today," she proclaimed. The teacher looked at her watch and said, "For twenty-five dollars an hour, you should be on time."

"Sorry," the girl apologized, went to the other side of the room, and climbed onto the table.

The teacher clapped her hands together and said, "All right, people, let's set up." The students all got out of their chairs slowly and into their smocks. Akemi lagged behind a bit. I guess she needed to follow what the other students were doing since she couldn't understand her teacher's English words.

Glad that the attention was now off me, I turned to leave. I looked at Akemi, who was standing in front of a cubby putting on her smock. I pointed at the clock on the wall to signal and let her know I had to go.

As I started to walk out, the girl model who had rushed in late, standing now on the table, casually pulled off her sweater and revealed her flesh, her neck and shoulders, her bare titties that went from white to pale pink, to pink, only to be topped off with purple nipples. What a creation, shaped so exquisitely! My eyes then rode down between her breasts and onto her soft flat stomach, then sank into her darkened belly button.

All I knew was I wasn't leaving no more. My legs weren't moving.

Swiftly she untied her wraparound denim skirt. There were no panties on that pussy, just a bush of sandy blond hair.

The teacher began instructing the model on how to pose properly. As the model tried to get herself into a position that pleased the teacher, she turned slowly, showing everyone her bare back and butt. She bent over, the crease in her behind widened some. Then she kneeled and eventually squatted, cocking her legs open, a slight scent escaping and awakening my always precise sense of smell.

The students, eight males and ten females, whose backs were all to me, faced their easels and the model. Nobody was saying nothing. They took her nudeness like for them it was an everyday thing.

Now the teacher was back on my case.

"You're welcome to stay," she said to me sarcastically, with a sly smile and her arms folded across her chest. The students turned toward my direction and began laughing once again.

Akemi, with her brush in her hand, just watched me closely with no judgment, simply observing my every move and maybe trying to read my thoughts. The intensity of her eyes unfroze my feet. Swiftly, I left.

In the cold breeze I broke out in a hot sweat. This was the first time I ever saw a completely naked woman up close and in real life, in all of her details.

There was no doubt that I felt what I saw. I started thinking crazy thoughts, like how come a girl can have straight hair on her head and nappy hair on her pussy, or red hair on her head and a blond bush between her thighs? And if this is how good a white girl looked naked, with a small, soft-looking white behind, then what did the Black females whose hips were wider, breasts more juicy, asses more bigger, look like fully exposed?

I kept seeing images of the gap between the girl's legs when I looked at her from the back. Every time I thought about it, I would never see the model's face or even remember what her face looked like or the shape of her nose or color of her eyes. I just kept seeing her body parts, one by one, like a slide show in my mind.

Before the dojo I dipped into the arcade. I played a few games of Street Fighter to try to get my mind back in the right position. There was no way I would be able to concentrate otherwise.

The whole scene back there reminded me of something Umma once said, concerning why me and Naja were not allowed to have a television in our Brooklyn apartment. She said, "No outsiders should control what my children see. Once you show a child certain things, you can never snatch that image back." I remember thinking that she was being too strict. Now I at least understood what she meant.

Luckily, when I was thirteen, after the fast of Ramadan, she brought me a television as a present during the Eid. She said, "There is nothing in this box that isn't happening right in front of you on these streets. You are becoming a man now. I have to believe that your father and I have raised you to separate yourself from evil." Naja, on the other hand, was still not allowed to watch. She was only five then.

"Your sandwich is in the bag," Ameer said, handing me what I knew was my joint. I put it in my gym bag and locked it in a locker in the dojo.

After our training, me, Chris, and Ameer hooked up. As we chilled in the back of the dojo, Sensei rolled up and asked me to step inside his office. Chris and Ameer looked surprised. Sensei had never singled one of us out before. If one of us fucked up, we were all expected to hear about it.

"It's your time now. I know you are ready," Sensei said calmly. He was standing behind his desk. His seven swords hung one beneath the other, mounted on the wall behind him. His deadly hands and knuckles gripped the edge of his desk. I wasn't sure what he was getting at. I knew not to interrupt whatever it was he had to say.

"Your weapons training will begin next week," he continued, searching for my reaction.

"Domo arigato gozaimasu, Sensei," I responded in my very limited Japanese, thanking him very much in the respectful way that we were taught to speak to an elder, teacher, and master. I was showing no emotion, but was very excited inside. Learning the Asian-styled weapons is what had drawn me here in the first place. But Sensei's

stringent standards and expectations were high and had kept him from teaching us weapons for the past seven long years.

I felt good that he thought we were now prepared. We had all trained so hard. Over the years, me and Ameer had never missed a practice. Chris missed practice every now and then because his father is a reverend who sometimes made demands on Chris' time.

"Just you," Sensei said as if he could read my thoughts. "My other two students are not ready yet." His words hit me hard. I stood still, weighing Sensei's words in my mind.

"Chris is still a follower. Ameer is a strong fighter, but he has a lot of work to do on his discipline," Sensei judged.

I thought about how in all of these years, us three never allowed anyone to say anything fucked up about each other without a fight. I was trying to accept that this conversation and criticism of my two best friends was not meant to be an attack on them that required my loyalty, or my foot to the face or head of the man who was my teacher.

Sensei and I had a few rough times like this one before. Sometimes we disagreed. When I first joined up, he taught us how the Japanese bow as a matter of respect. But I did not bow. It is against my beliefs. For the first two years, Sensei was bitter and sore because he felt I was being arrogant and stubborn. Four more years later, he realized that I had no personal disrespect toward him or his culture, but I had loyalty to my beliefs and the lessons of my father.

"When you were a very young man the first time you walked in here, you asked to see my sword. What did I tell you then?" Sensei asked.

Remembering clearly, I answered. "You said that a sword is not something you can just see and hold or play with. You said the sword was an extension of a fighter's spirit. You said that when you draw your sword, it must be used. You said that every man must think before he draws his weapon. To draw it, is to decide on death."

"Very good," Sensei said. "And for this reason, I have chosen to train you in weapons. I have watched you. You retain information that others forget. You have developed very nicely. I know that you have become a great fighter and independent thinker. I know that you are not a predator and will not abuse the knowledge that I will offer to you. You now show the discipline, the focus, and have the mind to become a great defender and protector of life."

After a long pause in which Sensei sat down and began looking at one of the many papers on his desk, he said to me, without looking into my eyes, "You do not have to decide anything here tonight. If you want to train in weapons, come next week on Tuesday at twelve noon. Your friends will be in school. Hopefully you will be here with me, one on one."

"Hai, arigato gozaimasu, Senseisan," I responded even more respectfully.

Outside, curiosity kept Chris and Ameer waiting on me.

"What happened? What did Sensei say?" Chris asked. Ameer waited intensely.

"Sensei said he is ready to train me in weapons," I admitted solemnly and truthfully. There was just silence. I knew they felt tight about it.

"Don't worry. Whatever I learn, I'll teach it to you. You know how we do," I promised.

"Whatever. Funny how he picked you for the weapons class. You already walk with your heat. What could be better than that?" Chris asked, still feeling cheated.

"No, don't sleep," Ameer said in a serious tone. "Sensei knows a thousand different ways to kill a man. You never know when you might have to defend yourself using more than your hands and feet, and can't get to your piece."

We stood there, thinking about what Ameer just said.

"Fuck it. We trust you. You're on our team, right?" Ameer patted me on the back and laughed. Chris' tension broke up. I looked at the two of them. I was grateful to have two friends in this foreign country. I thought of how my father's American friend and former roommate had left us stranded at the airport. I hoped that what we three had was something completely different.

Ten o'clock that same night, back on my Brooklyn block, the guns was clapping. I moved swiftly to my building, dodging and avoiding, imagining my mother and sister ducked down on the floor the way I taught them to do when they hear gunshots. I was certain that my mother had the blinds closed and curtains drawn by this hour. Hopefully she had on some music and couldn't hear the symphony of bullets.

My heart raced as my mind conjured up the image of a stray bullet piercing the innocence and beauty of my Umma or my young sister Naja.

I got home and showed my face and my love, so they could sleep.

Two and a half hours later, I was out on the ball court for self, in the thick of the night.

This time I saw him coming. I kept my eye on him as I dribbled.

"You fronted." It was Tyriq, disturbing my peace.

"I didn't promise you nothing," I answered.

"You could've at least came to check it out," he pushed.

"It's your thing. Have fun with it," I told him.

"This is your idea of fun, playing by yourself, wasting your skills?"

"You talk like you're offering me something more than a game," I told him.

"Maybe I am. But you gotta step up first. Friday night at eight P.M. We'll be at the gym again," he said.

• • •

Friday afternoon my mind was on finishing up at Cho's. After getting fresh I planned to walk four stores over on this same block to Akemi's job, to try to meet her people, introduce myself, and acknowledge my friendship with Akemi. I was uncertain about their beliefs and traditions.

When I stepped outside Cho's store, Ameer and Redbone was standing right there. I was tight about Ameer bringing her to another place I considered a permanent spot. At the same time, I figured if he showed up here at my job, which he'd only done once before, there must be some kind of emergency. I kept myself open to hear him out and help out however I could.

"What's up, man?" I asked him.

"Hello. How you doing?" she answered instead of him.

"I don't know about tonight," Ameer said. "We was thinking about going to the movies instead of hooping."

"Chris too?" I asked, since we all was supposed to meet up at the dojo on Friday nights as usual to hustle up a game in the nearby park.

"Yeah. We gonna go pick Chris and his girl up and head out."

"What you doing up on this side?" I asked him, wondering why he was in Manhattan at three on a Friday afternoon, when he attended Brooklyn Tech High School in Brooklyn.

"I took the day off. Been hanging out up here with her," Ameer said with a gleam in his eye.

"I was planning to head over to that high school with you and Chris tonight at eight. I found out there might be some business to make it worth our while in the basketball tournament they're having over there," I said to Ameer, knowing how serious he was about handling business. I purposely left out the name of the high school so Redbone wouldn't end up showing up there too.

"Fuck it, then. We can meet up over there for basketball. Afterward we can hit up the late show on Forty Deuce and meet up with the girls. How that sound?" he asked, pressing me to agree. But now I was looking over his shoulder at Akemi, who was walking up the block to see me.

Redbone, who was constantly staring into my mug, turned around to see what I was looking at.

"Sounds good," I told Ameer, agreeing and hoping him and his girl would step off before Akemi stepped up and they got even deeper into my business. But the two of them didn't move.

"So we can invite Homegirl, right? She really wanna see you anyway." Ameer smiled.

Akemi arrived. She stopped walking and stood about ten feet away from where we were talking.

Despite the normal New York crowds, Redbone was picking up on Akemi's presence. Her eyeballs kept shifting from Akemi to me and back. I didn't acknowledge nothing either way. I wanted her and Ameer to leave.

"Yeah, no problem." Quickly, I agreed to the homegirl situation to get them out of there.

"All right, tonight then at the high school. I'll let Chris know," Ameer said. They bounced. I watched them disappear around the corner. Redbone turned to look back as they turned the bend.

Akemi had a new haircut. It was now not as long as it usually was, but still more long than short. It was an Egyptian blunt cut with bangs running straight across her forehead, and the rest of every strand of her hair cut straight and lying on her back. It looked beautiful and set off her eyes in a whole new way. She had on brown tights that covered her legs, a short brown crushed-leather jumper dress, with a blouse beneath and gorgeous leather heels with a strap that wrapped around each ankle. The feeling of knowing she was dressing up for me felt good. The idea that anyone passing by could look at her also, didn't.

As I approached her, her pretty face went sour. She threw up her hand like she was saying, "Stop." She turned to leave, took a few steps, turned back facing me, and threw up her hands again as if to say, "Wait right here." It was bugged out, but I waited.

She came back up the block with a little girl around my sister's age or a little younger. I'm thinking, what's up with this? The little girl skipped up to me, struck a mean pose, one arm folded into the other like me and her were enemies. Akemi spoke some Japanese words to the little girl, pushing out each syllable with more passion than usual. The angry little Asian girl now facing me translated Akemi's fury.

"You didn't introduce me to your friends," the little girl said. I looked at her, then at Akemi. Akemi's big pretty eyes curved and then shrank with anger. I paused for a minute and answered.

"You didn't even introduce me to your parents," I told her.

The little girl translated. Akemi responded to her.

"My parents are in Japan. Your friends were standing right here between the two of us," the little girl said with even more attitude than Akemi.

"Your aunt and uncle and your store are four doors down. You never once invited me inside," I told her. The little girl translated.

"That's different. You and I are young. We have our world. They have their world," the little girl, now with one hand on her hip, said on behalf of Akemi.

"So what do you want? Do you want to keep our worlds separate? Or do you want to come all the way into mine and me into yours?" I asked. The little girl's eyes widened a bit. She seemed surprised by what I was saying. Believe it or not, I was surprised too.

When she translated my words to Akemi, there was a long pause. So I spoke instead.

"You can't have it both ways," I told her.

On hearing this translated, Akemi's anger softened. She looked at me, her eyes watery again, the kind of tears that don't fall. Softly now she spoke. The little girl interpreted more calmly.

"How about tomorrow at closing? You can come by my family's shop and meet everyone. Then maybe you and I can go out together once more?" the little girl asked in a more relaxed tone.

"Hai, ashita," I said, which means "Yes, tomorrow," in Japanese. Akemi bowed, just a slight movement of her head. They both smiled. Akemi grabbed the little girl's hand and they both left.

Believe me, I wanted to follow Akemi, her legs moving rhythmically, heels clicking on the pavement. I pushed off to Brooklyn though. I had to pick up Umma by five and my little sister also.

After a hot shower and a family prayer, a delicious meal of Umma's fish seasoned with a Sudanese hot sauce called shotta, soup, vegetables, salad, and fresh, hot homemade bread felt good in my stomach. Afterward, she served me some strong hot tea spiced perfectly with ginger and cardamom in a porcelain teacup. It raced around my body, warmed my blood, and gave me a complete and settled feeling.

When I left, Umma was just sitting down to her sewing machine. My sister Naja was reading her book out loud like she tended to do.

Dressed in my dark-blue Nike sweats, wearing a blue Jansport and a crisp pair of kicks, my hands gripping my basketball, I stepped into the dim hallway of my building and headed out to do one quick Umma Designs hat delivery and then over to the gym.

14

RECRUITERS

Late by half an hour or so, I came up on the backside of the high school, surprised. The entire parking lot was filled with cars. I knew something out of the ordinary had to be going down because the cars were mostly expensive, wearing a fresh wash and wax. Even the tires glistened with Armor All.

The crazy shit was how nobody parked within the yellow lines that outlined each space. Instead, people were parked however the fuck they wanted to. The kitted-up BMWs, Jeep Wranglers, Audis, Camaros, Saabs, and motorbikes, both Kawasakis and the dirt bikes, looked impressive.

Under the spotlight beaming from the lamppost, parked sideways, was the whip that caught my eye and made my jaw drop. It was the only Porsche parked on the lot. The color of the exterior was buttermilk. I walked closer to check it out. The interior was cream colored. The seats were soft buttery leather with gold piping. It was brand-new, the 959 PSK, which I knew from reading the car mags was so exclusive that Porsche only made two hundred of them to sell around the entire world. My face was pressed almost to the glass, and the dashboard of the Porsche was so pretty and high tech it looked like a small private plane instead of a car. The wooden stick shift was waxed, not even one smudge or fingerprint to stain it, as if no one even drove it here. The speedometer went up to three hundred miles per hour.

I imagined myself in this high-powered, high-speed

monster hugging a mountain road in Morocco doing 120 mph. I laughed, thinking I probably needed a fucking pilot's license to drive this machine.

On closer inspection, I saw the monogrammed insignia embossed into the driver's headrest. RS were the initials. This car had such a clean look, no junky attachments, lime-green fog lights, or press-on letters on the outside like I had seen some gaudy players do. As I stood up and stepped back, I thought to myself, *If I had the money to do it, this is exactly how I would do it.* It was deep to me, how you could always tell one man from another by his style. And it was rare for a man to break from doing a version of the exact same thing as every other man, and instead do something original of an even higher quality; something smarter, and better.

When a piece of light hits a real piece of gold, it glistens for less than one second of time. I caught the flash of genuine gold, a small but life-size pair of dark, solid-gold baby shoes, dangling from a six-inch, solid-gold link chain, hanging from the rearview mirror.

I was always on point about gold and jewels and their true content and value. My father consistently selected the best of everything and pointed out and kept away from the junk.

I was impressed with this dark-colored, twenty-four-karat gold and the craftsmanship of the shoes even down to the detail of the gold shoelaces. I had seen all kind of pendants and pieces, good and bad, but I had never seen a man mount baby shoes on a chain.

Somehow I knew for sure this ride belonged to a man. There were no feminine things to give it away, napkins, purses, lipsticks, hairpins, small pieces of wrapped candy, not even diapers or a baby seat.

Parked next to a cherry Beemer M3 with two hairy cloth dice on the dashboard, the style and build of the Porsche blew every other whip off the lot.

Music and loud talking was coming from the front of the school building. When I wound my way around there, I ran into hundreds of people standing in loose formed lines and tightly drawn circles, waiting. Bass lines and beats, do-rags, corn rolls, and bouncing balls, thick bodies, titties, and tight clothes—the niggas was out.

I pushed my way through the dark crowd looking for Ameer and Chris. As more people arrived I figured I better get my position on the line and wait to find my boys once we got inside the gym and into the light.

Tyriq had said, "basketball tryouts," but this looked like an organized and advertised basketball *game* was about to take place with some professional and well-known ballers and their devoted fans.

Easily I could've bounced, but because of me, my friends were out here somewhere in the mix. And besides, money was in the air. I could feel it.

Somebody rolled up blasting Just-Ice's joint "Cold Gettin' Dumb." The crowd jerked, excited from the beat. People started pushing and pressed up against one another.

Six big bouncer-type giants finally threw open the three gym doors and everybody tried to bum-rush Brooklyn style. The big dudes formed a wall and made everybody "Back up! Back up!" They made people walk in one by one. I was clocking their procedure real close. I needed to know if they was conducting a search or not. Or if they had handheld metal detectors or what.

It turned out they wasn't. I knew then there would be a gym full of guns, which was probably for the best. When everybody is packing, people are better at holding their positions, cautious of the consequences. Chaos usually breaks out when only one crazy cop or backward nigga is armed and the rest of the people are sitting ducks at his mercy.

Walking in, I heard dudes on the line talking about how they got "callbacks" from the first tryouts and how tonight

was the final cut. I put two and two together and understood
what was up.

Inside, the majority of the people filled in the bleachers
situated on either side of the gym. Everybody who planned
to ball remained on the gym floor. That made about two hundred teenage boys on the floor, no bullshit. I spotted Ameer
and Chris. They was way up the line. I was all the way in the
back. I stayed in position, knowing that to join or cut the line
up front was to draw attention to myself and set it off.

Tyriq appeared in sweats with a whistle and a couple of
big guys standing at his sides.

"Line up for layups," he shouted.

These youth must've known and respected him because
they did exactly what he said. One by one they took it to
the hoops while the girls and some mothers jumped up and
danced to celebrate this one or that one's skills.

In the back, still waiting my turn, I was scanning the crazy
crowd. I was bugging on how in this hot-ass gym, there was
groups of overdressed types in the bleachers, one in a full-
length rabbit fur wearing sunglasses at night and indoors.
Another one was wearing a full-length mink with a matching
mink hat. It was winter outside but summer in the gym, yet
nobody wanted to take off or check their coats.

A couple of grown-up cats playing the corners, dressed
in suits and hard shoes, were watching us closely like they
were professional recruiters. But these were Black cats from
the hood who, if pushed, could probably get on the court and
play a decent game themselves, not the official recruiter types.

When ballers would miss the layup, lose control of the
ball, or show sloppy style, Tyriq's big side niggas would sit
them down on the floor and out of the way. By the time I got
up I figured I better just dunk it. Nobody would remember
the last player of a group of over a hundred.

I caught a little reaction from the crowd.

After layups, we were tested on our jumpers, then our three-point shots. A lot of these cats were good but even some of the good ones were choking under the pressure of performance, the crowd, and the critique. The long line was thinning out as dudes got sidelined by Tyriq's men. Ameer and Chris were still standing. I wasn't surprised.

With the three-point shots, they let us shoot the rock till we missed one. If you missed on your first shot, they gave you one last chance.

I don't know what was feeding me. I wasn't sure that I could get paid from this shit, but I was trying my best. Maybe it was the crowd, faces plastered with one-hundred-percent approval and a joy so real they leaped out of their seats. For once, it wasn't hatred, stress, and put-downs. Black youths were actually cheering for one another.

I hit eighteen three-pointers before I missed one. It was easy for me. A real challenge would have been shooting the rock with my eyes closed. But that wasn't required.

When I finally missed on shot number nineteen, Tyriq put his left hand in the air. "A'ight, a'ight," he said, blowing his whistle and waving the spectators who had moved down onto the court back up into the bleachers.

Just then, I noticed Ameer's father chilling alone in the cut behind a group of men and up against the wall, looking serious and concentrating real hard.

After the whistle, we got divided into teams. Nothing was thought out, just the first five in the line on one team and the second five on the line on the next team and so on. Each pair of teams was told to run a ten-minute, full-court game. Tyriq had the stopwatch. The game was over when a team scored ten points or when ten minutes passed and the whistle was blown, whatever came first.

Some of the suited money cats who were casually standing and sitting around the bleachers earlier were now standing around the perimeter of the court reacting to the rebounding, the handling, the flying, the masterful dribbling and passing so slick that for seconds the ball seemed lost somewhere. They seemed like a group of gamblers at a race track or at OTB waiting for the results to come in.

For me this was a crazy experiment. Just as we got wound up, it was all over. "It's a wrap," Tyriq announced. The ball players who were still standing, blood was pumping and hearts were still racing. Our eyes were wide open as we stayed on the floor staring at one another and wondering what was next. My sweat was flowing into my blue terry-cloth head-band.

Instead of talking to the players, Tyriq hosted a meeting right on the court with the men from the sidelines. Their huddle was intense. Their backs were blocking out anyone trying to look inward. Seemed like they were consulting one another, and doing some arguing. It could easily have been mistaken for a big game of C-low. Whatever it was, we all could tell it was serious and knew to stay out their way.

Soon the girls started streaming down from the bleachers onto the floor. I drifted over to Chris and Ameer. Somebody threw on "Push It," a Salt-N-Pepa joint, and most of the crowd started dancing. About twenty minutes later, Tyriq started weaving in and out of the crowd tapping dudes, saying either "I wanna see you. I want to talk to you. You over here. You over there. Step up. Step out. Next time."

Security began urging, directing, and pushing the crowd toward the exit. A couple of fights got instigated then squashed immediately. Within fifteen minutes, only the chosen players were left in the room with Tyriq and his men.

They passed around a clipboard. We were asked to write down our names, telephone numbers, and addresses. We were told to meet here same time next week Friday for all the details.

"You little motherfuckers are Brooklyn's finest. Don't let it go to your heads. Practice, or the next man will jump in your spot. If you're still alive and free next week, you should be standing right here on the line," he said.

From the look of things, these cats believed in Tyriq and whatever promises he might have made to each of them. No one gave him any back talk or static or attitude about him having wasted our time or the lack of information and follow through. I figured maybe they all knew something that I didn't.

I decided even if Tyriq and them didn't do nothing for me, tonight was a good workout; proof that me, Ameer, and Chris, when compared to the rest, was no joke; serious contenders on the court; "Brooklyn's finest." Overall, I couldn't count it as a loss.

"You didn't write your name down, brotha," Ameer said to me, smiling.

"You invite us to some shit, let us sign up, and you don't sign," Chris added.

"They don't need my information. If I want to come next week, I'll just show up," I told them.

"What do you think we can get out of playing ball out here?" Chris asked me.

"Don't sleep. We can get a lot out of it. This is part of the Hustler's League, everybody knows that," Ameer revealed.

"Hustler's League?" Chris asked.

"Didn't you notice all them hustlers up in this spot? Even Crazy Eddie from the East was up in there. He's from around my way."

"You know him?" Chris asked.

"Everybody knows him," Ameer answered.

"Why didn't you say something?" I asked Ameer.

"I came here on *your* invite. I didn't know *who* you was dealing with until we got here. Besides, them motherfuckers is some real moneymakers. They saw how the three of us put it down in here. If they want us to play, they gotta pay," Ameer said with complete confidence. "I think it's dope, they started up a Hustler's League youth division."

"Your pops passed through here. Did you see him?" I asked Ameer.

"You fucking around?" Ameer asked me.

"Nah," I told him.

Outside the night breeze felt good. There was still cliques of kids standing out front playing the wall and the curb. We wasn't outside five seconds before a cluster of females started sweating us.

"Hey, in the green," one of the girls shouted. Ameer had on green sweats. Neither of the three of us turned around.

"They calling us like we the chicks," Chris said.

"Word," Ameer agreed. We kept walking.

Chris was bouncing his ball. Them girls were walking behind us close, talking so we could hear.

"You play good," one of 'em said. Ameer couldn't resist a compliment. He turned around to see what we was dealing with.

"Yeah, thanks," he answered the girl.

"Not you, him," a girl's voice said while the rest of them laughed. Chris stopped walking and dribbling and turned to look.

"Not you either." They laughed. It came clear that she was referring to me.

"What's your name?" the girl asked. I turned around but didn't say shit. So she kept talking.

"You kind of mean but I like it," she said. Her girlfriends giggled.

To tell the truth, I didn't like the reversal. I didn't like the idea of chicks trying to mack us.

"Just flow with it," Ameer said in a low tone, nudging me in the side with his elbow. Chris agreed with Ameer's plan with just an excited smirk on his face. We all three about-faced and walked toward them. Everybody broke into small sets, walked back, and sat on the stone wall outside the high school.

"You shy or something?" the girl who bigged me up asked me.

"Nah," I answered.

"I know that's right, 'cause you sure wasn't shy out on the court." She smiled.

"I did all right," I answered.

"No, you were the best." She smiled again, revealing pretty white teeth against the dark of the night and deep-dish dimples. "Let me give you my number," she said, digging into her pockets. She pulled out a half of a piece of paper and a Sharpie.

"What, you been giving out your number all day?" I asked her, 'cause that's what it looked like to me.

"No! I don't usually give out my number. Or if some boy pesters me, I'll give him the wrong number just to get him out of my face."

"So what are you doing right now?" I asked her.

"I'm giving you my number before you become famous. That way, I can say I knew him before he became a star." She laughed, then jotted down her number.

"Sign your name right here," she said, then turned her back to me, and dropped her jacket from her shoulders. "And put the date in case anybody try and say I didn't know you first. C'mon please, sign it."

She wasn't about to give up. I signed "Midnight" across her back and put the date.

"I live right here around the corner." She pointed. "Oh, and I gotta go." She jumped up suddenly like she had to pee or something. "I was supposed to be in the house by eleven. I got three minutes."

She ran off full speed like a track star. I watched her run. Her body was crazy, jeans so tight I don't know how she dashed so free and fast.

Ameer's pops strolled up toward the wall where we were sitting, moving slow and cool like he usually does. He had a can of beer wrapped in a brown paper bag in hand. He didn't have to say nothing. Ameer was off the wall and on his feet. Me and Chris followed him over to his pops, both of us probably thinking us being there would help Ameer out of whatever kind of trouble he was in now.

The other girls in the bunch just slipped away, the way teens do when adults come around. They caught the vibe and quietly left.

"What you got in your pockets, son?" That's how he started the conversation with Ameer.

"I got paper," Ameer answered. "About forty dollars."

"What else?" his pop asked.

"What you mean? I got coins but that don't count, right?" Ameer smiled at his pops, trying to break whatever serious vibe his father was delivering.

"You out here dealing with the hustlers, they got guns. You got forty dollars and some coins." His father just stared at him. "You out here with the girlies. They ready. You not ready. You got a condom on you?" he asked.

"Not right now," Ameer answered, then laughed.

"How about the two of you?" The father redirected his questions to me and Chris.

"I got some money," Chris answered.

"I'm good," I answered, looking him in the eye the way my father taught me to do. No laughter.

"Let's go," his father told us. We walked to the train station, the four of us.

That's how Ameer's father was, an ex-hustler who had a good little run for a little while and stepped out the game with nothing but his life in his hands. Now he works two jobs and spends his free time catching up and cracking down on Ameer. I never seen his pops yell. He wasn't that type. He just had his rules, about a thousand of 'em, each accompanied by a street tale.

"I'm not gonna tell you not to chase pussy. But bag up your dick every time. If you want to smoke weed come to me. I'll buy it. We'll smoke in the house. Don't try to buy it yourself. Don't smoke in the streets with nobody else. Stay in school until you graduate. Go to college. There's three type of men you got to avoid at any cost—the police, the army recruiters, the hustlers. They all want your life and that's all you got."

At the train station I asked Chris, "What about the girls? Are they on Forty-Deuce waiting for us to take them for the movie?"

Chris answered, "No. They not there. I called it off. I told Ameer we could kick it with the girls some other time. Why bring them around a hundred or more ball players? Do y'all think we could fight them all and win?" Chris asked. We all laughed, even Ameer's pops.

We all went our separate ways. Riding on the train alone, I thought about what Ameer's pops had to say. My head was cracking just trying to think about all the shit every other adult had to say and how their advice never seemed to match up. Where I come from, all the adults are living and pushing the same beliefs and ideas and ways of living.

In America, every other motherfucker got his own plan, religion, opinion, and ideas. And, like in the case of Ameer and his father, their religion, ideas, and actions could all be three completely different things. They were Five Percenters, who believed that the Black man is God. When I first hooked up with Ameer at the dojo, he said he was Muslim. But their idea of Islam and the Islam I knew and was born into were miles apart. I took the friend and left his religion and philosophy on the side.

The same with Chris. His family is Christian. As long as he went to church, his religion was easy. In both cases it seemed like neither of their beliefs required them to do anything, sacrifice anything, or fight for anything. In fact, I never seen either one of them pray, not in the morning, afternoon, or evening. Not when we were in deep trouble. Not even before or after a meal.

When they first saw me praying at the dojo, they walked up and interrupted. A few questions and a couple of laughs later, they never interrupted or allowed anyone else to interrupt me while I made prayer. It was bugged out though. It seemed like they believed that praying was only something that I do. Like it was part of my personality or something. Not something required of all human beings in a civilized world.

On the other hand, I liked that Ameer and Chris had my back while I made prayer. In my country we believed in that. We believed that men must pray, and while some men pray, some men must watch their back.

The aroma of Sudanese coffee mingled with the scent of Umma's oils late that night when I arrived home. She was seated at her sewing machine in her turquoise-colored silk pajamas, her thick hair wound into one long braid beginning at the top of her head and ending below her right shoulder.

"You seem victorious," she said to me in Arabic. "Shower and then tell me all about it. I have a few important things to tell you too."

Naja was asleep on top of a huge, soft pillow on the floor, curled up like a snail in its shell. "Yes, look at my littlest helper," Umma said.

I picked my sister up and carried her to her bedroom. I wondered if she could really be in such a deep sleep that she could not feel herself being moved from one room to another, or laid gently on her bed and covered. Or was it that she was just enjoying the ride that most kids no longer receive when they are six or seven years old and considered too big to be carried?

In the glow of a cinnamon candle, I sat beside Umma on the floor. My muscles were relaxed now and I was feeling fresh and clean and calm from my hot shower.

"Tell me," Umma said.

"It's nothing really. I tried out for a basketball team and was chosen. I am supposed to find out next week if there is any way to earn by participating."

"Why would anybody pay a young person to play basketball?" Umma asked. "It sounds strange," she added.

"No one would pay just anybody to play basketball, unless they was great," I said, smiling.

"Oh, I see!" She laughed.

"The game needs me," I kidded her.

"Of course it does!" she joked. "Anyway, remember our Ethiopian client up in the Bronx? The lady whose family moved here from Israel?" she asked.

"Of course. Remember how long it took me to scrub that emerald-green dye off your fingers after you custom designed her cloths?" I reminded her and we laughed.

"Well, she liked my work and received so many compliments that she recommended me to a Sudanese coworker of hers whose family has been living over here in America for some years. Their nephew is about to be married in some huge wedding and they require a wedding planner who knows and understands Sudanese tastes, customs, and traditions. There is a tremendous operating budget and a ten-thousand-dollar commission for me if I supervise and coordinate everything and also handle *all* of the aspects of design for the wedding including, of course, the garments."

"Ten thousand dollars?" I repeated calmly but in disbelief, thinking of how since we arrived to America, except for a handful of elite clients, we had to earn every penny very slowly. And poor client or elite client, in every instance we had to labor very hard. So far, Umma had done one dress here and another there, but this lump sum would bring in more revenue in one swoop than she would generate in six months' time working at the factory. Also, I thought about how completing this wedding successfully would put us right up close to our financial goal of buying our own home and property and getting ghost from Brooklyn.

"What do you think?" she asked me.

"I think that's great. Somebody finally recognized that your talent is incredible and almost impossible to find. No one else would work harder and do more for the amount they are offering. And even if they found somebody else to hire, their product would never be as authentic and attractive. If you give me their information, on Monday I'll call and set it up so I can collect at least fifty percent up front as a deposit on your commission."

"Five thousand up front? Do you think so?"

"Definitely. If they're serious, they'll pay some up-front money like any other client. I'll handle it," I assured her. Then she got quiet.

"There is only one thing." She hesitated. We both sat in silence for some seconds.

"I know." I paused. "You're worried and not sure if you want to work with a Sudanese family. I know they will be your first Sudanese clients since we have been living here in America. They will ask too many questions and believe that since you are working for them that you owe them the answers, right?"

"You are so smart," she admitted.

"But you said they have been living in America for some years, and we will be professionals. We will treat them nice. You will talk to the women about the art and designs and measurements of their dresses. I will speak and work with the men.

"When any other topic or something too personal comes up, you will do like the Americans and just tell them you have to go! Or we could charge them by the hour and that will cut out all of the talking!"

We had another good laugh.

Umma gave me the name and telephone number for the uncle of the groom, who was representing his brother's family. I would call him and confirm the business. Umma would do what she does best; make everything unbelievably beautiful.

After our late-night prayer together to make up for the one I missed today, I raised my forehead from the floor and went to my bedroom. Seconds later Umma reappeared.

"What about the girl?" she said sweetly. Then there was a long pause.

"Akemi?" I asked, already knowing.

"That one," she said, confirming.

"I am supposed to meet her aunt and uncle at their family business tomorrow."

"Inshallah," she said, meaning "If God is willing." Then she seemed lost in a thought as she leaned against my door.

"You cannot go empty-handed to her relatives. You know this, right?" she asked softly.

"Yes, Umma, you're right," I answered. She moved from my door and returned a little later with her hands full, just as I began drifting into sleep.

"Give these gifts to her aunt and uncle, on behalf of our family. It's not much. Yet they may enjoy them. I'll wrap them for you. Don't forget to take them with you in the morning."

"I will remember," I assured her. She switched the lights off and stood in the darkness. It seemed like her words floated on the air.

"Now that you are becoming a man, things will be more complicated than they have ever been," she said.

I did not really understand specifically what she meant.

"You will have strong urges and feelings pulling you in every way. But you should not become a servant to your desires," she said, her words cutting through the darkness before their true meaning could begin to sink into my tired mind.

She continued, "A woman is more than a powerful feeling or unforgettable taste, and a man should not try to eat from every dish. A good woman is a jewel from Allah for which a man must pay a heavy price. Be very careful."

She closed my door. Soon I heard her sewing machine start up again.

Her words were like a dish of cold water on my sleepy face.

15

GOOD INTENTIONS

Altogether, I was bringing three gifts. Umma's gift to Akemi's uncle was a sterling-silver cigarette case filled with her signature *bidis*. These were hand-rolled foreign cigarettes filled with a special tobacco, which Umma spiced up with her private herb recipe and wrapped in a scented paper. The taste and smell of the smoke usually fascinated all men who had the privilege to acquire them.

My father was not really a smoker, but he did smoke socially. He had a smoking room on our estate reserved for men. Many of his business, civil, and Islamic brothers gathered in this room to indulge.

The second gift was inside a maroon velvet box with a gold clasp. It was another homemade specialty, a crystal bottle filled with Umma's perfume elixir. The bottle was slim and short, containing only an ounce of the potion, which was so strong a woman need only use half a drop. It was hypnotic, this stuff. I remember even in my childhood finding myself following the trail of this scent when it was worn by one or two of my Umma's friends.

Both gifts were normally reserved for our customers who placed an order of three hundred dollars or more. Once a client received their special order of handmade cloths and garments, along with one of these elegant gifts, they became a customer of ours forever.

The third gift I picked out and purchased for Akemi. It

was less powerful than Umma's well-thought-out magic. I brought Akemi a Walkman and a Japanese language tape that she could listen to and, lesson by lesson, slowly learn how to speak English from a Japanese professor. I thought that right now this was what Akemi needed most. Of course, there was some selfishness in it too.

At Akemi's family business, they had a storefront, where items were for sale right outside the store door underneath a small, extended canopy. One of their workers always stood out there. I had first seen Akemi standing there. They served most customers outside. The customers asked for this or that, then paid and bounced with their purchases.

Once you got past the worker outside and the merchandise and entered through the glass store door, the whole vibe switched up to a family thing.

When I passed by their worker who was leaving and entered their store at seven that evening, I saw Akemi's uncle's body jerk, the way every shop owner trembles when a young, strong, Black man enters the door around closing time. Instantly, I noticed a pile of shoes off to the left of the entrance where I stood, so I removed my shoes also.

The aunt and uncle were in there standing, not sitting. They were both dressed plainly and conservatively. He wore gray slacks, a white dress shirt, and a blue vest. She wore a pantsuit, a whole lot of polyester. They were both wearing thick prescription reading type glasses.

The little girl with the spicy attitude who Akemi had translating for her the other day jumped off a low stool where she was sitting and scooted into a back room. Seconds later Akemi emerged.

She addressed her aunt and uncle in Japanese, of course, very respectfully and without a smile on her face. I didn't have a clue what she was saying to them, except for one word she used, *tomadochi*, which I knew means "friend."

When Akemi stopped speaking, her aunt dragged out a piece of a smile, then quickly covered it up with the palm of her hand. Her uncle stood stone-faced. The only thing moving was his eyeballs.

I greeted both of them in Japanese. Their reaction to my effort to speak their language was like what happens when a kid tries but fails to tie a knot at the end of a balloon. I could almost hear a small whistle of breath escaping slowly from both of them. They released some but not all of their tension, which was thick like pound cake.

In Japanese, they returned my greeting without any emotion. Even Akemi stood somewhat blank faced, watching. I lifted up the bag with the gifts. I handed a gift to the uncle, then to her aunt, and next to Akemi. The little girl pouted. I guess she felt left out. However, I did not know she was part of their family and still didn't know where and how she fit in.

"My parents speak some English. Why don't you say something to them?" the little girl said in her spicy American tone, as if she was snitching on her mom and dad.

"I'm a friend of Akemi's. I work four stores down at the fish market. I wanted to have this chance to meet you, so that you would know who I am. These gifts are from my family, to your family."

"Thank you for the gifts," the aunt said dryly in English.

"How do you know Akemi?" the uncle asked in English with a heavy accent.

"We met here in Chinatown," I answered.

"Are you a college student?" he asked.

"No. I am high school age," I answered, avoiding any pitfalls.

"What do you want?" the uncle asked boldly in an even tone.

"She and I are friends. So I thought it would be best if I knew you and you knew me. In my country, we do not avoid our friends' parents," I added.

"What country is your country?" he asked with a tone of disbelief, as though he had assumed that I was one of the countless men with no homeland, culture, or language. When I answered him, I watched his face muscles, intensity, and suspicion lessen another few degrees.

The relaxing of his face was a good sign that Akemi also picked up on. She smiled naturally. Then swiftly, she made her smile disappear. She began speaking to them softly once more in Japanese.

The tight encounter ended with one head shake from the uncle. After looking him in his eyes, I switched to Akemi. She didn't have to tell me that she couldn't come out with me tonight like I wanted and she requested. It was written on her face. Matter of fact, it was written on all of their faces.

I broke the strange staring contest and said, "*Oyasumina-sai,*" which means "Good night."

Umma laughed when I reenacted their cold stares and the stiff situation at the store for her at home.

"You see, this is what I have been pointing out to you," she said, her eyes bright and beautiful and smile so genuine. "If you go outside, you can find a thousand stones on the ground. They are lying around everywhere. You can just pick any one of them up anytime and put it right into your pocket, or throw it back onto the ground. Or do whatever you like with it. It has no value, so no one cares. But when a stone is a precious jewel, it is surrounded and protected. You'll have to work very hard to earn it and even harder to keep it for yourself."

After she and Naja had their fun with my situation, Umma assured me, "Don't worry. The perfume I have given to the aunt is very influential. If she applies it once, slowly, it will grow on her. Soon she will love it. When she doesn't wear it, her own husband will request that she put some on." Umma smiled knowingly. I listened, fascinated.

"The sterling-silver cigarette case I gave to the uncle contained twelve Sudanese *bidis*. Akemi's uncle will smoke the first one out of curiosity." Umma stood joking and posing as though she was smoking the *bidi* and was enraptured in its taste and scent.

"Soon enough his case will become empty." She frowned as though she were the uncle, out of *bidis*.

"He will have to come to you for more. There is no place else for him to go to get the exact same taste, fragrance, and feeling. He will have to return to you." She stood with her arms now extended and smiling.

Listening to Umma, the sound of her voice and depth of her thoughts and her dramatic theatrics, I was amazed by how every day she revealed more and more sides of herself. Her knowledge was gentle and her light humor seemed endless. Yet when I stared into her face, she still seemed very young and naive.

Without ever meeting Akemi or Akemi's family, she had chosen gifts that she knew would have an impact, and how they would impact. She had given gifts that she knew would linger and rebound.

My father was a scientist with a pile of university degrees. My Umma was a scientist of human nature, without having earned anyone's documents of approval.

In my room I hit the books for a couple of hours, unusual for me on a Saturday night.

Later that night when the sewing machine stopped and I could hear nothing but silence and the breathing of my sister and mother, I stepped out, locked our apartment door, and headed to the basketball court and hooped.

16

SUDANA

The smell of chopped peppers, garlic, onions, and tomatoes plus several secret ingredients of Umma's filled our apartment on early Sunday afternoon. After a great meal, Naja and I walked to the store to pick up various Sunday newspapers. When we returned, Umma excitedly announced, "Leave your shoes on. I have a chance to take some measurements from the family members of the wedding party."

"On a Sunday?" Naja asked Umma.

"I know. It's a rush job. Because of everyone's schedule, so many of us working two jobs, it turns out that Sunday is our best option. I just got the call from Yaella. The earlier I get these measurements done, the more comfortable they will feel. One of the women even works on Sundays. Now her sister says I have less than two hours to get over to the Bronx to take her measurements before the woman is off to work again."

Naja and I listened and waited. Umma spoke as she rushed around.

Ever since Naja was born, Sunday in our apartment was reserved as family day. The rule is, no matter what we do, we do it together on Sundays. Usually, we relax at home, reading, listening to music, or conversing with one another. In the spring and summers, we go to the park or to a special event that's of interest to us. On crunch time, Umma sews and Naja and I remain in the apartment along with her, doing one of our own hobbies. I never minded family day. Sometimes it was the only day where we could catch some real rest. Sundays slowed me down.

Once we arrived on our new Sudanese customer's Bronx block, without even looking at the numbers on the small houses I assumed their house was the white one with the aluminum siding and green trimming. It was the only house on the block with a gate around it. I knew if a Sudanese-born man came to this country along with his family, once he got a good look at the crazy Americans and the way that they live, his first priority would be to protect his family. Placing a gate around his property was a small way to separate or distinguish his loved ones from the influence and lifestyles of their American neighbors.

As we walked down the length of their block, my prediction turned out to be true.

"A-Salaama Alaikum," the voice came from the other side of the fence before we even reached to push the gate open. A Sudanese youth around seventeen years young with a soccer ball in his hand greeted all of us as he opened the gate and welcomed us in. A second, older son also ran up. They were all smiles, the sincere way people back home greeted one another. I had lost that all-day, automatic natural smile years ago, and now greeted most males with suspicion instead.

Their father welcomed us through their front door. Like many Sudanese men he was tall. Brown skinned, he had the nappy curls of a North African male. He embraced me, which was customary. At first I felt uncomfortable. When I'm holding I don't fuck around with no hugging.

Then I felt a warmth from my past, where men in a family and even in a neighborhood were all each other's security and not opponents. Where a man greeted a next man warmly and genuinely without even an ounce of perversion.

Most important, their father was respectful to Umma, and

praised her reputation and good works. He kept a respectful distance and a proper gaze and immediately brought forth his wife, who whisked Umma away to some rooms in the back of their home.

In an open area up front, he invited me to sit with him and his sons. Almost immediately a young daughter arrived to collect my jacket. She was covered from head to toe. I didn't even look directly at her. I did watch the direction in which she carried my jacket. I watched her hang it up in a closet, then close the door. Now that I knew where she was headed with it, I felt relieved. I wouldn't want her to find anything in my pockets that she could hurt herself or anybody else with by accident.

While Mr. Salim Ahmed Amin Ghazzali was there, we spoke only in Arabic, really a familiar Sudanese Arabic Creole.

"Business has been good for you and your family," he asked.

"It's building slowly," I responded truthfully.

"No, son, it was not a question. I know your business is good because I have heard and seen so many good things about Umma Designs."

"Thank you," I replied.

"Allah has blessed me to own two taxis. So I meet a lot of people in this city. One day I collected a very smartly dressed woman from Kenya. I recognized through my rearview mirror right away that she was wearing cloths with a Sudanese design and influence. I wanted to know, but did not want to ask her. Then I thought about the fact that my wife would surely want to know where she bought such nice materials. The Kenyan woman spoke so highly of Umma Designs, yet she did not have your business card available and could not remember the telephone number by heart.

"I thought to myself, 'Hey, that's how it goes. You pick up a passenger once and never see them again! If you don't get whatever information you might need from them right then and there, you lose out.' Believe it or not, this happened to me a few times with your company. After the third time, I looked up Umma Designs in the telephone directory, planning to order a gift for my wife. Eventually I dialed up 411. But, nothing!" He smiled, holding his hands up. He was one of those men who spoke with his hands.

"It's a small family business with excellent products and services. We haven't expanded as of yet. We have more than enough customers so far. Your account is very important to us. We are certain that you will be more than pleased with everything that Umma Designs has to offer," I said slowly and thoughtfully.

"*E-Wallah!*" he said, gesturing with his hands at his sons. "Well said! Are you boys listening? If I could only get the two of you to represent me like this young man represents his family business," he said, impressed.

"In the taxi business, father?" his older son asked. "But you have sent us off to school!" the older son respectfully defended.

"Yes, but there is after school," the father replied sternly.

"We must study, father. Even you have said this," the older son reminded him.

"We do work for you on Saturdays, father," the young son added.

"No matter! Your father will work four jobs, drive two cabs all at once, as long as all six of my children become doctors, lawyers, and engineers. Where do you go to school, son?" He turned his conversation toward me.

It was his first in a series of questions he hurled my way. I remained respectful and elusive. Each time I guided the conversation back to the business at hand, collecting the necessary information for his nephew's wedding. And, of course, working my way toward the required five-thousand-dollar deposit.

While their father spoke, his sons were almost completely quiet and obedient in his presence. In our tradition, a son cherishes his father. The most important thing a son can do after submitting to Allah is to listen to and obey his father and work very hard to become worthy of the father's love and acknowledgment.

I understood these two sons.

One of them had on red pants. The other was wearing orange pants. They better hurry up and figure out how to get with the New York styles, I thought to myself. They could not play behind the gate of their house forever. They would never be able to mix or survive in these hoods wearing bright colored pants, tight T-shirts, and bootleg sneakers. If the wrong niggas caught them in the wrong neighborhood, the first beatdown would be based on style alone, separate from whatever else the attackers wanted to steal or do them. They were easy targets.

Less than half an hour in, another sister appeared, fully wrapped in a mustard-colored thobe. She was a pretty teenaged girl named Sudana, who had beautifully shaped eyes, colored like an African wildcat's, hazel with a deep dark-brown perimeter. All I could see were her eyes and her smooth and flawless skin, the type that our women had from eating olives and dates and other natural foods. Her hair was completely covered. The whites of her eyes were brilliant white, just like her perfect teeth. Her slim fingers were wrapped around a wooden serving tray, which she placed in front of me, offering in English, "Would you like coffee, tea, or a cold drink?" all of which she carried in on the tray along with Sudanese sweets. I was not hungry. But I could not refuse her.

She reminded me of the incomparable beauty of Umma's female friends back home. They used to visit her on our estate, and because I was just a child, they would unwrap themselves, some removing their veils and relaxing in my presence. They underestimated me because of my youth. Yet I studied them and noticed every single detail and difference in each one of them—their eyes and even the length of their eyelashes, the curve of their cheeks and lips, the length of their necks, and the shape of their shoulders. I could even push it further and reveal to you that sometimes I closed my eyes and challenged myself to identify each one of them by their scent alone.

I developed a careful eye for feminine elegance. The way a jeweler could pluck just one clear diamond out of a fistful of flaws, I could look at tens and hundreds of women, I thought, and choose one whose cut, shape, and quality were superb on the outside, and clean and clear on the inside. For me, with observing and being attracted to females, everything mattered and measured: the look, the voice and sound, the rhythm of the walk, the manners of expression, the balance between modesty and beauty, the depth of the conversation, the words she spoke and the way she spoke them, the feeling of her presence, the depth of her concern and admiration for me, the way she interacted with my friends and family, and simple things like what she actually did with her life from day to day.

From being born Muslim, African, and Sudanese, I learned to enjoy seeing less of a woman and imagining more. So that in America when a woman shows me too much, or is too fast and too obvious, or too empty, it kills the power of her mystery, freezes my imagination, and poisons my natural attraction.

Some of the American girls seemed to think I was cold. But like a jeweler, I was a hundred percent certain when I was seeing something fake, flawed, or cheap. And I was not attracted to it, even though it might have one or two good parts.

I liked seeing Sudana. She made me feel at home. She was subtle, sweet, and careful, not a high-powered vacuum cleaner like the American girls who came at me all day long, titties first and ass out, nice looking but way too much way too quick, only to find out she's really nothing at all.

I figured Sudana was about fifteen. Back home, she and I could get married any day now, unless we chose to delay our family life and work by attending college. The thought made me smile. Seconds later, reality dropped on my head. We were all here in the U.S. and every single familiar thing we did and believe would be considered wrong and outrageous.

After serving me, the guest, and her brothers and father, she left the room.

We enjoyed our cold drinks, Mr. Ghazzali enjoyed his tea and we all ate the small homemade pastries. Conversations ranged from the high price of American living, to first encounters with Americans, the horror stories all taking place in Mr. Ghazzali's taxi cab. He spoke of meeting weird passengers such as women dressed like men, with male mannerisms and yet the breasts and hands of a woman.

He spoke of cursing, angry mothers and females who smoked outdoors and did everything else outdoors for that matter, which none of us had ever witnessed in the Sudan.

He spoke also of male passengers who were dressed like women, or dressed like men except for some strange feminine behavior or things like wearing two earrings and lipstick or eye makeup and sometimes even wigs. He tried but could not really imitate or begin to capture the way the men spoke and altered their deep voices as if they were the same as women. Or the way they giggled and blushed. After his first couple of fares with such "men," he admitted pressing on the gas pedal and speeding off whenever he saw such bizarre men hailing his cab. He'd rather lose the money than have them as passengers. "The American she-men are the greatest disgrace against everything we have ever known. And the Black ones in particular are most embarrassing," he said.

Growing more grim, he spoke of the African cabbie who got murdered by a shameless Black American drug addict who got away with twenty-seven dollars and robbed a father and husband of at least twenty-seven more years of life and love.

He spoke of monster mothers who threw their kids into his backseat and dragged them out when it was time to go. Also, mothers who screamed and cursed at even their youngest children and had no patience, and not even one trace of love.

His sons must have felt as bad as I was feeling now. The older one introduced the topic of the World Cup, which he must have known would excite his father, the soccer fan, and ease the melancholy mood he was falling into on that Sunday afternoon.

After a full hour, I saw the father check his watch. I assumed it was because of the upcoming afternoon Asr prayer.

"Yes, in America, I have to use the clock for prayer times." He laughed a little. "Back home, the call to prayer surrounded us all, didn't it?"

He stood up and made the call to prayer. We all washed our hands, face, and feet, which is required before prayer.

For the first time on American soil, I performed the salat standing and then kneeling beside Muslim men, three of them and myself. Seven women prayed behind us, his wife and four daughters, plus Umma and Naja.

I felt filled with emotion as we recited our prayers and did our *rakas*. To look to my left seeing the other Sudanese men, and then to my right reminded me of being with my father, brothers, and friends. I did not dare turn around and look at Umma. I knew somehow, she must be back there spilling two or three tears.

Mr. Salim Ahmed Amin Ghazzali and I wrote up a contract. It was nothing complicated, just a simple agreement using simple words. When it was complete, both he and Umma placed their signatures at the end of the document.

With no hesitation, he paid me the five-thousand-dollar deposit on Umma's services. He even made a joke.

"It's so much easier to part with my brother's money than with my own. Your Umma must be the best! For me, this amount of cash represents more than five hundred passengers, five hundred trips around New York, half of them just stuck in traffic. But my brother is a big man! For the wedding of his only son, he can give anything. All the best!"

Their son closed and then locked the gate behind us. We walked down the block toward the station.

"Did they ask you a lot of questions?" Umma asked me on the walk to the train.

"Not too many," I answered. "I took care of our business."

This time though, I was certain that she was not focused on the money. I believe she was thinking about how incredible her life was, everything she possessed, and the prominent and royal position that she had once enjoyed. Perhaps she thought about how back home working was a joy and a hobby for her, an option, not a requirement. Her money was just something on the side that belonged only to her, not to be touched or mentioned by my father who earned so much more. Probably she was dreaming about the thick love that she received each day and the friendships she shared and the beauty and pace of life compared to the one that she is living right now. I didn't say anything. I was just hoping that under these circumstances, my love and complete devotion to her could be enough.

Early Sunday evening, back in Brooklyn, we saw that the front entrance of our building was blocked off. There were police cars, a paddy wagon, and once again, the yellow tape.

We had to enter our building from the back. We stepped through the gray metal utility door into a dark stairwell, our feet crunching on glass with each step we took. Someone had busted all the light bulbs.

Back upstairs in our little Sudan I was feeling tight that from time to time my mother had to go through these fucked-up living situations. If anything was wrong by way of her, I knew I was responsible for it.

"Let me move us out of here now," I said solemnly to Umma.

"Before we are ready? In the middle of everything?" she said doubtfully.

"I'll do the work, find the new place, everything," I assured her.

She answered, "Sometimes I want to do just that. But the truth is we are less than six months away from our financial goal, *alhamdulillah*. With the blessing of this one wedding, we will be able to purchase our property and own it completely by this summer. Why should we spoil or delay what we have worked so hard to gain? Why should we throw our money into a realtor and new apartment that is not ours to keep? We should stick with our plan, *inshallah*, if we please Allah, everything will go fine."

It felt good to make those bank deposits on Monday morning. The usual teller stamped our passbook with the new numbers, representing our new balance. I held it in my hands and stared at it for a few.

I spent Monday afternoon working for Umma Designs, shopping for the supplies that Umma requested for this grand wedding. I was in and out of stores in both Brooklyn and Manhattan with a swiftness. I had been at it so long now that the vendors knew me by the name I gave them and by my reputation. When there was a good deal they would put things that I would usually order to the side and hold it for me. Sometimes if I had too many shopping bags to move around with, there were a couple of businesses where I was so cool with the owners that I could leave my stuff there until I was finished shopping in their area. They would store it for me until I picked it up and loaded it into a cab. The ones I trusted with it never skimmed my packages.

Umma didn't have any American credit cards yet, but we had credit. Those select foreigners who came to America and opened little spaces packed tight with the beautiful goods that we were accustomed to overseas, would extend credit to one another that they would not extend to Americans. Many of us had come from unknown places where a man's word was worth as much as gold. And, for Muslims, paying your debts is required, expected, and done.

17

AGREEMENTS

"My father said I couldn't play in the Hustler's League, but my mother said to go ahead and play ball anyway," Ameer told us casually. I didn't say nothing. It took me a few seconds to understand a mother telling her son to ignore his own father's instructions. I actually never heard of that before.

In fact, Ameer's mother did a few things I never understood. I remember when Chris decided to get an S-Curl in his hair. He wanted his shit to have a low cut with curly waves like everybody else in the hood. I told him not to do it. He laughed and said, "Everybody's doing it." And they were, the males roaming around pretending that their hair was naturally wavy and feeling good about it. This was something I could never understand.

Ameer told Chris that his mother knew how to put the S-Curl in. We trekked to East New York so Chris could get his secret curls. Ameer's mom opened the door wearing tight shorts and half a shirt, her legs and belly button and most of her breasts and arms completely exposed. I turned away, thinking that we must've caught her off guard by arriving too early.

She didn't move away though. She stood holding the door open after Chris had already walked inside. "Stop playing this shy routine and bring your tall ass in here," she said, to me smiling.

I walked in with my head down, eyes cast toward the

floor, seeing that everybody was still wearing their shoes inside the apartment.

Ameer welcomed us like everything was regular. "Y'all come in the kitchen." Chris sat in a chair by the sink. Ameer's mom massaged his scalp as Chris' head lay between her breasts.

I stood up and looked out the kitchen window. I didn't feel it would be cool to watch. That's why I could see Ameer's father coming up the walk three floors below. I didn't know what to do. I figured when he came through the door and saw his wife dressed this way with three thirteen-year-old boys in her kitchen, some shit was gonna go down.

"Janice, let me talk to you for a minute," Ameer's father said calmly after his eyes took it all in.

"What?" she said in a defiant tone.

"In the back room," he said, asking her for privacy.

"Honey, you must be kidding. This boy has the cream in his hair. He's on the timer. I can't leave him sitting right here," she said, still working Chris' hair. Ameer's father walked slowly to the back of their apartment looking disgusted. I heard the door in the back slam and the music come on, the volume increasing until it was blasting.

I was still staring out the window.

"Your moms is cool as shit," Chris told Ameer when we three was back at the dojo, Chris' low-cut curls shining. Ameer gave him a pound. "I know, my moms always been cool like dat," he agreed.

"I can play in the league," Chris said. "My father don't know nothing about who is running it. As long as it doesn't affect my grades, it's all good. Besides, now my father runs a group meeting at our church on Friday nights. What's the chances of him rolling up the way your father did?" he asked Ameer.

"The only fucked-up thing about it is, this Friday night we supposed to take the girls out. Remember?" Ameer asked both of us.

"We can take them out on Saturday instead," Chris proposed.

"Saturday's out," I told them, hoping to possibly meet up with Akemi.

"You owe us," Ameer said seriously.

"You right. I said I would do it," I agreed halfheartedly, wanting to get it over with. "Just once," I told them.

"You never know, brotha. Try it. You might like it," Ameer joked, then cracked up.

18

PRIVATE LESSONS

Weapons class with Sensei was intense. I felt the difference between sitting among many students and being seated with Sensei one-on-one in a room.

He had a chart of the human body posted on the wall and held a long wooden pointed stick in his left hand. He pointed out the eyes on the chart first.

"The eyes, the throat, the pelvis, the knees, and the ankles; these are the points of vulnerability on an opponent. These are the points of vulnerability on you," he said. By removing or disabling the eyes of your enemy, you win. He demonstrated the moves used to snatch or poke an opponent's eyes out of their socket.

"One simple strike to the larynx, executed properly, can kill any man," he said, then demonstrated how to execute the strike properly.

"The larynx?" I asked.

"The pipe that runs from here to here." He pointed out his own larynx in the vertical area of his throat.

After an hour of using his chart and then demonstrating the precise movements, and requiring me to prove that I understood the chart and could repeat the lessons and could duplicate his moves, he brought out his knives—the *kunei* and the *shuriken*.

My eyes were wide open, admiring the way his weapons glistened and were crafted. I wanted to confide in Sensei that I had my own set of *shuriken* crafted long ago, that I had been practicing using them on my own anyway, that I had made my own paper targets in my room, laid them across a mounted cork board, and taught myself to get nice with my knives. But I didn't tell him. Easily I could see that he was the master at this. I needed to watch him carefully and listen closely to take my own efforts to a much higher level.

He demonstrated how to hold each weapon properly. He said the ninja art is to appear that you are not holding or using any weapons at all.

"Holding and concealing the weapon is an art all by itself. Your enemy will not be able to defend himself against a weapon he cannot see and does not realize you are using."

Advancing through my first lesson, Sensei demonstrated how to execute the ninja attack, concealing knives and positioning them to penetrate or slice an enemy at points of vulnerability.

For some reason, this reminded me of a lesson from my father. He taught me how to kill a chicken and a sheep. Even though I was very young, my father said a man has to know how to feed himself and his family. My father said that men in the cities of the Western world "only know how to be fed, but don't know how to feed themselves."

He shared memories of guys he went to university with in Paris, London, and New York who had never slaughtered any animal to make themselves a meal, but in conversation, talked like my father was a savage for slaughtering animals himself.

My father said that these same men would sit in the cafeteria and eat chicken, pork, beef, or lamb, and feel more civilized because they had not slaughtered the animals themselves. He also pointed out how easily these guys would waste food.

Then he taught me to slaughter animals only in the amount that is necessary for yourself and your family, and not to be the type of man who hides from the realities of nature. "If you eat meat, be able to hunt meat and prepare it. If you are unhappy hunting and slaughtering your prey, then don't hunt and don't slaughter for meat. Eat only vegetables, fruits, and grains instead. But don't be the man who hides while other men do men's work, then appears for the feast after the work has been done."

My father said he even had friends who would go fishing, catch fish, then refuse to eat the fish they caught. He said this was complete foolishness. Either you go fishing and eat your catch along with your family, or you leave the fish in their living space alone. But to go fishing and catch a fish with a hook and then withdraw the hook from its bloody mouth only to throw it back into the water is not only a waste, it's cruelty.

"Nature works perfectly alone," my father said. "It is only the abuses of human beings that can alter that."

When it was time to slaughter an animal for eating, my father recited a brief prayer which is required for Halal meats for Muslims. Then using the sharpest knife I have ever seen up to this day, with one quick motion the animal's head was severed from its neck. We drained the blood, which is also required. We cleaned the animal. Then he showed me how it is more difficult to slice through the animal's bones. He demonstrated to me how the knife goes through with such ease when you place it between the joints and the cartilage of an animal, similar to slicing butter. When I used my knife to cut the chicken or the sheep into sections, I understood my father's lessons completely.

Facing Sensei with his incredible knife demonstrations brought this memory of my father back to my mind.

When it was my chance to demonstrate to Sensei my use of his weapons and what I had learned, I closed down my memories and focused one hundred percent on executing each new move with deadly precision.

Even though I paid for all my classes and use of the dojo and had been doing so for seven years, I had mad respect for Sensei for being a master teacher who gave each of us so much more than we could ever pay him for.

After two hours of receiving these private instructions in the dojo, I headed over to The Open Mind bookstore to do some reading. After two hours of having my head buried in a detective story, I closed the book and played a game of chess with the bookseller, Marty Bookbinder.

Ever since Bookbinder had asked me when I was seven years old, "Do you know how to play chess?" I decided to learn. I purposely went to a different bookstore, bought a book on how to play chess, and taught myself how to play on a two-dollar chess board I purchased from the local drug-store. By the time I was eight I was decent at the game.

That's how it was with me and Mr. Bookbinder. I hated to be underestimated and second-guessed by him. Even though he was an adult and I was a child, I wanted him to respect my intelligence.

Of course his respect came more easily when I became a teen, but not because of my age or size. His respect came when I invaded his castle, captured his rook, and defeated his queen, only to corner and checkmate his king.

19

CATCHING FEELINGS

Later, I was sitting at the top of the staircase at Pratt, uninvited, wanting to see Akemi even if it would only be for a moment. I knew I wouldn't see her Friday after work because of the League. I knew I wouldn't see her Saturday because of agreeing to meet Ameer, Chris, Redbone, and them. It had already been two weeks since me and Akemi enjoyed going out together. I wondered if she was missing me like I was missing her.

She showed up, climbing the cement stairs slowly, wearing jeans, dark-brown leather Nikes, and a tapered dark-brown windbreaker with a matching bandanna pulled tightly across her forehead like a gorgeous Cherokee squaw showcasing her dark eyes.

She had two long, brown, leather tubular cases strapped and crisscrossing on her back. On closer inspection, I could see from the red and green stripes on her leather cases that they were designed by Gucci. She looked like she was headed to an archery expedition, her bow and arrow strapped behind her. I realized that she was carrying her artwork inside the leather tubes.

As I watched her, she seemed trapped somewhere in her own thoughts. In that short space of time I wondered what she was thinking. I wondered how it was going with her aunt and uncle. When she looked up and realized it was me waiting there, her smile lit up so bright it cut through the evening dusk.

She locked her eyes into mine. No translation needed. I stood and held my hand out to assist her up the last step. She never let it go. We walked hand in hand like that toward her class.

I didn't know what my next move would be. I had suspended my thoughts and was moving only on feelings, something completely new for me.

Down the hall from her class, I pulled out a piece of paper and wrote out my telephone number, then handed it to her.

"Arigato." She ripped the paper in half and wrote her telephone number on her half, then handed it to me.

I felt foolish standing there with no words in the middle of a storm of energy moving back and forth between us. When more and more students brushed by, I placed my hands on her shoulders and spun her around in the direction of her classroom.

She spun back around to face me and threw up the "call me" sign, using her two fingers, the pinky and the thumb.

"Hai," I said, agreeing. We both laughed a little, then we both turned to leave at the same time.

It was even crazier when she called me late that same night. I picked up the telephone in my room. Instantly I recognized the rhythm of her breathing and her seductive silence.

She didn't say nothing. So I didn't either. She started to breathe a little harder then laughed lightly. Then I laughed too. After all, what did I expect by giving her my telephone number? Even when she called, we didn't have a common language to speak.

"Please," was all she said. Then *click*, she hung up.

I called her back. Her telephone line was busy. I hung up.

Four minutes later, my telephone rang again. It was her Japanese cousin with her American accent. "Akemi asked me to call you for her," she said, speaking in a low tone like she didn't want anyone on her end to overhear her.

"I'm sorry. I know it's late. But Akemi has no sense of time. She'll stay up all night drawing and painting and forgetting about how us normal people live," she said, sounding a little embarrassed.

"It's a'ight. Most of the time I'm up late too," I told her.

She took a deep breath. "So, I guess the two of you have become friends," she stated.

I don't know why I didn't like her way of choosing her words.

"Friends," is all I answered back.

"Okay, good. Well, anyway, Akemi wanted me to tell you that she won't be working at Uncle's store this weekend. She has to finish up her midterm art projects. She wants to know if you and she can meet up instead on the following week on Wednesday at two P.M.?" She didn't wait for my response. She started talking real fast and answering her own questions. "I told Akemi that you probably couldn't meet her then because you'll be at school on Wednesday at two P.M., right?" she asked and suggested at the same time.

"Tell Akemi Wednesday at two is cool. I'll pick her up at your uncle's store."

"Um, wait a minute, no. Meet her at that bakery like the last time you saw her," she said, assuming that the last time at the bakery was the last time I had seen Akemi. I could tell now that Akemi didn't tell her cousin everything.

"Wednesday at two at the bakery, a'ight," I agreed.

"Oh, so you're on spring break next week, too?" her cousin asked, still digging. "I didn't know if New York public schools are closed, but Akemi's college is closed and New Jersey public schools are closed too." She waited for me to tell her my business. I flipped it around on her and began questioning her instead.

"I thought you said that Akemi is sixteen, a high school student like us," I asked.

"She is sixteen. She attends the art college on a scholar-ship, Monday through Thursday in the evenings, and helps out Aunt and Uncle at their store on the weekends. She won a nationwide art competition in Japan. One year at an American art college was the top prize. That's why she's here in the U.S. It's her first time. You know, it's a very demanding program. Akemi really doesn't have a lot of free time." The cousin continued to meddle.

"You have an American accent," I said to the cousin to hear her reaction.

"Yes, thank you for the compliment," she answered like I figured she would.

"Why don't you teach Akemi how to speak English?" I asked, putting the pressure back on her.

"Akemi does whatever she wants to! Maybe now that the two of you are friends, she'll learn to speak English," the cousin answered strangely and defensively. "Listen, back home in Japan we are all required to learn English in school. But not Akemi! Her and her father make all of their own rules. Akemi speaks Japanese, Korean, Chinese, and Thai, that's it, no English." She laughed as though speaking four major languages was nothing if English wasn't one of them. She sounded like Umma's father, Northern Grandfather. He used to say, "English is the language of money. No English, no money!"

The cousin continued talking, seeming to enjoy the atten-tion being switched to her.

"My family moved from Japan to the States when I was six years old. My parents and my brothers, we are all fluent. Everyone except my mother's mother. She refuses to learn English too," the cousin said, looking down on her grand-mother's choice.

"So Akemi's mother and your mother are sisters?" I asked her.

"No. Akemi's mother is dead. She was North Korean. Akemi's father and my father and Uncle at the store are all brothers. Uncle just came to the U.S. two years ago. Akemi's father has never been to the U.S. He is big, big business in Japan, way too busy," she said proudly.

She had breezed by the statement "Akemi's mother is dead," just like the Americans breeze by heavy and serious and sacred topics with an ease I was unfamiliar with and could not understand as a Sudanese. As the cousin continued speaking, I was stuck back there.

It must be terrible to be motherless, I thought. It must be a loneliness that no one but a motherless child could understand, really. My world without Umma would be a world without sunlight or heat, without moonlight or music, without reason or love. It would be a cold place with no seasons, filled with complete darkness, no stars and no nothing. A strange sensation flashed over me. It felt like I had blacked out for a minute.

"He never remarried, Akemi's father. He is elder brother and Akemi is his only child," she was saying when I came back to listening to her.

Only child, I thought, no mother, brothers, or sisters. More loneliness.

"Okay, Wednesday at two at the bakery," I said, abruptly cutting her off.

"Oh," she said. "Okay," like her feelings were hurt.

"Thank you for calling me for Akemi," I said, hanging up.

20

SHOW AND PROVE

Me, Ameer, and Chris were seated on the gym floor with the rest of the cats who made the cut. Like everybody else, we wanted to hear how the competition was going down, and what the stakes were.

Tyriq and his boys, who stood solidly behind him, got straight down to business.

"Who provides the recreation in our hoods?" Tyriq started off asking us questions.

We the players was just kicked back, leaning on our elbows, one cat balancing his head on a basketball, another spinning a basketball on his finger, just looking at one another wondering if anybody knew what he was really asking us. No one said shit.

"All of you are right. The answer is, nobody provides the recreation in our hoods." He looked around to assess the effect of his words.

"If you young motherfuckers were not all sitting right here tonight, your asses would be outside doing nothing! I need y'all to remember that. Remember that we are doing something that no one else is doing for your black asses. Remember that when the stands are full, and the parks are packed, and everybody is watching and cheering for you!

"Don't lose your head. Remember who checked for you, who made it all possible.

"Everybody in here got on Nikes. Is Nike running this

League? Does Nike give a fuck what half a million niggas are doing on a Friday night in Brooklyn? Count it up! If you can count!" he said. Him and his boys laughed.

"One hundred twenty-five youth in here, including us up here in front, paid at least a hundred dollars for a pair of these joints. That's twelve thousand five hundred dollars' worth of footwear in this room alone. And you know Brooklyn gotta stay fresh! So us in this room all together, will spend at least twelve thousand five hundred dollars a month on kicks. That's a hundred fifty thousand dollars a year, just for us in this room.

"Outside on the streets, at least eighty-five percent of Brooklyn youth, male and female, are rocking Nikes. Yeah, I know, some paper also gets spent on Reebok for your girls and on Adidas. For Nike, that's half a million youth times twelve thousand five hundred dollars a month, in Brooklyn alone! How much is that in a year? Who can add that up?"

"That's seventy-five billion dollars," I answered in the silent gym.

"My man!" Tyriq shouted, giving me my props. "What's one percent of seventy-five billion dollars?"

"Seven hundred fifty million," I answered again.

"Are the rest of you listening?" he asked the players. "Nah, y'all ain't listening 'cause the numbers we talking, you never even thought about. Niggas is one hundred percent loyal to Nike, Reebok, Adidas, Puma, all them. But we can't get one percent return on our loyalty. You can't get none of these companies to put up even fifty thousand stinking, measly, fucking dollars to run this league, buy some uniforms, donate some surplus sneakers and a couple of balls. So remember who is right here in the hood with you, spending paper, making it happen, giving you something to do before you get a chance to kill each other."

One kid started clapping, then all the cats started cheering and clapping.

"Be grateful," Tyriq continued. "I hope not one of you is here looking to get something for nothing. You gotta work to earn. You gotta train to win. You gotta go hard and play hard. Got it?" Tyriq ended his pitch. He looked like he was feeling pretty good about himself.

I'm looking beyond the hype of his words, wondering if this meant the league was bankrupt and we wasn't getting paid shit.

Then he laid out the incentives. Ten thousand dollars each for the first-place team's five starting players. Bench riders get gift certificates for The Wiz, an electronics store. Next, two thousand each for the second-place team's five starting players. Bench riders get Foot Locker gift certificates. The most valuable player of this youth league gets twenty-five thousand, a custom-made diamond ring, and bragging rights in every hood in the New York area.

"For losing, you get the same thing you get for losing in life, nothing!" The players cracked up.

"We got no space or time for bullshit," Tyriq announced. Then he paced the gym floor, laying out the youth league rules. He started off with their "code of silence." He said since Nike gets our loyalty for free, we should at least let the league have it for the price of the prizes. The business of the league was confidential. He said any player who told anybody outside of the league anything about the business of the league, money changing hands and whatnot, would forfeit his winnings and position on the team.

"Don't ask us how we'll find out if you been running your mouth. We just do. And when we do, there won't be no lawyers or trials, if you know what I mean. And don't think that if you're one of the losers, that you got nothing to lose. You always have your life," Tyriq threatened. His words brought on a serious silence. When he felt the fear had sunk in enough, he laughed it off. But we all know he wasn't joking.

When he broke all 120 of us down into ten teams of twelve players each, we were seated into new groups on the gym floor. Some guys' faces were tight with the team choices, crews being broken up and different kids from different areas of Brooklyn being mixed in together, friends being divided, enemies being united.

"This is business," Tyriq said, cut and dry, responding to the tight looks.

He handed out each team's schedules for practices, scrimmages, and game times, dates, and locations. Each team got assigned a color instead of a team name. Needless to say, he had everybody's full attention and cooperation.

One of Tyriq's boys was assigned to each team. We now found out they were actually our team coaches. The cat who came my way was named Vega. Wearing a red Puma track suit, a crisp white tee, a cropped S-Curl, and red suede Pumas, he was swift and light on his feet and broad chested, like he had a committed daily workout. He squatted, signaled us all to squat, and spoke softly so we had to strain to hear his words.

"You looking at the winning squad right here," he told us. "I can feel it." He scanned our faces like he wanted our instant trust. "There's only one way to take control of this thing and that's this right here." He placed his hand over his heart. "Do you niggas got the heart?" he asked. We all stared right back at him, but nobody said nothing.

"Listen, I got tickets to the Saint John's college ball game tomorrow night at Madison Square Garden. This is the hot ticket, the Big Eastern Championship joints." He pulled the tickets halfway out and pushed them back into his jacket pocket. "I want all of you to meet me right outside the Garden in front of Roy Rogers tomorrow night at six-thirty. If you late, you fucked up. I need y'all to see how these players hustle, so you'll know what we need to do to handle this business. Don't bring no fucking body with you. I don't care who it is. From this night forward, we the team. Anybody ain't seated in this circle right here tonight, don't need to know and don't count. You got it?" He held out his hand. Everybody gave him a pound. He introduced himself, unfolded a sheet of paper from his pocket and tried to match players' names with their faces.

It was almost eleven P.M. when we 120 ballplayers got out of there. We walked out calmly, no crowd or music or drama like last time. Probably each one of us was still spinning the dollar numbers around in our heads and wondering if it was real or not.

I couldn't front. Vega didn't seem like a coach but he got me open with those tickets. I had never been inside Madison Square Garden, although I walked right past it often. Of course I've seen it on TV, the world-famous home of the New York Knicks. Back in the Sudan, at my father's apartment in Khartoum, we watched their games a couple of times on my father's satellite television. My father even had an autographed ball by old-school point guard Walt Frazier. Now my blood was pumping at the thought of checking out the championship game.

The police were circling the area of the high school gym like sharks waiting for an easy kill. It was a reminder to all us Black youth that we were born suspects. But for once, wasn't nothing jumping off with us teens. Cliques was regrouped and formed up and all walked off quietly in almost every direction. Tonight I could see that when somebody finally stops playing and starts talking real business opportunity to some young Black men, all that rowdy shit goes right out the window.

We three hung back a minute while everything cleared up. As soon as we went to push off, the girl with the dimples popped up out of the dark, walking swiftly toward us. She waved her hand with excitement.

"Hey, star!" she called out. All of us laughed. As she came into view I saw she had a T-shirt on that said MIDNIGHT in bold, dark-blue letters across her breasts.

"Where are the rest of your girls?" Ameer asked her right away. She didn't even look at him when she answered. She just said, "I don't really be with them like that." Ameer caught her intent.

"Anyway, I waited so long for you to call me, I got in trouble. I wouldn't let anyone in my house use the phone. I kept telling them, 'He's gonna call. He's gonna call.' What happened? Did you lose my number?" she asked, smiling, full of energy and rocking back and forth on her feet like there was no way for her to keep still.

"Nah," I answered.

" 'Nah' what?" she asked.

"Nah, I didn't lose your number," I said.

"All right, superstar," she said in a joking way. I smiled at her style. She had a nice complexion with smooth skin. Her hair was shining from the gel she used to swirl out her bangs.

"God, you got perfect teeth," she said, after I smiled. I really didn't know what to do with her comments. She seemed to say whatever was on her mind. She didn't give a fuck that my two friends were hearing her every word.

"I'm not gonna worry about it. You'll call me, I know it," she said. "I gotta run. I got one minute before my grandmother locks the door on me!" She turned on her Nikes and ran full speed in her denim miniskirt, leaving Ameer and Chris doing double takes.

"I think you need to call her, man," Ameer said. Him and Chris laughed.

"What y'all think about the money?" Chris asked. "Do you think the winners will really get paid like that brother Tyriq said?"

"Well if they don't pay out, what the fuck can anybody do about it? The hustlers are the sponsors. Who's gonna go to war with them?" Ameer asked.

"I think they'll pay out. I got a feeling about it," I told them.

"What kind of feeling?" Chris asked.

"You know, we thinking that it's all about basketball. But they gotta have something riding on it too. Otherwise, why would they do it?"

"Something like what?" Ameer asked.

"It could be anything. You see how they cut the groups into teams and gave every team a color?" I asked.

"So," Chris said.

"At least in the NBA you know who the fuck you're working for. Your uniforms got colors, but you know who owns the team, who manages the team, and who you running for. In this league, we can't see who's behind it. Tyriq is the front man. But who does he report to?" I tried to get them to look at all the angles.

"If you believe that they'll pay out to the champions, none of that shit even matters. We running for the money. That's it," Ameer said.

"But we all on different teams," Chris said. "Ameer's on the red and you on the black. I'm on the green," he pointed out.

"It don't matter," I told Chris. "It just increases our chances of winning. Whichever one of us wins some paper, we cut it three ways, no matter what happens. That's what up," I said.

"You right. That is what's up," Ameer agreed with me.

"Oh, yeah. I can't do the date with Homegirl tomorrow

night. My team got tomorrow evening on the schedule. It looks like if y'all still want to do it, I'm a have to do it on a weeknight, maybe a Thursday evening when we ain't at the dojo."

"Thursday evening," Chris repeated. "That's whack. But we'll do it. Girls are good on any night!" he said.

At the train station we went our separate ways. On the ride home, I kept breaking the basketball situation into separate puzzle pieces. Ameer was right, it is all about the money. And if I could get my hands on a chunk of money like that, even after we cut it up, I could match Umma's effort and speed up our move out of Death Valley, Brooklyn, into an even better house in a peaceful and safe place for her and Naja.

At the same time, I kept wondering what exactly the hustlers got out of it. Maybe it was a war over territory battled out on the court. Maybe it was all about ticket sales, concessions, or merchandising. Maybe it was a betting front. Maybe it was just a good-ass distraction from what the fuck was really going on.

After a while, I wondered if I was just thinking too hard. Maybe the hustlers was just some niggas with money to burn, who came up with a main attraction for Brooklyn cats to pile up at while they showcased their whips, jewels, and bitches.

21

VEGA

Seemed like half of New York was outside Madison Square Garden trying to get in. The New York City evening air was more cool than cold as spring approached, but some degrees hotter around the Garden where people gathered.

I took careful steps in my Clarks. I didn't want dog shit smashed into the grooves of my new soles. I didn't want none of these overeager cats accidentally stepping on my new shoes.

It wasn't hard to spot Vega. He was rocking a red Kangol and red suede Ballys, black slacks, and a red dress shirt.

The whole team and the coach had fresh cuts, including me. I could smell the scents of coconut oil and Afro Sheen and a strong cologne that I wouldn't wear cutting through the odors of grime, gum, and piss on the New York pavement. But the bright and colorful lights of Seventh Avenue, the crowd for the Garden, the rest rushing to shop at Macy's, made us forget any foul smells and made this the place to be. Besides, tonight we weren't outsiders. We were ticket holders.

Vega greeted each Brooklyn teen in our crew as they arrived with a hand shake and a swift survey of what they was wearing, saying only two words, "Nice, nice." He pinched the jute and burlap material on my tan dress shirt and said, "I like dat."

Vega used his eyes to keep a silent head count going.

Every few seconds, he checked his Hamilton watch. When the second hand hit the thirty mark, the last teen showed up. Vega waved for us all to follow his lead.

We ended up where the rest of the Garden crowd wasn't. We were at the VIP entrance to the Garden, where the college ballplayers were arriving in droves. There was a stream of Syracuse University players, over six feet tall easily, like it wasn't nothing to it. They climbed down from polished trucks and up out of new whips. We Brooklyn teens was all watching what they was wearing on their bodies and their feet. We even checked the gym bags they carried, some by Nike, by Adidas, Puma, and whatnot. Vega watched us watching them and said casually, "And they say there is no money in college ball, yeah right."

Three black vans filled with St. John's players, coaches, and personnel pulled up. These cats poured out of the vans singing, giving each other pounds, waving at the crowd, and giving the small gathering of spectators a show. I liked the way it seemed like those players had a strong camaraderie and spirit, one team, one goal. Dudes from my hood wasn't like that.

"See what I was telling you? You have to want it. Those niggas right there want it and tonight they gonna take it," Vega said, getting caught up in their hype.

I never seen so many people packed in one place before. There was mad energy and excitement. Not one seat was empty except when somebody ran to the bathroom. Can't front, quite naturally I started counting the black faces in this huge crowd. Most of the black faces were actually the ballplayers for Syracuse and St. John's. Otherwise there were small handfuls of Blacks sprinkled here and there up against a sea of white fans who were pumped up like their lives depended on it. The food vendors began weaving in and out of each of hundreds of rows with their Cokes and franks, peanuts, popcorn, T-shirts, and team flags.

We Brooklyn teens had good seats, not on the floor but close enough to it. The twelve of us plus our coach dominated our row. We remained standing though. We were too excited by the newness of being on the inside. Besides, there was about fifteen girls flaunting their blue-and-orange panties, cheering for their players.

Everything moving caught my eye—the way the players were being introduced over the powerful speaker system, their names and jersey numbers announced with pride, then echoing around the crowd of 25,000 cheering fans. I watched the way each player reacted differently, some soaking up the downpour of admiration, others playing it down, some looking up at themselves as the cameras caught them in a candid close-up and projected their faces onto the mega screen above the scoreboard, some looking anxious to get the game going. I felt that anxiety.

Just the strength of the lights shining down on the flawless triple-polished court, the unripped new white nets, and undented rims, got me amped. I imagined myself down there playing on that court for the love of the game. Maybe my entire team was thinking the same thing. Maybe that's exactly what Vega wanted us to be thinking. Well, if it was what he wanted, it was a smart plan. And these tickets must have set him back some. I saw scalpers hawking less expensive seats than we had for more than a hundred dollars.

It didn't matter who any of us was rooting for. Vega was rooting for St. John's, so if we thought anything different, we better had kept it to ourselves. He watched the game like he had money on it. The drawback was, when the first half was over his team was losing by thirteen points.

"Don't sleep," Vega said. "Get ready for the big comeback." He was talking to each of us, the strangers on his new team, but it was as if his voice was mic'd up to the ballplayers' earpieces, 'cause just when he called it out, they burst out with a new setup, new confidence, and an unbreakable fury. For sixteen straight minutes they flipped the pressure on those Syracuse boys, and all hell broke loose when St. John's player Ron Rowan pulled up and hit a fourteen-foot jumper with only eight seconds remaining in the game, bringing St. John's to a one-point lead over Syracuse. While everybody went wild, Vega stood cool, chanting, "Eight seconds, eight seconds, it ain't over, keep the pressure on, defense, defense!"

Syracuse player Dwayne Washington must've felt the same about the remaining eight seconds and the possibilities it left open. Washington drove to the basket with only three seconds left and was so sure his shot was on the money, he started celebrating before his feet touched the polished floor.

Just when him and his Syracuse boys thought they had it hemmed, St. John's player Walter Berry unveiled his wingspan and blocked the shot. The buzzer sounded. St. John's took it, the Big Eastern Championship, 70 to 69!

While our section of the Garden cheered and jumped and bumped one another, I stood still, thinking, Here is one thing that I'm real good at. This game is completely legal. And, everywhere in America, the whole country thinks it's okay for a young man to play ball. You can't get arrested for it. You can get paid and win props. You can get into a position to buy your moms a house, no problem, and save the family you love, while doing something that you love to do.

Vega told us to hang back while the crowd spilled out into the aisles, into the corridors and out of the building.

Soon enough, we were on the train together heading further uptown to get something to eat at a venue Vega chose. On the train each of us remained standing once again, leaving the seats for the other tired passengers. I don't think any one of the thirteen of us was scheming on any of the riders that night. We were all just thinking, hoping, dreaming that this night would work out in our favor and eventually put some paper in our pockets.

Our late-night dinner was at a spot on 175th Street and Broadway named Malecon's. Whole chickens were roasting in their wide windows. The streets surrounding the place were lit up now at 11:10 P.M., same as if it was early evening. The streets were packed with youth, adults, and even babies being pushed in carriages. Inside, the restaurant was popping. Almost completely filled, there was still a line of people, plus more arriving to begin ordering dinner at this late hour.

Our table must have been reserved, I thought. There was six small tables pushed together, six chairs on each side and one at the head. I took the corner chair by the side window. Almost immediately I noticed that same buttermilk Porsche with the buttercream leather interior and the gold piping. It was parked on the side block.

Brooklyn heads were pressed against Manhattan menus. Only a couple of them tried to find out from Vega what some of the Spanish words on the menu meant so they could get their food orders right.

Not focusing on the menu, I was scanning the restaurant. My eyes landed on one group of nine well-dressed young cats, probably in their twenties or late twenties. I could tell each of them had a different status by the quality of their jewels and clothing. Only one of them wore a Rolex. He was rocking a twenty-four-karat gold, thirty-six-inch chain with a unique piece, a solid-gold baby shoe. I realized immediately I had seen it once before. He was a top-quality cat. He was definitely the only one in the restaurant wearing a cashmere dress shirt and diamond cuff links. I glanced down at his Gucci suede driving shoes. "Top grade," I thought to myself.

"You gon' order, man?" one of the players asked me. I looked up at the thirty-something-year-old Boricua waitress stuffed in a tight dress, smiling down on me with her pad in her hand and pencil ready.

"I'll take the mofongo with chicken," I ordered and pulled out my twenty dollars and laid it on the table.

"I got the team tonight," Vega informed me. "Put your money away."

I held the twenty up toward the smiling waitress and said, "Just add this to your tip." Vega smiled quick and nodded. "A'ight." The waitress folded the bill, slid it in between her breasts, and left, smiling, and rushing to place our team's big order.

Instantly Coach went around the table trying to recall each Brooklyn teen's name from memory. He messed up right away and called one of our team members Mateo instead of Michael. The guys laughed at his mistakes.

"Who could do better? You niggas don't even know each other's names," Vega challenged. He laughed a little and pulled out a twenty-dollar bill and said, "Here goes twenty for whoever can call out the names of every team member, no mistakes."

Two players tried and failed immediately, causing everybody to crack up. Neither one of them knew my name 'cause up until now I never said nothing, never signed nothing. For some reason Vega turned toward me and said, "How 'bout you? Go ahead, give it a shot."

"Panama Black," I pointed out first. I remembered his name 'cause he was black like me and wore two gold-framed teeth in the front of his mouth. "Machete," I called out second, 'cause who's gonna forget a dude named after a deadly weapon? "Jaguar," I called out next. I remembered his name because I was always intrigued by people who named themselves after animals. My father named his friends and enemies after certain animals when telling a story, a technique he learned from Southern Grandfather. Whichever type of animal a guy picked to name himself after, I was sure it told something about his ways and personality. "Braz," I called out next. I heard him speaking on the pay phone once right before our last basketball meeting started. He was speaking Portuguese and that caught my attention. I wondered whether he was from Angola or Brazil.

I called off all eleven team members' names easily, ending with my own. "Midnight," I introduced myself.

I lifted his twenty-dollar bill off the table. A couple of guys clapped two times for me, gave me props. Next thing I know, Vega is telling the player Panama, seated right next to me, to switch seats with him. As the waitress delivered some of the food orders, the new coach sat on my side.

Eventually, Vega said to me quietly, "I see you got it." I didn't know what he meant.

"You want your twenty dollars back?" I asked him, figuring he was a sore loser like the cats on my block who fight and bust shots after losing a dice game.

"No. You won it fair and square," he said. "But let me tell you something," he said with a slight Spanish accent slipping into his Black English. "Always remember to make me look good. I take dis shit personal."

I didn't answer back nothing because I didn't know what he was talking about. I ate my food quietly and so did he, while the other players' conversations grew louder and louder.

I watched the sharp cat with the Rolex on the other side of the restaurant signal to Vega. Vega saw the signal then looked toward the restaurant door. Another cat entered the place carrying a bunch of Foot Locker shopping bags.

At one in the morning we were all standing on an outdoor Brooklyn ball court. Vega threw every team member who complained about playing ball in their dress-up clothes a new pair of shorts and sneakers from the Foot Locker bags.

"Did you niggas think you was on vacation?" he asked the team with a new seriousness. "You don't ever get something for nothing. It's time to run it."

I wasn't mad. This is around the same time I would normally be hooping it on my own. Now we were divided into two squads.

I went on and played it like I was on St. John's.

We had 24,989 fewer fans, but I could see the nine well-dressed cats from the dinner spot standing outside the fence, their cars shined up and double-parked, talking among themselves.

When I pulled up to take a jumper, I told myself, "If this one goes in, the light-skinned cat with the Porsche, Rolex, and diamond cuff links is the boss."

I sank it. It was all net.

Heading home at 2:30 A.M., coach and ballplayers on a train, the real hustlers riding in their cars, Vega asked me, "How did you do that?"

"Do what?" I asked him.

"Remember all those names," he said. I could see my little twenty dollar triumph was still fucking with his head. "Did you know some of the guys before the league started up?" he asked.

"Nah," I told him.

"Then how did you do it? In the gym, each player only mentioned his name once." He was staring me down for a real answer.

"I don't know," I answered. I wasn't gonna tell him that I study people, their names and faces, mannerisms and gestures, jewelry and possessions, cuts and bruises. I wasn't gonna admit that I am a ninja who is always anticipating an attack. Why should I tell him? Sensei taught me that there is an art to concealing my weapons. I could see now that my mind, my memory, and my observations are weapons too.

Rethinking the moment, maybe I shouldn't have exposed my weapons to Vega just to win his twenty dollars. Maybe I alerted him and caused him to pay closer attention to me in the future.

22

A SWEETER LOVE

My schedule now was tighter than it had ever been before. I realized that being happy about the ten-thousand-dollar wedding commission Umma and I had headed our way was only one level. The next level was the doubling, tripling, and quadrupling of our workload, Umma's and mine. I spent my days doing several more deliveries than ever before. I was traveling to new, faraway routes like Mount Vernon and even New Rochelle.

I encountered new businesses and new business people. Orders had to be placed, tents rented, painters hired. I even ended up at a midtown Manhattan music store renting band equipment from a request the wedding party made. I had to go deep into Brooklyn to locate the Tambour and Dallooka drums that are specific to the Sudan.

Even our Sunday family days were being consumed with all of us working side by side for that money. Naja was a polite part-time receptionist on the Umma Designs phone. She also was becoming skilled at mixing oils exactly how Umma taught her, and preparing the elixirs for the crystal bottles.

Squeezing in dojo practice, weapons training, basketball practice, and keeping up with homeschool work, it was looking real tight on me spending time with Akemi. But I was thinking about her five or six times every day.

Determined, I doubled up my efforts on Sunday, Monday,

and Tuesday. Even on Wednesday, the day me and her were gonna get together, my feet were moving fast on the pavement early that morning, so that by the time I met up with her, I wouldn't be focused on unfinished business.

Her eyes slowed me down and softened me. This was our truest form of communication.

Today there was no more winter whip or frost in the air, only a subtle wind. Coats were out and sweaters, hoodies, and long-sleeved T-shirts were in. It was March 21, the first day of spring.

I could see that she also had used her time well. She seemed real relaxed. Her skin and hair glistened. She was wearing a cantaloupe-colored jumper. It was a loose fit, not hugging or riding the curves of her shapely petite body. It looked fashionable but was too short. She had her legs covered with tights colored several psychedelic shades of tangerine, a style only an artist type would find and choose to wear. She had her little feet tucked into a creamsicle-colored pair of Pumas, a color I never seen before, foreign kicks.

Her Vuitton knapsack was riding on her back. The burnt orange leather straps brand new, hadn't darkened yet.

Her pretty neck was out. No jewels on her hands, and she had only the slightest tip of each of her fingernails painted in a sparkling orange polish with the rest of the nails left natural. Her hair was worn in a stylish side slipknot.

As she watched me finish checking out every detail, she smiled. Then we were both smiling and standing still among the busy New York travelers.

She slid her hand into her one odd-shaped front dress pocket and pulled out her used up, worn Japanese map of the New York subway system. She pointed out, using the tip of her nail, the location she wanted us to travel to today.

Her finger landed on the stop for Brooklyn's Prospect Park. My smile faded away and my mood changed, which she noticed immediately. She slung her knapsack to the front and rifled through it, pulling out another folded paper, handing it to me.

It was a flyer for the Cherry Blossom Festival, a Japanese cultural celebration of the arrival of the first day of spring. The paper boasted Japanese foods, Japanese drummers, and a Japanese Kabuki Theatre group in the Brooklyn park.

I took her map from her and pointed out a different location, Central Park located on Fifty-ninth and Broadway in Manhattan, a park that, from what I knew, every female couldn't help but love. Taking over, I grabbed her hand and pulled her along. She came easily.

On the train I sat her by the window on the inside of me. She placed her little foot right beside my foot, which looked so much larger than hers in comparison.

My mind drifted from the light and simple, fresh, citrus clean scent of Akemi's skin to that cold night in the Brooklyn bush at Prospect Park. Clearly, I recalled the image of the bullets rearranging the slow, confident, yet crooked swagger of Gold Star Tafari. The blast brought his bent style to attention before he folded and dropped down.

It was my last memory of what was a gigantic and wondrous park, miles and miles of natural beauty and public peace and privacy that sometimes made it okay to live in Brooklyn. Now there were real reasons why I stayed away from the place.

I had read in a magazine once, while chilling in The Open Mind bookstore, that the police expect and wait for a shooter to return to the scene of a takedown. The author of the article said that the police experts guarantee that guilt will bring every criminal back to the scene of his crime. The writer told a story of a case where a woman was strangled to death inside her suburban home. After the murder, the police on the case would drive through her residential area daily, just knowing that the guilty person would fit the formula and return to the scene.

One day on a random drive down the victim's block, a young kid came through zigzagging and popping wheelies on his bicycle. The officer driving the police cruiser waved him over. Casually the kid rode over, smiling and innocent. While he chatted with the cop, he rested his left hand on the roof of the cruiser.

"How come you're not wearing a bicycle helmet?" the officer asked him.

"'Cause I'm good on my bike. Didn't you see me?" Now the kid extended his arms, balancing himself on his bike, his feet on the pedals, yet standing still. He smiled with great confidence.

"I can even do a somersault on this thing! Watch!" The kid rode off and started showing off his miraculous bike tricks.

The cop gave him the thumbs up and his partner even applauded.

Next, they drove straight off to the lab and had the roof of their cruiser, where the kid had inadvertently placed his hand, dusted for fingerprints.

According to the cops, the lab, and the magazine article, the kid was the killer. The jury convicted him and the judge sentenced him to enough years so that no one would recognize him upon his release. He was a popular junior high schooler. The victim was his teacher, who chose to embarrass and expose him in front of his classmates instead of privately encouraging him to do better. Her constant demands for him to conform and comply with her, irritated his gangster.

He would have got away with it. One stupid error, placing one hand on the roof of the police car, got him caught. I learned from reading the details of that article to never return to a scene of a takedown. And I didn't and wouldn't. It was easy for me though. I didn't feel no guilt. There was no crime scene, and Gold Star Tafari was no victim.

I realized from living on my Brooklyn block that boys and even men in America expected and allowed strangers and motherfuckers to threaten, and fuck with, and play with their mothers, sisters, and women. They allowed other men to make false promises, to impregnate them, to make them cry and sometimes to even kick, slap, and beat them. Back where I come from we don't.

Akemi was staring into my face almost nose to nose, eyes to eyes, and lips to lips. She snapped her fingers to break me out of my spell. Softly she said, "Heeey!"

I came back from the hot spot where my anger is stored, and let her capture my attention once again. She wasn't the only one who showed up for our date with a plan. I had places to take her, things to show her all mapped out in my mind.

A little while later, her orange fingernail tips were pressed against the glass walls on the 102nd floor of the Empire State Building. Her eyes were looking down on the whole of New York City. Her face was filled with amazement.

We were 1,500 feet in the air. Still, she stood on her tiptoes. When finally her eyes had surveyed enough, she turned back toward me and flashed a natural smile across her face.

Kneeling down, she unbuckled her knapsack. I thought maybe she would pull out a camera like most of us who weren't born here would. Instead, she stood up holding a pencil and an unlined index card. Her pencil point was already gliding and sketching out something.

Everyone else up here had cameras—small ones, Kodak disposables, expensive Nikons, various-sized lenses, even zoom lenses. Akemi didn't seem to care for photography, I thought. She seemed to prefer capturing the details of what she felt and saw with her handmade, hand-drawn, or hand-painted pictures. I was impressed now that I saw her creating with a pencil her own styled postcards.

Giving her space and time, I stepped back, pulling my book out of my jacket pocket and picking up reading where I left off last.

Instinctively, I leaped up when I noticed a man aiming his lens at Akemi's face. By the time he pressed and clicked, he had nothing but a photo of my palm print.

"Jesus Christ! You messed up my shot." He grimaced.

"Keep it moving," I warned him quietly. "She's my girl, no photos." I blocked his view while using my peripheral to keep track of the Empire State security guard fidgeting on my left side.

"Let me ask her," the tall white guy photographer in the ball-buster dirty jeans pushed. Before anything else could be said or done, Akemi screamed out, "*Iie* nooo!" She gave him a flash of that spicy anger she gave me the other week outside of Cho's store.

Her shriek bought security over. All of the tourists stared our way. Immediately Akemi extended her arm and pointed out the white guy.

The security guard told the photographer, "The young lady said no. Leave her alone."

Pissed, the photographer repositioned himself to click photos of something that couldn't holla back.

On the elevator ride down, she stood behind me in the corner. I was the wall between her and the people packed and pressed into one another in the limited space.

On the ground floor, we both stepped into the same triangle of the revolving door.

Outside, we could breathe more easily.

Suddenly, the photographer reappeared.

"Listen, friend," he said, extending his hand, his business card dangling from his fingers. "You got me wrong. I'm willing to pay you for her photos. She's a beautiful girl and I work for—"

I grabbed Akemi and we disappeared into the crowded New York City streets. I wondered to myself why no man in this country understood how to pull himself back when it came to women. I was sure now that many men would be murdered easily because of this problem that they saw as being nothing. An image of me poking one of the blades of my *kunei* into that photographer's temple flashed before me. I was glad that in this instance, I had the opportunity to walk away.

Music surrounded Central Park. I could hear some African drumming coming from inside, the beats grabbing my attention and arousing my soul. With a closer listen, it sounded like the rhythms of someone lost. Every tap on the skins sounded like a question. I could tell that the drummer was an amateur, but still, every drumbeat is telling, saying, or showing something.

Outside the park there were sounds battling one another; radios, speakers, amplifiers, break-dancers, rollerbladers, roller skaters, musical gymnasts, silver-skinned human robots, people, monkeys, birds, you name it.

We willingly walked in and up the winding paths that seemed to turn everyone inside the park into characters and scenery from a colorful and elaborate children's pop-up storybook, the kind I purchased for Naja a couple of years ago.

Stinking horses trotted by dragging Cinderella carts loaded down with ripped-off tourists. The animals looked exhausted, unable to see to their left or their right. They only expressed themselves by dropping huge funky fucking piles of shit everywhere they went.

But the newly leafed and budded crab apple trees, maple and elm trees, and even cherry blossoms, along with the makeshift waterfalls and fountains, made it into a paradise.

Watching Akemi, I could tell that this park had the magic that cast a spell on females.

Seeing a set of swings, she took off running and jumped right on. Her legs lifted her higher and higher. Her eyes were shut. Her mouth dropped open. Her head tipped back. She leaned backward and was soaring.

Like an acrobat she suddenly stood up on the silver swing seat, pumping her legs and flying higher. In midair she jumped off and landed right on me. I seen she liked to live dangerously. What if, in a split second, I had moved? Luckily I didn't. She wrapped her legs around my waist and laid her breast pressed against my chest. Now her head lay on my shoulders. Her slipknot came loose and her hair brushed against my neck and fell onto my back. I carried her up the hill and down again, feeling and knowing only one thing. I had fucked around and fell in love.

By the Central Park Loeb Boathouse, I paid for a rowboat ride. Rowing on the fifteen feet of man-made lake water, I knew this was not the yacht named *Salaamah* or a felucca. It wasn't the Atlantic or the Pacific Ocean. In fact it was not a river or a sea and definitely not the Nile. But I was rowing and she was lying on her side, her shoes kicked off, her legs hanging off the side of the boat, each toe a different shade of orange in her strange and colorful toe tights.

She was listening to jazz music on an old five-inch transistor radio she pulled out of her magician's knapsack of endless Akemi stuff. As her music played softly, I noticed that the peculiarly shaped lake was surrounded by the most beautiful willow trees.

I rowed us past the other seven or eight boats to a secluded spot sheltered by the willows and near a muddy incline. When she felt the boat stop she sat up, clicked off her radio, went back into her magic bag, and pulled out what it took me a few seconds to figure out was a mini cassette tape recorder.

She stepped over and sat facing me as the boat rocked a little. She pressed record, then said softly, "Please."

I sat idle for about ten seconds before I said anything. I wasn't no poet.

My mind started pushing together a rhyme. I wasn't no rapper either.

I leaned in to be close enough to her little device. Slowly I said,

Akemi is a girl I met in New York City,
She's from Japan and she looks real pretty.
But more than that, she's talented and smart.
In just a couple of months, she stole my heart.
But Akemi remains a mystery to me.
She hides me from her family.
But the feelings she has for me she can't hide.
Every time I see her, it's all in her eyes.

I smiled, surprised at myself. When she realized I wouldn't continue, she clicked her recorder off.

In the park there were bridges with tunnels and caves beneath them, dark ones filled with nature and small creatures. We walked through one of the tunnels together. Because of the immediate switch from sunlight to darkness, all I could see in there was a silhouette of Akemi. She stopped walking midway. We were alone for a moment. Still we could both see some more walkers approaching, less than one minute away.

I could feel her hand reach up to the opening of my shirt. Her fingers began sliding across my collarbone. She moved them slowly across the width of it before she withdrew them. Then I felt both of her hands in mine. I didn't return her touches, which felt so good to me. I felt like if I started touching her, I wouldn't and couldn't stop. I was brought up not to be intimate in public. Yet I felt mad intimate within myself.

Another couple entered the tunnel. Akemi stepped away from me. I heard her click on her recorder. I never saw anyone do it before, but I guessed she was recording the sounds of nature. I could hear the frogs and crickets myself.

Southern Grandfather, my father's father, trained me to sit still for hours and listen to the sounds of the wilderness. Me and him weren't recording with any device except for our ears. He taught me to listen so carefully that I could hear the buzz of a mosquito, the ruffling of grass, and even the winding of a serpent.

Seated up high in the park on a rock, me and Akemi played a crazy game of charades together. How else could we do it? We couldn't talk. She would draw a quick, simple picture of what she liked. Then she handed me a card to draw what I liked. We communicated through these pictures. Only thing was, she was a great artist. I was not.

When I drew two fists on the paper to let her know I am a fighter, she looked unsure. I stood up and struck a stance and did some quick moves just for her. She clapped and smiled, delighted. I drew a basketball to let her know I like to hoop. I drew a book, then pulled my real book out and handed it to her to let her know I like to read. Last, I drew my version of a picture of her and flung it at her. She grabbed for it. Her face revealed that I was the worst artist of all time. She didn't get it. I pointed to her and said, "I like you."

She smiled and laughed. She held my drawing beside her face to show me how ridiculously off it was. Afterward she tried to slide my ugly drawing into her knapsack but I took it away from her and put it in my back pocket. I saw that she thought everything belonged to her.

On her turn, she tried to show me about herself. She

pulled out her little radio and turned it on. Suddenly, she began to dance while still sitting.

"You like music," I guessed. What else could she be telling me?

"Hai!" she answered. She started moving around again.

"You like to dance," I called out like I was competing on a game show.

"Hai!" She laughed. Then she jumped up and started moving her arms in a controlled motion, her fingers closed and cupped.

"You're a swimmer," I said. She didn't answer. Maybe I said it in a way she couldn't get it. "Swim," I said, using just the one word and gesturing.

"Hai!" She smiled. Then she dropped back down, took off her backpack, and handed it to me. Next thing I knew, she was positioning her body like a yoga guru. She struck a pose and shouted in her softest voice, *"Hanymansana!"* It looked wicked. Her legs were in a full split and her arms were extended like a graceful ballerina, one hand pointed to the sky. She didn't seem to care one bit that she was wearing a dress.

In an instant, she flowed out of this amazing position, right into another one. "Firefly!" she said. Both of her hands were on the rock holding her body up in the air and her toes pointed out. Her dress crept up her thighs. She flowed out of that pose and in her last exhibition she twisted herself up and said softly, "Scorpion," in her sensual accent. I looked at her. She was even more strange to me now and even more beautiful.

She lay down, relaxing on the rock and facing the sky, plucking small leaves and sticks off her dress. I faced east and made my prayer, first cleaning my face and hands and nose and feet as is required, using bottled water.

Some Ghanaians recruited me into a game of soccer on

the field. I wasn't gonna play, I was into something else right then. Akemi tried to encourage me by playing and pushing me with her body then her hands to go ahead. So I agreed.

She watched intensely from the sidelines along with some females who were there with the Ghanaians. I caught her eyes moving across the field with me. I felt good that she wasn't one of these girls with wandering eyes.

This was actually the first game of soccer I had played since arriving in America. It took a lot more coordination than basketball. After I warmed up, I played a good game. My eyes and my feet are quick anyway.

Watching the West Africans move with such passion and enthusiasm, I got into it. It was easy to look into one or two of their faces and to imagine I was seeing my father and his friends. More than that, it was relaxing to burn off the energy that had me exploding before I ran into them.

Coming off the field after the game, I didn't see Akemi. I gave the players a pound and a couple of them my Umma Designs business cards.

I walked around slowly. I stopped, figuring she wouldn't have wandered off this far. Then I heard her laugh. I followed the direction of her voice and saw her enjoying watching me look for her as she sat comfortably in a tree.

Why bother tryna figure out how she got up there or why? I stood below her and she came leaping down into my arms. She placed her nose against my neck, sniffing the scent of my sweat.

We both used our hands to brush each other off. I pulled a leaf and a couple of bits of bark off her. I even took some particles off her pretty stockings. So nicely dressed when we first started out, we were both looking like we had a mad and crazy good time.

Seated in a Middle Eastern restaurant called Medina Star on the east side of Fifty-seventh Street in Manhattan, I was sure I was introducing Akemi to some of the North African foods that I enjoy, which she had probably never tried. I ordered falafel with tahini sauce, hummus, and babaganosh. I ordered those purple Kalamata olives that I enjoy with cayenne-spiced onions and shotta. I also ordered a tray of chicken kebabs and warm pita bread, all of it for us to share.

When she returned from the ladies room all fresh and clean, her eyes danced at the spread on our table. She began trying each dish, her reactions showing up on her face each time.

I picked her mini recorder up from her side of the table. She was just sucking one of her fingers when I clicked it on and said, "Speak Korean." She must have had hot sauce on her tongue because her eyes immediately filled with water. Either that, or maybe she'd thought of her Korean mother. I knew this reaction was a possibility but I wanted her to know that I knew something about her family, that she was not a stranger or just a pretty face to me.

She spoke Korean softly into the mic. The flow of that language was completely different than her Japanese sounded in my ear. The Korean language sounded like a whining, every other word dragged out, the syllables moaned instead of spoken. The way she spoke it was erotic and it was nice too.

"Speak Chinese," I said next. Her watery eyes dried up. I saw she was delighted by games. She spoke some Chinese to me, which sounded nothing like her Japanese or Korean. It was a swiftly spoken language with a nasal twang. Last, I asked her to speak Thai and she did, easily.

Secretly, I was overwhelmed by her.

In the night she wanted to shop. She was the first person ever to take me into Bergdorf Goodman, which had to be the most expensive store in the whole wide world. I watched her drown herself in perfumes, checking with me on what scents

I liked. She looked at thousand-dollar dresses, shoes that cost several thousand dollars, and handbags so expensive they were locked in a vault. From Bergdorf's, she ended up only purchasing a couple of things, a pair of Prada kicks and seven pairs of stockings, beautiful and fancy ones. By now I could see that colorful stockings and textured tights was really her thing.

Afterward, she wanted to show me something else. We walked about twelve blocks before we arrived at a brick building on a side street. She pushed through the glass door and led me up six flights of narrow stairs to the third floor.

Up there were walls and walls and shelves of books, volumes of graphic novels, comics, and magazines. The catch was, everything was written in Japanese. I figured she wanted me to know that she liked books too and what kind. The place was kind of slick, I thought. I saw that the Asians were also good at re-creating their Asian world right inside New York City. I thought it was interesting how foreigners from the same land still manage to find each other in a sea of diverse people nine million deep.

She spoke nicely to the store staff, all Asians. But she remained focused on me. She never tried to place any distance between me and her while she was around her own kind or other youth. Yet in front of her aunt and uncle her vibe wasn't the same.

I bought one Japanese novel as a token. She bought three.

We ended up on a side street on Thirtieth. These were private Japanese boutiques. The store owner or a security guard had to buzz each customer in after a careful inspection.

Nobody had to tell me what one shop owner was thinking when she saw me standing there behind Akemi. She actually came to the door and spoke some Japanese to which Akemi answered only *"Hai."* I figured the woman asked, "Is this Black guy with you or should I call the police?"

After a while, I figured out that Akemi shopped there because they had the styles that fit Asian girls. Their body type was different from a lot of other women. These shops catered to them and also sold both the European and Asian high fashions in petite sizes.

Akemi took forever and then dropped a couple of grand on some items she selected in the Thirtieth Street shops. Despite the cost, all of her purchases fit into two decorative shopping bags, which she unfolded from inside her magical knapsack.

On Thirty-fourth Street a huge crowd had gathered on either side of the long blocks. I was surprised. There were hundreds or maybe even a thousand people standing there, side by side and back to back. When I looked up at the glowing numbers on the neon clock that sat in a billboard in the sky, I was surprised at just how late it was. Even Macy's department store had already closed. Police officers lined each side of the street keeping the crowd behind the barricades and keeping the streets clear.

Akemi walked behind me with one hand on my waist. When I found our way through to the front of the crowd, I thought I must have gone crazy 'cause I saw fifty huge, majestic elephants marching down the New York City streets, single file in a straight line. Akemi, standing behind me, could not see. I took her two shopping bags and secured them. I lifted her onto my shoulders, her legs dangling down on my chest.

"It's the Ringling Brothers and Barnum & Bailey Circus. They're bringing the elephants into Madison Square Garden. It's circus season," one parent explained to her teenaged kids.

"It's the Midnight March of the Elephants. They do this every year," another person said.

Akemi wouldn't move until the last elephant, clown,

monkey, horse and pony trotted off the streets. She was so fascinated I didn't move her or remind her that now it was the next day, 12:30 A.M.

When our cab arrived at Jackson Heights, Queens, she wanted to walk off on her own toward her house. I paid the cabbie and went with her, not trying to hear no sayonara. I wouldn't leave her to go alone at this late hour.

I walked with her right up to her front door. Their porch light was high intensity, high wattage, more like a searchlight and was the only light on the very darkened street. Her auntie pulled their door open slightly as though she had been seated right there on the other side of the door, just waiting.

I said, "Good night," to them both and made my way home. For me it was cool walking the late night–early morning streets of Queens, New York.

I could feel the love moving and spreading through my chest like an invasion. It was a new feeling, different from my love for my family. It was a good feeling too.

On the train I attempted to assure myself of a couple of things. Akemi was on break from school, so it was all right for her to be out late with me tonight.

But I knew that wasn't true. It wasn't all right in my beliefs and traditions. None of it was supposed to be happening. But what was up with her uncle anyway? I had introduced myself properly to him. I handed over the modest gifts from my family to his. I told him where I worked and where I came from. I was up front with him. But he was silent. If he had anything to say, or any rules to set, or any demands to make, the ball was in his court. I could respect any man who made himself clear about his family.

At our apartment I got some responses from Akemi's family. It came on my voice mail while I was listening to a few business messages at a low volume in my bedroom. The first call from them came from the night before at nine, while we were out shopping. It was Akemi's cousin looking for Akemi. Oddly, her message was spoken as if she wasn't the one who called me and set up the date between me and Akemi in the first place. She was talking like she had no idea what was going on or even if she was calling the right number. She was speaking as if she was unsure if Akemi was even with me. I replayed it twice. I paused it.

I decided maybe their uncle leaned on her about Akemi's whereabouts, and she pretended not to know where Akemi was, but still she called around searching. I wasn't sure about my theory though.

Her second voice mail came in at 10:30. "This is Akemi's cousin. My mother would like to invite you to our home tomorrow at one in the afternoon. She would like to meet you. Akemi knows where we live. If you agree, she will meet you tomorrow at . . ."

I would definitely show up. I could tell that now they were becoming more aware and interested in who I am and what I am involved in. I knew that them calling me over to their house was a chance for the adults on Akemi's side to take a closer look. All I knew was that I am a real man who is trying my best to be respectful of them.

Later that morning, I woke up hard as steel and remained that way for a while.

By ten A.M. I was freshly showered and dressed and standing outside the door of a Brooklyn wholesale flower shop named *Tropics*. I had some Umma Designs business to take care of, an expensive order of thousands of flowers for the Sudanese wedding.

This was the only flower wholesaler in my area that carried flowers imported from African countries as well as flowers from all over the world including Hawaii, Thailand, Brazil, Argentina, and so on. Besides, they boasted a money-back guarantee on the freshness of their product. But I didn't want my money back. I just needed them to get the job done right the first time. There would be no do-overs, take-backs, or second chances on the wedding.

I placed my order precisely as Umma had described it to me. The thousands of fresh flowers would arrive on the morning of the wedding.

I had an idea to double-check their business credibility. I put together an exotic flower arrangement and ordered it to be delivered to Akemi's family shop next week. I knew she might like these unusually beautiful and unique types of flowers that I selected for her. Perhaps her aunt and uncle would too. I would also get a chance to see if the flowers were delivered on time, if they were fresh and the exact arrangement that I had ordered.

By eleven A.M. I was in Manhattan at a candy wholesaler named *Sweeties*. I took my time looking at tons of candies and order sheets for exactly what Umma wanted.

I had the manager prepare a sampler pack for me even though I had already completed my order with them. I figured it was a small perk and nice gift to walk away with.

By one P.M. I was all the way on the west side of lower Manhattan to meet Akemi by the river as agreed, farther west than I had ever walked or traveled in NYC before.

Akemi was there waiting. She held up two tickets in her hand.

She was good luck for me, I thought. Once again, I found myself in a boat, a ferry speeding across the Hudson River. Yesterday a lake, today a river, tomorrow maybe she and I would be in the yacht of my dreams moving on the deep blue waters of the ocean.

My ticket said Edgewater, New Jersey. In script across the bottom of the ticket was the slogan "New Jersey, The Garden State."

As we rode side by side, she had her hand on my leg, playing with fire.

She wore a blue denim dress with the back out. It was covered only by strips of straps crisscrossing each other while exposing the beauty and curve of her back. She wore a pair of blue leather gladiator sandals that crisscrossed up her pretty, shapely bare legs, which I was seeing now for the first time. It was too much. She seemed as if she felt cold, the breeze on the river much stronger with more chill than on the warm spring streets of New York. I took off my jacket and covered her legs. Since I wore a T-shirt beneath it, I unbuttoned my denim Girbaud shirt, took it off, and put it on her instead. It was way too big for her pretty shoulders, but it did enough to satisfy me. She leaned against me staring off to the other side of the river, whispering, *"Arigato,"* but seeming trapped somewhere in her imagination.

There was not a large crowd getting off the ferry in Edgewater, a small town really on the edge, etched out between the river and the mountains.

I followed her. Soon we were boarding their version of the Brooklyn dollar van. We jumped in and stood right next to each other for the short ride to an unfamiliar market.

The place was named Mitsuwa. It was a huge complex framed by boutiques on one side and a Japanese restaurant called Matsushima, that sat farther back on the Hudson River. It had an authentic old Asian architecture, a design I had seen once in a film.

Inside the market, the aroma of fresh baked breads and pastries filled the air. Strangely, there were several separate businesses within the supermarket, open-stall bakeries, tea shops, spaghetti stands, and cafés. There was a huge seating area, high ceilings, and expensive benches and stools and chairs, not in straight rows but arranged like a jigsaw puzzle for small or big families and groups of customers to enjoy.

The grocery shopping section was well stocked and immaculate. Akemi grabbed a cart and began shopping. She looked at me before she pushed off, saying only one word, "cook." As we maneuvered through the vegetables and fruits, many of which I never knew even existed, she pointed them out and recited their Japanese names. When I saw items that I recognized, I told her the English translation for those too.

With two sacks of groceries, we walked out the side door, a different door than the one we entered. We stood in front of one of the boutiques and the Mitsuwa minibus arrived. We boarded a bus full of Asians, each one shorter and smaller than myself.

The driver sped up a winding road named River Road. I kept my eyes on the street signs because I always need to know where I'm at, how I traveled in, and how to travel the fuck back out.

Soon we were riding over the overpass to the George Washington Bridge. We entered a town called Fort Lee, and climbed off.

There were taxis there. We caught one. Akemi gave the street number and name, nothing more, nothing less. We traveled through expensive apartment complexes with terraces, and beautiful wooded areas and flowered paths. Soon we were weaving in and out of weirdly shaped and placed streets and alcoves, past mansions separated by acres, fences, tall trimmed and manicured bushes, and swimming pools.

The driver asked for nine-fifty. I paid him and asked, "What town is this?" He looked at me through his rearview first, then turned his head all the way around. "Englewood Cliffs," he said dryly.

We were at a dead end marked with two street signs. One said HONEYSUCKLE COURTYARD. The other sign read, NO EXIT. It was a cul-de-sac lined with a semicircle of cherry blossom trees. Akemi walked up a pathway to one mansion whose front lawn was a rock garden instead of grass. Each rock was carefully placed in a pattern. There were a few circular slabs of cement that served as a hopscotched path leading up to a bench oddly placed underneath their one beautiful purple-leafed plum tree.

Zooming out of their long driveway backward was an olive-green Range Rover. Akemi stopped walking and watched it pull off and away. She looked at me as if she wanted to say something that she couldn't express.

The bell chimed and it seemed that the sound was being amplified throughout their house and property. Soon her cousin opened the heavy and obviously expensive designer door.

Rapidly she began speaking in their language to Akemi. Then she turned to me.

"Come on in, welcome to my home," she said happily.

"Where are your parents?" I asked her instinctively while removing my kicks, which I knew was customary.

"Oh, yeah. Well, my mother is the one who really wanted to meet you but she just rushed off to the hospital," the cousin said, placing my kicks onto a shoe rack.

"I'm sorry. Is she very sick?" I asked. The cousin laughed.

"No, silly. She's a surgeon and her beeper went off. She hated to leave. She wanted to be here. But she had to go."

"And your father?" I asked.

Where I come from, when you enter a home, you are supposed to be greeted by the man of the house. If not, you seek him out and offer him greetings when you locate him. You always speak to the father first and then the sons because in every home there are rulers and rules and respect that must be offered. Back home, when the limits get crossed, the fists start swinging, the weapons get drawn, and heads get chopped.

"My father is at work. He won't be home until tonight around seven," she said.

Akemi exhaled, took the two Mitsuwa bags from my

hands, and strolled off somewhere. The cousin said, "Let me show you around and introduce you to my brothers and their friends."

The house was extremely clean, and not overcrowded with ugly furniture. There was mostly woodwork and steel, benches instead of chairs, wide corridors and high ceilings, good air circulating, open spaces and tall walls of windows, marble floors and granite counters, beds in the bedrooms lowered to the floor. There was a wide selection of artwork on the walls. There were several big rooms, nicely designed. I could tell her cousin wanted me to be impressed. I was, but I had owned and lived in much more back home, better and higher quality, sitting on much more land. I knew there was a huge difference between "a home" and "an estate." Besides, I was here because Akemi was here and this was her family and that was it. It could have been a tiny cabin. If Akemi was gonna be there, I would've showed up there too.

So far there was no trace of her brothers. When finally we arrived out back, I could see that this was where the real living took place. There was a greenhouse filled with plants, a small tree and flowers, and one old lady wearing a bizarre bamboo hat.

"She's my grandmother. The one who I told you doesn't speak any English" was how Akemi's cousin decided to describe her. But we didn't go inside the greenhouse to meet her grandmother properly.

Of course their basketball court caught my eye. That's where her brothers were, off to the side, getting a game on when we walked up. She introduced us. "Jiro and Kanosan, this is Akemi's friend Midnight. Akemi says to treat him like a king," she told them, laughed a little, then left.

Both brothers looked me over, gave me a pound, and introduced me to their two friends, two white boys. One was named Rob, the other Dave. Both of them gave me friendly greetings. I don't know why but as soon as I stepped up, they all forgot about the game they were playing and handed me the ball.

I took a few shots, all net. They kept passing the ball back to me. We talked about the New York Knicks and the New Jersey Nets. The guy Dave said his father got season passes to the Knicks and they went to the games at the Garden all the time.

Jiro asked me, "Tell us, how did you meet my cousin Akemi?"

"I work in Chinatown."

"That's really cool," Kano said and Jiro agreed.

Just as things was flowing easy, the kid Rob, who I figured was about seventeen years young or so, said some slick shit to me.

"So, you're dating Akemi? You're lucky, man. I been trying to talk to her ever since I first met her a few months back. I ended up with nothing." He was smiling and holding his arms stretched apart as though he couldn't understand his failure to attract her.

"You want to run one?" I asked him.

"Who me?" he said, just like a coward.

"Yeah. You and me, one on one." I threw the ball at him. "Check," I said. The other three backed off the court.

I humiliated him. I never let him shoot the ball. I smacked down all of his shots as soon as he tried to put them up. I stripped him, made him run around chasing a ball he could not see or catch. I knocked him over, then stuck my hand out to help him up. At eighteen points to zero he got tired of the beating and begged, "Enough."

I gave him a pound and said with a smile, "Good game, man."

His friends tried to hold it back, but they ended up laughing at him and looking at me with amazement. It was not like I felt good about it. It was easy for me to dominate them on the court, even without my kicks on.

Just then I noticed Akemi watching me through a window. Then I couldn't see her anymore.

I thought to myself, it's bullshit for people who can't play the game and don't love the game to have season tickets. Meanwhile, in our hoods, the game is pumping through our veins and living in our hearts, yet most will never get to go to the Garden, much less sit in the seats right on the floor.

"Let's get some waters," Kano said. We all followed him to his kitchen. He grabbed the waters from a stainless steel refrigerator that was filled with bottled waters. He tossed them across the room to each of us. I finished off mine and asked for the bathroom. Jiro pointed the way, which I remembered anyway from their sister's tour.

I washed my hands and face in a sink shaped like a large dish. It was made of marble. I stood still a moment, thinking.

When I returned to the kitchen, Akemi and her cousin were standing there. For some reason, the dude Rob was in the kitchen too, even though Jiro, Kano, and Dave had moved on. He said to me, "You was gone a long time," and smiled slyly.

Rob was one of those dudes who could never survive in Brooklyn. The type who never learns how to play his position and shut the fuck up until he's bleeding from his mouth. He was their guest. Yet he carried himself like he was the man of their house, having too many words to say about every small or large situation.

Akemi pulled me out of where my energy was moving. I followed her to the other side of the backyard, up some stone steps, and into a private area under a trellis.

There were vines and plants hanging down from overhead, and on three sides, plants made walls where there really were none. Only one side remained open and was clear to see in and out.

It was breezy. Akemi had the small barbecue going. She had sliced and placed chunks of salmon on sticks with onions and green peppers with seasonings. She was turning the sticks now but I could tell they were cooked and ready.

The outdoor table was arranged with love. There were miniature dishes of sauces and spices, carefully placed. There were green porcelain rectangular plates of varying sizes, a table offering salads and vegetables, and steaming brown rice in a rice cooker. There were two black metal kettles, one filled with soup, the other with tea. After I looked at everything I looked at her. She was waiting for my reaction. I smiled and then sat. She smiled, relaxed, and served.

The spoons and even her maroon glazed wooden chopsticks were beautiful. It was a table with nothing ordinary to offer. I could tell she wasn't sure what I would eat, so she had prepared a lot of simple but thoughtful choices. I liked it all.

Her fingers wrapped around her chopsticks. Her nails today were clean with only a coat of transparent gloss. She stared at me while she chewed. Her stupid transistor radio was playing piano tunes. Her taste in music was obviously diverse, same as my father's.

The meal she served didn't weigh me down. It was light and satisfying. Afterward, I pulled out my candies and spread about nine of them across her table and pointed for her to choose one. I wanted to know what kind of flavors she liked.

She picked them up one by one and looked each of them over, but didn't select.

I opened the Hershey's kiss and held it to her mouth. She bit the tip. Then she went through each of the eight pieces of candy and licked each one, sucking her own tongue afterward to bring down the flavor. I guessed she was looking for the right taste, but at the same time she was driving my blood up. She licked the caramel twice, but settled on the honey.

She took it in her mouth and kept it. She took my hand. She said one word, "Go."

I think she meant "Come." I picked up the caramel candy that she had licked. Caramel had always been my first choice. I followed her. We stepped around the trellis. She disappeared into a path behind it and into the woods behind her cousin's house.

We walked for about six and a half minutes before I saw an easel and a chair off to my left. I realized she must come out here sometimes to paint. I could see why. There was nothing out there but the beauty and sounds of nature, no humans, except for us.

Surprisingly, she turned to the right, walking away from the easel. She stopped in front of an old oak tree with deep roots, a huge wide trunk, and branches that stretched to the sky forever. The new spring leaves were every shade of green.

She leaned up against the tree. She locked her eyes onto mine. She started speaking Japanese to me. She placed her palms underneath my T-shirt. When her skin touched my skin my whole body heated up. I stepped in to her. I put my hands on her shoulders, then moved them down her bare arms. She caught goose bumps and began breathing intensely. I locked my fingers into hers.

She brought both our hands up to her breasts. She unraveled her fingers from mine, then dropped her hands to her sides. My hands were still there on her breasts, the size of mangoes. I began to caress and gently squeeze her titties. Her nipples raised up through the denim. She breathed even louder. I leaned in and kissed her, still touching her titties. It was lips to lips at first. Little by little her mouth opened. She licked my lip. My tongue found her tongue. She began sucking my tongue like she wanted to have all of the caramel for herself, like she wanted to consume me inside of her mouth. It felt so good. I picked her up to hold her closer to my body, to feel her. Eye to eye, I held her in my arms, her butt seated in my hands, her back up against the tree, her bare legs wrapped around my waist. She rubbed my head. Even my scalp was on fire. She touched my face, my chin, my neck.

I began sucking her neck. She started moaning softly. Soon she was back to suck on me too. Her body gave in to the feeling. The taut grip of her legs loosened. Soon enough we were both on the grassy ground, her legs slightly open in her short blue denim dress. Her chest heaved up and down like she just completed a strenuous marathon.

She sat up, pulled her body to the tree and leaned up against it. I sat up beside her. We tried our best to slow it down. But she took my hand back into her hand. She was massaging my fingers. I ran my other hand up the inside of her thigh. I had never felt anything so soft and so good. Her cheeks were flushed and her eyes were so excited, wide and beautiful. Her left leg was shaking some. I couldn't believe the power of my touch, but her breathing and moaning made it true.

Under her dress, I could feel her panties. They were the only thing that separated me from her bush, which I could feel raised up through the very thin material. I didn't try to pull them off. I just touched the outside, rode the contour of her body with my fingers, gently exploring. Her moistness soaked through almost immediately. She whispered only one English word, "Please."

Her legs dropped open now completely, I imagined like a beginner's yoga position. Both my hands were raising up her thighs and holding her hips. Soon I was holding her small, bare waist in my hands. She laid back down slowly, but before I could slide her panties down, we both heard her cousin's voice screaming out her name.

Her cousin's voice interrupted something so sweet and powerful and yanked me out of the momentum of something so new and incredible. Reluctantly I stood up and held out my hand so that she could grab on to me and hurry and get up too. Akemi tried to pull me closer on to her. She didn't want me to stop. I definitely didn't want to stop either but her cousin's voice was drawing closer.

Her cousin shouted out some words in Japanese. Akemi answered back in Japanese. She turned around and said, "Go." I knew she meant "Come."

I jogged behind her the seven minutes back to her house.

In the cool corridor of the house, her cousin was looking both of us over. The light was dim but even I noticed the purple passion mark I left on Akemi's neck. I wanted everybody else and everything else to disappear for a while. Then I would pursue my passions and put my marks all over Akemi's body. Instead, I took a deep breath and looked away from my attraction.

Her and Akemi kept talking back and forth. The telephone rang. Her cousin looked at her and without words her eyes instructed Akemi to answer the phone. Akemi picked up the telephone. Her voice switched into respect mode. I could tell she was speaking to an elder.

Her cousin was standing by me. "It's our uncle calling," she said. "This is his second call," she added.

"Is something wrong?" I asked, completely out of guilt. A leaf from the woods fell off Akemi's dress and came zigzagging down onto the marble floor.

"No, it's just that our uncle is responsible for Akemi. He is both of our fathers' youngest brother."

Looking very disappointed, Akemi hung up the phone and began speaking to her cousin. Her cousin interpreted for me.

"Our uncle says that Akemi cannot have a guest in our house if neither my mother or father are at home," the cousin announced. "I tried to explain to my uncle that Mom was supposed to be here and that she should return soon enough. But our uncle said that this is no good because when he called the first time, Jiro could not even find you and Akemi."

"It's no problem. I'll get ready to leave," I said.

"Ask Akemi for my jacket," I told her cousin. She translated.

"Akemi says come and get it," her cousin informed me.

As Akemi walked down the corridor then up three indoor stairs, turning into a bedroom, I followed her easily. But her cousin also followed me.

In the bedroom she picked my jacket up from the bed and handed it to me. The look in her eyes was too powerful. But I could also feel her cousin's eyes burning a hole in my back, to hurry up and leave. I took the jacket and turned to go.

Akemi spoke to her cousin. Her cousin said to me, "Akemi said she's coming with you." Looking at her cousin instead of her, I answered, "Tell Akemi I said to stay here. I don't want to cause her any more trouble with your uncle."

"You tell her. She's a rebel. She won't listen," her cousin said, then translated. Akemi checked my eyes to see if I refused her coming. I shook my head no to show her she could not come with me. She pouted and folded her arms over her chest. Her cousin said, "That's better anyway. Akemi's staying over here in Jersey for the next week instead of being at home alone in Queens. Uncle said so."

"Isn't she working at the store?"

"My older brother is home from college for the week. He's working at Uncle's store. Akemi will be right here with me."

"Until?" I asked.

"Until her vacation ends, one week. She'll return to Queens on next Sunday." Akemi was leaning against the wall, looking mad and even more pretty.

Before I put my sneakers back on, I asked about Jiro and Kano.

"They're in the basement," her cousin said. She led me to the basement door.

"All right, Jiro, Kano, I'm about to bounce. Good meeting you two," I said.

"Later, man," they both said. Then Rob and Dave yelled up, "Later, dude."

"They would've come upstairs to say 'bye, but they're playing video games. You know how it is," her cousin said.

I walked to their front door, pulled my sneakers off the rack, and put 'em on.

Ja mata, Akemi," I said. It meant "I'll see you next time."

It was a long walk to the nearest bus stop. I kept my pace swift, didn't want to inspire any policemen, although I had not seen any so far.

The sun was warm and bright. There was nothing but peace and solitude. The trees swayed and the birds were busy. I could see why they called this The Garden State.

After a trek there were several buses headed right over the George Washington Bridge. It was the quickest way for me to get back into the city. I decided to save the ferryboat rides for me and her. I jumped on the bus instead.

Seated in the back window seat, I pressed my head against the glass. As the bus pulled off, I could see Akemi pedaling fast on a boy bike she must've borrowed from her boy cousins. She was wearing a sweater, a T-shirt and capris, and kicks now. Her hair was in a wild long ponytail. She was covered with a light sheen of perspiration and looking all around for me.

Allah is good, I thought. Akemi could not see me and it was too late for me to get off the moving bus. I knew if I were to encounter her again today, there would be no stopping the momentum of our feelings. The scent of her was still on my fingers. I had no desire to remove it. It made me feel as if my hand were still moving up the inside of her soft-as-butter thigh. The scent enticed me almost as much as she did. I couldn't think straight, at least not as straight as I usually could.

This day had been a series of firsts. First time to New Jersey, first time being inside of Akemi's family's home, first time sliding my tongue into a mouth, first time running my hands over a female's breasts and thighs and touching her panties. First time I felt like something felt so good that I couldn't stop myself.

I knew I had to sort it all out. But for now, I did something I never do while traveling or standing still in the streets of Brooklyn. I closed my eyes.

23

THE INSULTS

Fresh, I was fresh when I picked Umma up from work. Still I imagined she could see Akemi's passionate prints all over me like a purple ultraviolet light exposes lint on clothing that the naked eye cannot see. But she didn't say one word differently than she usually would when I met her in the early evening.

"Let's get a cab instead," she said. "I have the address of an Egyptian jeweler. His jewels come very highly recommended."

On the ride over, Umma explained. "I want you to convince the jeweler to agree to a private showing of his bangle collection at the executive apartment of the father of the groom. The father and his son, the groom, will be certain to select something exquisite for the bride."

It turned out that the groom's father, whom Umma never spoke to directly, is an important Sudanese dignitary. He would arrive in New York tonight from Switzerland. His business this upcoming week would require his presence at the United Nations. He could accept a meeting with the jeweler at his Manhattan apartment across from the U.N., but his schedule would not permit him to make the trip out to the various jewelers' stores.

"Sudanese brides," Umma said, "expect their bangles to be incredible. The jewels on a bride's arm on her wedding day are so much more important to her than any ring being

placed on her finger. The bangles will be hers to cherish forever. And believe me, they are only a small part of the dowry
that her groom must provide to her and her family."

"Sounds expensive," I said.

"These are not poor people we are working for,"
Umma informed me. "The groom has graduated from a
prestigious university in Cambridge, Massachusetts. He is
working now for some U.S. corporation. His auntie told
me that their nephew has gained all of the money that he
ever wanted, but he has lost his tradition." Umma made
a sound with her teeth, expressing how shameful she felt
the loss of tradition is.

"Our job is to make sure that the groom and his family,
who have been living in Europe and America for all of these
years, are properly prepared for his wedding to a Northern Sudanese Muslim woman whose Sudanese family will
expect a traditional Sudanese wedding and will be completely
insulted by anything else."

We stood outside the Egyptian jeweler's door. A big
sign in the window read OPEN. The lighting inside the
store was bright, yet the door was locked. An Arab woman
looked at us from a distance behind the jewelry counter.
An Arab man emerged into view and looked us over too.
He walked toward the locked glass door and stood still for
some seconds.

"You're in Brooklyn, motherfucker! Open the door," I
thought to myself. Who did he expect to see as his customers? My Islamic mother was standing right there covered
from head to toe.

He signaled to the woman, who remained behind the
counter. She reached her fingers to the wall behind her and
pressed the buzzer, unlocking the door. He pulled the door
open before I could push it. He stood in his doorway blocking us from entering.

"Salaama alaikum," I said. "Are you open?"

"Nom," he answered, which means "yes" in Arabic. "Do you want to spend some money today?" he asked us.

I didn't like his question. It was a subtle way of saying, "Do you two have any money, or not?" Or, "Why bother?"

"We want to arrange for a private showing of your bangle collection to a dignitary from our country." I handed him our business card.

Without even looking at it, he said with clever sarcasm, "He can come here to the store. We will show him our collection privately." An older Arab man emerged. He was standing a few feet behind him now, watching. I assumed he was the man's father.

"He's an important client for our business. We need to make it convenient for him. It will be profitable business for you too," I assured him. "You won't be disappointed."

The Arab stepped outside his store. The door closed and locked behind him. Umma stepped back. I remained standing there in his face.

"You see the pharmacy there?" He pointed. "Go and buy a camera and bring it. I will snap some photos of our bangle collection. You will show him and return with his money and his choices," the Arab said.

Umma stood silently, listening, watching. If she were not standing here with me, I would have stopped this conversation before it ever started, before he decided after too long a wait to move closer to the door. But I wanted to please Umma.

"All right, if we can come in, my mother can look over the bangles. She will know the tastes of our client," I said, preferring to work it out that way.

"Is she buying or is he buying?" the Arab said curtly.

I touched Umma's arm. We turned and left. I heard him spit on the ground somewhere behind me.

• • •

Running suicides at basketball practice wasn't nothing
for me. I needed to do something physical and extreme to
burn off energy. So I did. After Vega's whistle, I was still
running suicides. The laps Vega called for, I doubled. The
drills, I drilled. I wasn't tryna impress anybody. I was trying not to kill anybody . . . else. But the disrespect was too
constant.

Three hours after practice began that same night, the
entire team was seated together on the gym floor, drenched
in sweat. Vega wasn't sweating. He was plotting.

"All of you are making me look good tonight. Keep it up.
We'll look good together," he said, talking fast and clapping
his hands twice.

"For now, you need to choose a team captain, a leader, a
point man. I'm gonna walk away. In three minutes when I get
back, you all tell me who it is."

"Who wants to be the captain of Los Negros?" Panama
Black asked. So we all knew he did. Nobody was stepping
up. Then the kid named Braz said, "That brother right there
should be our captain," pointing at me.

"Nah. I'm just a shooter. Let Panama Black be the captain.
He hustles hard. I'm not a leader. If I'm in the clear, feed me.
I'll sink it in the hoop," I told them. "A'ight?" I asked.

They all nodded their approval or said, "Yeah."

Panama Black smiled, revealing his framed gold teeth.
"You know it," he said, accepting the new position.

On our way out, Panama threw his arm around my shoulder and kept it there too long for me. "You a cool motherfucker," he said with a straight face. "Where you from?" he
asked.

"Brooklyn, same as you," I answered.

He laughed once and said, "A'ight, I hear that." He knew

we were both from different countries. I was just being polite enough not to tell him to mind his fucking business.

Panama thought I was doing him a favor, stepping out of his way so he could shine. I looked at it the other way around. The way I saw it, Vega was about to dump a heap of responsibilities on his head as team captain. Panama would have to be accountable for every player on the team, their whereabouts, and getting them to act right and show up on time. When a next player fell short, he would take the weight. I didn't have the time. For me the league was strictly business. I was glad to give him that position and move out of the light where I preferred to be.

Our team stepped out of the gym and into the red and blue lights of the popo, pulled up and parked on the curb in front of the gym. They was eyeing us with a hatred that didn't mean shit 'cause it was an everyday thing. "Keep walking," a cop's voice blasted out over the megaphone. "Keep walking, clear the area, get back to your buildings," the voice ordered. Only one team member made the mistake of turning around and looking back toward the police cruiser. The cop on the driver's side jammed the gas pedal. The police cruiser jumped and sped up to where we were walking. One and a half seconds' worth of siren rang out then stopped immediately. "We're looking for a black guy in jeans and a T-shirt. Is that you?" the cop asked sarcastically, throwing his voice over the megaphone from inside the cruiser. Our whole team was wearing sweats and kicks. We just kept walking, our backs to them.

Vega walked with us too, toward the train station. I knew he had his reasons for walking with the team, because earlier, I seen him roll up in his car, which he parked in the opposite direction. I noticed Vega wasn't saying nothing either. The cops followed us slowly, still sitting and riding behind us all the way to the station. They disappeared when they were sure we were all going down into the subway and out of their area.

"A black guy in jeans and a T-shirt," I thought to myself. That fits the description of every male youth in all our hoods.

I had two guns, four knives, and eight hundred dollars on me that night. Close call.

24

ISLAM, LOVE, AND SEX

In our Brooklyn apartment, late, clothes and cloths hung on hangers everywhere. There were white sheets laid across the length of our living room, a strategy Umma used to keep the cloths she was working on clean. Umma was seated on the floor with six yards of a brilliant red cloth laid across her lap and an open box of beads, sequins, and tiny jewels. The lampshades had been removed from our three lamps. The hundred-watt bulbs were radiating blinding light and extra heat. I knew she was really doing it.

When she gets in this intense creative state of mind, she stares at the cloth as if she sees something there that no one else sees. She pulls out her spool of gold thread. She lifts up her needle, threads it the first time without missing the impossible needle eye. One by one she sews on the beads, sequins, and jewels in a pattern that only she has in her mind. With great patience she sews on five hundred to five thousand adornments, never breaking her pattern, until the thobe is perfect.

I removed my sneakers and walked around the perimeter of the living room wearing socks, not saying too much, trying not to break Umma's concentration.

Before I could reach the door to Naja's room, Umma stopped everything and looked up at me. I was disappointed with myself for being in her way. I knew that whenever I was in the same room with her she began to focus on me.

"You'll need some rest tonight. The next eight days will be a *haboob*," Umma said, which means, in our Sudanese Creole, a "sandstorm." "Tomorrow, I will need you to place the fruit order at the wholesaler. Go there and make sure that everything there is fresh, completely fresh. If it turns out to be a quality wholesaler, and *inshallah* it will, place our order and make sure he schedules the delivery to arrive on Sunday morning, the morning of the wedding, fresh. Double-check, since the wedding will be held on a Sunday. Some of these businesses are closed on Sundays and I don't want the fruit to be delivered on Saturday."

"No problem. If their fruit or the delivery date is no good, I know a couple of other places to try out," I assured her.

"And, while you were at basketball practice, I spoke to Temirah Auntie," Umma said, referring to Mr. Ghazzali's wife. I could see that from working together, she was feeling much more friendly with the first Sudanese family that we'd met here in America. I'm sure she was also relieved to be working for people who spoke her language. Because of this, she was handling more responsibilities than usual, jobs normally reserved for me.

"Ms. Temirah will arrange for the groom and you to meet and visit a variety of jewelers. His father and his uncle will not be able to accompany him. They are both working and unavailable. You'll need to stick with him until he makes his final purchases. I know that you know jewels. I promised Temirah this," she said, very sure of me.

"When you accompany him shopping, just think of it as if you were purchasing these jewels for your own bride," she said, so soft and calm and clever while looking at a gold bead smaller than a child's teardrop.

I smiled. "No problem, Umma. I'll do it."

"You have their telephone number. Do it on Monday. This way, if the groom turns out to be stubborn or to have poor

taste, we will have time to save the situation before the signing of the *agid*. Oh, and I will need you to come along to the
mosque for the ceremony," she said.

"The wedding?" I asked.

"No, not exactly. A Sudanese wedding takes place over
several days. The signing of the *agid* is the contract between
the groom and his new wife and both of their families. It will
be a much smaller ceremony than the actual wedding, but it
is extremely important.

"You see, when you choose, or your family chooses your
bride, it is the marrying of the two families together. It is not
just one person doing whatever or however he pleases," she
said.

And then there was silence, the Umma kind of silence.

"So, what did you do today before you came to pick me
up?" she asked, so sweetly, and full of innocence.

"I saw Akemi. I went to her uncle and aunt's home in
New Jersey, a very nice place. But the aunt and uncle were not
there," I said. Then I explained about the aunt being a surgeon,
and the uncle being away on work. I knew that Umma would
disapprove of my visit to Akemi's family's home without the
elders being present. I knew she would look down on the
elders for allowing it. Then Umma responded with one of her
truth-filled bombs.

"Not everyone in the world believes the same beliefs,"
she said. "But I know that what we believe is true. Allah has
given us a way of doing everything. It is a way that is right
for any people who want what is best for everyone over what
they may think is best for only themselves."

"I'll get you some water," I said, walking to the kitchen to
keep my brain from exploding.

I came back with two glasses of water, both filled with
ice. I thought of my father, who never took ice in any
drink. He disliked ice and air conditioners or anything like

that. In one-hundred-degree weather, he seemed to feel cool and easy.

"She can come," Umma said, bringing me back to the here and now.

"Who?" I asked, blindsided.

"Akemi. We will let her see what we believe and how we live at the signing of the *agid*. We will watch and wait and see how she feels about it," Umma said.

What could I do besides agree with Umma? Of course I wanted to see Akemi as much as possible.

"So, the two of you were alone in her uncle's house?" Umma asked.

"No. Akemi's grandmother, cousin, and her two brothers, and two of their friends were there too," I said truthfully, but feeling like I had just lied.

"Very well," Umma said, returning her attention to her work.

In Naja's room, the lime-green lights of her alarm clock read 1:15 A.M. She was asleep under one sheet and one very light blanket with her quilt turned down at the foot of her bed. Her bookbag was packed and placed in the corner as usual. The glow-in-the-dark stars and crescents on her bed-room ceiling were all lit up. Everything was good with her. So I closed her door.

"Naja has been saying that she needs to spend more time with you. I reminded her that we are all working hard when we are away from home," Umma said.

"On Sunday I will keep her right by my side. I'll make her feel special, even when I'm working," I promised.

In my bedroom after my shower, I turned the volume down and pushed the button to play my voice mails. I wrote down the new business inquiries and contacts into a small notebook I used.

Ameer's familiar and excited voice was the last message. It

came through at a greater volume than everyone else's voice.

"Wednesday night, you, me, Chris, and the girls. Say no, and I swear I'll bring all three of them to the dojo. Hit me back. You know the digits." *Click.*

I looked at the clock, realizing how few hours I actually had remaining before I would have to wake up and hit the pavement.

I lay still, surrounded by darkness. Akemi's pretty eyes came to mind. I thought about her touch. For me she was more than a sexual desire, although that desire was strong and real and growing stronger with each day. I liked her whole style, admired her talent, respected her thoughts, and was completely drawn in to the way she went about show-ing me love too. I felt a genuine love growing that was never within me for any person outside of my family. It was a completely new and different kind of love and a real good feeling.

I felt possessive over her. I wondered what she was doing right then. I wondered how long Rob and Dave stayed in the house along with her. I wondered if she was talking with that fool Rob or not. I wondered if she was talking to any man, period, who wasn't her blood relation. It all mattered to me now, and really, I wanted her right here by my side.

I heard my doorknob turning.

Umma was standing there now, stepping halfway into my darkness, and halfway remaining in her light.

"I wanted you to know that there is a reason why in our faith we hold back from making love until we are married," she said softly.

I was thinking to myself, *How can it be possible for her to know even my unspoken intimate and private thoughts?*

"Once a man has knowledge of a woman's body, almost nothing or no one can stop him from seeking that pleasure over and over again. You should not pretend that you are the first man in the world to be feeling what you are feeling right now. You have to acknowledge that there were millions of men who lived before your life was even a thought. The outcome of your feelings and experiences is already clear. Your lovemaking will bring forth new life. New life is a beautiful blessing, but should be brought forth into a complete family, a mother and father, a husband and wife, and both of their families also. New life should come *after* the union of marriage is secured. Allah requires this from us, and Allah is the best knower of all things. Allah has arranged it, that if the believers follow true to the Quran, they will experience better lives.

"Don't be stupid like the American boys, who pretend to be shocked when their women become pregnant, and then run far away. Never accept women like the American girls who have sex with anyone, then make all of their babies disappear."

A silence fell.

"What about condoms?" I asked. My eyes and embarrassment were both shielded by the darkness of my room. I wished I were talking to my father right now instead of Umma. I remembered Ameer's father's advice about sex and condoms.

"Do you think you will stop your feelings each and every time to put one on?" she asked me comfortably.

"It will be easy for you to do if you don't know, don't love, and don't trust the girl who you are with. But where there is real love and deep feelings, it will feel too good. You'll go in naturally over and over again and natural life will be born.

"What then?" she asked, still leading the conversation. "Are you prepared to marry and bring forth new life with this girl? Is she the one for you, for us? Or will you touch her, then abandon her, like the men in this country who abandon their families so easily?"

I knew that what Umma was saying and asking me to consider was right. And I knew that whatever I chose to do meant the world to her. But, at that moment, I felt like five different things—a boy, a man, a Muslim, an African, and a son trying to grow up in America without being fucked up like everybody else.

25

VIRGINS

Fawzi pulled out his brown Dunhill wallet and flipped it open. There were eight slots inside. I checked out that each of the eight slots carried credit cards, beginning with his American Express Black card.

The Indian jeweler whose genuine dark gold and elegantly designed, thick, wide bangles we selected was patient and pleasant but firm. He was the sixth jeweler we had visited that day. We left the arrogant Arabs in Brooklyn. We fled from the jive Jews in Manhattan and landed in Queens with the dark man from India, who understood how to take his customers into the back room and line his bangles up on a soft black velvet cloth, unafraid that we were gonna jump up and scream, "This is a holdup, motherfucker. Get on the floor."

Of course he had an armed guard in his place who was definitely another Indian, I guessed, probably one of his cousins. But I respected that.

"Discount is always possible with cash. Cash is always good," he said, smiling swiftly and rocking his head from side to side the way Indians tend to do. Then, he pulled back to seriousness.

Each gold bangle cost somewhere in the vicinity of six hundred dollars. Fawzi had selected ten bangles, each with a different design. I had already pushed the jeweler to apply a ten percent discount because of the quantity of the purchase.

The total price tag for the twenty-four-karat gold bangles was now at fifty-four hundred dollars.

The ten diamond bracelets that Fawzi then selected cost somewhere in the vicinity of six thousand dollars for each one. I sat blank-faced but in shock of how easily Fawzi made decisions. I wondered if the jeweler really expected us to spread almost sixty-five thousand dollars in cash onto his glass counter.

"Easy," Fawzi told the jeweler. "You have already applied the ten-percent discount for my overall purchase. So I don't mind paying the tax for the jewels. I will also need a receipt. I will have everything appraised and insured in any case." He slid his black card onto the counter. Before the Indian jeweler could cast any doubt, he slid his driver's license next to the card.

I saw that both Fawzi's and his father's name were on his credit card.

The jeweler ran his credit.

It was only then that I felt fucked up. Not about Fawzi, but about myself. I mean, I was seated there with a pocket filled with my own hard-earned cash. But Fawzi had legitimacy and backup.

He was in the position I should be in easily, a son fully set up and financed by his father. A son who still studied hard and worked nonstop and pushed hard to make his own name in this world. He must love this woman a lot, I thought. Even if his father is backing up his spending, it was still a lot of paper to drop in one sitting.

As the jeweler cleaned and boxed the jewels and prepared the paperwork, Fawzi turned to me and said, "I think you are right. My new wife is going to love these jewels more than she loves me." He smiled.

He was wearing a tan leisure suit and hard shoes. He was much more confident and laid back than I had expected. He could flow in Arabic, English, or Sudanese Creole, although he spoke English the majority of the time.

The jeweler returned with the cases, opened them one last time to reassure us. He closed them, locked the clasp on each of the boxes, and placed each case into one black velvet sack. He put the sack inside a gold-embossed shopping bag. He asked, "Do you need an escort to your car?" He glanced at his armed guard.

"No, we're good," I stood up and answered for Fawzi. I took the shopping bag, turning to Fawzi and saying, "Let me carry this for you."

"Don't try to get away," Fawzi joked. "You are probably much faster than me, but I am a long-distance runner. Way after you run your fastest race and run out of breath, I'll keep coming and find you wherever you're at." He laughed. I didn't.

"And when you catch up with me, what will you do?" I asked him solemnly. I saw he felt a wave of intimidation. He was six feet. I was six one.

"Lighten up. I'm just joking. My uncle told me that you are the perfect businessman, solid, reliable. I trust you," Fawzi said, still smiling. I remembered then how comfortable money, family, and status makes a male youth feel. I relaxed some.

I had about fifty questions I wanted to ask him. He was twenty-four years old, I calculated from the birth date on his driver's license. He was only ten years older than me. He must have felt some of my same feelings about a female, or gone through some of my similar situations.

He was already fully established. He was from my country and my religion. Maybe he could tell me something different than the shit that everyone else here was talking that didn't sound right in my ear.

I wanted to know if he was fucking these American girls while he was living up in Massachusetts. Or if he was waiting until marriage the way Muslim men and women are supposed to do. I wanted to know if he kept one secret girlfriend up there with him. And, if he did, what would he do with her after his wedding? Would he cut her off? Did he love her? What did his father require from him?

I knew I needed to think before I spoke. I knew I had to put my words together right to ask about women, marriage, and personal things that every young man wants to know and should learn from his own father. I knew this would prob-ably be the last time that I saw Fawzi, alone and man to man. After this, he would be swept up into a wedding whirlwind and beginning his new life.

Outside, we walked. He suggested McDonald's. I think he thought it was for my benefit. I laughed and directed him into a nearby Thai restaurant. It was 4:30 P.M. now. I had just enough time to have an early dinner with him, then deliver him and the jewels to his father.

Before we were seated, I placed a call to his uncle, Mr. Salim Ahmed Amin Ghazzali, the one who hired us for the wedding and paid out the deposit. I gave him the address of the restaurant so that he would send a car to pick both of us up.

"If Fawzi locates and purchases the jewels today, give us a call at once. We don't want him walking the streets or riding the train with the jewels. We'll send a car to wherever you are," Mr. Ghazzali had instructed me in advance.

I had insisted that it wasn't necessary. Mr. Ghazzali insisted that it was.

When I went to join Fawzi at our table, he was sur-rounded by the smoke from his cigarette and finishing off his Singha, a brand of Thai beer. I figured this was what Umma and his Auntie Temirah had been discussing concerning Fawzi's "losing his tradition," because Muslims don't drink alcohol.

I didn't say nothing about it.

"How long have you been living in America?" I asked him, taking my seat.

"Let's see. I completed my B.S. and master's degree in five years at MIT. My Ph.D. took only two years at Harvard, that's seven years."

"Before that, were you living in the Sudan?" I asked.

"No. I did boarding school in Switzerland," he said, matter-of-factly.

The waiter interrupted. We placed our orders. "And bring me another beer," Fawzi told him.

"So how was it being away from Sudan? Did you like it better?" I asked.

"I do as my father says. When he sent me to a European boarding school I was twelve years old. I graduated at the top of my class and got recruited on a full, five-year master's program scholarship to attend MIT at age seventeen. By the time I was twenty-one, I'd graduated MIT and got recruited by a military firm in Massachusetts while completing my Ph.D. at Harvard. Now I've been hired by a firm here in New York and am set to get started working there next month. Not bad, right?" he asked, smiling and tapping his next cigarette on the tabletop, then lighting it up.

"Then how did you meet your wife? She's from Sudan, right?" I asked.

"Oh, I see. You want to talk about women." He smiled. "You are living here in New York, obeying your traditional Sudanese parents, and your balls are turning blue and you can't take it anymore." He cracked up with men's kind of laughter.

"You too are Muslim, a believer, right?" I reminded him. He leaned back, balancing his weight now on only two legs of the four-legged chair. He took a long drag from his cigarette and turned suddenly serious. "You know, when I first began studying engineering it was extremely difficult. Our professors would always tell us that most of us wouldn't make it, never graduate. I didn't want to lose my academic scholarship either. I had to keep my grades up. My father required this also.

"I and a couple of my classmates would sit up sometimes for three or four nights in a row, crashing our brains together to solve just one math problem. Just looking for one right answer," he said, wandering in his own thoughts.

"That's how it was for me when I first left Sudan. Everything European and American seemed wrong, backward, crazy. At first I would think about it real hard and all of the time. I was searching for explanations and answers.

"In my heart, I am a Muslim man. Yet they have a saying here in America that you may have heard before, 'When in Rome, do as the Romans do.'"

Our waiter served our food, Fawzi's Singha, and my juice.

Fawzi said, "The only thing the Thai are missing is home-baked bread. I wish I had some aseeda now," he said, referring to a Sudanese bread that Umma makes so expertly.

"Living over here in the U.S., if you want to be respected, you need to acknowledge and accept the American God. And his name is 'money.' Nothing matters more. All of their religion, rituals, and beliefs are entertainment, just something for them to say and not mean. Something to say to make them feel all right with themselves. Something they can squeeze into maybe one hour or two hours per week and that's it. But every day, every hour, every minute, every second they are awake, they are doing something, anything to make money. And when they are asleep, they are even dreaming about money.

"It is the opposite of Islam. America is the opposite of Sudan, where even if you are wealthy, you wake up to the call to prayer to praise Allah. You bend your knees in prayer five times in only one day. You stop everything and place Allah first. Back home, we say it, we believe it, and we do it. We serve Allah.

"But, believe me, brother," Fawzi said, gripping his fork and pressing it through the white tablecloth into the wooden table below, a nervous habit, I guessed. "If you get in the way of this white man's money, they'll kill you. They can do anything for money. I mean anything. I've seen their arsenal. I have even been part of a team that designed a few of their latest, deadliest items. They have weapons that can make you and your family evaporate into thin air. No one would ever know that any of you were ever here."

He was getting too heavy for me. I really wanted to speak about females.

"You see I'm drinking this beer. It's my second one today. I've learned to drink alcohol while living beside them. You have to. If you continually say, 'I don't drink,' it makes them feel suspicious. They'll start asking you a lot of questions. Next thing you know, you'll be isolated and thrown aside, completely alone. They'll spread rumors that you are some kind of foreign guerrilla or terrorist, even. It's crazy."

"And the American females . . ." I led in. Suddenly he relaxed and changed completely.

"Hey, they are a truckload of fun. They'll do anything, but they are garbage."

"So you have been with them?" I asked, carefully moving toward my real questions. He laughed.

"Oh, yes." He leaned in now. "They beg to suck my balls, so I let them. These American girls suck the stress out of my life and I don't have to give them anything. I just speak politely and thank them for it." He laughed, seeming to reminisce.

"The first time it happened for me, I was a college freshman. The girl was too. She was from California, my lab partner. Late one night, two of the study guys fell asleep. She started caressing me, and tugging on my zipper. When she got on her knees and put her lips on my big boy, oh, what a feeling! After that night I was hooked. I just convinced myself it was okay to get it because it wasn't actually sex or even fornication. I didn't have to enter the woman's womb." He put his cigarette out, smashing it well after the fire was extinguished.

"So do you fuck them or not?" I asked.

"Never," he answered, with only one word and a solid straight face. It was the shortest answer he had given to any one of my questions.

"I could never slip up and *have* to bring even one of them home to my family. My mother would die. My father would disown me. So I don't ever get myself into a position where any of them could get pregnant by me. Besides, the suck is good enough."

"Are you talking about the white girls or the Black American females?" I asked.

"They are all the same, the American women. I'll give you ten thousand dollars if you can find one single virgin American female who is not a child." He was leaning forward and staring me dead in my eyes. "Each of them should be made with an odometer on their foreheads, like every car has. When you look at the high mileage on each of them, you wouldn't even want to be bothered.

"You won't find one virgin. And this is only one of the many reasons why my parents have found me a Sudanese bride. She is Muslim, cultured, raised properly, and yes, a virgin, of course." He leaned back, more relaxed now.

"I will see her for the first time this Thursday when she arrives in the U.S. along with her entire family. But even then, she will be in *niqab* and *hijab*. Only her eyes will be available to me."

For three minutes I sat there, my mind blown away at

how he could put so much care and finance into a woman he had never seen. It must have been easy for him to read the rare, confused look plastered onto my face.

"I talked to her over the telephone for six months. She is seventeen years young and so sweet," he emphasized. "She studies music and plays the violin. And she reads a lot too. She reads books I don't ever get a chance to even look at. She prays for me and ridicules me when I miss saying my prayers, which is often. It's gotten so I can't get a good night's sleep without hearing her voice. My phone bill is so crazy you couldn't imagine."

"Are you worried at all?" I asked him seriously. He laughed again.

"Why don't you just ask straight out, how the Americans would ask. You want to know what if she's ugly or fat or disappointing, right?"

I wasn't thinking that, but now that he mentioned it, it was a funny but good question.

"Well, she would never have gotten beyond my mother's inspection if she wasn't right for me. The two of them were all the time meeting in Sudan and talking, even writing letters to each other when Mom was traveling. My father approves of her too, and he always protects my interests. I trust their judgment completely. I am sure I will love her. I am already very connected with her. After our wedding, she will belong to me forever." The waiter brought the check. I took it before he could lay it on the table. I tucked the balance plus twenty dollars' cash as a tip inside the billfold.

"Hey, if I didn't know any better, I would think you were planning a wedding for yourself also." He smiled. "What age are you anyway?" he asked.

"Fourteen," I answered.

"Man, you had me fooled. Fourteen and still you're taller than me." He looked at me. "Fourteen, the year of curiosity," he said, seemingly speaking aloud to himself and remembering something.

"It seems like a Sudanese wife is a major expense," I said carefully. I knew it was true.

"She doesn't have to be. A lot depends on her class, her family background. If she is from a wealthy family, then she and her family will expect more. If she is a poor girl, she'll be happy with handmade jewelry and hand-picked flowers from her groom's backyard. If she's rich or poor, if she loves you, she'll follow wherever you go, even into a mud hut. Right?" he said, tossing the question my way. "What is shit to one man, is fertilizer to another." He pulled out one more of his cigarettes.

"Your wife's family is wealthy, then?" I pushed.

"Not really. But if my family has it, why not give it to her? She'll become the mother of my children, *inshallah*. When I give her something, in some way, it still remains with me. It's still mine, because she is mine. Besides, if she is happy, my life is so good. No intelligent man wants a miserable wife," he said, his cigarette dangling and unlit.

"Do you think living in this country might change your wife too?" I asked him.

"No. She will follow my lead. I will love her. She will care for our home. This will give her so much to do. Anything she wants, I will provide. I'll work for it. I will bring it home to her. My mother will stay on in the beginning and help her. Her auntie, a widow, will come and stay with us also.

"My wife will have one baby every year for five years, *inshallah*. And by the time my first child is five, I will be set up in business in such a way that I will hire engineers to represent me here in the U.S. Then I will move with my family back to the Sudan, working my Sudanese office. This will be best for my daughters to be surrounded by the right kind of culture.

"But for now, there is trouble in the Sudan, political trouble. And political war is a bad time for earning money. No stability, unless you are the man selling the weapons to everyone on all sides!" He smiled.

On that point I became silent. There was no way for me to discuss Sudanese politics without mentioning my father. And eventually, anyone from the Sudan discussing the details of politics would have to mention my father too. I wasn't prepared for this side of the conversation. This is the reason I rarely asked questions, because when it came my turn to give up answers, I would refuse.

He finally struck the match. The fire burned down almost to his fingers before he actually lit his cigarette.

"You are more mature than I was at your age. You are already a businessman. I can tell that whatever you want, eventually you will have it.

"Islam is good. In fact, there is nothing better. But here in America, you have to have two faces if you want to succeed. One you show them. The other you show only to those whom you love."

Riding in the car reviewing his words, I could catch the cracks in his story. Easily, I could point out his contradictions. But I liked the fact that the things he said seemed to be what he really believed, based on some experiences that he actually had. And he didn't try to cover up his flaws.

26

SENSEI

Hyped up real strong, that's how Ameer and Chris showed up at the dojo.

"My whole team is crazy," Ameer said. "You should see these guys at practice tryna fuck each other up while we tryna run a practice game. We got three East New Yorkers, and a couple a dudes from 'the Hook.' They be tryna settle beefs on the gym floor. I be telling them, 'Look sons, we on the same motherfucking team. How we gone get this paper if y'all keep brawling?'" Ameer had his arms stretched out. His eyes were excited. He loved that type of chaos even though he knew it wasn't a winning strategy.

He continued, "Finally, Coach just told some bench riders, 'Go guard the doors. Don't let nobody in.' Then he made the East duke it out with the Hook. These kids was beating the shit out of one another, slamming each other around like it wasn't nothing. I was straight laughing. I said this ain't no fucking basketball team.

"Later, the three kids from the East posted me up in the rusty ass locker room, talking 'bout, 'You a motherfucking perpetrator,' like I was supposed to jump in and hold them down 'cause I'm from the East too. I told them straight up, 'I ain't got no beef with the Hook.' Everybody in the East knows that out here on these street, unless we bonded by blood or money, it's every man for himself."

"Oh, so we three is only bonded by money?" Chris challenged.

"We brothers. We family. Y'all know how that go," Ameer said.

"How's *your* team looking?" I asked Chris.

"We a'ight but we need that spark, that fire, you know?" he said.

"Then *you* gotta bring the heat. *You* be the spark. Let them rally around *you*." I amped him up truly believing that he did have what it takes to hold his own in a leadership position.

"Word to life," Ameer agreed.

Ameer borrowed twenty-five dollars from me. "I'll give it back to you on Thursday night when we take the girls out," he promised. "It ain't nothing," I told him.

"Yeah, I'm tryna get where you at. Where twenty-five dollars 'ain't nothing,'" he smiled.

"You could've borrowed against our car fund," Chris said, like a real banker.

"Yeah, I could always borrow from our car fund, but the three of us can't fit on a minibike together. If I keep borrowing from the car fund, that's what it's gon' be, a motherfucking tricycle or a minibike." We all cracked up laughing.

Later that night I practiced throwing my *shuriken* against the corkboard in my room. I wasn't sure if Sensei was planning to test me at weapons training the next day. But if he did, I planned to be well prepared.

Tuesday morning after *Fajr* prayer I was on the move. I had to do business errands before my 12:00 weapons training class.

I flew through the dojo doors in a hurry. Sensei required all of his students to be on time. Once I got inside, the whole vibe switched up. Sensei's energy was calming. I slowed my breathing and put my belongings in the locker. Sensei had tea brewing, which was unusual. He seemed to want to talk. After we exchanged greetings, he said, "Pour yourself some tea. Today we are going to begin by discussing vulnerabilities."

"The eyes, the larynx, the pelvis, the knees, the ankles," I said, assuring him that I had studied and retained the information. There was no need for review.

"*Eedis*," he said, which is a Japanese word meaning very good.

"But today we are not focusing on physical vulnerabilities. We are focusing on emotional vulnerabilities. Just as a ninja must know where on the body to attack, he must also learn when is the best time to attack his opponent to achieve complete success."

Sensei's use of the word "success" triggered a thought in me about Fawzi.

"Senseisan, one question, please," I said, then continued. "We are here for weapons training. What would you say if another man said to you that he works for a military weapons company and that he has weapons, which could completely wipe out your entire existence as though you were never ever born? Would it make you feel like everything we are doing here is nothing?"

"It would reinforce my understanding of Sun Tzu's teaching. 'War is deception.' You see, an opponent who can attack your mind and disable your confidence and skill, has won before you have ever thrown one weapon, one kick, one fist. This person who flaunts his military superiority over you or your people, is trying to immerse you in fear. He knows, and they know, that fear will guarantee their success and your defeat. They will have conquered you in your mind first, to minimize their chances of losses on their end."

"And what if these deadly weapons they say they have are real?" I asked.

"Most probably they are real. Men have devoted centuries' worth of time to perfecting machines of destruction, bombs, missiles, even chemical warfare. Yet, even though some countries have these weapons, they have gone to war against people who have no fear of death, but have the spirit of determination, love of preserving their future, and the power of being on the right side of truth. When a mass of people has this, the training that I am offering you is the same training that they will need. If properly trained, people who seem to have no chance of victory can disarm their invaders, strip them of their weapons and use their own weapons against them. They can even set traps, use the elements to their advantage or appear to be passive while poisoning their opponents. For survival, they can do anything. This has happened before, in Vietnam and Korea and other places. Let me recommend a book to you." He reached for his pad and pencil. He paused as if going back into his mind. He wrote down, *Dien Bien Phu* by General Giap.

"In Vietnam and Korea a lot of good men were defeated too?" I supposed and asked at the same time, while looking at the title of the book Sensei had written down on the paper for me.

"Yes, of course. In war there are always losses. The victor is the one who can cut his losses when compared to the losses of his enemy, and emerge with the possibility of rebuilding his team, or village, or civilization according to his beliefs, philosophies, culture, and interest," Sensei stated.

"A Buddhist friend of mine would ask, 'What is death? If the idea survives, then the dead live.'" Sensei smiled a rare smile.

I heard the voice of my father woven in those words somewhere. Although my father, the scientist, was even more specific and precise. But since Sensei's words had components of what my father might say if he were standing right here, right now, I respected Sensei's opinion.

It seemed that our talk motivated Sensei. He went about the two-hour training with intense enthusiasm and care.

I listened intently when he taught me the importance of knowing when to attack an opponent. He described a man's emotional vulnerabilities as happiness, sadness, sexual arousal, and altered states of mind.

Sensei said, "If an attack can be properly planned and launched when a man's mind is altered by the emotion of happiness; for example, at the birth of his child or at the excitement of a sporting event, or at a party, he is an easy vulnerable target."

Sensei said, "If an attack can be properly planned and launched when a man's mind is altered by the emotion of sadness; for example, a funeral or at the moment of great financial loss, or during illness, he is an easy and vulnerable target."

Sensei said, "If an attack can be properly planned and launched when a man's mind is altered by the emotion and action of sexual arousal; for example, while watching a sexual display, pursuing sex, or having sex, he is an easy and vulnerable target."

Sensei said, "If an attack can be launched while a man's mind is in a self-induced altered state; for example, while drinking alcohol, smoking opium, or using drugs, his defeat by any ninja is certain."

Sensei did not waste even one of his words on me. I listened. I understood. I locked them into my memory.

After a half hour of talk, we went into action. I learned the art of the rope. Sensei instructed me on how to tie and bind a man in such a way that if a man tried to become untied, his own movements would cause him further injury instead of escape. It was deep.

Sensei dragged out of his closet a life-sized dummy to demonstrate. I watched him tie it down, each precise move, loop, and pull. He did it twice. Then he asked me to tie up the dummy, in the same manner.

As I got my chance, I replayed the process he used in my mind. It was as though I had Sensei's fingers caught in the close-up of a powerful movie camera lens. I tied the dummy the same way I had seen Sensei tie it. My eyes were looking from the dummy to Sensei, from Sensei to the dummy. Yet, Sensei's silence made me doubt whether I had done it correctly.

Breaking his silent pause, Sensei asked, "What is the problem in this lesson?"

I thought for a moment. I kept staring at the dummy, looking for mistakes in my method. After careful review, I was sure that I tied it perfectly. Still I paused.

I admitted that I did not know the answer.

Sensei answered for me, "The problem here is that a ninja must always expect the unexpected. Therefore, the enemy who you are tying down will not be a dummy." Sensei pushed me with force, small hands, small man, still I fell from the force. It was my mind that was off guard.

"Your enemy will be trying to fight you," Sensei said, kicking me. I pulled my body out of his way. Yet, I was still on the floor at a disadvantage. "Your enemy will be trying to destroy you to free himself," Sensei said, attacking. "He will not be still like this dummy. He will be moving and responding to your every move," Sensei said, still striking me. Now I felt like the dummy. I got my head together to fight back against the master teacher.

Within thirteen minutes he outfought me, had me down, constrained me, and then bound me to the chair.

Then he smiled. "You made two major mistakes," he said calmly, not even seeming like someone who had fought an opponent bigger and taller than himself for a prolonged amount of time. "First, you failed to survive my sneak attack. *Panic* can have fatal consequences. *Panic* shuts down your thought process and renders you useless." He lifted up his teapot.

"Second, you showed your opponent too much respect and it led to your defeat. When you fight, every time, you must think and move and fight to win."

He had me sit there tied up while he poured himself a second cup of tea.

27

HOOD CHICKS

I was tight for the rest of the day. I had nobody to be mad at other than myself.

So, I followed through on handling my business as usual.

At 7:00 P.M. I showed up for a scheduled basketball practice on the outdoor court outside of the high school gym where we usually practice. I don't think Vega was worried too much about us sweating inside of the hot-ass gym. I don't think he moved us outside to enjoy the spring breeze. By moving us outside, he put us under the pressure of performance for the random spectators who showed up to watch. No player minded getting barked on at practice in front of his teammates. But no player wanted to get barked on outside in front of the hood. I saw that it did cause a couple of our players to step up their effort and their game.

Ever since the clocks were pushed forward by an hour for the spring season, the sunlight lasted much longer than it had during the winter months. That night at 9:00 P.M., right as the sky grey got overtaken by the blackness, the temperature dropped by ten degrees and she came running in with the night breeze. She crashed into the metal fence that surrounded the ball court and then whistled like a man. She caught everybody's attention.

"I wanna talk to you," she said. Most of the players who were just finished packing up started heading over towards her. I stood still.

"Not all y'all. Don't even try it," she said boldly. "He know who I'm talking about." A couple of players looked back. Panama stepped up from the rear saying, "Who else but the team captain?" He started to move towards the fence where she was leaning now with her breasts pressed against the wires.

"Panama," I called out. "She's looking for me, my bad," I said. They all turned back around going on about their business. Practice was over now anyway.

Walking over towards the fence, I asked her, "You looking for trouble?"

She smiled and said, "I'm looking for Midnight."

"Why you always calling me?" I asked her.

"Why you never calling me?" she asked. "I gave you my number."

"What would you have done if the rest of the team came to meet you at the fence? What then?" I asked her.

"Then I would've waited for you to look out for me just like you did," she said, smiling. "Besides, I got two legs. I would've ran. They would have to get around this fence first. They wouldn'ta never caught up with me. I'm fast. I would've dashed right down that side alley." She pointed. "They don't know that way. That's my secret. Then I would've ended up right at my bedroom window." She smiled.

All I could do was laugh. She was so excited telling her little story to me.

I walked her home because it was dark, she had a bag, and she had already drawn too much attention onto herself. I really couldn't guarantee what Panama had in mind.

"I know you got a girlfriend," she said, walking.

Before I could say anything she threw her hands over her two ears, closed her eyes and started saying, "No, no, no, don't tell me. Don't answer." When she opened them up and noticed I wasn't saying nothing she pulled her hands down.

"You're crazy," I told her and meant it.

"It's okay because if you would've met me first, I know what would've happened," she said, looking at me with a side glance.

"What would've happened?" I asked her.

"You know." She smiled even harder.

"What?" I asked.

"You know!" She started jumping up and down in place then stomped her foot. "Instead of me looking for you, you would've been looking for me." She struck a pose. I kept walking and carrying her bag.

"If I stop walking you gotta stop walking too," she said. "You don't even know where my house is," she said, challenging me now with both of her hands on her hips.

"Yes I do," I said, still facing forward. "You already told me." I kept walking.

I waited in the alley under the only ground level window. For two minutes I held her lightweight groceries, before she showed up. It was a dark narrow path between two four-story brownstones.

I heard her hurried footsteps approaching. I was thinking she must've figured out that her temper tantrum didn't work on me. I handed her the bag. I doubled back and disappeared. I could hear her calling out her phone number, "7-1-8-. . ."

All I could do was laugh. This girl was nuts, but her little prank loosened me from my fury at my fighting failures of the day.

Late night, I waited to hear the sound of Akemi's voice on my voice mail. Out of nine business messages, not one was from her. I would've been satisfied hearing her say one word.

Her silence wasn't pushing me away. Every day I didn't see or speak to her, my interest, thoughts, and feelings were just escalating.

• • •

Shower and a fresh cut, I cleaned up nice on Thursday. All brand new, I was wearing my suede Ralph Lauren dress shirt, Polo jeans and even cracked open a fresh pair of dark brown leather Lo boots with the gold buckle.

I was going to The Palace, an elite hotel in Manhattan, where they dress the doormen up like fools, so the rich could be sure by looking at them, that *they* were definitely the servants.

Fawzi was staying in this hotel for the next ten days, in a room that was actually an entire apartment. There was a kitchen, living room, a master bedroom, and three bathrooms. The apartment even had a separate doorbell that chimed.

Following Umma's instructions, I was delivering his new bride's new dress, the one she would wear to the mosque for the signing of the marriage contract. I had the scented garment hanging and wrapped and nicely placed in a long silver garment bag.

I took a taxi to the hotel to avoid having the garment tossed and crushed on an overcrowded morning train. I thought about how Fawzi, a Sudanese groom, was responsible to provide everything for his Sudanese bride, and I mean everything.

I was to deliver the dress to him so that he could present it to the bride's mother, along with each item they had already negotiated and agreed upon, including the jewelry. Monetary sums would also change hands from Fawzi's father, to the bride's father. Everything the bride received according to our traditions would become hers. It is not proper in Islam to take back anything a husband has granted to his wife in the contract. But I guess Fawzi was right in some small way, whatever he gave to his wife remained with him, because she would remain with him forever.

I was relieved to hand the garment, in perfect condition, over to him.

Afterwards, I had to hurry to collect deposits on two Umma Designs side orders which customers had placed with the understanding that because of the wedding account we were involved in they would have a longer wait than usual.

While working, I ran across an odd little place called "The Helium Hub." Since it looked like an interesting business with unique offerings, I walked up in there. I would at least collect a business card from them and drop off one of our cards as well.

Inside, there were three walls covered with uninflated new balloons of every imaginable color. Every two inches of wall had a different color balloon sample pinned up.

"How many colors?" I asked the lady up front.

"We have 240 different colors. That's three times the amount of colors offered in the deluxe Crayola crayon box. Each balloon is fifty cents except if you buy in bulk, which is an order of one hundred or more balloons. Then it's twenty-five cents each." She smiled.

"One hundred balloons," I repeated, skeptical.

"You'd be surprised. Some businesses and events order tons of them. They make a plain place look exciting and women and children love them."

Looking around I figured they had to be selling something besides balloons to turn a real profit. Although I could see from the extremely small size of the space that the rent they were paying couldn't be too much.

"What else you selling?" I asked the lady.

"Just balloons," she answered. "But our balloons are filled with a special helium solution. The balloons from the other stores will die out in an hour or two. Ours will last for forty-eight hours or more," she said.

"Forty-eight hours?" I repeated.

I ended up ordering one hundred balloons from their elite line, the psychedelic ones with the crazy colors that I knew she would like. They would match her strange stockings and tights. They cost double the price of the basic colors. There was also a twenty-five-dollar service fee for the short guy whose job was to pump 'em up. Then there was the twenty-five-dollar delivery charge to have the balloons delivered to New Jersey where Akemi was staying for the week. I was starting to see how the Helium Hub made their profit. But I didn't care about the money. I wasn't gonna walk around the city holding a bunch of balloons like some kind of clown. Yet, I grabbed the opportunity to do something special that she could feel. Once she received them, I would invite her to come out to the *agid* ceremony with me on Saturday. Umma wanted to meet her and Naja was going to be there too, so it meant the world to me.

"Each balloon will be knotted and then tied with three colorful twisted ribbons," the lady said, after collecting my information and my money and completing my receipt.

"Would you like to write anything on the card? It's complimentary with your delivery." She pointed to the small card collection in her counter case.

I chose a lavender-colored gift card and wrote inside.

Akemi, I would like you to meet my family on this Saturday at five o'clock. If you say yes, I'll come and get you from wherever you are and bring you back safely afterwards.
  Mayonaka

I knew it would be her cousin reading the note aloud to her, or someone else in her family. So I wanted it to be short and simple and decent. Then, I would wait for her or someone in her family to give me a call and hopefully a favorable answer.

In the evening, I showed up on the Deuce to meet with Chris and Ameer and their girls as promised. Forty-second Street was all lit up and bursting with people and tourists, same as it would be late into the night, same as it would be almost twenty-four hours a day. Our meet-up spot, the arcade, was three floors of fun for teens and tourists, and con men and pimps looking for teens and tourists. In New York, that was unavoidable. It just came with the territory.

Chris was inside the picture booth behind the curtain with his girl. I recognized him by his kicks.

Homegirl was alone and bent over on the pinball machine. Her face changed as soon as she saw me roll up.

"I thought you was gonna leave me hanging," was her greeting to me after all of this time.

"Is that what I should've done?" I asked her.

"Oh, and you got a smart mouth," she said.

"Did you show up to watch or do you wanna play?" I asked her.

"Yeah, let's do the air hockey, I'm good at that," she said. I put the dollar in. We grabbed our handles and started slamming that plastic puck around like our lives depended on it. She was mean on the table. I imagined she was looking at that puck like it was me. She was banging that shit with a vengeance.

Every time she leaned in, those 34 Ds bubbled out of her Danskin body shirt. I could see the white body powder in her cleavage. She had her leather belt drawn tight around her small waist and wore jeans that couldn't restrain that ass. I was part playing the game, part checking her out. Her ten-karat gold knocker earrings dangling from her ears. She rocked Reeboks.

As I looked around the place, every teenage female had on the same thing, tight jeans, tees, and kicks, nice-looking bodies, okay faces, but not a lot of originality, style, or variety. I thought to myself, I could pick any one of these girls. It seemed like no matter what, I'd end up with the same damn thing.

After a while, I let her win the game but didn't tell her that.

"I told you I was good," she said, grinning.

"Let's play Pac-Man," she suggested. I followed her over, not really interested in the little girly game. I dropped in two quarters and she pushed "two players." She got ate up real quick because she couldn't be calm and steady. Pac-Man is a simple game of nerves.

All six of us ended up lined up side by side, driving the race cars against one another. I don't know about the girls but me, Ameer, and Chris was definitely competing to run each other off the road and race to the finish line. Chris had his hands gripped tight on the steering wheel, his face all screwed up like this shit was for real. He was in a zone like he gets in a good basketball game. Ameer was serious at first, then lost focus laughing at Redbone, whose car was crashing into everything including the walls and even driving backwards from the finish line. Homegirl was looking over at me when Chris won the race.

"Let's go somewhere and get something to eat," Redbone said. Chris jumped in immediately and said, "Pizza." Me and Ameer both laughed, knowing this cat was constantly concerned about the budget.

At the pizza store, Chris slid his girl some money and a motherfucking buy-one-get-one-free coupon! He told her,

"Get two pies and drinks." We laughed again. The girls went up to get the food. We hung back and took the chance to talk.

"What's the plan?" I asked.

"We'll take them to the 7:45 P.M. show at the Roy-Al. The seats lean back," Ameer said, smiling.

"I brought a bag of candy in case they ask for anything," Chris said, cracking up.

"Damn, you can't break down and buy her a bucket of popcorn?" I asked him.

"Not when I can get twenty pieces of candy for a dollar and popcorn at the movies cost five dollars," he said.

"You too cheap, man," Ameer barked.

"The more I save, the more we save. You'll be thanking me later when we taking turns driving our new Testarossa."

"Word up," I agreed.

Homegirl and Redbone came back with two pies. Chris' girl carried the drinks in a cardboard tray.

I sat there staring at the two pork pepperoni pizzas before I just stood up and walked away from the table. I'm thinking that Redbone and Ameer been together now for a minute. She *been* chilling at his house and him at hers. He *been* bringing her around to all our spots. Didn't she know he considered himself a Muslim and that *we don't eat no God damned pork?* I wasn't hungry anyway. Still I didn't want to sit over the pig on the pie.

I realized these chicks didn't really know us. Even if we explained ourselves to them, they either wouldn't understand or wouldn't care, or better yet would think we was on some bullshit.

I heard Homegirl ask her girlfriends, "What the fuck's wrong with him now?" Chris jumped up and grabbed the two round trays with the pies untouched and took them back to the counter.

Next thing I know an argument broke out between Chris and the guy up front. The angry Italian was refusing to take back the pies. "Once the pie leaves the counter it's yours," he barked.

Me and Ameer stepped up. As soon as he saw us coming he picked up his telephone receiver and threatened to call the police. The girls ran up, talking about "What's wrong y'all? There ain't nothing wrong with this pizza." Each of the three of them grabbed a slice for themselves and started chomping. The angry Italian hung up the phone. Now the girls were sitting with the pork pies back at the table. We fellas were still standing, our jaws tight, estimating what could be done about the rude Italian.

I knew the girls thought they was helping us stay out of a fight or from getting arrested. But I was burning anyway.

"Forget it. They didn't know," Ameer said, defending the girls.

"I can order one without the meat. Nobody told them to put pepperonis on it anyway," Chris said.

"Nah, I'm good," I told them. "I'm not hungry." We went back to join them at the table. I sat sideways in the chair just cooling out my temper. Homegirl was staring at me outright. Redbone was getting her secret glances on. Then they would signal each other. None of it mattered to me.

At the movies I hung back and got some popcorn and a Coke. When I walked inside, I seen everybody was paired off and seated in separate rows and sections. I handed the popcorn and the drink to Homegirl.

"Thanks," she said.

In the dark theatre Chris and his girl, and Ameer and his girl, got it on. For them, it didn't matter what the fuck was on the screen.

After just ten minutes Homegirl got real aggravated. For some reason she started squirming in her chair and looking around. She wasn't interested in the film, I guessed. She started exhaling real hard, then folded her hands across her body. I looked at her. She was rolling her eyes.

I don't know what she was thinking, but I was thinking, to me she was average. Her personality didn't shine through. She had a nasty attitude and her conversation had my mind wandering off all over the place.

Redbone's face was buried in Ameer's lap. As he leaned back in the flexible theatre seats, her head was bobbing up and down. I thought to myself, no wonder this brother was pushing so hard for me to get with Homegirl. If I wasn't here to keep her out of Redbone's face, he would've lost out.

"Can I say something to you?" Homegirl asked.

"Talk," I told her.

"What the fuck did I ever do to you?" she asked.

"I don't know what you're talking about," I answered calmly. But I could tell without even turning my head towards her that she was getting real wild up.

"Since you first met me you been acting like you too good for me. What's up with that?"

"You don't really want to know," I told her, still calm.

"If I didn't want to know I wouldn't even ask," she shot back with attitude.

"When I first met you, you was with some other dudes," I told her.

"So," she said. "I didn't know you yet."

"You didn't know them either," I answered her. She sat quiet for a minute.

"Then, after you was with them, you switched up and rolled with us," I reminded her.

"So? Your man liked my girl!" she explained.

"Right," was all I answered.

"Right what?" she asked with fury.

"He picked her. Chris picked your other girl. But I didn't pick you," I said calmly. She didn't have no quick response.

"I told you that you didn't really want to know," I said.

After a few seconds, she asked, "If I wouldn'tve been with them other niggas first, and you just met up with us like a coincidence, would you have picked me?"

"Nah," I told her.

"Why?!" she screamed.

A couple of people in the theatre turned around saying "sshh" loudly.

"Relax," I told her. Then I didn't say nothing else.

"Why the fuck not?" she asked, getting loud all over again.

"I'm not saying nothing else. You getting too crazy," I told her.

She stood up and in one unexpected motion dumped the Coke and emptied the popcorn box on me. As I sat there drenched in soda syrup and popcorn butter, I saw myself standing up and choking the shit out of her.

I didn't have to be able to see my Ralph Lauren suede shirt to know that it was ruined. Now I would have to throw away a garment that cost me two weeks' pay. The Coke was all over the already dirty movie theatre floor, mixing with the dirt and grease, and making a paste on the bottom and sides and in the ridges of my Lo boots.

But, my father told me, "Never beat a woman; if she gets crazy, just restrain her." I thought about his words and I thought about getting out of there before this chick got so loud that next thing I would be up against the wall getting patted down by the popo.

Ameer and Chris was on their way over towards us. I got up calmly and told them. "Don't even worry about it. I *knew* I didn't want to fuck with this crazy broad. I'll check y'all tomorrow." I moved to roll out and Homegirl stuck both her feet forward to block my path. I stepped over her and left.

Back on the Deuce, wearing a wet and stained shirt in the night chill of spring, I walked right into a nearby narrow Army & Navy store. I picked out a new crispy green army shirt and pants and popped the tags and put them on. At the register I paid cash and regretfully dropped the Ralph Lauren and my wife beater into the steel wastebasket.

Outside I cleaned my boots off with a bunch of napkins and bottled water I copped from a frank stand.

28

CONFLICT

A lot of cats were milling on my Brooklyn block that night. Springtime brings everybody out who was either hibernating or hiding for the winter.

I was walking through on a humble, home much earlier than I planned to be, maneuvering to stay out of any one guy's path or clique. Still I was watching, catching everything going on to my left and my right, as well as directly in front of me.

Of course I seen Kelvin, aka Conflict, hosting an outside conference in the corner in the dark. I had noticed his black Camry first, with the white leather interior and the big Mercedes-Benz sticker he had plastered across his back window. DeQuan was standing with him in a tight circle of four, his brand new Kawasaki bike parked close by with one of his brothers standing on post to make sure nobody fucked with it.

Conflict broke his quiet conversation off and called me over. Instinctively, I ran my hand over my Caesar cut, paused for a minute then walked over slowly. They all slanted inwards, converting their circle into a semicircle with everybody facing me. Conflict was doing all the talking.

"I see you wearing fatigues tonight," he said. I didn't respond 'cause it wasn't a question and what the fuck did he want anyway? His ten-karat so-called gold, hanging from his neck, was a poorly crafted pendant of a gun.

"Are you a soldier?" he asked me.

"What's up? What'd you call me over for?" I asked him solemnly. He broke a half smile. The other three of them, including Ronald and Rolland Smash, were straight-faced.

"Nah, you ain't no soldier 'cause soldiers know how to get in line," he said. DeQuan cut in. "Nah man. He's good. Lil' man is good," he said firmly.

"You still calling him 'Lil' man' and now he's bigger than you," Conflict reprimanded. The other two laughed. I remained solid.

"This man is about to spread his wings and take flight," Conflict said to the three of them.

"If you don't want nothing, I'm gonna push on," I told Conflict.

"You checking him out?" he asked the other three.

I folded my arms in front of me and looked Conflict in the eye. My green army shirt rose up a little so the metal on my piece could flash a warning into his eye. I knew he was holding. I knew DeQuan was holding. I could see Rolland was holding too. They were all nine or ten years older than me but my nine milli made us even.

"I see how you walk through here styling every day. What I don't see is how and where you earning," Conflict said, sporting his two-piece corduroy Lee suit and brown suede Wallabees.

"So?" I answered.

"This is my hood. I hold it down. You should already know that. Anybody earning out here gotta run it through me. Ya know what I mean?" he threatened.

"I got a job. I ain't hustling," I said dryly. There was a pause and a standoff.

"What about a woman?" he asked out of left field. "*Every time* I see you, you for self. You got some sugar in your tank?" he asked, still serious faced.

"What?" I asked, not knowing what he was asking me. Ronald and Rolland busted out laughing. DeQuan and me remained silent and straight-faced.

"Go ahead, man," Conflict said to me. "And stay in your lane."

I pushed off knowing one thing—this dude, who acted like he already had the best of everything, was hiding some kind of jealousy towards me. He was like a nervous, deadly, and dangerous rattlesnake. I knew he had plenty of bodies under his belt. In fact, he was one of the main cats raising the corpse count in our building.

In the jungle, a rattler, python, mamba, and boa are all poisonous creatures. A tap from the tooth, a too-tight squeeze and death comes quickly. But as my grandfather would say long ago, "There is a mongoose for every snake, a hyena for every lion. Never underestimate anyone."

Upstairs Naja heated up the dinner that Umma had prepared and put to the side for me. She served it out nicely and sat beside me while I ate. Umma was in the living room placing finishing touches on a few items.

"So how are you feeling?" my little sister asked, smiling.

"I'm good. What about you?" I asked, turning it back around.

"Oh, your life is so much more exciting than mine," she said knowingly. I smiled.

"Is that right? Tell me all about it," I asked her since she looked like she knew something I was supposed to know but didn't.

"Somebody came looking for you today," she said.

"Who?" I asked, surprised. "Somebody came up to our door?" I asked again.

"No, she came down to Ms. Marcy's place," Naja admitted.

"Ms. Marcy let someone in her place?" I asked, concerned for real.

"Ms. Marcy was asleep when the girl knocked on the door," Naja said. "I opened the door for her and she came inside," Naja said.

"That couldn'tve been what happened because you know better than to open anybody's door. You know not to speak to strangers or let them in the house. I know you know. I taught you that," I said, growing tight.

"She's not a stranger. She spoke to me three or four times before. On the way to the bus stop sometimes, but usually after school," Naja said.

"And where is Ms. Marcy when all of this is going on?" I asked her.

"She says hello to Ms. Marcy too. Every time she asks about you. She likes you a lot," Naja added.

"Give me her name and stop playing around," I said firmly.

"She has a strange name, Heavenly Paradise. Isn't that the same thing?" Naja asked. "Aren't Heaven and Paradise the same place?" she asked again. "I know in the Quran, Heaven and Paradise are the same place."

"What did she ask you?"

"Once she asked if you have any girlfriends. I told her no. Then she asked what school you go to. I told her I didn't know the name of your school. That's not a lie, is it?"

"Anything else?" I pressed.

"She asked how old are you. She asked how come you're never home. She asked if me and her could be friends. Today she asked if I could give you something for her," Naja said.

"Is that it?" I asked, wanting to collect all of the information while Naja still remembered it clearly.

"One minute, I'll go and get the letter." Naja dashed to her room. She returned. "Here, Heavenly said to give this to you. She said to make sure no one else sees it." She handed me the envelope. I opened it and read:

I'm ready to make you my God. Stop frontin' and come see me, apartment 8F. Peace. It was signed, *"Heaven On Earth."* Even without her signature I would've known it was her by the words she chose.

The Five-Percenter females covered themselves with what they called "three-quarters of cloth." But what difference did it make if she was covered and *still* living foul?

"What does the letter say?" Naja asked.

"Don't worry about it," I answered. "Just sit down right here so I can tell you the rules again. You have to listen carefully to what I say. It's for the security of our family. Do you understand?" I asked Naja seriously.

"That's not all," Naja said strangely.

"What?" I asked.

"Heavenly gave me a gold chain. She put it on my neck so I wouldn't lose it. She made me promise to give it to you and no one else," she said sweetly.

"Where is it?" I asked, worried about how the story kept spreading out more and more.

"Umma has it," Naja answered. She might as well have hit me on the head with a brick.

"Heavenly said to give her chain to you and if you wear it, then you're her God and she's your Earth *and* she's my sister. She said, 'If you don't want my chain, you should bring it back to my apartment and only give it back to me in my hand.'

"She asked me to tell her what you said the next time me and her talk together!" Naja sat there really seeming like she thought Heavenly was her friend. I wanted to tell her that no seventeen-year-old girl's gonna hang out with a seven-year-old child who she's not related to.

"I wasn't gonna mention anything about the necklace to Umma, because Heavenly said not to, but when I took off my *hijab*, I wasn't really thinking about the chain. Umma saw the necklace right away. Then I had to tell Umma the whole story," Naja said, looking worried that she had gotten me into some trouble.

"Listen, Naja, this girl is not your friend and she's not mine either. None of these people around here are our friends. None of these people around here are like us. They don't believe what we believe. They don't live how we live. If you love this family, then you have to understand what I am about to tell you. You have to understand the rules and you have to remember. And there is no space and no time for any mistakes, understand?"

"Yes," she answered, with tears now falling from her big eyes onto her little face.

"I love you. Umma loves you, that's it. Your friends are your same age, the little girls who go to your same school *only*. Anyone who asks you to keep a secret is not your friend. There are no secrets for you to keep away from Umma and me. Ms. Marcy is your sitter. She is supposed to take you to your bus every morning and pick you up every afternoon. If she is ever not there when your school bus drops you off remain with Sister Fatima, your bus monitor. She knows to call Umma in any emergency situation. Don't go anywhere with anybody else, no matter what. Don't talk to anybody else no matter what. Don't take anything from anybody else no matter what. In Ms. Marcy's house and even if you're up here in our apartment don't open the door. Keep it locked. Always let an adult answer the door or leave it alone. No secrets with anyone outside of our family, no one, no matter what. You got it?" I asked her seriously.

"I got it," Naja promised.

"Now repeat it," I told her.

"*The whole thing?*" she asked.

"The whole thing," I ordered her.

She repeated it and repeated it well. She was no dummy. In her school she had to learn long *suras* from the Holy

Quran. After she learned them, and the teachers discussed them, she had to recite them in front of her classmates. I made her recite the rules back to me three times. Then I sat her down so she could write them out as well.

In her room I had her post her writing up on the wall above her bed.

Umma finished up around 1:00 A.M. After straightening up her work area she came into my room.

I had spread newspaper across an area of my floor. On top of the newspaper I had the ones, fives, tens, and twenty-dollar bills separated. In another area, I had separate piles of coins. In another pile were the few receipts I carried for the day, a pile of new orders and inquiries, a short stack of new business cards and my thin notebook of contacts, phone numbers and addresses.

"Who is she and what does she want?" Umma asked, holding up the fourteen-karat gold chain with the word "Heavenly" written out in script letters at the center.

She's nobody," I answered. "She's nobody to me," I assured Umma.

"Every female is somebody," Umma said solemnly. "Every female you involve yourself with leaves her trace on you, good or bad. Did you encourage her?" Umma asked.

"Umma, my word to Allah, I said nothing, did nothing with this female."

"Then she is a desperate woman and desperate women set traps. Make sure you don't lower yourself to her."

I was disappointed. I worked very hard for Umma to trust that there is no greater love or respect than the love and respect that I have for her, and now it seemed that this one silly girl had brought in the only moment of doubt about my character that Umma had ever felt.

At least I understood now what kind of problem Conflict had with me. Like the sucker he was, he couldn't keep his girl in check. Did he really believe he could eliminate every cat she craved? There were many before him and he obviously wasn't even the end of her line. Even if he tried, her cravings would still be there. Then what would he do?

As for the small matter of her chain, damned if I move, damned if I don't move. If I didn't give it back, she'd come on to me even stronger. If I brought it back to her, somebody would see me at her door and start sounding the alarm. Either way, word would get out that she was thirsty for me. Someone would lie and say I was fucking with her. Word of mouth in the hood is stronger than the beat of the drum in my grandfather's village.

All I could see was more conflict with Conflict for no real reason at all.

29

THE CONTRACT

Thursday dissolved so quickly. The day just flew by filled with usual and unusual errands and familiar and unfamiliar faces.

For the first time, Umma and Naja were not sleeping at home. I had escorted both of them to The Palace Hotel. Umma and Naja would remain there with the family of the bride, who had arrived earlier in the day from the Sudan. There were five rooms booked under the bride's father's name, and three rooms under the groom's father's name, not including Fawzi's incredible suite. There would be an Islamic gathering, males hosted separately from the females.

The goal was clear for Umma. She was working for the groom to make the bride's family feel comfortable in an unfamiliar place. She was to do what she does best, make everything look and smell and feel beautiful.

I felt relieved after I left them safely in The Palace. I told myself that I could feel relieved like this every day, once I had both of them out of the area in Brooklyn where we lived. I had already decided that the week after the wedding, we would begin looking at various affordable properties, since we would be in clear reach of our financial goal.

My day was spent traveling and meeting up with and checking in on independent contractors who were retained to perform some service or other for the huge wedding ceremony on Sunday.

However, even training at the dojo and practicing with

the basketball team, I felt lighter with Umma and Naja safely tucked away and surrounded by people who at least, in general, believed the same exact things, no surprises.

Late night alone, I played my music in the apartment. I could walk around with my shirt off. I could exercise in my underwear. In my bedroom, I could throw my knives without a second thought, with the bedroom door open. After my repetitions, I could collapse on the floor staring at the ceiling thinking about Akemi.

Her phone call began with her silence, then just her breathing, then words, "*Mayonaka hansamu arigato gozamasu.*" She was thanking me. That part I could tell.

Those were the only words she said that I understood. The words that followed were all in Japanese, but she seemed so sure about speaking her language to me. I just listened to her soft sound, which slowed down and then sped up, suddenly excited. I decided from her rhythm and melody that she received the balloons, maybe even the flowers I had sent to her uncle's store, and that she would come along with me on Saturday after work to the ceremony.

Her call ended strangely with her silence. Then I could hear her breathing, a pause, and then the words "*Mayonaka Aishiteru.*" The next sound was the click.

I wanted to know the meaning of her last word, but I didn't. I wanted to know from where and what time to pick her up, but I didn't.

While I was thinking about whether or not to call her back this late at her cousin's house, my phone rang again.

"Akemi insisted on calling you first. Now it's me." It was her cousin.

"How are you?" I asked her.

"Okay, I think," she answered. "Anyway, there are balloons everywhere, all over my house," she said.

"Do you like them?" I asked her.

"It doesn't really matter. Akemi loves them. She is thrilled and no one can even talk to her. They're very nice really," she admitted, reluctantly it seemed.

"Will she be able to come on Saturday?" I asked.

"Who can stop her? She was supposed to do something here at our house with our family. It's been planned for so long since we are all out of school and work. But she will come to you on Saturday, no doubt. Uncle has said that if Akemi wants to go along with your family, then I had to go along with you two. I don't want to cancel my plans, so I don't know what is going to happen. I'll let you know," she said.

"One question." I caught the cousin before she hung up the phone.

"*Aishiteru*, what does this word mean?"

"Did Akemi say this to you?" the cousin asked. I paused instead of answering her question.

"I don't know. Maybe you are pronouncing it wrong," she said. "I have to go now." She hung up.

On Saturday at 5:00 P.M. when I rounded the corner to The Palace Hotel, she was standing there. Even though her cousin had phoned me at the very last minute to ask me about the address, I was still stunned.

She was standing taller than usual, and the first thing I noticed were her incredibly expensive black ostrich skinned stiletto heels and matching black ostrich clutch bag. She wore a silk black dress, which was well tailored to her figure and cut short just below her hips. She wrapped her waistline with a beautiful silver grey scarf causing her mini dress to ride up even higher. Thankfully she wore matching black silk capris underneath, covering her legs. Her dark eyes came out more, with the coordination of her clothes. They were like an endless sea of beauty.

Her natural nails were manicured immaculately with a clear polish with a hint of a grey sheen that could only be noticed if you looked closely. Her jet black hair, the way it flowed and surrounded the jet black dress, and the way her jet black eyes peered from her face—I was floored by her. I felt everything shifting within me. Still, I managed to appear cool.

Playfully, I walked past her as if she wasn't standing right there. She called out my name softly as if I could have missed seeing her standing there. She followed behind me quietly. Even the sound of her heels against the pavement caught my attention and aroused me. Yet, it was impossible for me to follow my natural instincts.

I should have ordered a magic carpet. Her shoes, alone, were too expensive for the ground, I thought to myself.

In the lobby of the hotel, I pulled the silver grey scarf she had wrapped tightly around her waistline of her dress and put it over her hair instead, tying it in the back. She was still and allowed me. We were standing so close that her scent gave me fever.

The way I tied it wasn't a Muslim style of wearing the scarf, but it was fashionable the way Akemi would rock it. It complemented her, while covering her hair as all of the women in the ceremony would have their hair covered. Truthfully, I wanted to cover her hair. I had begun to feel that it was mine, for only me to see, and that she was mine also.

The elevator door opened, revealing Umma and Naja.

Umma was a radiant star. Her silver thobe, made of an elegant and fine sheer cloth, was a sparkling outer garment to her long silver grey dress beneath. During the two and a half days of our separation, she had applied a beautiful henna design to her fingers, hands, and feet. Her style and beauty had everyone passing through The Palace Hotel lobby in complete awe. Two curious and fascinated European ladies interrupted her, delaying her from reaching us.

I introduced Akemi to Umma and Naja in Arabic. Instinctively, Akemi bowed her head down to Umma. When she raised it up, she reached out to Umma's hands and flipped them over, feeling her palms with her fingers, her eyes showing complete amazement at Umma's henna art. Even after several seconds, Akemi was still staring and holding Umma's wrists.

Umma smiled, adjusted her hand to hold Akemi's, and began walking away with her, only saying to me in Arabic, "We will see you tonight at the ceremony. I love you, son."

Naja held back and said, "She is sooo pretty."

"She doesn't speak English," I informed Naja. "And she doesn't know what's happening here today."

"Well, she should fit right in!" Naja laughed.

I gave Naja a kiss on the cheek and told her, "Take good care of Akemi," then sent her on her way to catch up with the ladies.

In Fawzi's suite, I warmly greeted the Sudanese men gathered there in the living room. I felt like I was not myself. Right then I was my father in his private area of our estate, greeting his guest and business associates, a gathering of men in the finest suits and most elegant traditional wear as well, surrounded by swirling cigar, cigarette, and *bidi* smoke. The quiet murmur of the men speaking only the important words, following through on previous agreements and making new plans and deals, filled the suite.

In the foyer, I pulled out a heavy wooden chair, with a dense cushion, that was covered by a thick upholstery embroidered with a scene of the bland British ancients. I sat down. I needed to be seated close to the telephone. Discreetly, I began calling business numbers on a long checklist that I had prepared to make sure that every detail was absolutely covered for tomorrow's wedding.

There were the tent builders, who had already constructed

the wedding site. I needed to confirm the tent takedown and final payment date. There were the painters, two Sudanese and two Iranians whose services Umma and I contracted. I needed to push those guys. They did great work but were scheduled to complete their job yesterday morning. Yesterday evening when I phoned them I found them, "still finishing up," which delayed me from arranging their payment. The fruit, flower, and candy deliveries for tomorrow morning needed to be reconfirmed, even though I had confirmed them yesterday. The portable commode people needed a confirmation as well, and then there was the company where we rented the chairs . . .

I had an hour and a half before the limousines would arrive here at The Palace. So I used my time effectively.

When the groom's uncle, Mr. Ghazzali, arrived he and I would get squared away with all of the checks that needed to be issued to pay the various independent contractors. We would go over the details once more so that everything would flow as planned, *inshallah*.

Limousines lined the cluttered streets of New York and brought the business at The Palace Hotel to a standstill. Seated inside of one of them, I watched Umma, Akemi, and Naja entering another limo with some women from the bride's family. Akemi was the last to get in. She stood watching everything as though she were not a part of it. She looked left to right, stared at the women from head to toe and eventually gazed up at the sky.

I traveled with Fawzi, his father and uncle, and two male cousins. Fawzi's father was intense and pensive, the way powerful men (like my father) tend to be. He and his son were dressed to the nines in tuxedos. I had chosen a clean black Armani suit. All of our white shirts were glistening. Uncle Ghazzali and his two sons all wore white *jelabiyas*. Believe me, they were looking sharp and crisp as well. There was not one speck to blemish the bright whiteness of their cloths. On the floor of the limo were six pairs of brand new shoes, ranging from Mr. Ghazzali's JCPenney's to Fawzi and his father's mean and authentic black crocodiles. I felt powerful seated among all of them, although my status was the same today as it was yesterday.

"A small ceremony at the mosque for the signing of the *agid*," Umma had said. "Nothing compared to the actual wedding ceremony."

The spacious, medium-sized mosque was filled up with the groom and bride's relatives. Despite the expensive wears, when the call to prayer, the *Azan*, was sung out, in complete unity, the *ummah* bowed their heads to the ground and made *salat*. The feeling was so unexpected and awesome, to be welcomed into a mosque and make prayer among an international, Islamic community right here in America. I felt overwhelmed.

There was such incredible power in the call to prayer. It humbled even the richest of the believers. The words entered the body, aroused the spirit, and soothed the soul. They caused the knees to willingly bend, and the head to touch the ground in a way that no believing man would bow for any other reason any other time.

Imam Musa was in *jelabiya*, his head wrapped in a turban. He was a tall Sudanese African. He sat facing the *ummah* and in front, but between the bride's family and the groom's family. He had a small table at his side, and a Holy Quran mounted on a carved wooden stand. After his salutations to Allah, he offered the *khutba*, which is the "spiritual message," exclusively in the Arabic language.

"It is the responsibility of a Muslim man to be the guardian of his wife and family. In today's times, the non-believers scream, " 'Why marriage? Why limit myself? Why bother?'

"In Islam we have always had a tradition of marriage.

We marry however, not because it is a tradition, but because Allah requires this from us and Allah is the best knower of all things, and Allah always commands us to do what is best for us, whether we know it or not.

"The arrogant will scream, '*I know* what is best for me! I don't care what is best for everybody else!'

"But, a person who is arrogant is also ignorant. Otherwise, arrogance would not be his chosen way of life.

"We marry because a complete family is the foundation of life and civilization. Where there is a man who willingly bows down to Allah, and voluntarily obeys Allah's laws, there is a man *capable* of respecting limits, of being a good husband, the responsible party and good father. *Not* sometimes, but each and every day.

"A woman who bows down to Allah, and obeys Allah's laws, is a good woman who is modest, wise, and mature of intellect. Women who are wise, are the opposite of boastful, conceited, and flagrant. And a boastful, conceited, and flagrant woman is never necessarily intelligent.

"Where there is a humble man who accepts the limits imposed on him by God, a man who bows his head in prayer, thought, and praise along with a modest woman who observes her limits and bows her head in prayer, thought, and praise, happy children can be born to live happy and balanced lives. Happy and balanced children respect their parents, because it was their parents who cultivated their knowledge of Allah. Happy children, in turn, bow their heads in prayer, thought, and praise as they witnessed their parents do.

"Among the arrogant, ignorant, proud, and boastful nonbelieving people there are born nations of unhappy children, living unbalanced lives, drowning in depression and anxieties, children who love things more than they love the womb which bore them.

"Arrogant, ignorant men make horrible husbands to their

wives whether they are rich or poor. They make horrible fathers to their children, are full of fancy and deceitful words and promises. But they are only capable of the 'no show.' Even with a pocket or bank filled with money in their name, they can only pay out in pain and sadness. There is a short life for them on Earth, and an eternal and roaring fire in their future.

"Immodest, boastful women of no shame and no limits make horrifying wives and mothers who can only make themselves look and appear good. But, they are rotten on the insides and in their wombs is only misery.

"But enough of this, today is a celebration of this Muslim man and this Muslim woman who together will bow their heads in prayer and thought and praise to Allah, who have both agreed to live their lives and conduct themselves in accordance with Allah's laws. And *inshallah*, they will bring forth many happy children who will live good lives and do good things and humble themselves in prayer and thought and praise of Allah too."

Each of his words fell like large rocks on my shoulders and head. I was reminded of what I must do and in which order I must do it. But I was not a hundred percent confident that I could get it right.

My eyes surveyed the people in the room, as Imam Musa carried out the asking and answering of the questions to the bride and groom. There was Fawzi and his father and mother seated beside him. I could see now that he also had three sisters who were older than him as well. He was not only the only son, he was the baby of his family. Still he looked strong seated up there with his family, including his uncle and aunt and their two sons and three daughters.

This scenario reminded me of my father posing for a rare photo we had taken at our estate on the last day that I saw him. It was my father standing beside Umma, his first wife, and Amata, his second wife, and Hanifah, his third wife. My northern grandfather was there, my Umma's two brothers were there with their children, cousins of course and babies, brothers and sisters and an unborn Naja lying safely in a welcoming womb.

In the delight of the completed signatures and *agid* agreement, I caught a glance of Akemi, who held on to Umma as if they had known each other for years. I thought to myself, *Ain't nothing wrong with that.*

Mr. Ghazzali and I had to go. He said we would take one of the town cars and head to Westchester, which was the wedding ceremony site. We needed to check with our eyes to assure that everything was perfect for tomorrow. "This evening was the spiritual seal," he said. "Tonight is the party for the groom and his male family and friends, and another for the bride and her female family and friends. Tomorrow is the splendor." He had a genuine energy, excitement, and happiness about his nephew's wedding. Even though I could easily see that the greatest portion of their extended family's wealth was in his older brother's hands, I felt nothing but love and commitment coming from Mr. Ghazzali towards all of his family members.

I thought, however, that the splendor would be when the groom finally gets to lift the veil of his wife in privacy and gets to know his peace.

Umma's eyes moved over me carefully as I stood before her and Akemi. Then her eyes moved over Akemi as well, then back and forth like a Ping-Pong match.

"Akemi can remain with me while you go handle the business," she said. "We have to return to The Palace for the bride's *hennana*," she said.

"*Hennana?*" I asked, wondering.

"It's the party for the bride, women only. We will bathe her. I will prepare her and paint on her henna. You will see the results tomorrow night at the wedding ceremony," Umma said, speaking only in Arabic.

"And Akemi? I have to bring her back home to her family tonight," I said.

"When you are finished working, return to The Palace. Phone up to the penthouse. Akemi and Naja will come down. You can take Naja along with you as you return Akemi to her home," she said softly. No matter how gently she spoke, I knew this is how it needed to happen, no negotiations.

The smooth ride of the Lincoln town car lulled Naja to sleep. Of course she sat in between Akemi and I, falling off into Akemi's lap the same as she would if it were Umma.

As the driver sped around the deep curves of Edgewater and up into the cliffs of Englewood, Akemi placed the palm of her hand onto the back of my neck. Through flashes of light provided by ignited signs and random street lamps, we looked into one another deeply.

Her hair was down now, falling mostly on her left shoulder. The scarf was in the palm of her left hand. Her million-dollar shoes were off. Her pretty feet rested on the car carpet. Her toes were nicely shaped, nails clear with the hint of a polished grey tint like her fingernails. Her feet looked soft and beautiful like the inside of her thighs.

Sensations were flowing through my body as she caressed my ears and touched the side of my face. The West African driver appeared oblivious to everything except the road. If she kept it up, I would not be able to stand up when the car stopped. Right now the only thing separating me from the long sermon of Imam Musa was my respect for my young sister and the wrong impression I would've caused if she woke up and saw me all over Akemi, giving in to my intense feelings.

I knew I could not hold on to this warm sixteen-year-old female by keeping her waiting and desiring and in a holding pattern.

Finally, parked in front of the plum tree on Honeysuckle Lane, the driver shifted gears into reverse and landed us in front of the long path to her cousin's house, which was lit up by small metal lamps that led to the front door. The driver hopped out to open my door.

"I got it. Good looking out," I told him, so he would get back in his seat. I got out instead and moved around the back of the car to her side. I opened the door and helped her place her pretty feet back into her shoes.

I awoke Naja to free up Akemi's lap. She climbed out dazed and dizzy. She awakened slowly as the spring night chill alerted her senses. I extended my hand for Akemi. She came willingly.

"Pop the trunk," I told the driver, grabbing Akemi's shopping bag of items she had collected at the bride's party and probably from Umma as well.

We three walked up her path quietly, Akemi's hand held onto the back of my belt. Her body was brushing against my back with our every step.

"Nice house," Naja said. "Are we going inside?" she asked.

"No, the driver is waiting for us. I'll take you right back to The Palace with Umma," I told her.

In front of the door, I reached into my inside jacket pocket and pulled out an engraved wedding invitation. I handed it to Akemi and said, "If you would like to come to the wedding tomorrow, I would love to see you." I smiled at her in the dark, knowing that she could not understand. She smiled at me too.

"She doesn't speak English. I thought you already knew," Naja informed me.

Half a second later, her cousin pulled open the front door.

"Whose car is that?" she interrogated without a proper greeting.

"Ours," I answered.

"It's almost midnight," she said. Instantly, Akemi began speaking to her softly in their language.

I interrupted them. "I have to leave now, good night," I said.

"Good night," her cousin said hurriedly like, "sure go."

"The wedding is tomorrow evening. If Akemi would like to come, we can meet at The Palace in the lobby at 3:00 P.M. We were there today. Akemi knows where it is," I said to the cousin as I grabbed my sister's hand to leave.

"Wedding!" her cousin raised her voice. I smiled, realizing she didn't know.

"Not me and Akemi's wedding tomorrow. Maybe some other day," I teased. "Just look on the invitation. Akemi has it in her hand," I said. "If she can't come, it's okay."

30

THE WEDDING

The next morning at 8:00 A.M. I was on the grounds of the wedding ceremony. In true form to Sudanese weddings, the gathering would not begin until 5:00 P.M., in hopes of really getting it moving by 6:00 P.M. Sudanese are known to work hard, but when it came to celebrations and parties, the festivities started late and would go on well into the early morning.

I put in six hours, accepted the deliveries and squared the independent contractors away properly. Umma was given six or seven workers to carry out her instructions for the day. She told me and then I told them exactly what to do.

When everything was the way she wanted it, I called the car service and we were taken back to The Palace Hotel.

We needed to shower again and dress there. Our clothes were in Umma's room, and Umma had to ride back up to the wedding with the arriving bride, after making certain she was a perfect vision.

Fawzi's barber hit me with a fresh line up at the hotel, the last in a long line of priority heads.

The shower water refreshed me. I was feeling exhausted from the past week's heavy workload and brief sleeps. I was glad this was our last day of service to the wedding, especially since I had only one more tailored suit. You see, no Sudanese would wear jeans, no matter how expensive they were, or kicks to a special occasion.

Fresh dressed, I pressed the button for the elevator. When

the doors opened, I got on. Standing in the corner, also riding down, was a pretty face and familiar set of eyes. It was Sudana, who served me the Sudanese sweets in the Bronx, the daughter of Mr. Ghazzali.

She moved her eyes from mine and I did the same, as was customary. She spoke.

"*Salaam*," she said. "I saw you yesterday evening at the mosque."

"Yes, I was working for your father," I admitted.

"You were looking very nice for a worker." She smiled. "And today . . ." she continued.

"Today you are looking very nice as the cousin of the groom," I said, swiftly interrupting her compliments towards me and showering them onto her instead.

"That's funny," she said with a laugh. "Do you really mean it?"

The doors opened. Akemi was standing there poised to enter the elevator. She smiled brightly.

"Akemi," I said, stepping out into the lobby.

"Nice shoes," Sudana complimented Akemi, looking down on her authentic dark blue alligator open-toe high heels, the straps crisscrossing across her pretty feet and up her ankle. Those shoes were more than "nice."

"She doesn't speak English," I told Sudana.

"Your girlfriend?" Sudana asked me with a coy half smile. She knew it was a trick question, since she and I are both Muslim and are both not allowed to date outside of a marriage.

"Friend," I replied.

"She looks like more than a friend to me," Sudana said comfortably, knowing that Akemi could not understand her. But looking at Akemi, I was certain that even though she could not understand the words, she could understand the moment.

"No worries," Sudana said sweetly with a woman's sarcasm. "We are living in America now and I have heard that in America, you can do anything, no rules." She smiled, penetrating me with her Sudanese wildcat eyes, the rest of herself covered in a Sudanese forest green thobe, which accentuated that untamed feeling she let off.

Breaking the moment, I chose to introduce them. "Sudana, this is Akemi. Akemi, this is Sudana."

They each said something, but both of their sets of erotic eyes were really doing all of the talking.

Just then, Akemi's little angry translator from her uncle's store skipped into action. "What's going on here?" she asked, with her two fists balled up and on her hips. I was surprised to see her. She was dressed up like a sweet little princess, with a bunch of ribbons in her hair. I didn't let her childlike looks fool me though. I knew she was a firecracker.

I put my arm around Akemi's waist. Sudana looked at me hard and said, "See you at the wedding."

"All right then," was all I said.

I took Akemi and her cousin up to Umma before the rumor spread that I was embracing a female in the lobby.

"*Mayonaka*," Akemi placed her hands gently on the little girl's shoulders, "*Saachi*," she said, introducing us.

"*Konichiwa*, Saachi," I said.

"You know I speak English," the little girl said with attitude.

"You're right," I said.

"And you should thank me," the little girl pushed.

"Why is that?" I asked.

"Because without me, Akemi wouldn't even be here today. My father said—" Akemi's hand was over Saachi's mouth. It was the only thing that stopped Saachi from talking since she appeared in the hotel lobby.

She knelt down to the little girl's height level. The curve

of Akemi's legs pressed against her soft silk wave skirt, which covered most of her legs but was cut on a seductive angle. I admired the deep blue authentic alligator sash that crossed over her soft ruffled blue blouse, and held her alligator-skinned knapsack in place on her back. It matched her shoes exactly. She must have gone shopping in that vault at Bergdorf's, I thought to myself.

I couldn't overlook that she had covered her hair today. She wore a deep blue Hermès silk scarf tied tight to hold in her thick hair. Somehow, with some scissors, I figured, she had shaped the extra material into the shape of a flower blossom, a head wrap unlike anything I had ever seen. Her sense of style was unique, attractive, and flawless.

She spoke Japanese to the little girl. Whatever she told her, the little girl made a mean face at first but then straightened up.

I really didn't want to cause Akemi any problems with her family. Yet I had been working so hard over these past few days and that was what I had to concentrate on, to complete the job and reap the reward for Umma and my family.

Naja was excited to meet Saachi. Saachi greeted and treated Naja better than I had seen her treat anyone else. I escorted them to Umma. I left them, all my ladies, there together.

I got right back into work mode.

There is this sound that Sudanese women make with the waving of their tongue that causes everyone everywhere to stop, listen, and take notice. I had not heard it in seven years. I was hearing it now. Not from one woman, but six hundred females from the youngest to the eldest, tongues waving a shrilling high sound. The wedding was about to begin.

The piercing call of the women brought on the frantic

drumming from the men. The scent of Umma's perfumes and elixirs intoxicated the air. Lemongrass was used to repel the insects. Sandalwood and jasmine were to lure the people and hold them there.

There was an explosion of colors, every shade, pattern, and blend imaginable except red and gold, which was traditionally reserved for the bride. The Sudanese women were the only ones more beautiful than the ten thousand gardenias, orchids, and roses, which were hanging, sprinkled, and dangling everywhere.

The Sudanese men, tall, strong, and adorned in fabulous fabrics, some with turbans, some with kufis, some bareheaded, moved in the procession with an excited coolness. It was an army, I thought to myself. Yet I wondered where they all had come from, and why were so many of them living here in America now. I smiled, realizing that only a wedding could draw them out in these great numbers. Otherwise, these proud Sudanese men would all be hardworking, hidden, anonymous and invisible to everyone except their families because of the way we tend to separate ourselves from anything unfamiliar. Still, we were all here living in America gathered at a wedding, enjoying yet wishing we were back home, I'm sure.

No one except Umma could have created a beautiful Sudanese village right there in Westchester. The sea of genuinely happy and excited people opened up under the curved tent that was the size of half of an American football field. It was not a standard white tent. The inside walls were adorned with red, yellow, and gold murals, painted with passion by the two Iranian and two Sudanese painters. The explosion of colorful art made an already warm evening feel warmer and extremely welcoming.

As the drumming eased down to a soft simmer, the people sat down in waves, some in chairs, some on stools, many on the huge royal red carpet, which stretched across the lawn.

Sixteen young Sudanese teen girls decked in tangerine thobes sang a song of prayer all together, their voices filled with emotion. Their hands were wrapped around thick circular gold candles. Hot wax gathered in a small pool at the top of each candle yet below the flickering flame.

Sixteen young Sudanese males all dressed in brown and gold recited the *Fatiha* all at once.

The bride appeared, shimmering. She stood out like Sirius, the brightest star in the universe. The intricate gold embroidery brocade that lined her royal red thobe was unmatched. The red sheer cloth, which draped over her hair and body, had the gold beadwork carefully placed to highlight her beauty. On her face were a line of gold beads that stretched across her forehead featuring her exquisite green eyes which were outlined with black kohl. Her cinnamon skin color was a perfect canvas for Umma's artwork.

She tilted her head downward and placed one hand over her face. Her fingers, hands, and palms now revealed the elegance of Umma's carefully drawn henna. Her wrist was glistening with the ten diamond bangles, which not one of three thousand eyes failed to notice. Prisms of colors sparkled from them and were dancing throughout the crowd. Her other hand, down at her side, jingled with ten twenty-four-karat gold bangles, which were banging also.

The soft light cloth of her garment suggested a beautiful figure but did not give it all away. Fawzi is fortunate, I thought. So far, his parents had not disappointed him.

The bride was facing both her mother and father. She dropped down and kissed their knees as an acknowledgment and show of respect. Also with her were her four younger sisters, and four brothers, all of whom had come to the U.S. for their first time and only for their sister's wedding.

How powerful their father must feel, I thought to myself; to have brought forth nine children, to have raised his eldest seventeen-year-old daughter properly under his careful eye, to give her hand in such a grand gathering to such a successful man and family. The father had been a careful planner. Allah had given him a great sign of approval.

I believed every person was either reflecting on their own wedding, or dreaming of what was to come and hoping that it could be half as perfect for them also.

Right across from the huge tent was their newly built home, a sturdy American mansion made of bricks. Fawzi and his wife would be the first to have ever lived in the house, which Umma had wrapped in a three-foot-wide ribbon that was also twenty thousand feet long, culminating in a huge bow that was mounted on their front door.

Outside of their new home was a stone water fountain that continuously sprayed water into the air, caught it on one of its stone shelves, and let it flow down dribbling and gurgling like a stream.

Of course there was a huge black iron electric gate that secured his acres. But the gate was wide open to everyone for today. A Sudanese wedding welcomes the community to the happiest day in a man's life outside of the birth of his daughter or son. Even curious neighbors would not have been turned away on the wedding day.

Fawzi and his bride sat on a king-sized mattress blanketed with a wickedly patterned red and gold crocheted cover, which Umma stitched. On top of the crocheting were pounds and pounds of rose petals. At the center of the tent they sat declaring their oaths to one another under the guide of their guardians and Imam. The word "*Qabul*" was spoken by Fawzi and his bride, then repeated by many in celebration, signaling the completion of the official aspect of the wedding.

Umma stood up front and off to the side watching every-thing with a critical eye. I thought it would be impossible for her to find one flaw. She had done a tremendous job of expressing a culture that she knew and lived so well. Wear-ing sky blue, she was behind both her *hijab* and *niqab* today, her identity shielded, just an incredible set of eyes, an artist, a supervisor, a worker, a woman who wanted to be left alone with her memories, feelings, and thoughts more than she wanted to be recognized and commended.

As the live band played, every comfort was made avail-able to the huge crowd courtesy of Fawzi's family finances and Umma Designs. There was an elaborate stretch of tables covered in fine cloths, which offered all Sudanese foods, catered by the North African Food Company. There was a spread of breads, cheeses and chutneys, sauces, soups, beans, lentils, olives, salads, vegetables, and stews. There were grilling stations offering chicken, beef, and lamb. There were dessert stations offering creams, custards, car-amels, yogurts, finger cakes, and sorbets. There were fruit stations offering mangoes, guavas, dates, oranges, apples, hibiscus, and lemon. There were Sudanese drink stations offering Aradib, Maaza, Carcaday, Mirinda, and Stim. There was the tea lady and the coffee bean fryer. There were water and ice stations. People could become full on the aroma of this elaborate feast alone.

In business mode, I worked the crowd as the party jumped off. I introduced myself as part of the wedding plan-ning team while handing out business cards to brothers, sons, uncles, cousins, and fathers. In some instances I collected their cards as well.

The bride performed an erotic celebration dance for her new husband, surrounded by a curtain of colorful cloths held up by her female friends, and I could hear their cheering.

As I continued my networking, I would whiz by people

speaking all kinds of different languages and dialects. Parts of conversations would capture my attention.

"Yes, he had the house built. It was one million dollars for the property and another million for the house." "U.S. dollars?" They chuckled at the unimaginable sum for the average worker. Years ago, my father's wealth was viewed with the same type of awe, when compared to the amounts earned by the average Sudanese family living in the Sudan.

"Back home, for that amount of money, he could have lived forever like a king, owning land stretching as far as he could see."

"Look at the few acres such big numbers buys him here!"

"*Inshallah* he will survive this purchase. What he'll pay each year in property taxes alone will be more than I pay to rent my entire apartment for the year."

I was listening carefully. Now I realized that the house and the property could cost two separate large sums. Even after you officially buy and own the land, you still have to pay the U.S. government a large property tax. It didn't sound fair, yet it sounded true.

"No worries. The bank gave him a huge loan. When he pays the mortgage, the price of the loan repayment, the interest on the loan, house insurance, and property tax costs are all included."

"That's not free money. You make it sound so easy."

"Well, he's got thirty years to pay it back."

I felt myself sinking into the lawn under the weight of these words. I could feel that they were not exaggerated. They were the details that men discuss between themselves. These were the burdens that men must carry quietly.

"He's a big man, son of a bigger man, from a good family! He will do fine," one of the men speaking said, gesturing wildly like he was speaking to the deaf.

It was the eldest man of eighty years or more who made

the startling prediction, "When he adds up the price of a Sudanese bride, clothes, jewels, the honeymoon, and the six kids that will come out in the first six years or less, he'll go crazy and die of an American heart attack at age thirty-four."

"Allah forbid!" the others said all at once.

"He has a Ph.D. in Chemical Engineering. He will be more wealthy than he is right now in no time. America will pay him handsomely to make bombs for them to drop all over the world!"

"Even on the Sudan?!" the elder asked. Everyone grew quiet.

Sudana snuck up on me. "I saw you from across the room. You looked thirsty," she said offering me a glass of guava juice.

"Thank you. You seem to always be seeing me."

"Can I prepare a plate of food for you?" she asked.

"No, thank you," I told her. She looked disappointed. She paused then regrouped. Standing beside me, but with her body turned away as though she and I were not actually conversing, she said, "She's pretty and she's probably smart too, must be. But, is she Sudanese?" she asked.

I smiled, knowing she was speaking about Akemi. I didn't answer. I knew where she was heading with it. Every Sudanese will tell the other, "Marry Sudanese and no one else! Only a Sudanese woman will share your beliefs, language, traditions, and know what is expected of her. Only a Sudanese woman would know, most importantly, what not to do."

"Is she even Muslim?" Sudana said softly.

"She doesn't have to be. You know a Muslim man can marry a non-Muslim woman, because she will follow his lead. But you can never marry a non-Muslim man because he will surely mislead you," I said, smiling.

"So clever," she responded and walked away into the crowd.

Not as clever as you, I thought to myself. I wasn't mad at Sudana. But I wouldn't play with her either. Sudanese women receive our highest respect. She is also the daughter of the man with whom I was doing the biggest business our company has ever done. Why should I lie to her when my whole everything was caught up and locked into Akemi so tight?

Sudana couldn't possibly know, I didn't pick Akemi because she was not Muslim or not Sudanese. Akemi just happened to me like how a day radiant with sunshine converts into a downpour of rain in seconds. Now I was drenched and I liked it. Akemi felt good and true and right for me in every way.

As I walked, I spotted the imam head on. I also saw Sudana place herself right beside Akemi on the other side of the tent. They stood together like two gazelles.

"*A-Salaam Alaikum*, Imam Musa, I have a question please," I asked respectfully.

"*Alaikum Salaam*, young brother." He nodded me on.

"What age does a male have to be to marry?" I asked. He smiled.

"The wedding has inspired you?" he asked.

"I was inspired before the wedding. I heard your *khutba* last night. I want to do what is right, before I do what is wrong. Do you follow my words?" I asked him.

"Of course," he said solemnly.

"Your Holy Quran does not give an age for marriage. It is only that you are required to be of the age of puberty," he said, watching for my reaction.

"Then it is legal?" I asked. "Can a fourteen-year-old take a wife?" I asked again.

"There is a difference between Allah's law and the law of this United States," he said. "Allah requires that you marry a female before engaging in sexual intercourse. Sex with any woman who is not your wife is *harom*, forbidden.

"The United States does not require marriage for sexual intercourse. It simply requires that an adult not have sex with a child.

"In this State of New York, legally you may marry at age fifteen with your parents' permission, and the permission of the parents of the bride if she is also young. At fourteen, however, you cannot marry legally in the State of New York.

"What is the rush?" he asked. I didn't answer, just looked into his eyes solemnly. As a man, more than an imam, I was sure he knew what the rush was about.

"Self-restraint can be achieved through fasting," he suggested. "If you fast, Allah will reduce your desires so that you might control yourself. In my view, the opportunity to have sexual intercourse freely should not be the only reason you take a wife."

He waited for me to say something in response. But I was racing into my own thoughts. In July, on the twenty-seventh, I would turn fifteen years old. This was only three months away. Yet I didn't know when Akemi's birthdate was. And then of course the permission of both of our parents was the problem. I could barely get an audience with her uncles, and the fact that her father was overseas was a huge dilemma. How could I win his confidence that I am his daughter's match?

"Take a look around, son. Fawzi's father has been working, planning, and saving for this great occasion since his son's birth, for more than two decades. Even the groom has done his part. He studied diligently and worked very hard. It takes patience and determination to attain certain things and levels in life," the imam said.

"But a poor man may take a wife and marry and love her. If he is a good man, she will follow him even into a mud hut?" I asked, borrowing Fawzi's lines.

"A good woman will marry a good man and follow him

wherever he may lead. This is true," the imam offered. "Two male witnesses or one male and two female witnesses and to recite the *Nikah* and gift the *Mahr* is all that Allah requires."

"And if a poor man who has reached puberty chooses a wife, he can still work hard and achieve wealth and the blessings of Allah, can't he? Choosing a wife does not make him poor, right?"

"A good wife makes the poorest of men wealthy. You are right," the imam agreed.

"*Shukran*, Imam Musa," I said, thanking him. He gave me his card.

Saachi dashed by. Naja chased her. Some woman must have fallen in love with Saachi and draped a *hijab* over her head. Now Saachi's hair was covered just as Naja's was.

By the night's end, the guests were filled to the brim. The children were exhausted from running, clapping, singing, playing jump rope, double dutch, and double orange. The males were checking their watches and easing their families away in preparation for Monday morning. The beautiful ribbon was cut, the bow busted open. Fawzi escorted his wife into their new house for her first time.

"In his new house, Fawzi will remove her shoes and wash her feet," Umma said, standing beside me, seeming to reminisce.

Mr. Ghazzali appeared, resting his hand on my shoulder, smiling and sighing with great approval. "It is time to settle our accounts, young man. I have to travel back to the Bronx with my family. There is work and school tomorrow. For you too." He checked his Timex. "It's already the next day, really," he said with a tired smile.

After I counted and recounted the final payment of five thousand dollars cash in his presence, I pulled out his receipt, which I had already written up. Our business card was stapled on top.

"Thank you for choosing Umma Designs," I said. "We are forever grateful for your business. If you are satisfied with our work, please do not hesitate to recommend our services to a friend or coworker." We shook hands.

"Your work will recommend itself. Everyone has personally witnessed what your company has done. You will have an abundance of business in the near future, I'm sure."

He leaned in with a laugh and said, "Maybe I should fire my sons and hire you."

"The cleaning company will arrive in the morning, and the canopy company, the commode company, and the North African Food Company representatives will come to collect their supplies. Would you like me to meet you here in the morning?" I asked.

"Wah! You have the money in your hands and you are still offering your services? Join me!" he said with a new burst of energy and a slap to my back.

"Thank you for the offer. But I'm good working for Umma. You know, family comes first," I told him. We were both speaking in Arabic. He leaned in again as though he was about to share a big secret with me.

"The driver of the town car number nineteen, out front, will chauffeur you and your family back to The Palace Hotel, courtesy of Mr. Ghazzali. Get a good night's rest. Check out at noon tomorrow. Your duties have been completed, *Allah Hafiz*, son," he said, meaning may Allah keep you well.

"*Shukran*," I told him, meaning thank you, in Arabic.

Umma, Akemi, and Naja were patiently waiting for me while Saachi skipped around the entire empty tent still bursting with energy same as if it was midday. I gestured and told them, "One more minute, ladies." As I walked away to the three-foot-tall vase where I stashed my gun underneath some wood chips earlier; to my surprise and alarm, it wasn't there. I searched again. I stood up thinking and worrying and reassuring myself that no one saw me drop it in there and that there would be no reason for anyone to go digging in one of the wedding props either. It didn't matter though. Either way, my joint was still missing.

Sudana walked over, distracting me at a bad moment. Akemi saw Sudana from across the room. She was walking over toward me as well. Umma and Naja watched. Saachi was singing her version of one of the wedding songs she heard earlier.

"I wrapped this up for you," Sudana said, handing me a gift.

"It's okay, Sudana, Umma Designs provided the wedding gifts to the guests. So I don't need one." Akemi arrived. We stood there, the three of us.

"Oh, I think you'll need this. I'm sure I have *what you are looking for*," Sudana said, her wildcat eyes changing colors right before me. I stared at the nicely wrapped gift box in her opened hand. Akemi stared too.

"I would have held it for you all night if you asked me to," Sudana said. I took the gift. Now I knew it was my gun.

"Thank you, Sudana, really, and good night," I said, relieved.

"There is no thank you between us," she said with a smile. "There is no thank you between friends." She smiled even more. "And, we three are all *friends*, right?" she asked, then turned towards Akemi. "And, good night, Akemi. Thank you for coming. It was a pleasure to meet you."

As she walked away, she waved politely, believing that Akemi could not decipher her flirtations. But I knew she was underestimating Akemi.

Out front it was fairly dark. I looked around, my eyes adjusting after having been in the bright lights in the yard.

As soon as the town car pulled around, directly in front of Umma, I opened the door for her. I took her shopping bags. She got in. As Akemi stooped to get in with her bags, I grabbed her hand discreetly and pulled her towards me. I told Naja and Saachi to get in the car first instead.

I took her shopping bags also, then walking Akemi around to the trunk, I knocked on the trunk door, signaling the driver to open up. As I packed in Umma's two full shopping bags, I tilted my head in the direction of the Japanese dude standing way across the street, in the dark shadows, underneath a newborn tree with slim branches.

Without words, I was asking her if she recognized him.

Akemi exhaled as she stared off in the Japanese guy's direction.

By this time I could see that there were three other dudes seated in a black Infiniti sedan parked over there, although I couldn't make their faces.

She wasn't saying nothing and for some reason, neither were they. I walked Akemi to our car door, and pushed her inside the car with Umma. I left her shopping bag on the ground. I leaned in through the front passenger window and told the driver to give me five minutes.

I stooped down as if I was tying my shoes and tore the paper from the gift and pulled out my twenty-two. I left the box on the ground, stood up, and tucked my joint in my belt. I walked over there slowly, stopping halfway in the middle of the street, standing on a weird angle not to give them any advantage. I did not know this dude. But from what little I could see, I knew I didn't like his looks.

In the dark I asked, "What's up?" There was no wedding welcome or smile on my face or in my tone of voice.

"I came for Akemi," he answered in a firm emotionless voice that didn't sound right in my ear.

"Who are you to her?" I asked. Now I had my right hand on my tool.

Their back car window rolled down revealing the profile

of Jiro and Kano, the two Japanese brothers I played basketball with in Jersey.

"It's us, man. Uncle sent us to pick up Akemi. It's okay, right? No problem?" He seemed intimidated and was asking in a purposely polite tone with an innocent grin. The other cat under the tree still wasn't smiling, intimidated or saying nothing.

"Who is he?" I asked Jiro.

"Our elder brother Ichiro," Kano answered. My tension eased up slowly. I walked over to our car, tapped on the top of the car, and Akemi and Saachi crawled out.

"Your family has come for you two," I told her.

Akemi looked at me as if she wanted to stay with me. But I was sending her back home. That's how it goes. She belonged to her family unless I step up as a man the way the groom did today, and take her away properly. And when a man takes a woman for his wife properly, no man can come take her anywhere or even speak a word to her without the husband's permission.

Akemi reached in and hugged Umma. "Sayonara," she said softly and smiled with regret. Umma kissed Akemi's cheek through the window. I handed her the shopping bag. Saachi ran over to her cousin's car skipping happily, shouting, "Good night, Naja! Next time I won't cheat! I promise!"

The elder brother snatched the *hijab* off of Saachi's head as though a simple piece of cloth could turn her Muslim.

Akemi walked over and extended her hand forward toward him and he handed the *hijab* to her. Akemi folded it nicely and placed it with everything else she had collected. She waved good night to me. She got in the car. The elder brother jumped in the driver's seat and sped off.

As I got into the front seat of our car, Mr. Ghazzali and Sudana stood watching in the distance on the grass. I adjusted my frame of mind and gave them a second good night.

In the car, I told the driver to take us to The Palace Hotel in Manhattan. He responded, "No problem," then pulled off slowly. I knew if I had announced our Brooklyn address instead, he would've been making excuses just to keep from traveling into the area.

The clock on his dashboard read 12:49 A.M. Naja wasted no time nodding off up against Umma. Umma rested her head on the headrest, her eyes closed but not asleep.

"You did an incredible job, Umma," I complimented her. She smiled with her head still tilted.

"I got a business card from the wedding photographer. I convinced him to take some close-ups of the clothes you designed. I gave him a thirty-five-dollar deposit. He said we can pick up the photos next week. I set it up so you can use the pictures as samples of your work for your new clients. After tonight, you'll definitely have some new clients," I assured her.

She opened her eyes finally and took a good long look at me. I could tell she wasn't thinking about her business at the moment. But she also knew I wasn't ready to talk about Akemi right then. My mother is smart and sweet. So, she let the topic go, and just said, "*inshallah*," in response to the possibilities of the new business ventures.

At The Palace Hotel we didn't get settled in until around 3:10 A.M. I didn't see a possible way for Umma to awaken for work at 5:00 A.M. as she usually would.

When I phoned downstairs for our wake-up call, Umma said, "Tomorrow, no work, no school." I was surprised, because since we arrived in the U.S. and she began working, she had never missed one day of work. Even I had not missed one day of work at my part-time job at Cho's.

"I am working the night shift starting tomorrow, 4:00 P.M.

until midnight, Tuesday through Saturday. I arranged this in advance, switched shifts with my Lebanese coworker. Only for one week," she said, drifting off to sleep.

From the floor where I laid, I answered, "No problem. I'll take you every afternoon and pick you up every midnight."

"*Alhumdilallah*," she said softly, meaning praise Allah.

The next afternoon, Umma and Naja were still sleeping. I stepped around the hotel room quietly, washed up, and dressed.

At the front desk, I checked us out and off of Fawzi's father's tab. I asked the front desk clerk the price of one additional night's stay.

"It will cost two hundred and seventy-five dollars per night for our single room," he answered. "Three hundred for the double like the one you checked out of."

"Are these your lowest available prices?" I asked.

"Absolutely," he responded. "Our rooms range from two hundred seventy-five up to five thousand per night for the penthouse, *this week*," he emphasized. He seemed to get an extreme charge out of reciting the fees. It was like he enjoyed crushing the customer who couldn't afford it. I was sure that he couldn't afford a room in this hotel where he worked either.

I went into my pocket and pulled out my personal money and laid it on the counter to check back into the same double room at my own expense.

I knew it was only one night and not an investment that offered any financial return. However, I found myself feeling fucked up about possibly having to wake my family and rush them back onto our Brooklyn block. The thought of returning home made my muscles tighten. I felt Umma deserved so much more after the immense job she had just completed. And, if she took a day off, along with Naja, I would help them to relax and feel good and be happy, my treat.

As she slept, I glanced at her, my Umma. I wanted to give her something. I found myself asking myself, "What can you give a woman who has already experienced a tremendous love?"

Later, on the midtown Manhattan streets, Naja and I searched high and low for a bathing suit suitable for a little girl. Almost everything in the hotel shops were for grown American women. Three blocks over and eleven blocks down and across, we found one right style and price.

Naja didn't mind the long walk. She was just excited to the extreme from all of the celebrations, new acquaintances, and also having her brother to herself, as Umma relaxed in privacy at the hotel.

We had the hotel pool to ourselves and I taught her how to swim that one afternoon. She wasn't afraid of the water, so she caught on easily. I knew that for her to really become comfortable and good at it, she would need some daily or weekly practice. These were the kind of things I wanted to be able to offer my sister. It wasn't about the cost. But, it mattered what kind of program I would put her into, who was running it and what kind of kids participated. I wanted to keep her ways pure.

"Did you know that Umma can dance?" Naja asked me when we finished swimming and were on the elevator riding up.

"Oh yeah?" I responded, wondering.

"At the *hennana* she danced for the ladies. She taught Maha how to dance for her new husband Fawzi. I watched her. I couldn't believe it was Mommy," she said. "And the clothes she wore. You should have seen. She wore a bra with silver glitter. It shined. She had a necklace around her belly and a jewel right here." Naja stuck her finger in her own belly button through her towel and swimsuit.

"Did the ladies tell you to tell everybody what went on at their private ladies' party?"

"Nope," she answered. "But I never saw Umma have that much fun before. All of the ladies were clapping for her, us little girls too. There were five of us," she said. "I saw the bride naked. Umma massaged her skin in oils, even her feet. I wanted to do her hair, but they wouldn't let me. I hope that when I get married, there will be so many friends there to treat me so special and help out."

"You're still telling all of the ladies' secrets," I scolded her.

"But, I'm telling you. You said there were no secrets between me, you, and Umma."

As we walked down the hallway towards our room, Naja stopped telling her story of the *hennana* party, which made me believe she knew from the start that she wasn't supposed to be telling in the first place.

In the room Umma was still in her pink satin pajamas, her hair out and down her back, and feet exposed. It was strange to see my mother from a different angle, the one that Naja was trying to show me. I always knew that she was so beautiful. I always had the privilege to observe that. But since we lived back home in Africa, seeing her in love with my father and playful with him and he with her, I had not thought of her as more than a mother. And a mother is as close to a supreme being as a human can be. So to imagine her hips swinging and swaying, hypnotizing the younger ladies with her charms, was a foreign thought.

We showered and made afternoon prayer together, the three of us.

Umma changed into a pale yellow dress and a startling yellow thobe, no *hijab* or *niqab* today, yet still covered of course. She wore a two-inch-heeled brown leather shoe and matching bag. I could tell she was feeling good, relieved, and free.

I took them out for pasta at a nice Italian restaurant. The food was so enjoyable but there is always the problem of the Italian men's hostility towards the African male and fascination and lust for the African women. I turned down the table they offered. I sat Umma in the corner table sitting opposite her to block their view.

Our server was captivated by the designs on Umma's hands. I thought to myself there will be two more months of this unwanted attention. That's how long Umma said the henna would last.

"It's so nice out," Umma remarked. "We should take advantage of this week and find ourselves a house," she said.

I pulled the folded portion of the newspaper out of my pocket. "I circled the ones that are in our price range," I said, laying the newspaper on a free space on the table.

"Did you know that the land and the house could be two separate prices? And there are still the property taxes to pay?" I asked her.

She smiled. "It's okay. We are not buying the kind of property and house that Fawzi purchased in Westchester. We are looking for something small. A small piece of land, with a decent sized backyard for Naja to play in, a fence of course, and three bedrooms. One bedroom is for me, and the other bedroom is for Naja. The third bedroom will be where I get my sewing work done and keep my supplies, like an office." She paused and sipped from her water glass. But then, she didn't say anything.

"And your son?" I asked. "Where will your son go?"

"From the looks of things, my son will go wherever Akemi goes." She smiled. Naja laughed. I broke out in an uncontrollable smile myself. She definitely took me by surprise.

"Perhaps there will be a finished basement or attic for the two of you. After you recite the *Nikah* together, you will both be welcomed there, of course," she said, blowing my mind.

"I spoke to the imam. He said the New York State law requires a man to be fifteen to marry, and only with both parents' permission," I informed her.

"There is New York State law and there is Allah's law. Allah's law is the highest law. It is best for you two to recite the *Nikah* and for you to take a wife than to corrupt yourselves and bring forth a 'chaos baby,'" Umma said. "Two or three witnesses and it is done. You two will be married." She drank from the water glass once more. "Yes, you are young. But you are mature, really. There is no finer young man in this country than you, my son. And we are business people. We make our own money. We make our own way. I am certain that you *can* and *will* provide nicely for our new household." Naja's eyes and ears were wide open.

Today was a day of firsts. Later on was the first time I saw Umma working out in a gymnasium. She ran on the treadmill with her eyes closed, wearing pants, one of my long shirts, and a scarf.

I pushed the weights, worked the circuit, while Naja tried to walk across the floor on her hands.

Late night while Naja slept, Umma and I sat on the floor together diving into the details of our real lives, no fantasies.

"Wherever we move, Naja has to have a good school. I really don't want to take her out of Islamic schooling," Umma said.

"We can ask at her school if they have information about other Islamic schools in the state," I added.

"True. You know Temirah Auntie has told me that there are many Sudanese people living in upstate New York and in Philadelphia and the Washington, D.C., area. They must send their children somewhere to be properly trained. But Temirah Auntie said that the daughters of African people, especially in Washington, D.C., are down there losing their dignity."

"So you and Temirah Auntie are friends now, or just business acquaintances?" I asked.

"She could be a friend, I guess," Umma ventured.

"I could arrange for us to see some properties on Wednesday very early after we drop Naja off."

"Good," Umma agreed. "And there is the small matter of getting our citizenship papers. You remember, we completed our applications together and went for fingerprinting?"

"No one forgets being fingerprinted," I said.

"So it is time to go in and get our citizenship papers," she reminded me.

"Yes, I remember. I'll go to City Hall and get the updated list of requirements," I promised.

"Good, because since your sister was born here, she is an American citizen. Allah forbid something crazy or unexpected happens. You and I would get deported and only she would have the legal right to remain here. They could force us to be separated from Naja." She said these words so seriously, it seemed that she was experiencing a piece of the pain from the thought alone.

"I'll get the papers for us," I reassured her.

"And you should consider taking an English course," I said to Umma.

"You're funny," she said, laughing. "Your mother speaks only Arabic. Your love speaks only Japanese!"

"True, and both of you will have to learn if we're going to stay in the U.S. Otherwise you'll both worry me to death," I said seriously. She hugged me. "I'll do it for you," she said.

The young bank teller who sat at the same window every day broke out of her mechanical routine and got soft and friendly when I handed in the dough. When she looked up and smiled at me, I gave her that mechanical look she usually has plastered on her face. As I turned to leave, I thought to myself, *it must be the money.*

In the taxi waiting for me outside, I handed Umma the

passbook. I pointed out the new stamp, confirming our new bank balance, eighty-five thousand U.S. dollars.

We dropped Naja directly at *Khadija's School For Islamic Girls*. Afterwards we directed our cab to the address of the dojo. I needed to speak directly with Sensei about rescheduling my weapons class. He was strict about his students keeping their word and honoring their agreements. So was I.

We rescheduled and agreed on weapons class for Thursday at 8:00 A.M. until twelve noon. I think he considered my punishment for rescheduling to be the extra early morning class and the extra two hours of instruction. But there was no punishment in it for me. I was ready to learn whatever he was willing to teach.

At home we unpacked and resituated things.

I showered and jumped back into jeans and kicks and a Polo shirt.

We prayed.

By telephone I made the appointments for us to see some properties tomorrow.

In our building, I spoke to Ms. Marcy about our scheduling changes for the week due to Umma's temporary night shift. She eagerly agreed for Naja's sake and the extra earnings as well. I spoke sharply to her about getting enough rest so she wouldn't leave Naja unsupervised while she slept. I reminded her that only she should answer her door and even then, there was no reason to open it.

I escorted Umma to work by 3:45 P.M. She went in fifteen minutes early.

31

LEARNING HER BODY

I had some downtime until basketball practice at the gym, so I headed to the bookstore feeling all right but with a whole lot of shit on my mind.

"Long time," Marty Bookbinder said. "Don't I deserve a rematch?" he asked me.

"A rematch is cool. But I hope you been practicing," I joked.

"All day! I got nothing better to do." He smiled.

"Thursday then. I'll come by. Today I need to do some reading."

He watched me as I changed from my usual path, which was to check out the mystery books first. I turned and looked back at him, jarring him so he would mind his business.

All of the adult magazines were covered up with paper so you couldn't see the images until after you made the purchase. They were always there in the bookstore in the same "Adults Only" section. But I never messed with them or even stopped to try and look.

Now, curiosity had me open. It wasn't really the pictures I wanted. I wanted to read about females, what they want and what they like. I wanted to learn about how to make them feel good. I wanted to know when I put my finger on her panties, why did she suddenly get wet? I wanted to know why on the phone, and whenever I was near her, she breathed so hard. I wanted to know why she moaned and what really triggered it to happen. I wanted to know everything about women without having a conversation about it.

I knew I could just rely on my instincts about what to do. I could just deal with each situation as it came up. Yet when I looked into these females' eyes, they stared at me like I was gonna give them the most extreme amount of pleasure imaginable, the highest high. Truthfully, I wanted to be able to do it right and smooth so she could feel real, real good. When she thought of the best earthly feeling in the world, I wanted her to think only of me.

I knew that when I kissed Akemi, she started sucking on my lips and tongue. It felt so good to me that I found myself recalling the feeling and re-experiencing it when I was all alone. Her kiss alone left a deep craving in me. I wanted to be kissing her all of the time. I didn't need no magazine or book to feel and react to that. Still I was curious about the female body, the inside and how it worked. I wanted the upper hand, to be in control of the lovemaking even though I didn't have the experience.

I left out of the "Adults Only" section and found a human anatomy book instead. It was corny, dry, and factual. The drawings of the human body in there didn't seem real. All of the women were red. All of the men were drawn blue. It was hard for me to look at their drawings and transform them into what I saw when I looked at a real female.

I read the words anyway.

I discovered the clitoris, a woman's pleasure point. It was all news to me, a small spot like a button at the opening of the vagina, which a male could touch, even just lightly with a finger, to bring a female a great rush of pleasure. And what if I put my tongue on it and moved it back and forth? I thought.

I read about how a female's pussy gets moist as she

becomes excited. And that a female's pleasure is related to how relaxed, safe, and comfortable she feels.

I read about women's nipples and how they're also highly sensitive and become erect when she is excited. I was fascinated that even a light wind could cause a nipple to plump up. I thought it was amazing of Allah to design our bodies to reveal our true desires. Both of us, the females and the males.

I learned about a woman's orgasm, the point where her pleasure becomes so intense and unbearable that she experiences an internal explosion and showers down fluids and feels an unbelievable release and peace. Wow! That's something I can't wait to cause to happen. I want to watch and see what her face looks like when I am there making it happen to her.

I read about the difference between foreplay, touching, kissing, fingering, sucking, and actual sexual intercourse. I had to put the book down for a few to think about it all, and for other reasons.

I started wondering if foreplay and sex could actually be separated. I did not think so.

A kiss didn't seem casual to me. It seemed crazy intimate and erotic and powerful. When we kissed she aroused me and made me feel aggressive as though I could not stop myself.

And, in one conversation I had with Umma, she didn't think any of this was casual either. The way Umma talked about it, after the first touch and feel of a woman's body, everything else is an avalanche. After the first touch, the momentum alone pushes and pulls and drags you to engage in and enjoy and finish.

And what did the Imam Musa believe? I never read anything in the Holy Quran forbidding kissing, although I read about how it forbids sexual intercourse before marriage. So is kissing sexual, and a part of sexual intercourse? Or does it fit a different category like this book says, "foreplay"?

Could a female suck a dick and still be considered a virgin? I wondered. If I allowed a female to do me, does that mean we didn't have intercourse because I never actually went inside of her? Like Fawzi said?

I read that a virgin has a "hymen," a thin piece of skin over her vagina opening. The first man to go up inside of her bursts the hymen and some blood should come streaming down. I never knew that before. I just knew in the streets, a busted cherry meant a girl's first time having sex. Now I knew why.

My mind wandering, I wondered about Akemi. I always thought of her as a virgin like myself. I always thought of her as someone who was into me and only me. She never gave me the feeling or any evidence that would lead me to think differently, not even a glance or interest in another man. Of course she is a virgin, I assured myself. *She would have to be a virgin to become my wife.* My wife, that's deep.

I started thinking about my life, religion, and culture. Our Sudanese females are virgins until marriage. It's considered a woman's honor. I wondered why it didn't matter to American girls. Even American men didn't seem to give a fuck if their woman was a straight-up, used-up whore. I wondered if maybe it didn't matter to anyone else except the Muslims?

After a couple of hours of reading and thinking, I was only certain of one or two things. Based on what I felt under that big tree in Jersey, when the touching and sucking jumped off, I would not think about any of the shit I read this afternoon.

The foreplay and the sex would all be the same thing to me. It already was. When I looked at Akemi, or any beautiful woman, it was sexual. I guessed that's why the Muslim men and women are required to turn their eyes away from one another and dress with modesty. If I just watched Akemi moving her legs on the swing, in an incredible yoga pose, walking, even just talking, it was *all* sexual and alluring to me.

If I wanted to do things right, in the required order as my family believes, I needed to get married swiftly. The only other alternative was for me to do nothing at all. I'd have to stay away from Akemi because the love would ease right into the touching. I'd have to stay away from even the females who I didn't love but whose physical presence turned me on. Once the seduction started, I noticed, it was getting harder and harder for me to just turn away.

Or, I could just roll with it. Be all in. Be like an American man would be, and just start fucking without thinking. Just follow the pleasure feeling.

In the book, I read about erogenous zones, other parts of a woman's body that might not be obvious, but brought her great pleasure. But I discovered that for each woman, the erogenous zone could be in a different location; the crease in her inner thigh, the inner ear, the back of the neck, the toes . . .

I was liking reading the part on aphrodisiacs. Aphrodisiacs are things which increase and intensify the feeling to want to have sex in the first place. The natural aphrodisiacs were things like various hot sauces and certain fruits like the pomegranate or "Chinese Apple." Even chocolate is an aphrodisiac. I laughed to myself at how we all running around all day aroused, and not even knowing we intensifying it by the items we choose to enjoy. Akemi had a pomegranate tree growing in the greenhouse in New Jersey. A whole tree dedicated to arousal.

Afterwards, I found a small book, smaller than my hand. The cover and the pages inside were all colored black. The drawings were white. It was titled *Positions*. I opened it up. Each page showed a different sexual position, a different way to enter inside of a woman. I looked at each of the fifty pages carefully. I wondered what was the difference between these positions and the yoga positions I saw Akemi do in the park. It all involved a great amount of flexibility. I knew that Akemi's body was as flexible as a rubber band and light. As an athlete, I could lift her body easily and move it however she wanted and liked it to be moved.

32

BANGS

I walked over to the pharmacy. I planned to do everything the right way. Yet, there's no excuse for being unprepared. I knew that.

I stood in the section with the condoms. Of course I had seen the boxes before, although I had never purchased one and never even seen a condom outside of a sealed wrapper. I bugged out when I seen they had flavors, sizes, and styles. I began picking up different styles and types and reading the boxes. I probably looked stupid reading over everything trying to figure it all out. I didn't care. No one around here knew me. This wasn't my neighborhood.

"Supastar!" a female voice yelled. It was the running girl who up until now, I never saw except in the dark of the late night. She was standing over at the pharmacist's counter. I eased away from the condoms and walked over to her.

"What's up?" I asked her casually.

"You're too cool for me," she said. "Here I am, picking up my grandmother's medicine. I'm trying to hurry up all worried that I might be missing your phone call. And you walk over here like it ain't nothing."

"You're crazy," I said to her, smiling because she really was funny to me.

She put both of her hands over her eyes like she was shielding them from a bright light. Then she placed one hand over her heart.

"Ooh ooh, now you're killing me with that smile of yours. Stop it! I can't stand it!" she dramatized, which only made me smile some more and laugh too.

"Am I supposed to believe that every time you see me, you go crazy like that?" I asked her.

"You can believe whatever you want. But every time I see you my heart starts thumping like this," she patted her hand against her left titty real fast. I cracked up.

She slid the pharmacist her card and some money. He passed off a white bag stapled shut, sealed with a prescription paper.

"Come on, walk me home," she said touching my arm. "C'mon," she added. I extended my hand to carry her books. Easily, she handed me her book bag. I threw it over my shoulder and walked out with her.

It was a nice day. She wore tight pants and a yellow V-neck. I could see her clearly now. She was all curves. There was not one ounce of fat. I took a closer look at her face as she spoke to me. She had pretty lips and deep-dish dimples. In fact, her face was all dimples because she couldn't keep herself from smiling, and the dimples popped up every time she smiled. Plus she was hyper, swinging her arms, moving all around and even fidgeting while walking.

In the sunlight I saw that she was a natural beauty, no makeup, just grease shining on her combed down swirling bangs.

"I can't believe I saw you today. Got you all to myself, walking around my way!" she said, celebrating.

"I'll walk you home but I can't stay," I told her in advance.

"Why, because you got a girlfriend?" she asked again, still playfully.

"What does that have to do with anything?" I asked her.

"Okay, so that means yes," she said. "That's all right, because we can be friends, right?" she asked. I wondered if she even needed me to participate in this conversation. It seemed like she could ask me all the questions but was too jumpy to listen for my answers. Or maybe she really didn't want any answers, I don't know.

"What were you buying in the pharmacy? It looked like you was about to get into a little something," she accused, then cracked up laughing, entertaining herself.

"Anyway, now that you know the way to my house in the daylight, you can stop by and see me. You already have my phone number. Or should I give it to you again? Come on, say it with me now." She started reciting her phone number like it was a song. I couldn't really do anything but laugh again. This girl was straight comedy. She turned into a stoop with stairs leading into a brownstone row house.

"We walked the long way home 'cause I wanted it to last," she confessed. "What do you think my name should be?" she asked me, another crazy question that no one ever asked me before. "C'mon, look at me, then make something up. Whatever you say, that's what you can call me from now on," she pushed.

I looked at her closely, thought to myself, she could be called, Crazy, Curves, Jokes, Pretty, or the most obvious name, Dimples. I didn't tell her all that. I just looked at her hair and answered, "Bangs."

"Bangs?" she asked. "Now that's wild!" she said. "Okay, only you could call me Bangs.".

I handed her the book bag. She said "Ooh, thank you!" I laughed.

"How old are you?" I asked her.

"Fourteen," she said. "But I can be older." She gave me her first serious look.

"Is your father home?" I asked her.

"Why you say that?" she asked me.

"Say what?" I asked her. It was getting confusing.

"I live with my grandmother," she said.

I didn't want to ask anything else about her family. It seemed like that changed her happy mood, which so far was the best thing about her.

"Want to come inside?" she asked me.

"Might as well. You two been standing outside not caring if my kidney falls out," another voice said. I stepped back to trace it. It was a much older woman. I assumed it was her grandmother posted in their front window. The window was positioned at the top of the stairs, so the grandmother could use it to see anyone who was entering their home, no surprises.

"See now you have to come in and meet my grandmother," she whispered while pushing open her door. We went in.

It was a big but narrow house. There were no lights on inside. The blinds were drawn and shutters closed. Everything on the inside seemed old. It had probably belonged to the grandmother for many years. We walked into the living room. The grandmother appeared out of what I assumed was her bedroom. She closed the door behind herself and stuck her finger up to her mouth as if to ask us to be quiet even though we weren't saying nothing.

"Grandma, I want you to meet my friend Supastar!" Bangs said.

"Jesus Christ! You kids and these names," her grandmother complained. Bangs ran out of the room.

"Nice to meet you, Grandma," I said.

"Oh, you can call me Ms. Kelly. Cut out all this grandma stuff," she said.

"Pleased to meet you, Ms. Kelly," I corrected myself.

"Oh, I like you already. Got you some manners. More than I can say for the rest of them," she said. Her every word sounded tired and heavy, like a complaint.

"The rest of who?" I asked.

"The teens your age, that's who. The ones I watch running up and down the block acting nutty all day, that's who," she explained. I was glad she made herself clear because I was about to dash out of there if what I thought she was saying about her granddaughter was true.

Bangs returned with a tall glass of water and three different pills in her hand. The grandmother grabbed up the pills, threw them all into her mouth at once and gobbled down the water.

I thought it was nice of Bangs to care for her grandmother. Then I remembered that each time I saw her, she always mentioned her grandmother. I erased some of my suspicions and distrust about her and told myself, she's probably a decent female.

"I guess I'd better go lay down," the grandmother announced. Then she went straight back to her room and closed the door.

"C'mon in. I stay in there," Bangs said, pointing and walking over towards a different room across the hall from her grandmother.

Standing in the middle of the living room, I looked around and noticed every door leading anywhere in this house was closed. There were also some steps that led to the upstairs.

"Who stays up there?" I asked.

"No one," she said casually. "Sometimes my uncle visits but that's it. No brothers or sisters living here."

A house with no men, I thought to myself. Here's a real pretty girl, living alone with a really old and sickly lady. How could this ever be good?

"I gotta go," I told her. She collapsed on an old dusty couch and began shaking.

"Please don't go," she said.

"I definitely gotta go." I turned and walked right through the door. I swung a sharp left and headed out through that side alley I used before. She cranked her bedroom window open before I could walk past it. She must've ran through her house, I thought. She's always running.

"This is my secret pathway. Who gave you permission to come through?" She was smiling, her chin resting in her hand. I thought it was nuts, a bedroom window facing a brick wall and nothing else, no sky or direct sunlight or trees or flowers or grass. Just a couple of metal trash cans.

"Now climb up and pay the toll," she demanded, closing her eyes and sticking her lips out.

"You're crazy, Bangs, for real," I said walking off through the narrow path, another narrow escape.

"Hey! Catch!" she yelled. I looked back to something hurled flying a crooked path through the air down the alley. I caught it and took a look. It was a box of Magnum condoms.

"You looked like you was about to get into something back there in the pharmacy. Maybe you ought to take these with you. Ya know?" She smiled, pushing her head out of her window as far as it could go without her losing her balance and falling down.

I walked back to her window, probably what she wanted anyway. She pulled back a little, relaxed now, seated in her window, still staring at me.

Her condom box was opened. I didn't know if it was before she threw it or not. I turned it sideways and dumped the packs into my hand and counted, fifteen condoms. I flipped the box around. It read on front, fifteen condoms. I stuffed the packs back into the box and I handed the box back to her.

"You take it easy, Bangs." I smiled. She dropped out of the window and onto her bedroom floor, I guessed. Then she jumped back up immediately and screamed, "You got that killer smile. C'mon say my name one more time," she begged.

I was already gone.

She wanted me to know that she's fucking. Now I knew.

I walked straight over to the high school for the scheduled outdoor basketball practice.

33

LOOSE ENDS

Wednesday after situating Naja, Umma and I went on a house search. There were four properties lined up for us to check out. We were smarter now, she and I, than when we first got duped into renting out our apartment in the fucked-up hood we still lived in.

The Bronx house we went to see had stairs that were caving in. The owner described it as a "fixer-upper." The Brooklyn house wasn't too bad construction-wise, but it was situated next to an active weed spot, so many different faces kept moving in and out just in the half an hour we were there. The Harlem house was across the street from the projects. Strangely, it was the only house next door to so many buildings. The last house was sturdy but was attached to three gutted-out buildings, no good.

These were the places that listed the prices that we could afford. Umma was disgusted. We both agreed that there was no reason for us to move out of a horrible place into a terrible place. If we were gonna make a move, it needed to be a real improvement or else what's the point of parting with our hard-earned capital? I was feeling kind of low.

Still, I picked up a new issue of the New York *Daily News* and *The Amsterdam News* as well. In a random bodega on the side of the Bon-Ton bin, I picked up a pamphlet listing "Houses For Sale By Owner," throughout the State of New York.

I marked down the most decent possibilities presented in those papers.

We sat silently on the floor with all of the other fighters at the dojo. Sensei was up front setting up the class, then walking down the rows of his students, various ages, young and old. Sometimes us young ones were more advanced in skill than the few eighteen- and nineteen-year-olds. But the two old guys who showed up to the dojo regularly, they were not to be slept on.

Ameer was seated one row across from me and one row back. I saw he had a cut on his face, but I could also tell the two-inch wound running vertically under his left eye and beside his nose was in the beginning phase of healing. He had his hands on his knees and they were all scratched up. He had a fight with his girl, I figured, some next, stupid new shit.

Chris tried to gesture something to me but Sensei's eyes were swift, so he pulled back and waited until class was over.

"What happened, one of them girls flipped out on you? All three of them girls is fucking crazy," I said to Ameer, referring to Redbone and them.

"Where you been?" he asked me. "You missed dojo Monday night, first time!" he said.

"I had to do something for my moms," I said.

"I got your money, the twenty-five you lent me last week. And I got some money for Chris to hold towards our car fund," Ameer said, pulling out a small stack of singles. He counted out twenty-five dollars and handed it to me. He counted out a hundred dollars and handed it to Chris.

"Now what y'all got. I know y'all ain't stop hooping for paper just 'cause we in the league now, right?" he asked me and Chris.

"We could head to the park right now and hustle something up, but I been mad busy for the past week," I told both of them.

"We better do that 'cause I ain't got nothing to put in this week either," Chris added.

"Yo, the red team is crazy," Ameer said with emphasis, us three walking.

"That's your team," I said.

Chris laughed.

"The coach didn't show up for practice the other night. So as a team we agreed, 'Fuck it. Let's run it anyway.' " Ameer began telling his new story from the red team.

"So I told everybody, 'Let's just run it the same way we been running it when Coach is here.' So the Red Hook nigga on the team was like 'Nah, fuck that.' I was like 'Fuck what?' Because he didn't have no reason to disagree. He just wanted to disagree and shit. So he said, 'You ain't the coach and you ain't team captain.' So I told him, 'We about to vote for team captain tonight after practice like Coach said.'

"So he said, 'Fuck it, let's vote right now.' So this nigga asked, 'Who don't want me to be the captain?' So nobody answered 'cause of how he asked the question. So he said, 'Good then, I'm the captain.'

"So I said, 'Wait a minute. That's not how you take a vote, by asking who don't want something. We supposed to find out how many people want to be considered to be captain and then vote from among the candidates.'

"He said, 'Too late, nigga. I'm the captain. Nobody raised their hand up when I asked the question so there you go.'

"I said, 'Let's just let the best player on the team be captain and everybody knows that me.' So this nigga swung on me. I ducked and it was on. We started fighting. The other two niggas from East New York told the rest of the team to chill while we two fought it out. I knew they wasn't gonna jump in on my side 'cause I didn't jump in for them two the last time the team had a fight. Now this Red Hook nigga got two long nails on each hand like a bitch. I'm fighting this dude straight up. He fighting me like a motherfucking girl, scratching and scraping me up and shit. When he scratched my face, it wasn't nothing to me. But when I put my finger on it and drew back the blood yo, I was vexed.

"I hit the motherfucker with my *right hook* and sent his ass flying all the way back to *Red Hook*," Ameer said. We all three cracked up laughing.

"So what happened?" I asked.

"Ameer's the team captain," Chris answered.

"Hell yeah," Ameer said. "And when that nigga got up off the floor, the Red Hook niggas wanted to jump bad together and fight me too. That's when I set the bet up. I told them, 'Fuck fighting 'cause y'all ain't gonna shoot a fair one. Who got some paper?' I asked them. Everybody had a little paper on them except the motherfucker who I knocked out. He had nothing but dirt in his pocket. So he bounced. I didn't give a fuck. 'I'll play any one of y'all niggas for whatever you got in your pockets,' I told the rest of them.

"I took 'em on one on one, one by one, made two hundred dollars by the time practice was over. The dude who I fought came busting back through the door almost two hours later talking 'bout he had fifty dollars and a turntable, just like a fucking crackhead! He said he'll play me for whatever amount I already won. I acted like I was backing down on the bet. He made a whole big rah rah like he was gonna win back all the money for the whole team and take over the captain's position too," Ameer bragged.

"So, what happened?" I asked.

"Ameer's still the team captain," Chris said with a laugh.

"How you gon' get it?" I asked.

"Get what?" Ameer asked.

"His turntable," I said.

"I got it already. That nigga brought it in the gym with him when he came back that same night. No bag, no box, no wires or nothing. Just bare-handed carrying the shit like it was a book or something. When I told him, 'Pay up the fifty dollars,' he slapped a leather wallet in my hand and a watch fell out his pocket. I looked through the wallet. It had fifty dollars in it and some white man's driver's license. I looked at this fool and realized he just went outside and found somebody who he could beat up and knocked him over the head. I don't know where he got the turntable from though. I know he stole it 'cause like I said when he first got to practice, he was empty-handed and didn't have no money," Ameer said.

"So you seen him since then?" I asked.

"The next night we had practice. The coach showed up this time. At first we was all cooled out like nothing was the matter. Then Coach said, 'It's time for y'all to choose a team captain.'

"Then another dude said, 'Ameer is our captain. We chose him last night.' Then the nigga who I fought had the fucking audacity to say, 'Nah, we should do it over 'cause Coach wasn't here.' The whole team started arguing. These idiots started running their mouths and snitching on one another. Then the coach squashed everything. He said we ain't supposed to play each other for money. We supposed to play the *other teams* for the *big money*. Coach said, 'Y'all some two-dollar niggas.' I said, 'Nah, I'm a two-hundred-dollar nigga and it's right here in my pocket.'"

We all laughed.

At the park, I hung back while Ameer set up a bet. As I watched him doing all the talking, all I could think was, somebody gonna clap my man. He puts himself out there too quick and easy. He humiliates other cats with his skills. It never mattered much before. But I knew being on the red team with some desperate-type youths and making enemies out of each of them wasn't gonna end right. I told myself, I needed to watch his back better. There wasn't nobody else around to hold him down when he was shooting off at the mouth. I was surprised that the kid he fought didn't show up the next night on some bang bang shit. I didn't think Ameer ran into the grimy kind of niggas that be on my block, the kind you couldn't leave half-dead 'cause the shit wouldn't be finished until there was one or two bodies laying on the ground.

"Yo, I'm sorry about Homegirl and shit," Ameer apologized after a close game. "I'mma make her pay you for your clothes. You was chillin' that night. I know they cost you a grip."

"Get it if you can. But if I have to meet up with her to get it, she can keep it. That's one girl who can make me catch a bullshit case," I told him.

"Word to the mother," Chris said.

"I got a new girl anyway and she got some new friends!" Ameer said.

"No thanks," I said. Chris laughed knowingly.

Late at night I moved around the apartment quietly. I showered and made my prayers.

My finger pressed play for the voice mail messages. The first message was from her. "Akemi, *Aishiteru*," and then all I heard was the click. After listening to four other calls, all of them business, it was that first message, her message that kept playing in my head.

My heart said I would show up to check Akemi at Pratt tomorrow night. My head reminded me that I needed to set limits and not go too far. My body said, "Stop fucking around and go get your girl." I wanted to see Akemi as soon as possible.

34

REPUTATION

Sensei wasn't going to catch me off guard today, I decided. I arrived at class five minutes early, eyes peeled and ready to fight. I had already conditioned my mind to understand that Sensei might pose as my enemy and that if he did, I would fight him like any unknown attacker from the streets.

But once I got inside the dojo, Sensei had a card table stacked with hundreds of cards. I tried to switch tracks in my head. I knew he was about to play some kind of mind game. Besides, the lights were off and it seemed like he wasn't even there. Of course he was. Otherwise how would I have gotten inside of the opened front door of the dojo? I walked around the perimeter slowly, poised for his sneak attack.

As I walked past his closed bathroom door I figured he was just using the bathroom and I was making something out of nothing. I walked over to the light switch. Before I could flip it up he came swooping down and was standing right there in front of me.

"It is a common mistake," he said in place of a greeting.

"People tend to never look up. A ninja must always look up and in every direction, even beneath his feet."

I guessed he was hanging there on the ceiling in the dark like a bat. I knew ninjas could do these types of maneuvers, but I also thought it was because they were usually small-sized Asian men. I didn't see myself as being able to hang on to the ceiling hidden away at six foot one unless he had some way to show and convince me that I could.

"*Ohayo*, Senseisan," I said, offering him the Japanese morning greeting.

"*Ohayo, gakusei*," he returned the greeting to me the "student."

"In ancient times armies of warriors had rules of confrontation that they abided by. Most would rather die than break the rules of war as they understood them, and as they were trained to follow them. But this is not the way of the ninja.

"Other warriors pride themselves on confronting their enemy face-to-face and fighting honorably. But this is not a ninja's honor. A ninja is usually the outnumbered, the underdog, the underestimated. Therefore he must fight in such a way where winning remains a possibility. One of those ways of fighting is invisibility. It will be hard for an enemy to fight what he cannot see and did not foresee. A ninja must be a master of strategy.

"A ninja, unlike the ancient warrior who loved confrontation, open combat, spectators, and ceremonies to cheer him on, always seeks to hide his plan and execute his plan in secrecy whenever possible.

"It is not above a ninja to stab an enemy in his back," Sensei said in a calm but deadly serious tone. "Or to poison an enemy in such a way that he kills himself with his own hand, by a substance slipped into his drink or food or carefully placed on his personal belongings. Or to set a trap for his enemy after studying his usual movements and habits."

I listened very carefully, seeing Sensei from an angle I never looked at him from before.

"The object is to win at all costs. The meaning of the word 'ninja' is 'one who remains alive, one who preserves his life, the one who plans and fights and struggles through any circumstance no matter how difficult, and remains standing at its conclusion.' Therefore, in this complicated world, a true ninja of today's times would have to be a careful but extremely swift thinker who uses everything within his reach to achieve his goal."

"A thinker," I repeated.

"Yes," he confirmed. "This is why a fool could not be offered this knowledge which I am offering to you. A fool doesn't think matters through. A fool does not know the difference between his enemies and his friends. So with these skills that I am teaching to you, a fool would destroy everyone, including himself. Your ability to think through situations is what gives you a great advantage and a great civility. You can kill, but you are not eager to kill. You won't kill your friends or family. But you will kill your enemies and you will be a thousand-percent certain who your enemies are because you have been thinking and watching and observing them all along."

"But what about a man who makes himself my enemy on the spot, without warning?" I asked.

"This is not probable. In most cases, your enemy has been there all along, just as I was here in this room all along. Your enemy has most likely warned you, through his words or gestures or his energy even. You just failed to recognize the warning signs. You just failed to see him as you failed to see me," Sensei said calmly.

I didn't like this word, "failure," that Sensei had thrown around in my last two weapons sessions. I did not want to be called a failure. I did not want to actually be a failure either.

After his words, Sensei taught me how to "size up" a room whenever I entered it. He had me search the back room of the dojo. At first, I thought it was useless. Other than the card table and chair, which had never been in the room before, the room was empty. But rather than fail, I took a much, much closer look.

After an hour, I discovered the secrets of the construction of the room. I found the door in the ceiling that Sensei dropped through. I found an unmarked exit that appeared to be a smooth wall. I found a floorboard in the corner that when pressed at the right point, led to a downstairs closet I never knew existed after seven years in the dojo.

"Is there anything else?" Sensei questioned me. I had been observing and searching an empty room for more than an hour. Other than the dummy and items Sensei had stored in his closet, I was certain I located everything.

"Do you think your enemy will give you the luxury of time to search his place?"

"Of course not," I responded.

"Then you must become more swift with your observations." Sensei pulled something from below the silver card table. It was daytime and the lights were bright but I could not see what he was maneuvering. He tossed it. "You would have been dead." His concealed mock *shuriken* hit my chest and fell to the floor.

When I checked underneath the card table, there were two real knives taped beneath it. There was no way to see them without crawling directly under the table.

I guess I was becoming more aware and alert than ever before. As I was being trained, I began to look at every item in the room no matter how small it was. I began to think of how each item could be converted into a weapon or a defense.

Of course I noticed Sensei's rope hanging on the wall, but that was too obvious. I am certain he left it out there purposely to encourage and challenge me. He did well because I planned to tie him up to a chair as he did me. But I would have to work on my technique and execute it when he least expected it.

The second two hours of weapons class had me tight. After a strenuous workout, Sensei ordered me to take a seat at the card table. He instructed me to build a house from the hundreds of cards he had there.

My mind and heart was already sped up from the morning challenges. I did not want to slow myself all the way down to build a house of cards. Besides, I didn't want to be an artist or architect. I am a fighter and a businessman.

I sat there staring at the cards.

"Do not leave, until you have utilized every card, and built a house which is standing," Sensei instructed me. Then he walked out of the training area into another room, probably his private office.

Even bricks are held together by cement, I thought to myself. How would I build a house of cards, no glue, no nothing?

It took a half-hour for me sitting there to move beyond my anger.

Sensei was right when he said, "Anger blocks success, because anger shuts down a person's thoughts, which paralyzes a person's skills." I could've got up and left. I didn't. I picked up two cards to see how I could lean one against the other and make them both be standing when I removed my hands.

Four hours later, I was still there, stuck in weapons training with no food, no water, and no break for six hours total. I had to block out the sounds of the fighters in the main room of the dojo.

I put the last card on my four-story structure, hoping it wouldn't cause the entire roof to cave in. There had been two thousand cards in total.

I eased my chair away from the table slowly and carefully. I walked out of the room to let Sensei know I had completed the task. I was ready to go.

Sensei walked back into the back room where he trained me. He stood looking at the house of cards from a distance. He asked me, "What does this house symbolize?"

Tired, I wanted to respond by saying, "I don't know." But I didn't want to fail or cause this session to drag on. So I thought about it instead.

"Effort," I responded.

"Okay," he said, seeming to want me to use more words in my explanation.

"Discipline," I added.

"I see," he said apparently not satisfied yet.

"Patience and respect," I tried to add more words to my tired explanation. He just grunted instead of using any words to let me know if I had gotten it right.

"Hard work takes careful effort," I said.

"It could be," he said moving towards the table to take a closer look.

As he got to the table, his leg bumped the edge and the whole two thousand card house collapsed.

He turned to me and said, "The house symbolizes your reputation. It takes forever to build a good one. It takes a second to blow it all away."

35

MY HEART

On the train, I wondered if Allah only talked to me. Or was Allah speaking to every man, planting thoughts and requirements and boundaries inside of his heart and head? If he was talking to every man, how come there was no evidence of this fact in each man's actions? If Allah was speaking only to me, or even only to a handful of men, why was I, and the few of them, if they existed, chosen to be and do so much more than the others? Why was Allah's standard so high?

Maybe I was bugging, light-headed because I was hungry.

After a pizza slice, I arrived at City Hall, the building with what seemed like hundreds of offices. There was someone in charge of every question anyone could ever ask. I just had to figure out how to get one of the workers there to listen first, give me a straight answer second, and get up off of their asses to do what they get paid to do, third.

I collected the one hundred questions Umma and I would need to study to accomplish receiving our citizenship papers. Since we had already completed every other part of the process and had lived in the country the required amount of time, we could come down to City Hall on any Monday or Wednesday with our green cards and paperwork, get on line, and get this entire process finished by answering some questions correctly and reciting some shit that we needed to memorize. Then we would be citizens of the United States.

I finished up early so I headed over to Akemi's family store instead. She was outside standing under the canopy, selling their accessories.

Akemi smiled. She was back to wearing her jeans and kicks, standing much shorter than when she rocked her heels. She wore a turquoise colored top and a matching turquoise sweater.

As she walked down the two steps in front of her store, she took the sweater off and tied it around her waist. Now her turquoise top was sleeveless, today no bra.

Her hair was pouring out of the back of her bandanna. She kept her hands in her back pockets which made her mango-sized breasts poke out on her petite frame. Her jeans rode the curves of her hips. I pushed myself to concentrate.

We were both kind of frozen there, aware that her uncle was watching us through the glass door. Saachi stood watching us too. She hurried outside bold and unembarrassed at staring into my mouth. I guess she was preparing to record my every word to report back.

"Let's walk?" I asked Akemi, pointing. She nodded yes and ordered Saachi back into the store. No sooner had the little girl left than she returned with her uncle, who stood outside his store and under the canopy looking in our direction blank-faced and pretending nonchalance.

Saachi kept him company doing cartwheels and flips outside in front of his store, causing the walkers to move out of her way.

"You have paint in your hair," I told Akemi. She looked at me puzzled. I touched the bottom of her hair and brought it around to her face so she could see the yellow color. She laughed. "*Arigato*," she thanked me. "Art," she explained.

She pulled a paper out of her back pocket, brought it out in front of herself, and unfolded it for me. It was an advertisement, a huge Ferris wheel at an amusement park. She pointed to herself and then pointed towards me. It was easy to see she wanted me to take her there.

"Saturday?" I told her. I held up four fingers. "Four o'clock." Then I pointed down towards Cho's to let her know where we should meet.

"*Hai!*" she said, meaning yes. "*Aishiteru,*" she said with excitement. There goes that word again, I thought, but didn't know the meaning.

Her eyes were searching me for emotions. Her uncle's eyes were searching me for a wrong move.

I started to turn and leave. I paused instead. Sensei's lesson today had reminded me to use everything within my reach to win.

What was really happening with Akemi and me? It was only the language that made every move so difficult. It was me depending on either her older cousin or younger cousin to translate what was going on inside of their family's heads and Akemi's world. Yet I was standing there with this beautiful and creative girl who spoke five different languages easily, in a section of town known as Chinatown, where almost everyone spoke at least one of the five languages that she speaks.

As she stood there waiting on me, a plan was born in my mind. I walked back over to her uncle. I felt her following.

"*Konichiwa,*" I greeted him. "I want to ask if I can take Akemi to get some ice cream. It's two blocks over and three blocks down, here in Chinatown," I explained.

His expression shifted out of his usual blank stare.

"You go now. Akemi has half hour only. Bring her right back," he said.

"I want ice cream," Saachi sang. I ignored her.

"No problem, *arigato,*" I thanked him.

He said something to Akemi in Japanese. She thanked her uncle and followed behind me until we disappeared around the corner.

Once we were out of his eyesight, she bursted in delight.

We walked together silently, our feelings boiling in our hearts.

Since I said we would go for ice cream, we went for ice cream. I took her to this Asian hole-in-the-wall, known for its unusual ice cream flavors like green tea, ginger, pumpkin, black sesame and red bean, or vanilla soy ice with corn flakes and maple syrup drizzled on top.

The place only had six small tables and twelve wooden chairs. Mostly everybody ordered their creams to go. Usually this place was packed, with a line out the door and halfway down the block. That's how I discovered it in the first place.

It was after lunch time but before dinner and before the after-dinner dessert rush. So the place was kind of empty as I thought it might be. I led Akemi to take a seat while I went to put my plan into action.

"Do you speak Japanese?" I asked the girl behind the cashier counter.

"No, Chinese," she answered.

"Would you sit with my girlfriend and me and translate a little bit?" She stood on her tiptoes and looked over at Akemi.

"She's not Chinese and I'm working," she said in a neutral voice.

"Ten minutes, ten dollars," I said. "She speaks Chinese. I want you to just talk for me and nothing else," I reassured her.

"She is your girlfriend and she cannot understand you?" the Chinese girl asked.

"No, she understands me. She just doesn't understand English," I said.

The girl looked confused. I took out my ten-dollar bill and slid it across the counter.

Just as I was about to double my offer to twenty dollars, she said something in Chinese to the second cashier.

She stepped from behind her register and walked over to the table where Akemi was watching and waiting for me to return.

Akemi looked surprised and posted up a little towards the girl.

"She is Akemi. Tell her for me that I miss her," I said, and the girl translated.

Akemi smiled so bright. Then she answered the girl in Chinese.

"Akemi says that she misses you every second." I felt a heat flow. I was happy and embarrassed. But on the outside I remained cool and steady.

"The other day at your cousin's house, we came so close," I said, purposely being vague. The girl translated.

"I was so lonely when you left. I wish it were only you and me, and that it was our house," Akemi said, bringing her emotions out into the clear.

"Tell her I want to see her after work on Saturday."

"Akemi says she wants to see you every day." I broke out in a natural and uncontrollable smile. I dropped my head and rubbed my Caesar cut. I lifted my head and looked at this pretty girl, her eyes so filled with passion and her words so soaked in emotion, I could feel the heat coming off her body.

"This is crazy," I said in a low tone to myself but did not want the girl to translate.

"Tell her I want to marry her," I said in a heated rush. But the translator did not translate.

"You cannot ask her in this way, in this place. Where is the ring?" the Chinese girl challenged.

"I don't have one on me, but I can get one," I said.

"Well get it first, then come back. I will say it so nice for you two while you put the ring on her finger."

I sat there motionless for a moment. Akemi was looking at us like, "What are you two saying?"

"Please ask Akemi if her family is against us being together." The girl translated my question.

"Akemi says, 'No one can stop the force of nature.'"

"Tell her that in my religion, there is an oath of marriage that we must take before we can be together." The girl translated.

"Akemi says, 'Like you, your religion is so beautiful. So what are you waiting for?'"

Blown away, I sat still for some seconds.

I tried to remember every question I had been wanting to ask, and every word I had been wanting to say to Akemi. The Chinese translator looked drawn into our love story and mesmerized too. She was waiting patiently along with Akemi, for my next words or question.

"Ask her when is her birthday?" I said, and the girl translated.

"Akemi says, 'She was born on December 31st.'"

"Tell her I was born on July 27th." The girl translated for me.

"Akemi says, 'She is sorry. She knows that you are younger. She wishes that you and she were born on the same day at the same time, but she is sixteen years old, and she is one and a half years older than you. She hopes you do not mind.'"

"Ask her if she has any other boyfriend. Or if she has been with any other male before, in the past?" I said.

"You can't ask her that," the Chinese girl raised her voice.

"Ask her," I repeated. The girl cast her eyes down as she asked the question more softly than the other words she had spoken. She listened intensely to Akemi's response. Akemi spoke softly and slowly as if every word she chose was special and serious.

"Akemi says: 'The first time I saw your face, I knew I belonged to you. It is the first time I felt what I have never felt, and still feel. The first time we kissed was my very first kiss. I was feeling that you would feel that in my hunger and in my touch. The first time that we make love will be the first time that anyone has made love to me, although you have already made love to me in my dreams.'" The Chinese girl loosened the top button of her uniform and wiped some new perspiration from her forehead. I leaned back and let Akemi's poetry soak into me.

Akemi sat looking directly into my eyes as if the translator was not even in the room with us. I went into my pocket and pulled out my small notebook where I kept information for Umma Designs. I opened it to a clean page and told the Chinese girl to ask Akemi to write down the address of her father in Japan.

After Akemi heard my request she hesitated. The mention of her father was the only thing that she seemed unsure of.

Suddenly, she picked up my pen. As Akemi's pretty fingers glided across the small sheet of paper, writing out her father's address, I thought of how I had fought many men in my lifetime, but I never felt as strong a challenge to my manhood as her placing her life into my hands so willingly. Being close to her was like being underneath a natural and powerful waterfall. There is no way to resist the current of the water pouring down from every angle and forcing humans and even the hugest animals to move with its flow.

"Tell her to leave everything to me. I'll need some time. But I will still meet her on Saturday at 4:00 P.M. after work." The girl translated.

Akemi answered, "*Hai!*" Meaning yes.

I thanked the girl for helping my life. I gave her a ten-dollar tip.

"Aren't you two going to have some ice cream?" she asked me.

"Maybe some other time," I said, not wanting to get her

back to work late. As we turned to go, I asked, "One more thing, will you ask Akemi what '*aishiteru*' means?"

"*Aishiteru?*" the Chinese girl repeated.

I told her, "Yes. *Aishiteru.*"

The Chinese girl translated my question to Akemi.

Akemi answered her.

"Akemi says, '*Aishiteru* means, I love you.'"

As we walked back to her family store, I could feel my heart beating in my eardrums. I could feel her heart beating in the palms of her hands.

In a love daze I bounced back to my Brooklyn block to scoop up Naja. Even though Ms. Marcy was all set up to babysit, I preferred to have Naja with either me or Umma before the sun went down each evening.

Naja knew how to sit quietly and be calm. Besides, this little schedule change would only last for one week, small sacrifice from me.

"I like the way you fly," Naja said to me after watching us train on Thursday night at the dojo.

"Do you think girls can fly like that too?" she asked.

"Anyone who trains to fight can learn to 'fly' as you call it, male or female," I answered. After a pause I added, "like the girls who do gymnastics, they can 'fly' too right?"

"I've never seen them," she said, unconvinced.

"Well then, I better find out where they are and take you to see them," I offered. "Would you like that?"

"Definitely!" she said.

"But I don't want you to fight," I cautioned her. "I'll fight for you. I promised. And when you grow up, *inshallah*, your husband will fight to protect and provide for you."

"But what if you're not there when it's time for me to fight? And what if I'm not married yet?" she asked.

"You are never left alone," I reminded her. "Someone who cares for you is always watching over you," I said.

"But it's not the same thing. No one can fly like you, except your friends," she said, like she had thought about it and was so sure.

"Okay, good point. I will train you to defend yourself in certain ways," I said.

"When then? When does my training begin?" she pressed.

"On Sunday, family day," I promised.

She made a frustrated face and huffed, "Always only on a Sunday."

We met Umma at her job ten minutes before midnight just to be sure.

On the train ride, I showed her the one hundred questions we needed to study to pass the test for our citizenship papers. I translated the information and pointed out how easy the test would be, simple questions like who was the first United States president, and who is the current United States president, and little things to recite and facts to remember.

"Don't worry, we'll study together," I assured her.

"And I'll test you every day," Naja said in her sleepy voice.

At 1:30 A.M. in our little Sudan, I confided in Umma as always.

"I have something else to recite," I said to Umma. She sat waiting for me to explain.

"The *nikah*. I would like to take Akemi as my wife," I said solemnly.

"Does she agree?" Umma asked.

"She does."

"*Mubarak!*" Umma said, meaning "Congratulations!"

She got up from the living room floor where we were sitting and disappeared into her bedroom.

She emerged holding her silk scarf in her hands, the one she wore on the last night that our entire family was together in the Sudan.

Sitting down, she untied the scarf bundle, revealing the contents I knew were inside, her treasured and exquisite jewels, the ones she was wearing on her last night of seeing my father.

With the jewels in close view, glistening under Umma's night lamp, the seriousness of my taking a wife sunk in even further. It was deeper than Akemi's beauty and charm and intelligence and creativity and passion. If my mother sat poised to part with those items which my father selected and purchased specifically with Umma, his first wife and love of his life, in mind, then this was a huge responsibility and a very warm acceptance of Akemi into the fold of our family.

"Give her these," Umma said as she separated the jewels that she would give away from the ones that she would keep to herself.

As I watched her pretty fingers maneuvering, I saw the uniqueness of each of her bangles, the engravings and designs, the careful attention to details, the specially selected charms that dangled from a particular one of them, the clear princess diamonds and trillions as they sparkled.

"I cannot separate you from your jewels, Umma."

"Oh, you can give yourself to Akemi. She can give herself to you. Yet I cannot give her some jewels, when you are worth so much more?" She sat waiting for an answer. I didn't say one word.

"I can be moderate, then. I'll gift her four diamond bangles, four gold bangles, and my pair of earrings." She rearranged the jewels to match her words.

I looked at her beautiful enthusiasm. Umma was big-hearted. Her jewels were worth even more than the jewels that Fawzi purchased for his new wife. And, of Umma's chest of jewels that were left back in the Sudan, these pieces were the only ones she had with her here in America.

My father did not have to go through India to acquire authentic gold and clear diamonds. They were pure and original in Africa, buried in the soil, drifting in the waters, mined and sold in our shops.

"The bangles yes, but not four of each. Two diamond, two gold, and you keep these earrings for yourself. I'll purchase some earrings for Akemi myself," I told her.

"You keep the bangles and the earrings for her. Use your money to purchase a ring for her finger," Umma insisted.

"You keep your earrings," I said solemnly as we went back and forth over what were "pieces of my father." Or at least, pieces of our memories of him, her deep love and my awesome admiration.

I had seen Umma refuse to pawn these same earrings once before when we were in Egypt. An Arab offered her ten thousand pounds for them, when they were actually worth fifty thousand pounds. I saw my mother pick them up from the counter, pleased that the Arab was unfair in his business. This way, she could keep the earrings for herself as my father had always intended for her to do.

"How about this ring?" I asked, selecting something much more modest.

"This is small enough to fit Naja's finger," Umma said. "But, it is not suitable as a wedding ring."

"I know, but if you don't mind, I'll take it," I said.

"And what of Akemi's uncle and family?" Umma asked.

I thought for some time before answering. I recalled Akemi not exactly answering this same question earlier this afternoon in the ice cream store when I asked her.

"They may not agree," I said truthfully. "But she will agree," I said confidently.

"If I could speak any of their languages, I would go and

talk with them. It is better when families have agreement, but as a woman I can tell you that Akemi will follow her man. As a Muslim, I can tell you that you and she are both of age. She agrees and you agree, recite the *nikah*, three witnesses and Allah agrees." Umma crushed her hands together lightly, a gesture which meant, "and it is done."

As an afterthought Umma said, "And if the *nikah* were not recited and the marriage left undone, the love and desire would still be there. A child would come and the adults would be guilty of forbidding and breaking what would have been a complete family, as Allah requires."

Umma left and returned with her Holy Quran and her calendar. We both looked at the dates on the page of this month, and selected Saturday, April 26th, as the evening Akemi and I would recite the *nikah* and be married.

Umma smiled, her slim finger resting on the calendar date. "This is sixteen days from now. You can use this time to prepare yourself. *Inshallah* we will find a good house to buy at least to begin the process of moving away from this place. In this time you will become an American citizen, which may work out better for Akemi as well. But son, do not go into her until the *nikah* is recited and the wedding is complete."

"I plan to see Akemi tomorrow. I promised to take her out," I admitted.

"The proper thing is to wait. Even Muslim men who are older than you have to stew in anticipation of their bride. They don't go about dating her. The more you see her before the *nikah* ceremony, the more you increase your chances of slipping up. Allah requires that things be done in proper measures," Umma said.

"To marry is a sacred thing," Umma said. "Your entire life together with your wife will be a constant discovery. The Americans want to know everything of their mates before they marry. The American fiancé takes full knowledge of his woman's body before she becomes his wife, if she ever really does become his wife. But they exhaust, drain, and use one another before even their wedding day.

"By marrying young, you are not doing a wrong thing. You will be fascinated every day for a long, long time. You will share something with your wife that you have not shared with anyone else. Each thing she reveals to you will excite and amaze you more and more. You will learn her. She will learn you. You will both teach and learn. You will grow together, struggle together, celebrate together, suffer together, create, and guide new life together, *inshallah*.

"You two will lock out the distractions of Satan and this world, and the temptations of the liars." Umma was dropping bombs and our living room was a scene of constant fireworks in the black of the early morning.

"Tomorrow I'll write a letter to Akemi's father. I think it is the right thing to do," I confided. "I am not asking for his permission, because the Quran does not require this. But I want him to know who I am, how I feel about his daughter, and that he can be certain that I am a good man with a true intention to secure her and be her husband for a lifetime."

Umma spoke of the ceremony she would set up. We both agreed to keep it short and very simple. As her lips continued to move, my mind drifted towards the reality of the inevitable fight, Akemi's uncles and her male cousins. I knew they would come to snatch the jewel from me, as I had somehow snatched it from them. It was not how I wanted it to be. It's just how it was.

On our estate my father once said to his friend in a gathering of men where I was seen and not heard, "You will know that you love a woman when you will do anything to woo her, win her, and keep her, when you would even protect and defend her honor with your own life."

• • •

On Friday I mailed a three-page letter that I wrote in the passion of the late night, to Akemi's father. After the introduction, I put it plain and simple: "I respect your daughter and I thank you for bringing her into and bringing her up in this world . . ." I maintained a humble tone, as I believed I should have. I explained about my faith and its requirements and our love. I explained that we planned to marry according to my faith. I told him about our boutique company, "small but profitable and expanding every month." I assured him that I could and would take care of Akemi and that furthermore, I would enjoy doing it. That she and I would continue to grow and learn together as husband and wife. I invited him to write back and share his thoughts. I told him that we would both love his well wishes and that the State of New York wanted his permission. That Akemi and I were not planning a big ceremony, just a simple exchange of vows.

The next day I placed the marriage form and the letter in an envelope and posted it to Akemi's father.

36

THE BLACK TEAM

"Even though our first game is just a scrimmage, we need to go in there and set the tone of dominance. We got home court advantage. The game will be right here on the outdoor courts, new nets, but everything else is the same." Vega was squatting while we were sitting on the gym floor after a serious and thorough practice on Friday night.

"I'mma run down the starting lineup, but y'all already know the deal. You know who the strongest players are. If you're not one of them I don't want no back talk, just get your game up," Vega said.

He ran down the top five, started with my name and then Panama's name and on down the line. By now, Vega had all twelve team members' names by heart, and had even given a couple of dudes new names.

"You seven who ain't in the starting lineup, this is no time to chill. You might hear your name called next Friday night at the game and if you do you better hustle hard like you one of my top five, got it?" Everyone agreed.

"We gon' practice every day next week," Vega ordered. The team groaned. "Whatever else you into, you gotta put it on pause. Get into this. You gotta make me look good," Vega said, like he had something big riding on the game.

"We playing the red team," Panama said.

"Red vs. Black," another player said.

"Coach, you gon' have to wear all black next Friday night

'cause every time we see you, you got something red on," Braz said. "You can't be repping for the other side." The team agreed.

"I'mma be in pocket. You make sure you young ones is in pocket. And let's get some paper in our pockets!" Vega pressed.

"Word up," everybody said.

"What about these fucking police? Seem like they be just wanting something to jump off when we be leaving the practices some nights," one player asked.

"What you expect? We the black team!" Vega said. "And look at Midnight, Panama, and Jaguar. I mean we really the black team!" Everybody laughed. "When they first showed me y'all I said, 'Ah shit they set me up.' I knew the police was gonna keep fucking with us," Vega joked.

"Yeah, but we pull the girlies," Panama hit back. "Most of y'all yellow niggas can't hold 'em." He reversed it on Vega.

"Seriously, fuck the police. We ain't giving them nothing to go on. We 'bout this here basketball hustle right now. Just move together as one team, and when you see them motherfuckers don't say shit. Keep it moving and keep your mouths closed. Got it?" Vega said with a dead serious looking face. I thought to myself, that's exactly what Vega did last time, walked right past his own car and away from the police. He kept it moving and didn't say shit until we was all down in the train station.

In the men's locker room, Panama pulled a flyer off the wall. "High School Jam," he read. "Yo, listen up, check this out. There's a party next Saturday night right here in the gym. After we smash those red boys on Friday, our whole team should show up to this Saturday joint and scoop all the honeys up. Let these niggas know who runs this motherfucker."

37

THE FERRIS WHEEL

Cho hit me with my cash on Saturday. His store was mad busy from early morning so he was caked up. We worked his spot like we been together for years, served each customer swiftly and moved them right out. At 3:00 P.M. when my shift ended, a next wave of customers showed up. I stayed and grinded with him until it all lightened up and cleared out.

He counted out $180 and put it in my hand. It was the most I ever drew in one day of work at the fish spot. It amounted to $20 an hour on a 7:00 A.M. till 3:00 P.M. shift, plus one hour overtime.

Akemi showed up. I saw her through the window. Cho saw her too.

"Japanese girl looking for you," he said and flashed a rare funny smile, closed lip and revealing none of his teeth, the corners of his mouth pushed up.

I ran down to the basement, showered, and changed. I had to be fresh all over. When I came around the corner, she was on the side of the building like when I first met her. She switched her style up again today. She had her hair zigzag-parted like a ghetto girl and pulled tight. The long ends were braided and wrapped around in two wicked braided buns that sat on both sides of her head like ram's horns.

No gloss or lipstick, just a splash of glitter that made her eyes sparkle more.

Soon as she saw me, her pretty natural lips parted and her smile spread wide. She stopped leaning on the wall and stood waiting.

I wanted to take her to the store and buy her some pants to wear underneath the white linen dress she was rocking. But I took her to the jeweler and bought her some diamond studs instead.

"No gift wrap," I told him. "Just clean 'em up with the machine and get me some alcohol wipes."

I took her earrings out, cleaned her ear lobes with the wipes, put some alcohol on the stems and poked them through her two holes, which had healed nicely.

When I looked at her, it was perfect. Diamonds rock with linen, and expensive clothes like the ones she wore needed to be complemented with authentic jewels. They looked clean. She looked clean.

It set me back, money-wise. I had to dip into the money in my left pant leg that I usually keep just in case. But I was learning that when you are really in love with a female, you don't give a fuck about spending your money on her.

Fingers, not chopsticks, that's what we used at the Ethiopian restaurant where I took her for dinner. Now she was addicted to flavor. So she was real excited by the dishes of spicy foods. She dipped two fingers into a tiny sauce bowl and sucked them. Her pretty eyes filled up with water from the heat of the peppers.

I could tell she loved the scenery, the pictures, and cloths in this African restaurant. Her eyes shifted slowly from wall to wall and carving to carving. Everybody's body swayed some to the voice of Bob Marley seducing his girl to "Turn Your Lights Down Low."

On the warm streets of New York, her legs looked pretty in wedged Espadrille heels with a thick, pale-pink ribbon that crisscrossed around her ankles and up until just below her knees, like a ballerina in pink toe shoes.

We walked in and out of some of the Manhattan shops, her curiosity constant, me waiting on the sun to ease down. Amusement parks always looked better in the night.

On the train I sat her on the inside. We rode hand in hand to Coney Island, home of the greatest ghetto amusement park. I passed on the idea of dropping two or three hundred at Great Adventure in New Jersey. Besides, in Coney Island, there were no searches or metal detectors.

She didn't mind. When she saw the rides, the lights, and the swarms of people her eyes lit up. She was having a blast and wanted a little taste of everything. She wanted some cotton candy to try. I bought it. She took two bites and that was it. She ate a tiny piece of funnel cake, but mostly slid her finger in the confectioner's sugar then sucked it. I bought two medium-sized colorful lollipops. She left them in the wrapper, stuck one on each side of her braid buns and rocked them just like that.

Most of all, she wanted to ride the Ferris wheel. We got on line. The metal cages swang down one by one, with couples jumping in and threesomes stuffing themselves in then being ordered out.

I helped Akemi inside, then climbed in myself. The joint rocked back and forth.

"Pull the safety bar," the attendant reminded us. He left then to hit the switches.

The wheel jerked and took off. While the wheel spun around, we looked at the people way down below and the colorful lights that lit up the area. We could even see the dark waters of Far Rockaway Beach. I thought about how this was the first time in a long time that she and I had been alone. Now we were hanging in the air, swinging back and forth trapped in a cage.

• • •

She put her hand on the back of my neck. We started kissing. Between the rocking, and the light wind blowing into our faces, and her breathing, and the spinning, and the feeling of dropping when the ride swung down, the sensation was crazy.

The metal bar held our bodies back in one crazy uncomfortable position. But I could feel her tongue and her lips, and I was sucking her soft, smooth, and pretty neck.

When I touched her bare leg, she moaned. It was a kind of whining like a cat. She leaned her head back like the feeling was too much. Then suddenly, the ride jerked then stopped. We just sat there.

"Come on out. It's over," the ride operator said.

We were back on the ground. We walked a little.

The music from the DJ booth of the Himalaya ride was blasting. It was loud, crowded, and fun.

Next we hopped on the line for the El Dorado bumper cars. It was a mad rush like everybody had the same idea at the same time and wanted to get on the same ride. But as we stood there, I could see that every ride was packed with people tryna get on. It was a slow moving maze. Some people was pushing. Some people were cutting the line. The people on the line closed in tighter, trying to stop the cutters. It was a Brooklyn crowd.

Akemi was pressed against my back. When the heat from her body disappeared, I turned to her. Akemi gasped, and I figured someone had stepped on her foot. Then I saw that a female had her hand around one of Akemi's braided buns and was pulling her backwards by the hair. She was falling. Just as I grabbed her away from the girl, another girl's fist came crashing down on Akemi's face. Akemi dropped to the pavement.

"You picked this Chinese bitch over me? You must be

fucking crazy," the enraged girl screamed. Her face was all contorted like a evil comic-book monster. I took one real good look at her. It was Homegirl, backed up by a group of her female friends, including Redbone.

Hurt and shocked, Akemi held both of her hands over one eye. I picked her up from the ground and put both my arms around her. I froze. If it was a male attacker, I would've killed him. A group of boys, I would've fought 'em all. But, it was a group of girls led by one crazy broad.

On instinct, I pushed Homegirl out of the way so I could get Akemi out of the overpopulated, fenced-in line. Homegirl fell backwards but up against the bodies of her friends, who caught her. They all started screaming and three of them threw their drinks onto Akemi's dress.

"That's what you get, bitch!" Homegirl yelled.

"Fry me some chicken wings, bitch," Redbone screamed.

"Paint my toenails, bitch," the other one barked.

"And Brooklyn don't wear white before Memorial Day, bitch!"

I held three of the girls back. But one of them snatched the lollipops out of Akemi's hair and started beating her with them. A group of girls started leaping over the rail. They Brooklyn mobbed her. Akemi ducked down by the bottom of my leg where they couldn't reach her. I kicked one of 'em with my one free leg. I pushed the rest of them down one by one. The crowd started spreading and splitting, until we was out of there.

Everybody watched the whole thing happen. They talked. Some cheered. Others laughed or screamed. Some fools even tried to block our exit to keep the fight going strong. There were no cops around. That was a good thing. The Coney Island ride attendants were caught up watching the brawl, so the bumper cars were at a complete standstill.

I grabbed a pile of napkins from Nathan's. I was wiping

the soda off of Akemi, but it was sticky on her skin. Her hair was unraveled and fucked up from all the pulling. Now her right eye was swelling.

At a small clothing booth, I paid ten dollars for a blue XL "I Love Coney Island" T-shirt and pulled it over Akemi's stained wet dress. We hopped in a cab. "Jackson Heights, Queens," I told the driver.

"Are you okay?" I asked her, not knowing what else to say. I felt like shit. I had failed to protect her.

"*Hai*," she said softly, but I could see her eye was already blackening.

I did not know what the fuck to do. Her dress was soaked in Coke, which looked like diarrhea on her expensive linen cloth. Her eye was black. I could also see how I had left a big purple passion mark on her neck. It looked like I had fucked her up, abused her, beat her with my fists.

I had to either take her to the hospital, or take her to her uncle's house. Either way I was fucked. Trained not to panic, I took deep breaths. Calmly, I told the driver, "Turn around." Then I gave him my Brooklyn address.

"For that address pay up front, twenty dollars plus whatever the meter says when we get there," he said. I put my twenty-dollar bill in the metal cup attached to his shield that separated the driver from the passengers. He grabbed the money, made the turn, and sped off.

As we pulled up on my block, I saw Conflict sitting in his parked car, Heavenly at his side. They were both stretching their necks like giraffes to see what I was doing. I held Akemi close and tight on an angle away from the two of them. I walked her past and up the walkway into the building.

As I unlocked and entered the door to our apartment, I was already explaining myself to Umma. Naja was excited to see Akemi, but instantly her face went from joy to complete shock.

In rapid Arabic I recounted the events for my mother.

Akemi stood with her head down. Umma stepped in and put her hand below Akemi's chin and pulled her face up. Umma's eyes brought tears to Akemi's eyes. Once she saw Umma's expression, she knew exactly how bad it was. Umma took Akemi into her room. Naja followed them.

I went for the telephone. It was still early, 10:10 P.M. I was hoping to speak to Akemi's cousin to control the damage on the other side. I could easily see this thing blowing up into all-out war and complete mess and disaster.

Luckily the cousin picked up. I started putting my quick plan in place.

"I need your help. Don't say my name please," is what I asked her. The cousin was quiet on the phone for a few seconds.

"Are you in a room alone or with others?" I asked her.

"I'm alone now, why?" she asked.

"Listen, Akemi is all right. She is with me. We went to a park and she got jumped by some girls."

"Oh no, why?" she asked.

"I don't know, jealousy, robbery, something," I said.

"Where were you? How could you let this happen to her?"

"I was with her. But, there were a lot of people there in a crowd and we got separated. I'm sorry. But she is at my house now and I am taking care of her," I said.

"She has to go home!" her cousin said, raising her voice.

"I know, but she can't leave just now. Her dress is ruined and my mother is helping her. I just need you to do us a big favor. Please call your uncle and tell him that Akemi is spending the night with you," I asked her.

"I can't do that! If this is some kind of joke, or if you two are trying to spend the night together, don't include me. Akemi will get into sooo much trouble. Put her on the phone please." The cousin was tensed.

"Listen, first. I'll put her on. I called you because you know me and you know and love Akemi. This ain't no joke. We need you to do this. It's not a trick or a game or nothing. It's more of an emergency."

"Please put her on the phone," the cousin insisted. I knocked on Umma's door and asked her to hand Akemi the telephone.

As I listened to Akemi speaking fluently in Japanese, I couldn't tell either way. She spoke so softly. As I watched her, I could not detect anger or fear or anything in her tone of voice. I returned to the living room and picked up the phone to listen in. There were three voices now all speaking Japanese, Akemi's, the cousin's, and the uncle's.

I pictured myself in my imagination, standing at the door of the uncle's house holding Akemi's hand. When the uncle opens the door and sees the bruises, he draws his sword, the real deal one like Sensei's, and chops off my fucking head. I don't move. I let him. I deserve it. If it were my sister standing there at my house with some guy who failed to protect her, I would do the same.

Then I heard the click. I put the phone down worried.

Then the phone rang again and I picked it up. It was the cousin again.

"Midnight, I put Uncle on the three-way. He believes that Akemi and I are here at my house together. It's fine as long as he doesn't happen to speak to my parents before tomorrow. If this thing backfires I am so dead. I did this for Akemi's sake. But she promised me she wouldn't . . ." Her voice trailed off.

"I won't," I promised. "My mother and sister are here too. I have some respect, you know," I reminded her.

"Bring her to her uncle's house in Queens in the morning at 11:00 A.M. No one will be home, because they will all be in Chinatown at the store by that time. I'll leave my house early and meet you two there. I'll take care of the rest." Now she sounded confident.

"Thank you. Don't worry. Call back if you have to," I told her.

Umma had Akemi lying down on her bed. She had prepared a solution in a silver dish, and was dabbing it onto Akemi's eye. Then she placed the ice bag she prepared over her eye. Naja watched intently. Akemi seemed relaxed and somehow to enjoy the attention and affection. I understood. Umma had that effect. As I stood in the doorway looking in, Umma said to me in Arabic, "She'll be okay in time." I took it as a cue for me to leave. I went to my room.

An hour later, I looked out my door. Naja was washing Akemi's hair in the kitchen sink. She had her bottles of Umma's female potions, rose water and lavender and tangerine. She seemed to be thinking of Akemi as one of her dolls. I could tell by her expression that she was having the time of her life.

Umma was smooth at working her magic. Now the white linen dress was soaking in the bathtub in some type of cleaning solution. I didn't think anything could remove those dark-brown stains. Meanwhile, Umma was speed-sewing. I've seen her do it before during some important rush job.

Akemi ended up sitting on a huge pillow on the floor, freshly showered and wearing one of Umma's beautiful robes. Her hair was still moist. She had her arms wrapped around her legs, her long hair covering the blackened eye, the other eye peeking out. She still looked beautiful to me. Some scars and bruises are erotic if you could just look at them and block out how they got there. Plus she had ten perfectly shaped unblemished creamy toes.

I walked near her and went into my jeans pocket. I sat down and placed the small diamond ring onto one of her pretty toes. I raised up.

Umma looked up from her work, caught me staring at Akemi, and smiled. She said, "This is how you got into this trouble in the first place." I thought to myself, she's right. Luckily for me, her and Naja are home, or there would be some more trouble to get into.

Akemi walked straight back to my room. My door was left wide open. I stood in the doorway so Umma could see I was not doing anything she wouldn't approve of.

Akemi looked around. She put her hand on my bed and ran it across the length of it. She bent over and smelled my sheets.

She stopped and checked out my book collection. She pulled open my drawers and flipped through my T-shirts. She took one out and smelled then caressed it and said, "Akemi's."

She saw my Ninjitsu gear folded on my desk. She assumed a fighting stance and smiled. I felt like a fraud and was embarrassed after what happened tonight.

She picked up one of my dojo flyers, looked it over, and put it down. Then she picked it back up, and said, "Akemi's."

Soon she was sitting on my floor rummaging through my closet. I waved her to come out of there. She pulled out one of my sneaker boxes instead and opened it.

Her face switched when she saw one of my guns lying on top of the tissue paper inside the box. She held the box in one hand staring down at it. Then she stared at me. I stared back at her. She put the box back.

She opened the leather fold that held my custom-made *kunei* knives. I shook my head no, to signal her to put them down. She pulled one out, examined the art and design of the *kunei* handle. She kissed the blade of the knife, probably admired the special craftsmanship. She slid it back into the individual slot and closed the leather fold.

When she looked at me I could not see or feel any worry

inside of her. Strangely all I could see and feel coming from her was a deeper love.

She breezed by me smelling like sweetness, holding one of my T-shirts, my dojo flyer, and a couple of other things in her hands.

She put her items down on the table in the living room, then joined Naja on the floor, helping her to put together one of her five-hundred-piece puzzles. They both fell asleep on the pillow.

Umma did not sleep. She sewed and guarded. When she was finished sewing, she moved Akemi into her room, and Naja into hers. She slept in the living room, separating me from my temptation.

In the early morning Umma and I made *Fajr* prayer together. I asked Allah for forgiveness for what I allowed to happen to Akemi. I wondered if my kissing and sucking on her, before the two of us were properly bound in marriage, contributed to this situation going all wrong. I thought about it. Then my mind let go of it. There was no way for me to rearrange what was already done.

The smell of Umma's breakfast cooking roused Akemi. She looked out of Umma's bedroom door with her bright smile like a sneaky cat.

Her right eye seemed even worse. It was half-black, half-green with a blob of blood floating in the white of her eye. I felt bad. I didn't know what the day would bring.

Umma said, "That's the way it heals. It gets worse before it gets better. Soon it will be gone altogether."

We enjoyed breakfast, the four of us. Akemi's fingertips were covered with spices, pickled peppers, and onions. She enjoyed the fish and yogurt, and ate cheese and hot bread. When I told her we should be leaving, she was sucking on a slice of green mango. She wasn't moving. She seemed like she wanted to stay.

Umma had Akemi looking fine in a newly made wine-colored chiffon minidress, the stylish kind she observed that Akemi liked to wear. It was a soft, elegant material that Umma had kept for a long time to use for herself. She cut and stitched it perfectly for Akemi's petite yet shapely body. The compromise was the matching pants, which were precisely tailored and went nice with the wedged heels and the pale pink ribbons that Akemi wore out yesterday.

Umma threw her heart into that beautiful outfit, even though it was too dressy for this casual day. From knowing my mother, I knew she saw it as a small means of apologizing on behalf of her son and his family.

She embraced Akemi and Naja did too. She handed Akemi one of her shopping bags, which Akemi immediately stuffed with more items she collected from our place.

As we left out, Umma surprisingly pulled her pair of black Gucci sunglasses out of her silk robe pocket. These were her nice ones, which she wore long ago, when we were in Egypt. She placed them over Akemi's eyes, kissed her cheek, and we left.

We rode down the elevator with the drizzle of project churchgoers. It was early enough in the morning that last night's partygoers were still all locked inside of their apartments.

We taxied to her house in Queens.

"She does not look hurt." Her cousin stood up from the curb where she sat waiting for us to arrive. They spoke some. Then Akemi removed her glasses. The cousin gasped then covered her mouth with one hand. She looked at me suspiciously. However, the peaceful and happy look on Akemi's face contradicted whatever her cousin was thinking.

Akemi walked on by and used her key to open the front

door. I turned to leave. Akemi said, "Please," and waved me in. The cousin looked nervous. Akemi said something brief to her. "She says she has something to give you," the cousin said.

We all stepped out of our shoes, which we left in the foyer, and into the darkened living room area.

Inside they used the telephone and called their uncle. They both spoke to him.

"We got away with it," her cousin said to me after hanging up the phone. Next the cousin called her house to say good morning to her parents, who were sleeping late on their day off.

"Yes, Akemi and I are at Uncle's house now. Akemi wanted to complete some artwork. We'll be here but don't call back. You know we won't be able to hear the telephone in Akemi's studio. Talk to you later."

She took a deep breath. "See what you two have turned me into?" she asked me.

I was grateful to the cousin, but I didn't trust her. She was working too many angles all at once. My mind raced ahead.

I kept getting the feeling that this might be the last day I would see Akemi because of everything that went down. I did not know what to do to change things for the better. I was already standing in another man's house without his knowledge or permission. I knew I was wrong. Yet I was still doing it.

"Please," Akemi said. I followed her. She opened a closed door and descended the metal staircase. I looked back at the cousin. I went down. The cousin was still standing at the top of the stairs.

Fourteen steps down and we became part of a separate world. I stood in a large room with a wall of water. There were three ordinary walls but the fourth was made of glass. Behind the wall was hundreds of gallons of water, home to two astounding blue octopuses. On the bottom were purple, blue, and orange rocks on which sat some beautiful seashells of every color, shading, and blending, along with some coral. Against the glass there were starfish of all shapes and sizes and colors. I imagined it was like standing on the floor of the ocean, but being able to breathe normally. It was a beautiful sight and the collage of colors cast from the lighting of the life-sized tank was calming.

Across from the wall of water was a unique circular kitchen table. It had a metal frame with chunks of colored glass as the tabletop. It looked like an unfinished stained-glass project.

There was a small, rectangular, orange-tinted window that let in a slight ray of colored light from outdoors. She had three new mismatched small-sized sneakers sitting on her windowsill. On a closer look, I realized she was using them all as flowerpots. She had soil where the heel would usually rest, and was growing peppermint leaves inside of them.

She was still wearing her sunglasses, but moved around in the colored dark with familiarity. She pulled a small chain and a Tiffany lamp lit up the kitchen area. "Go," she said, inviting me to sit down.

In the chair I stretched out my legs, admiring the bleached wood floors. The craftsman had done a perfect job of laying it down and bringing out the natural grain of the wood with just a light coat of shellac. My grandfather did amazing woodwork too, I remembered.

She broke off a peppermint stalk, sprinkled it with some water, and placed two leaves in each of three ceramic teacups. She poured bottled water into a small black cast-iron tea kettle. She turned the fire on and placed the kettle on top.

She gestured to say, "one minute," then disappeared through another door.

Her cousin, now sitting at the top of the stairs, reminded me that she was still there.

"Akemi's father had this basement designed for her, months before she arrived in the United States. Everything you see is what *she wanted*," the cousin stated.

I looked around the wide and long open space. There were no walls to separate the kitchen from the living room or bedroom area. In fact, I did not see a bed at all.

Instead I saw a swing. An indoor swing? I had to get up and check it out. The swing seat was made of the same metal as her table frame and staircase. It was sturdy and wide enough to sit, stand, or lay down on. The chains that held it up were heavy metal links. The whole thing was bolted into the cement ceiling. I yanked the chains a bit to see how strong they really were.

I guess since I moved out of my chair, her cousin came walking downstairs.

"She creates on that thing," her cousin said. "She sits there with her eyes closed, and swings back and forth sometimes for a long time. That's where she comes up with all those crazy ideas for her artwork and everything else. Then she goes over to that table and draws whatever she saw in her mind."

The cousin pointed out the adjustable tabletop desk, which was slanted upwards. It was a drawing table where there was a large sketch pad, markers, pencils and small tools, little erasers, protractors, and rulers.

Above the table in the cased-in rectangular windows was her book collection: a few Asian history books, Japanese novels, and the rest mostly manga series.

"Where are her paintings?" I asked the cousin.

"The garage outside was renovated into her art studio. That's where she is most of the time. She works late at night. She works on her big pieces and everything for the Museum of Modern Art show that she has coming up in the beginning of May."

I listened to her cousin's careful descriptions and explanations. I knew she had not turned suddenly friendly, or forgetful of what happened this weekend. I understood what she was attempting to do. She wanted to prove to me how important Akemi was, and how ridiculous and unbelievable a distraction I was in her life. Somehow she thought, if she could convince me, maybe I would just do them all a favor and go away. I got the message. How could I miss it?

How could I provide all of this luxury for Akemi anytime soon? It would take a lot of hard work, big clients, and big commissions.

Akemi returned wearing a tight tee that gathered at her waistline, and a pair of blue capris. Her hair was pulled back, fully displaying her bruises, which I felt was her rebellion and her intention. The sunglasses were off. She began pouring the steaming water into the cups.

Her sound system was wired to fill the entire basement with music, I noticed. I flipped through her album collection. It was vast and varied. The oldest were her John Coltrane collection and Monk and Miles. She had Donny Hathaway, Al Green, Minnie Riperton, Marvin Gaye, and Roberta Flack. She had Carlos Santana, The Sugar Hill Gang, Full Force, and Eric B. & Rakim. I plucked out an old Pat Benatar joint, a singer I only knew by this one single called "Love Is A Battlefield." I held it up to show her my choice. She smiled. I tried to make myself feel less tense, and more comfortable. I played the record for us.

Immediately, she started moving her body to the beat. It was hot to see that she had some rhythm. She didn't smile. She just stared into me, into my soul. The music soothed me. Her world aroused me. I danced with her. It was my cool dance, a lean here and there, my head moving some, my feet moving very little, but always on the beat. I wasn't the pop-locking, bouncing, trembling kind of wild-dancing man. I don't do no fucking headstands or back spins.

The cousin looked bewildered. The music helped to hide, or even remove, the energy that she let off, which interfered with the perfect energy between Akemi and I. When the needle danced off and the song was through, the cousin seemed glad it was over.

I sat now and watched Akemi pouring the tea. Even that was sexy to me, her hands holding the hot kettle, pouring the hot tea, and even the style of the teacups she selected and the unusual sexy curve of her Asian spoons. She served all of us our tea. They sipped, the only conversation happening through all of our eyes.

My eyes were saying, "I never meant for you to get hurt." Akemi's eyes were saying, "I wish we were alone." The cousin's eyes were saying "Give him the gift so he can get out!"

"You know, in Japan, everyone says Akemi is an artistic genius. They write about her talents in the newspapers and even the magazines. Everyone was proud when she left for America to do her art. Everyone is expecting her to do great things. Instead, she does what she wants to do. It would help us if you would just let her go." The cousin had finally said it.

My face must have revealed my shame and my pain. In Sudan, shame and pride are both too heavy to carry. I was ashamed of letting Akemi get attacked. I was in pain over the thought of losing her.

Akemi jumped in, sensing that something was wrong.

She exchanged words with her cousin. She was still speaking softly, but she was pushing her words out forcefully. I could feel her anger. Both of them stood up.

Akemi pulled her chair around to face me directly. She took her cousin's chair and faced it away from hers so that the cousin would have her back to Akemi and her face to me. I was just sitting there, checking out what they were doing and how they were doing it, wondering how I got myself all involved in this strange situation.

"What are you two doing?" I asked.

"Akemi has some things to say to you. I will translate," the cousin said, exasperated.

I felt my heart drop. I felt this was it, her good-bye. Afterwards, it would be like everything unique and special between Akemi and I had never really occurred; something that could never be forgotten, to be forgotten.

Akemi sat down in her chair, so closely facing me that her legs were woven into mine. First my leg, then hers, then mine, then hers. The cousin was on the outside of the two of us. I could see her, but Akemi could not, on purpose.

If anyone could have seen the three of us tightly pressed together in such a small space in such a large apartment, they might have thought we were involved in something bizarre and freaky.

Akemi began to speak in her soft, musical, sultry voice.

Her cousin began to translate, sucking the nectar out of Akemi's Japanese words and placing them into English for me.

"I was twelve years old when my mother died. She always told me to follow my heart and enjoy my life, to do as I please. She was Korean, a great writer, so great that my father fell in love with her words before ever seeing her face or even meeting her.

"The rest of my family is Japanese, but my mother is the one who gave me these eyes and the fire that burns within them.

"My father loved her a lot. So, he holds on to me too tight. I wish he could see that I am as my mother was. Since he loved the freedom in her, he should love the freedom in me also.

"My family loves me and my art, yet they keep trying to

put out my fire. I keep telling them, without this fire, there is no art." Akemi turned around and shot a mean look at her cousin.

If I could catch a snapshot of that mean look, the squinting of her big eyes to half their size, and the way they slanted across her profile. She was too much.

Akemi jumped up and left the room. Her cousin remained stewing, but eased a little when she saw Akemi return with the gift that was to be given to me so I could get out.

Akemi placed the gift, which was inside of a Bergdorf Goodman shopping bag, over on the tabletop. Then she walked back over to me and bowed down.

Her cousin lost her composure and began screaming at Akemi. Akemi screamed back at her. I stood up, as the second girl fight was about to jump off in my presence.

"She is not even supposed to be bowing down to you," her cousin yelled. "The Japanese bow down as a display of respect for their elders, or when people are meeting each other for the first time. She is older. You are younger. So why is she bowing?"

I didn't have no answer for her. She and Akemi were back at it in their language. Akemi must have won, because her cousin dropped back down into the chair. I believed that Akemi must have told her cousin something that she wanted to hear. Even if it was some small concession coming from Akemi, it was enough for the cousin to jump back into the translator's shoes.

Akemi began speaking as she sat down. The cousin translated.

"Your mother is a goddess," Akemi said.

The word "goddess" swirled around my head. Muslims don't use these terms to describe human traits. Yet I understood that Akemi was in awe of Umma. So was I.

"I like your apartment. It is filled with so much love. No one is holding their love back. No one is disguising their love at your place. You three are showing it all the time. I wish I had a mother here to love me the way that your mother loves you and Naja," Akemi said.

The cousin reached to the table and pulled the shopping bag down after she translated those last words about Umma. Akemi ignored the bag and continued speaking for her words to be translated.

"Thank you for taking me to the wedding. I have never seen more beauty and passion in a people. You never told me that the women from your country are so beautiful. At the wedding I began to wonder why you even bothered about me."

"No one is like you, Akemi," I answered. "Not even your own family," I added. The cousin translated my words to her, I hope.

Akemi responded in Japanese to her cousin.

Her cousin leapt up and her chair fell down on the floor. I stood and picked it up. Akemi jumped up, they went back and forth. By now, I understood that Akemi had said something else that her cousin did not agree with and refused to translate.

Then all of a sudden, the cousin spit out, "Akemi said she wants you to make love to her." Now her eyes were red and tears were welling up in them. "But I wish you wouldn't!"

I knew this was it. It was time for me to go.

"Look, calm down, I'll leave. Just ask Akemi one last thing. Ask her, if she changed her mind about what she said yesterday in the ice cream store."

"What did she say to you? How *could* she say it?" her cousin asked me.

"It's nothing, really," I lied. "Just ask her for me." I was staring towards Akemi. Akemi's answer came back through her cousin.

"What I said to you yesterday will never change," Akemi said.

I looked at Akemi, overwhelmed by her intensity and loyalty. Then I even felt relieved by her forgiveness. I was realizing that I didn't like the way one small situation could be used to sum a man up and throw him in the garbage without consideration of his truth and his intention. In the Quran, a person's intention is so important.

For the sake of her cousin, the only one who stood in between myself and Akemi's uncle, whose home I was standing in, I accepted the gift, picking up the shopping bag, and said, "Sayonara," walking across the floor to climb the stairs to leave out.

Akemi called out something. I looked back. She was holding a knife in her hand. I dropped the bag and jumped to her. In one quick wave of her hand, she cut her hair off. She stood there holding a tight fist filled with about twelve inches of hair. Now she only had a foot and a half of hair left on her head, shoulder length.

She tied the bundle in her hand into a slipknot, as I had once done for her. She tossed the tied bundle of hair across the room and it fell right into the shopping bag.

Word life, I didn't know what the fuck was going on. Was this some Asian tradition or just a woman thing? I don't know. I took the knife from her hand and tossed it to the floor. I pulled Akemi into me and kissed her. She relaxed some and seemed relieved. Maybe she and I were both believing that the other would quit trying. In my embrace her body felt soft and warm. She was using her tongue to convince me to stay.

Her cousin stormed up the stairs. I picked up the shopping bag and followed her and left out before she rang the alarm, the phone call to her uncle or the real one.

Walking out through the Queens residences, the white

sun lighting up the light blue sky, I saw a couple of signs lodged on lawns, HOUSE FOR SALE. While my family could not afford even this middle-class New York neighborhood, the for-sale signs jarred my memory of the fact that Umma, Naja, and I were *supposed* to go looking at potential homes today. And, I had promised to teach Naja some lessons also. It is family day.

Then my mind drifted back to Akemi.

After the scene in her basement apartment, I knew that realistically, I would need to have some suitable housing in place soon in case she ended up thrown out of the good graces of her family. Also, because to take a wife, I should have shelter set up for her.

I smiled as I thought of how Akemi was saying she liked our apartment in the hood. Maybe Fawzi was right. A woman in love will follow her husband even into a mud hut.

38

HEAVEN OR HELL

On a sidewalk on Main Street, the main road that runs through Jackson Heights, Queens, I picked up a girl's bicycle from a sidewalk sale for forty dollars. I would gift it to Naja, to make up for stealing her time on family day to deal with Akemi. I would take her outside for a while, and teach her to ride.

"Bergdorf fucking Goodman," Conflict said, when I came through the block with the shopping bag from Akemi, and pushing Naja's small bike.

"Look at this motherfucker," he said to his man who was sitting on the chain as Conflict stood next to him chewing on a toothpick. I kept it moving at my same pace.

"I heard you came through here last night with some sexy Chinese bitch. Now that's something we could split two ways," he called out behind me. "Let me find out you got something moving around here and ain't telling me," he said. I was up the walkway on my way past DeQuan's benches and into the building.

I rescheduled the house appointments till first thing in the morning.

Umma and I practiced the one hundred questions and answers for our citizenship papers. We planned to cram and take the test and recite the words at City Hall next week.

Around four o'clock, when the shifts changed on the block, and niggas who been standing out there all day would be replaced by a next set of familiar niggas to stand in their exact same spots, I took my sister downstairs and taught her how to ride her bicycle.

She was thrilled. She almost never got to play on our block, unless I was downstairs to watch her. For the first time, she played with two other little girls who were out there on their own, ready and willing to make friends so they could get a ride.

I let her share with them as long as they all stayed within my eyesight. They took it. It was better than nothing.

Standing still on the block always had its price. I saw Heavenly Paradise and a couple of her friends coming out the lobby of the other building. Wearing her spring colors and everything brand new, she left the other two girls waiting, threw on her mean walk, and headed over towards me.

"I feel like I haven't seen you in months," she said. "Where you been?"

"Working," I answered her with one word.

"You got something for me?" she asked.

"Nothing," I replied.

"Matter of fact, I did see you the other night, right?" she asked.

"I don't know," I told her.

"Well I know," she said coyly. "You know where I stay, right over there in apartment 8F. You should come see me," she said, shifting her stance to give me a closer look, while I was looking at Conflict pulling up, double-parking and looking at us.

"You better go," I told her.

"Oh, I got him. Don't even worry about that. But come through with my gold chain. He bought it for me and he's been asking about it. If I get a chance to see you, I'll tell him I lost it, and you can keep it. He'll buy me another one. If I don't see you . . ." she said, waving to Naja as she tried to balance herself on her new bike. Now Conflict was inside his car with the windows down. He was cursing and leaning on his car horn.

I knew it didn't matter what she said. The worst damage was already done.

After we took the bike upstairs, Naja and I washed up. We all three prayed and enjoyed Umma's meal.

Afterwards, I took them both to the Open Mind bookstore with me. I was feeling uncomfortable leaving them in the building alone, even in our triple-locked apartment. I had some business to take care of with Marty; in the meantime, they could both find something to read and enjoy.

As Umma flipped through various magazine pages, I asked Marty what he knew about real estate.

"That's a big question. What do you want to know?" he asked.

"Which newspapers or magazines might advertise houses for sale in a decent neighborhood for a reasonable price?" I said. Marty laughed.

"Planning on moving?" he asked.

"Maybe," I answered.

"Brooklyn has everything. And I'm not saying that just to keep you close. Although I can't afford to lose my best chess rival," he said, smiling. He walked off and returned with a real-estate newspaper. "You might want to take a look at this," he said. "You just have to decide what your family is really prepared to do. You must want a mortgage with a good interest rate?" he asked.

"What if we didn't? What if we just wanted to buy the house directly?" I asked.

"Nobody does it. Why use up all of your money buying a house on your own, when you can spend other people's money instead and then invest your private money into something smart and make your money make more money?" he asked.

"A mortgage is a thirty-year thing, isn't it? We would be in debt for thirty years and if we missed a payment or two for any reason our house would disappear like it was never ours, right?" I asked.

"Right you are. It's the American way." He was laughing but I needed him to take me seriously.

"There are other options," he said. "You could rent to own. You could find an owner who is willing to sell you his house, but the owner rents it to you instead and applies a certain percentage of your rent payment to the overall purchase price of his house. This way, at least your rent is going towards you owning the house one day. Then you can keep your private money freed up to do something that makes your money make more money." He made it sound like it was easy business.

I stood and thought about his words. I always thought that he had to be involved in some other kind of business, because over the years I rarely saw him receiving any customers. Yet he was always here, always smiling like money wasn't the point. I never understood how he could keep his store door open without multiple daily transactions and sales.

I owed him a game. So we sat down and played chess.

"You are a masterful player, my friend," Marty said after his defeat on his own chessboard. I thanked him for the compliment.

"No, it is not your chess-playing I'm complimenting. It's your strategy in life," he said, smiling.

"What?" I asked, not following his logic.

"Well, I won three games and you won three games," he pointed out.

"I won the last three games in the last three weeks," I corrected him.

"Yes, and today you brought your queen along with you to my palace. You knew that no man could concentrate with a beauty like her in the midst. And what a lovely scent she has brought into my store. You created a diversion, captured my queen, and assassinated me all at once." He smiled, glancing at Umma.

"She is my mother, Marty," I said solemnly.

"I know. You've won. So don't show off," he said resting his hand on my shoulder.

I paid for Naja's two books. "Don't forget my order," I reminded Marty. "Put a rush on it," I pressed.

"If there's a book in the universe that I can't find . . ." he said.

"Then I'm not Marty Bookbinder." We recited the last part together.

As the three of us got on the train together and headed back to our building, I replayed Marty's statement in my head, the one statement that I would have normally forgotten, "Don't show off."

It was crazy to me, how I make it my business to mind my business, to lay low, to keep my mouth closed, to play my cards straight, but somehow, people, all kinds of people still think I'm showing off and shining. How could I dim my light? How does a youth keep from shining when it's a natural thing? And why isn't it enough that I don't mess with nobody else's women, money, or things? Still men wanted to have their things and my things too. Wars are made like this.

Late that night, I put on my black khakis, my black boots, my black tee, my black gloves, and my black hoodie. From the rooftop I watched my block. I needed to know how this cat was moving this week and where his most recent weak spots were located.

All kinds came and went: cops, strippers coming home from Squeeze, jugglers, scramblers, dealers, regular night-shift workers.

When Conflict's black Camry Benz pulled up and parked, I could see a male approach his car and lean in to talk with him. But I couldn't tell who it was. So, I headed down. I knew he would sit in his car and run his mouth because he was the type who could never say something just once and never considered just shutting the fuck up anyway. On the ground level, I exited the building, shot straight across to Heavenly's building, opened the elevator door, and pressed every button so the elevator would stop on every floor.

When Conflict came up the stairs from the ground floor, he was cursing. "Wait till I catch the little motherfuckers who busted the light." When he came around the wall separating the second floor from the third, I plunged my *kunei* down into the top of his head. He never saw the tiny and extremely sharp long blade. The ice pick-like weapon pushed through his scalp like it was pound cake and into his brain, or the space where his brain was supposed to be at. I twisted it one good time. He dropped down onto the stairs, spilling his Chinese fried rice and rib tips, and dropping his nine millimeter. These were the things he was holding before death made his muscles relax. He must have been suspicious about the fact that someone had busted all eight light bulbs on all eight flights of stairs leading to his Heaven. That must have been why he had his gun drawn. I flicked the small key light I carried on my key chain and checked his face. If only he could see how uncool he looked, he would've been disappointed in himself. There was no blood unless it had soaked up into his hair. Next I saw just a tiny droplet of blood falling down onto his forehead, only the amount that could fit through the small hole in his head, which was still jammed with the *kunei*. I pulled my *kunei* out. I stepped around his body and disappeared. The whole caper had been executed without my hands or my gloves ever touching his body. He had so many enemies anyway. I'd let the authorities kill themselves trying to figure it out, if they even wanted to bother.

39

THE CALM

Early morning, we took the Greyhound to Connecticut to see about a house. We sat in the back of the bus, Umma at the window, Naja right next to her, me right next to Naja with my legs stretched out into the open aisle. With my two ladies tucked safely on the inside, I slept till we arrived.

By now, I knew I would be able to tell which house we would choose by the expression on Umma's face.

While in Connecticut, I never saw that expression.

I dropped her to work on time. I grabbed up Naja and went about my day. She read her first book, then read the second. She did her homework quietly at the dojo.

I did not return to our block until 12:45 A.M. Monday night or Tuesday early morning depending on how you want to look at it. After picking Umma up from work, we all three walked together from the train station to our block and into our building.

Tuesday was tight and it was the last day of Umma's night schedule. We dropped Naja to school, then went to see a couple of Brooklyn houses for sale.

From 12 noon until 2:00 P.M., I threw my full attention into Sensei's weapon class. The theme for the day was poisons. I found it amazing how regular items like flowers and plants and everyday household chemicals could be used to end lives. I also thought about how important it is who you allow into your personal space and trust. A woman you love, or your favorite restaurant owner, or anyone who could serve you food or drink or handle items that belong to you that you will in turn touch has the power to poison you in a way that authorities might never trace.

I thought of Umma, who was a woman of herbs, oils, potions, and elixirs. Most of them contained ingredients that could be considered secret, in the sense that she was the only one who knew about them, their portions and combinations and effects. I knew she probably already understood and knew the power of natural poisons, which were some of the lessons Sensei was giving today.

I thought of Naja. She wanted me to train her in self-defense. Poisons seemed like something a female could get into. I guess it's the same as spraying pepper spray or mace into an attacker's eyes. It's one of the few ways a sixty- or seventy-pound girl could slow down a two-hundred-pound attacker.

I believed that if I gave Naja a knife, even if I taught her how to use it, an attacker could too easily take a weapon from a small girl and use that same weapon to hurt her real bad. I cringed at the thought.

I decided I would prepare a poison, which could be thrown by a little girl to blind or temporarily disable an attacker, and give it to Naja as a first lesson.

Later when I thought about all of the beautiful flowers like the African Lily and the White Oleander, and the wedding flowers I ordered myself, I thought about Heavenly Paradise. How she talk so nice, dress so nice, could look so nice, like a blossoming flower, and be so poisonous on the inside?

I dropped Umma to work, picked Naja up, then went to basketball practice, then the dojo, then to dinner, then to pick Umma back up and back on the block late night over again.

Wednesday, the next day, was a relief. After I dropped Naja and Umma in the early morning, I returned home and slept. Six hours later, I walked down to DeQuan's apartment, something that I had not done in months. I needed to put my ear to the ground. Besides, I thought I had the perfect pretext.

"Must mean jihad," DeQuan said when he opened his door for me. "First time you come by my place it was jihad. The second time you came to my place it was jihad," he said, referring to the time when I bought a four-five and a silencer off of him. "Now this is the third time. What can I get for you?" he asked. "They say omens come in threes," he added.

"No jihad, no beef. I stopped by to put you up on something. You know I'm playing ball over at . . ." I told him the whole rundown on the teen league minus the money involved and about the upcoming scrimmage on Friday night.

"I thought you might want to check it out. There might be some business opportunities, some heavy players out, you know what I mean?" I said.

"Yeah, I knew about the Hustler's League but not about the junior division. You should've told me sooner. I would've put my brothers on it."

"A'ight." I turned like I was leaving.

"So what you think about this shit with our man Conflict?" he asked me. I turned back.

"What's new with that cat?" I asked.

"He returned to the essence Sunday night, dead," DeQuan said, looking me in the face for my reaction. But I knew better than to seem sad, happy, or even concerned. DeQuan knew I didn't like that sucker. I knew DeQuan didn't really like his ass either. Matter of fact, there was a bunch of cats that hated that dumb-ass tyrant and only affiliated with him because he was Superior's brother.

"That must've freed up some of your money then, right?" I said. DeQuan smiled.

"You a cold motherfucker, man," he said.

"Not as cold as you," I answered. He gave me a pound.

"You coming to the game?" I asked, like it really mattered. I, of course, knew that DeQuan loved games, any type of game where men competed and somebody got conquered fair and square.

"Shit, I want to, but the wake is Friday night. Everybody from around here gon' be there double-checking to make sure that nigga is really in the box." DeQuan laughed. I didn't. "Plus, Superior will be checking to see who pays their respects."

"A'ight man. Do what you gotta do. Check the box, then roll through at half-time. The game should be crazy," I said, and bounced.

As I reached for the door to leave, DeQuan said, "You came a long way from sandals. I see you every day chilling. I'm proud to see you shining. I'd like to think I had something to do with that."

"You left me no other choice," I said solemnly. "I guess I owe you some appreciation," I said. "Thanks, man." I gave him a pound. He wanted a hug. We embraced. I left.

Outside I saw Conflict's parked Camry Benz. It was dirty, bird shit everywhere, with three parking tickets placed under the wiper.

40

THE CONNECTION

Wednesday night at the dojo me, Ameer, and Chris got to talk. It was the first time this week I had showed up without Naja, and didn't have to pick up Umma late at night. Her work schedule was back to normal.

"Now don't go catching feelings when me and the red team come rock y'all blacks on Friday night," Ameer joked. But I knew he meant it.

"Whatever happens happens," I said. "I either get half of yours, or you get half of mine," I reminded him.

"Not half, thirds," Chris reminded us two. "We got a game too, on Friday night. It's the green team vs. the whites, over in Brownsville." He was serious but we all laughed anyway at the sound of it.

Umma was already studying the one hundred questions when I arrived home. Naja was her tutor. I showered and joined in. I didn't need to do too much studying. I already knew the majority of the answers.

I went to bed early, resting up for the game and whatever else was coming my way. If I could get two good nights' sleep, I could be at the top of my skill set.

I wondered what Akemi was doing, how she was feeling, how she was looking, and what her family was saying or telling her to do. I drifted off wishing she would call, but not even considering calling her before I knew what verdict was coming from the men in her family.

On Thursday, I went on my own to see a property I found in the newspaper Marty Bookbinder had given to me. It was located on Beach Nine in Far Rockaway, Queens. It was a "For Sale By Owner" and the cost was $80,000.

The seller was an elderly, short Jew with thick glasses and a slow walk that added twenty extra minutes onto every undertaking. At first he didn't want to open his front door. I'm sure I looked frightening in my everyday fresh gear.

He peered through the body length rectangular window beside the door. His hand was shaking as he held back his white lace curtain. I pressed the newspaper, ironically called *The Connection*, up against the glass. He was encouraged to open the door, at least enough for him to talk through the three-inch space that was open but still chained.

"Good morning, I saw your advertisement for a house for sale in this newspaper. I'm the one who called and made the 11:00 A.M. appointment. Well it's 11:00 A.M. now and I'm here," I said politely.

"Who gave you this paper?" he asked.

"What paper?" I asked.

"The newspaper!" He responded like he was quick and I was slow.

"Oh, Marty Bookbinder, he's a friend of mine. But the paper is on sale to the general public at Marty's bookstore," I said. He slid the chain off.

"Come in, come in," he said as though I had suddenly given the correct password.

Automatically, I hated the furniture and the stale smell of the place. It was a house that had, more than anything, been lived in. There were things packed up and piled up everywhere in uneven stacks, in every room.

I loved the house. There were three bedrooms, a small study, a living room with a fireplace, a small dining room, two and a half bathrooms, and a basement. The paneling in the basement was old and out of style, but the basement was finished and even had a small kitchenette. I couldn't really see the kitchen, which was so small you could miss it if you didn't look hard, because they had boxes and papers stacked even on the counters and floors in there.

There was a backyard, about fifty feet by fifty feet. More importantly, there was a fence. There was an unused clothing line I knew Umma would like, and a deck where a family could chill and grill or just read a book. It had electric heat and no central air-conditioning, but the owner had a big, antique air conditioner in his bedroom window, which he claimed worked well, but he would be leaving it behind.

The house sat right next door to the house on the left of it, but it was at the end of the block. There was no house to the right of it, only woods. But the beach was around the corner. And the street had trees and privacy.

"Who lives next door?" I asked.

"Good people, the Arnoffs, but they'll be selling soon too. Everybody's going south to Florida," he said.

"When are you prepared to sell?" I asked him.

"If the money is right, we can vacate by the first of June," he said. "No more New York winters for me," he complained.

When my tour of his house was over, he asked, "Who's got the money?" He revealed his teeth, which looked like they had fifty thousand dollars worth of dental work done on 'em.

"My family," I said.

"How long will it take for you to get clearance on the loan?" he asked. "I can't wait forever." Then he added with a laugh, "I guess you can tell!"

"How long will it take for you to get the inspections?" I asked.

"Fuck inspections, lawyers and all those other God damned thieves!" The man had an outburst. "Why should we give them a piece of our money? My son's an attorney, the lying bastard! I'm an old-timer. If you want to buy this house, then buy it. If something is broke when you move in, fix it. I'm a straight shooter. I'm asking for $80,000, not a penny less, not a penny more."

Wondering if this guy was legit or some kind of senile lunatic, I asked some follow-up questions. "You have the deed, right?"

"Of course!" he said. "No deed, no sale. When I bought this house, they gave me a deed. You buy this house, I give you the deed, plain and simple."

I stood thinking. "How fast can you get the money?" he asked again.

"I'll have to let my family see the place first," I told him.

"Your mother, right? It's always the mother!" he said.

I smiled. "Yes, it is always the mother. No doubt," I agreed. "We can come by on Saturday around 5:00 P.M.," I said. "Is that good for you?"

"Listen, whoever gets here with the money first, gets the house first. I don't care if you carry it in here in a plastic bag. Money is money. Coins are good too. My wife loves the casino," he said. "As long as it adds up to $80,000."

"Okay, I hear you," I said.

Despite the old guy being a bit unstable, I left the house with a good feeling. If I could get a comfortable expression on Umma's face, we could buy it. Although, in the back of my mind, I was thinking how once we paid out the eighty grand plus whatever side expenses it involved, we would not have one penny savings left in our Umma Designs account. I would only have my small savings and Umma's jewelry as collateral or emergency fund. I also thought about the "rent to buy option." Yet I knew this wasn't available with this guy who obviously had a little bit of time left and big plans for the money from the sale of his little outdated home.

The MVP prize money at the Youth League was looking more and more appealing and important to me.

"It needs work," I told Umma. "But, it's close enough to Naja's school. We wouldn't lose any of our customers, and I walked around the neighborhood. It's mostly older Jewish people, mostly quiet. The backyard is all weeds, but once you put your touch to it, everything will blossom. I know it."

"And what about Akemi? Will she like it?" Umma asked.

"Akemi likes me. I guess that's good enough," I said, smiling.

"Ooh," Umma said. "You must be right." She was smiling.

"You are both artists. Eventually the house will become too small to be home to two tremendous talents. But for now, we can make it work," I told Umma.

We agreed on Saturday at 4:30 P.M. for a visit. I imagined that no one else would rush there with eighty grand stuffed inside a Hefty for the old man.

41
GAME

Friday I felt powerful, well rested, and optimistic. I raised up early, showered, and then placed my head to the floor in prayer.

When I walked past Akemi's family store, the metal gate was only halfway up.

All day long working at Cho's, I looked out for Akemi. By noon Cho's store was crowded with customers. From noon to two, I watched for her to do her sneaky walk by. By 3:00 P.M., quitting time, I felt bad that she didn't show.

Of course I wanted to rush into her uncle's store, charge into the back room and grab my girl and dash out their door and never return. But, I knew better. My one big fuckup, the beatdown and bruises, had placed her family ahead of me in some way. I wouldn't worry. She said she loved me and I knew she did. "Tomorrow," I told myself. "She'll show tomorrow. We'll go see the house together, Umma, Akemi, Naja, and me, *inshallah.*"

Locking my apartment door, leaving Umma and Naja and my longing for Akemi on the inside, I made my way to the game. Now it was about total concentration.

A sold-out concert, that's what the park was like. All the spaces and seats on the outdoor bleachers were taken. On both sides and down front as far as they could reach

without interfering with our game, the fans stood shoulder
to shoulder. Real hustlers, in new rides, parked all around
the perimeter. Little boys, pre-teens waiting for their
chance to rock and shine, hung from the fences like monkeys so they could see past all the adults who wouldn't let
them squeeze in.

Everybody was cleaned up nice like a fashion show, the
models and the onlookers. There was music, all kinds of
music, none of it official by a hired out DJ. Instead it was one
man's musical tastes battling the next man's musical tastes.

No one was selling franks or peanuts and popcorn like
The Garden, but people were brown-bagging beers. The smell
of herb made ghetto clouds, and the females was swinging
hard 'cause they smelled money.

Coach Vega was amped all the way up like a coke fiend.
But he was drug free and hell-bent on his squad making
him look good. It was the first time we ever seen him not
wearing anything with the color red in it. He was dressed up
more so for the after party, or in his mind the victory celebration. He had enough cologne on for all the dudes seated
in the first row of both bleachers. I swear I doubted this cat
had ever played basketball himself. But he was three parts—
passion, personality, and style. And for whatever it was worth,
he made every member of our team feel like he gave a fuck
for real.

We warmed up. The red team showed up looking like
a bunch of niggas in a lineup. They had eleven players, not
twelve, and about seventy-five people trailing behind them
going nowhere, 'cause there wasn't more seats available. Their
rowdiness caused a melee. It took about five to seven minutes
to clear it up. Ameer was in the middle of everything. All I
could think was, *That's all he needed.* These people are like gas-
oline to his match, and he was loving it.

I slapped myself in the head to jar me out of friendship

mode. I came to play. I came to win, and somebody had to leave defeated, no doubt.

After the first quarter, I had the whole schematic figured out. Based on Ameer's funny stories about his teammates, I pegged who didn't like who, who was hogging, who was hating, and so on. In our huddle I put Panama up on the setup. I would take care of their captain, Ameer, he would check their number-two man, Specialist, and we would leave their man Noodles wide open 'cause he was no good.

Panama accepted the plan then told me he was gonna break their center's eyeglasses 'cause he couldn't see without 'em. Then we would have two men on the court that posed no problem at all.

Vega paced but didn't interfere. The crowd hung on our every move. A lot of showboating went down, but by the end of the game it was 87 to 69, our favor. Panama "accidentally" broke the glasses and pulled down twenty-eight points. I pulled down thirty-four, the rest of our team stepped up and did their thing as well.

We got some instant cheerleaders stomping on the court. Female teens made up a team song on the spot. With their T-shirts flipped over and pulled down to make halter tops, tight jeans, cutoffs, and miniskirts, they cheered and bounced for us, the hook ringing throughout the park, " 'Cause we're Black, Hey! And we Dominate, Wooa!"

Vega had us in a tight pack. He was tryna set up the after celebration. But cats were telling him they wanted to scoop up the girls and go their separate ways. Panama leaned on cats that we could scoop up the girlies tomorrow at the jam. "It should just be the fellas tonight."

I was looking over towards the red team. They were in the process of blaming one another and fucking each other up before they even got all the way off the court. Ameer wasn't running no risks. He was off to the side, had his arms around two girls and his back towards me.

I told my team, "We did good but this wasn't even officially game one. We gotta keep the pressure on them."

"On who?" Mateo, one of our team members, asked me.

"On every team we play!" I answered, feeling the rush of adrenaline.

Vega threw his arm around me. Vega, me, and the whole team walked. I told the coach I had to go to work early in the morning so I had to break out.

It didn't help my story that Bangs was standing beneath the lamppost in a sparkling white tee that said MIDNIGHT in big bold blue letters plastered over 34 Ds.

Panama looked, smiled, and said, "I see where you headed and I understand." He laughed, his gold frames around his white teeth standing out.

I walked over to Bangs. I would have been crazy not to.

"I can't believe you're standing still," I said.

"I got three minutes before I start running." She smiled now, shifting her pretty legs back and forth, and her deep-dish dimples spread.

"I know you're gonna walk me home, right?" She smiled again.

"Of course," I told her, bouncing my ball.

"Did you tell your girlfriend about me?" she asked.

"What's there to tell?" I teased.

"Don't break my heart," she said. "And when you smile look the other way, my eyes and my heart can't take it." She placed her hand on my face and mushed it in the other direction away from her.

"What you wanna do, Bangs?" I asked her, stupidly believing that if I stepped up she would take some steps back.

"I wanna do whatever you doing," she said and smiled again. "You should see me at my house laying on my bed wondering where you at and why you ain't calling and what you doing now and who you doing it with." She would pull on a new finger with each question she was wondering about.

"Don't you have anything better to do?" I asked her.

"Nothing that I really want to do," she answered. We arrived at her door.

"You coming in, right?" she asked.

"Oh no, I gotta go. I gotta work in the morning," I told her. I walked off hard as a brick. The urge within me was growing stronger every day. It was the adrenaline from the training and the sports, the hordes of girls, the cheering and the encouragement.

My mind switched to what was real. Every day I was yearning for Akemi. I might not have said it aloud, but I really wanted to touch and feel *her* womb with my fingers, with my tongue, my dick. I didn't want nothing in between me and her flesh; no rubbers, no plastics, no creams, no patches, no pills. Just natural body to body, I wanted to be all over her and I wanted her all over me as her body flowed into some of those hot-ass yoga positions.

Late night I listened for Akemi's voice on the voice mail. It wasn't there. Instead, aside from our regular and new business customers, both Sudana and Ameer called.

"Good game," Ameer said when I called him back.

"Man you gotta get those knuckleheads on your team to knuckle down," I told him.

"Them motherfuckers is embarrassing," Ameer said. "Never in my life . . ."

"Yeah, but you the captain. You gotta provide the leadership. You conquering them guys instead of building them up."

"You right, I gotta go, man. Check you Monday night. I got a slimmy on my side," he said.

• • •

Saturday there was no Akemi in sight. I was feeling miserable now. It had been seven days and six nights and I couldn't hear a word from her.

I called her house knowing her uncle wasn't home and therefore wouldn't pick up her phone. I knew he was right down the street in his store.

Her phone rang and rang and rang.

I called her cousin's house knowing I shouldn't, but I did anyway.

"Is Akemi there?" I asked.

"No, she doesn't live here, as you know," her cousin said smartly. I took a deep breath, knowing that I wouldn't get nowhere fighting the cousin. So I tried to be easy.

"Listen, I know you're mad with me, but I really love Akemi. I just want you to tell me if she's okay and what's happening, that's it."

"She's okay," the cousin said, softening a bit. I didn't respond. I figured I'd give her space to talk if she was willing.

"She's locked up in her art studio. There's no phone in there. She's mad at all of us because of you," the cousin said. "She fights for you, you know. And she is in so much trouble."

"What kind of trouble?" I asked, really concerned.

"It doesn't matter. If you really love her as you say, you'll leave her alone. She has work to do. She has to finish up her projects for the show," she said. "It's a big deal, you know. You act like it's nothing. But it's everything to her father."

"So, that's what you decided, huh?" I asked.

"I decided?" she asked.

"Yeah, you're the one making all the decisions. You're the one speaking to everybody, me, Akemi, all the families. You're in control! I see that now," I said, leaning on her.

"Oh, believe me, Akemi does whatever she wants to do. She knows where you are, doesn't she? If she's not coming around, maybe she doesn't want to anymore," her cousin said, sounding pissy.

"You got it," I said. "My bad, sorry to bother you. Later." I hung up.

42

YES

Umma's facial expression finally said yes.

Naja said, "It's gonna take us a year to clean this mess up and paint these walls and it stinks in here." She was right.

"We'll have to let a lawyer look at the paperwork first," I told the old man.

"It's your money. Spend it how you like. The first one who gets here with—"

"I know. We'll contact you first thing next week," I promised.

At home, we sat on the floor reviewing the paperwork and organizing the details of the steps we needed to take before purchasing the house. We both wished that we could finalize the purchase of the house, yet we both knew from experience that only fools rush in. A lawyer would cost some fee; however, a good lawyer might save a lot of agony in the long run.

Afterwards, we studied the one hundred questions, agreeing that we would go through the citizenship ceremony on this upcoming Wednesday. It would be nice to have the citizenship in place, prior to the purchase of the new home.

43

DOING IT

Chris called. "Me and Ameer are going up to that party at the high school tonight where the black team practices," he said. "You want to meet us over there?" he asked.

"What time y'all running through?" I asked.

"About 10:00 P.M. tonight. It ends at 1:00 A.M., you know how it is," he said.

"I'll be there at ten. Y'all be easy till I get there," I told him.

"We got it," he said. "Yo, yo, yo, my team won, did you hear?"

"I knew you would," I said. "You'll keep winning until you meet the blacks!" I said. We both laughed.

The beats in the music were so powerful I could feel them vibrating in my chest. It was dark like nighttime inside of there. Only the light from the DJ booth and a random beam from the flashlights of the four or so chaperones had any impact on the darkness.

Looked like every teen in Brooklyn was packed in the space of the gym. Each person was body to body, booty to booty for real. I stood still in the crowd waiting for my eyes to adjust to the darkness, smelling hairsprays and perfumes and oils and sweat.

The DJ threw on a Doug E. Fresh, Slick Rick joint and the crowd jerked like a train pulling off from the station. It

was a good feeling in the atmosphere. I walked around looking for my boys but there were at least two hundred fifty cats
up in there and three hundred girls.

By the time I walked all the way to the far wall, I still
hadn't seen them.

Bangs was there though. She found me before I found
her. The DJ threw on some sexy-ass song named "Doing
It" by a black chick who sounded like she was fucking and
rhyming at the same time. Five hundred hips were grinding
simultaneously. Bangs slid herself against the wall and right
in front of me. She leaned her body back on it and started
grinding on me. I put my arms around her waist and pulled
her even tighter. We were pressed together like what.

The music did something no one could ever do, sucked my
mind right out of my head.

Her body felt good from her shoulders on down, all
curves and valleys. She was holding me so tight, like she
would die before she would let me go. Her hands were rubbing all over me, no shyness, no restrictions.

The DJ changed the joint, sped up the pace, and flipped the
vibe. I pulled back some. She pushed back in. I whispered in
her ear, "Go home." She let her hands drop from me and stood
on tiptoe to whisper back.

"Why?"

"Because I said so," I told her.

"Will you come?" she asked me.

"I don't know," I answered. "But you go," I told her. She
started cutting her way through the tight crowd. I followed
her but she wouldn't know. It was too loud, too crowded, too
dark, too confusing.

Once she pushed through the doors of the gym, I waited a
few and walked out.

I watched as she made it out to the sidewalk, then took
off in a mean sprint.

It was 10:45 P.M. I knew she had to be home to her grandmother by 11:00 P.M. anyway.

When I went back in, I found Ameer in a dance battle against five dudes, all six of them freestyling and surrounded by a triple layer of girls cheering them on. It wasn't long before I spotted Chris up against the wall wrapped around some girl like a pretzel.

This was the perfect crime scene, I thought to myself. Everybody all pressed together with the lights out. Nobody really controlling shit. No gun check at the door. Everybody dressed in their best. Scared niggas with their chains tucked. Bold niggas with their chains dangling, in plain view. If I had beef with people in here, I could stab them up easily and get away with it too.

Apparently, I wasn't the only one who thought so. I seen a line of niggas collecting and swerving through the crowd like a train that ran off the track. They was being led by none other than the red team idiot from Red Hook.

I went and plucked Ameer from his good time and stripped Chris off of an unknown girl. "It's about to go down," I warned them. The Red Hook niggas started shouting Red Hook, which made the teens from this hood, which was Bed-Stuy, start screaming Bed-Stuy. Brownsville spoke up, then East New York sounded off with a crazy loud unruly crew. People started pushing and splitting up.

"C'mon," I told Chris and Ameer. They followed me.

Before we could get to the door, a fight broke out. Some chains got snatched. The Red Hook nigga knocked a couple of people over then shot through the doors with the jewels. A crowd of hundreds got panicked and everybody tried to stuff themselves through the gym doors at the same time.

The sirens were screaming and police lights were spinning by the time we hit the open air. Everybody started running. I mean flying and jetting and zigzagging. Chris and Ameer was gone and so was I. The cop cars were accumulating, careless and confused.

As I ran down the dark path to Bangs' window, I heard eight Glock shots let off. I heard the separate siren sounds of the ambulances screeching.

Bangs had the window open. I jumped in. The lights were off in her room. I closed her window and felt around for the window lock.

"It's at the top, but it's broke," she said. I sat down on the floor where she was at. It was warm inside.

"It's so nice to see you," she said calmly. She struck a match and held it up as though it could light up her whole room. It burned down and heated up her fingers instead. She got up and started searching for something as my eyes adjusted to her darkness. I heard her strike a match again then saw her light a candle.

She put the candle, which was waxed onto a plate that held it up, on the floor. Then she went and lit another one. There was one candle on her side and the other candle on mine.

Now I could see her pretty smile and deep-dish dimples. Still, my mind was on my boys and I could hear the running and chasing drama still going on outside.

"It's nothing, Supastar. This shit happens all the time around here. You in Bed-Stuy," she said, smiling, seeming much calmer than I had ever seen her.

"Where you think I'm from? The police is the police," I told her.

"They'll bring the paddy wagons around in about five minutes, start sweeping everybody who's outside on the streets right up into their custody," she said casually.

"Somebody got shot," I told her.

"Better hope it's not a cop. They'll go door-to-door tearing everything up, pulling everybody out. Better hope it's just some nigga shot in the leg or some'in," she said even more casually.

"Chris and Ameer is out there. I rather it be a cop than be one of them," I said.

"You want me to go get 'em and bring them inside here?" she asked.

"Why would I send you out there?" I asked her.

" 'Cause I live around here and it ain't nothing to me. I'm a girl and they ain't looking for no girls and won't fuck with me. And even if they say something I can just say that's my house right there. All they gon' say is, 'Well get inside and stay inside for the rest of the night,' " she said softly.

"Damn. How many times did this shit happen to you?" I asked her.

"It doesn't happen to me. It happens around here. That's what I'm saying." She got up and put on her jacket.

"I'll be right back," she said.

In ten minutes she came back. I had stashed my gun by that time, just in case.

I got off the floor when I saw Ameer step up. He was smiling like this whole thing was a game.

"Brother, you really are a fucking disappearing magician, ninja secret agent, ain't you? Look at you, you got a *girl* and a *house* and all that shit. Who the fuck knew? I'm supposed to be your best friend and I didn't know," Ameer joked. Bangs laughed too.

"Where's Chris?" I asked him.

"I don't know. You seen what happened, everybody broke up and split off and went they own way," he said.

"I found him in the fried chicken store on the corner," Bangs said. "Right where I knew he would be."

"We gotta go and get Chris," I told Ameer.

"The cops had a bunch of boys in the paddy wagon and some boys in the back of their police cars. I think I saw your friend Chris in the back of the police car, but I'm not all the way sure. If you go out there now, you gon' get rounded up. I'm sure about that," Bangs warned.

"Wherever Chris is, that's where he's at," Ameer said. "It's not like he's still out there running or looking around for us." I thought about it for a minute.

"A'ight, let's just lay low in here for a minute," I told Ameer.

"That's right, 'cause they out there, the police, the paddy wagons, the whole nine," she warned.

"A'ight," Ameer said. I could definitely chill right here.

"Go out in the living room," I told him. Bangs pointed him to the couch.

She came back in and closed the door. As she went to sit down, Ameer came back in.

"If y'all about to get into it, could I at least get a blanket and one candle?" he asked. "Somebody didn't pay the electricity bill!" He laughed.

Bangs got up. "Sit down," I told her. "You don't get nothing, Ameer. Just chill on the couch for a few. You scared of the dark? What you think this is?" I said. I got up and closed the door. I discovered there was no lock on her bedroom door either.

"How did you know where Ameer was?" I asked her.

"Because that's how dudes around here do it when the police is chasing them. They blend right in with whatever everybody else is already doing. The ones that just keep on running on the streets are the ones who get caught," she said calmly.

"How did you know which one was Ameer?" I asked her.

"Because he was the only one in there with green eyes," she said matter-of-factly. But her words got me tight for some reason I didn't immediately understand.

"I'm saying, he was with you when I first met you. So I

knew who you was talking about. But that's it. The only reason why I know him is because he was with you, period," she explained herself passionately.

I looked at her real good in the pieces of light offered by the candle. I'm thinking to myself, at least she left the party when I told her to and went straight home like I told her to do. She didn't give me a lot of attitude and static. At least she was smart enough to leave the window open for me. At least she was bold enough to go outside and find Ameer. She was cool, I decided.

After some minutes she asked, "So what about us?"

"You know I got a girl, right?" I asked her, being serious with her about the topic for the first time.

"Yes," she said, straight-faced for the first time on the topic.

"You might have figured out that I love her a lot?" I said, watching her closely.

"Okay, that hurt," she said.

"Do you want me to lie to you?" I asked her.

"Yes," she said and smiled in a mature way, like a woman instead of a fidgeting teen. "I'm saying, just don't talk about her. Just don't mention her. Don't even tell me her name. Just when you see me, see me. We can be like real cool friends," she said.

"Friends?" I asked her. "Could you really do it like that?" I asked her again.

"Could you and me really only be friends?" I pressed her. "And how many friends like me do you have?" I pushed.

"None," she answered swiftly. "I don't have a man and I definitely don't have any friends like you," she confessed.

I thought to myself, this girl doesn't know me, not even a little bit. When that love works its way into my chest like it did with Akemi, I feel too close, so possessive, so crazy. I can do anything at that point. Same as I need to have Akemi completely, every single inch of her, mind, body, soul, spirit, and anything extra, that's how I would be with anyone who I loved. Now she wanted to be a part of it. But I knew she wasn't ready.

"Supastar, I can make you feel good," she sang, bringing back her excited ways.

"I can make you feel good too," I answered feeling challenged by her.

"Well, come on then. Stop teasing me," she invited.

"Then what?" I asked her.

"Then if you like it and you like me, you can come again," she said, smiling.

"And when I'm not around, what will you do?" I asked her.

"Wait for you," she said.

There was a knock at the door, too soft to be Ameer. It was her grandmother.

"The baby is hungry now," she said. Bangs jumped up and walked over and took the newborn into her arms. Her sleepy grandmother walked away, closing the door. I could tell she didn't even see me sitting right there on the floor. The door pushed opened again but this time it was Ameer.

"Man, I got to give it to you. You got a baby too? That's it. You're good," Ameer said, still joking around and interfering.

"Close the door," I told him. Bangs laid the baby on her bed. She pulled her T-shirt over her shoulders and unsnapped her bra and took it off. She picked the baby up and turned around. She bent over and handed the infant to me. "Hold her for a minute, please." Her breasts, the size of two ripe grapefruits, were dangling when she went to pass the child, and sweet milk started shooting out of her nipples onto my face.

When she sat down on the floor, she took her baby back. The child latched on to her bare breast and started sucking on her nipples. The baby's fingers were pressing into her titty.

The baby was breathing as if its mother's body and milk were the closest thing to ecstasy.

"Now what were you saying?" she asked me.

I didn't know if this was a test. I never seen or read a chapter in the Holy Quran that taught a man how to deal with a situation like this. And how strong is a man supposed to be when even the Quran says in one or two places that men are weak?

"Where is your baby's father?" I asked her.

"Dead," she answered. "He got hit by a drunk driver."

"Sorry," I offered.

"The newspaper article is on the back of my door. You can see it next time, when the power is back on."

The flame from the candles cast an erotic silhouette of Bangs feeding her baby onto the wall. I felt like clamping myself onto her other breast.

"So this is why you're always running, for your grand-mother and to your baby?" I asked her.

"Yes. I run because my milk builds up while I'm at school. If I don't get home quick enough to let her suck, my titties get too swollen and sometimes they hurt and sometimes they start leaking too." My body was turned on by her. But I reminded myself not to spill my seed into her.

"How old is she?" I asked about her baby.

"Three months," she said. "But her father died before she was ever born," she explained.

"I wanted you to see her anyway. That's why I always invited you in. I know some men run away from babies," she said sweetly with regret.

"What kind of a man would run from a baby?" I asked her seriously. She just stared at me like she had just that second fell into a deep love.

But I had to pull myself out. I had to pull myself out carefully. I didn't want to damage anyone or anything. I sat watching her until the baby finished the suck. Then I raised up to leave. She didn't seem surprised.

"At least give me a kiss," she said. She stood up. My body wanted to. Her lips were thick and smooth and moist and really pretty.

"Nah," I told her. "If I get started, I won't stop."

"That's cold," she whispered. Actually it's the opposite, I thought to myself.

I walked over to her bed and picked up her bra.

"Burp her," I said, remembering Naja as a baby.

"Okay," she said. Afterwards she laid her baby down and faced me with her full pretty titties. I helped her back into her bra and snapped it closed. Then I slid her T-shirt back over her head.

"If you're gonna go now, at least change your shirt in case they got a description of your clothes from earlier when you was running. And leave your heat here. You don't want to get caught with it. That's an automatic five," she said casually.

"Who lives in this house?" I asked again.

"My grandmother and me."

"And your daughter," I added. "Anyone else?"

"No one else."

"I already stashed my piece," I admitted to her.

"I knew you would," she said. "And I knew you was holding. I felt it when we were dancing."

"Yeah, thanks for that dance," I told her. She tossed me two Champion hoodies. I opened the door and tossed one out to Ameer and told him to throw back his shirt.

"I'll come back through for my joint. Leave it where I left it. Don't fuck with it, you might hurt yourself or somebody else," I said. "And thanks for looking out, I appreciate it, really."

"When you coming back?" she asked, her eyes and her body calling me.

"When I come back," I told her. "Like you said, you'll wait for me."

"We gonna have to go check for Chris," I told Ameer.

"We can just call him," Ameer said.

"No we can't," I said.

"Why not?" Ameer asked.

"Because let's say he got away and made his way back home. If we call at two o'clock in the morning, then by ringing the phone, we are blowing up his spot with his father. Let's say he didn't make it home. Well, we don't know where he is and even if he's okay then we would still be blowing up his spot with his father. Or say he already called his father and told him one thing, then we call and . . ."

"Damn, I get it," Ameer said.

"We'll head up to his father's church in the morning. If Chris is okay, that's where he'll be."

"A Muslim and a Five-Percenter in church," Ameer doubted.

"Man, if something happened to me, wouldn't you come looking for me no matter where I was at?" I asked him.

"No doubt," he answered.

As we walked swiftly yet calmly through the streets of Bed-Stuy, headed for the train station, we were both silent, trapped in the thoughts in our heads. I told myself I should make a prayer for Chris. If anything happened to him, I would feel personally responsible.

"Brother," Ameer said, breaking the silence. "That's a nice piece you got back there. I can see why you hid her." He was referring to Bangs.

I didn't say nothing in response. Commenting on other men's women is purely an American thing.

44

FRIENDSHIP

The Christian church was a first-time and strange experience for me. In a lot of ways, it was the opposite of the mosque that Muslims attend.

I found it odd that the Christian women of the church could not cover up themselves for at least one day, their day of worship. Instead they arrived decked out in tight, short clothing. Mothers and daughter alike had their necks, cleavage, breasts, thighs, and legs exposed to some degree slight or completely bold and obvious. There was no difference between the thirty-year-old women and the fourteen-year-old girls back on my block. I doubted that any man could concentrate on God in this setting.

At the same time, the men were all well-suited, dressed, and completely covered up, escorting their mothers, wives, sisters, and daughters who were half naked. I couldn't figure it out.

Everyone in their church entered through the same doors and prayed together sitting down or standing up and in the same space.

In the mosque, the men either prayed in front of the women, with the women praying behind them, or the prayer areas were side by side or in separate spaces. We believe that prayer is supposed to be devoted completely to Allah, with no diversions or lusts or preoccupations working their way into the eyesight, mind, or thoughts of the Muslim. Besides, we start off standing when we pray, but we conclude completely bent over with our heads touching the ground in complete respect and praise of God.

Chris' father, the Reverend, who Ameer and I have seen over the years, looked different in his church robes. I mean he was always a conservative and quiet-moving man who I never seen rock a pair of jeans, not even once. Outside of his church when we would see him, he usually wore some style of a hat, hard-bottom shoes, dress shirts, dress socks, and slacks, even at sporting events and on weekends.

Now he looked much more removed, like an American Supreme Court judge or a Black pope. He was raised up on a higher platform than his congregation, speaking in a loud tired voice that was projected from the microphone though it really wasn't needed.

The sermon, which we Muslims call a *khutba*, was a story from their Holy Bible, Luke Chapter 15, about a son who makes wrong choices in his life despite his father's advice and teachings. The son runs away to another town to live the way he wants to live outside of the eyesight and reach of his father. The son ends up spending his monies foolishly and is forced to take a job working with pigs. The son finally realizes that he needs his father and should have respected his father's wisdom in the first place. The son returns to the father begging for forgiveness. The father forgives and accepts his son, even though the son really didn't do anything good or right or respectful to show and prove that he deserved his father's forgiveness.

After listening to the sermon, I knew that Chris' father knew all about what happened at the party last night. The disappointment was felt in his words and stamped on his tired face. I also knew that Chris would be forgiven. However, the point seemed to be that he would have to do something to win back his father's trust.

All me and Ameer could see was the back of Chris' head. He was seated in the first row of the church and we were seated in the last row of the church.

Ameer said, "Let's just walk up there and go get him."

"We can't start walking around while the brother's father is speaking," I said. "Let's just chill till the end, then we can get at him."

Some people who were seated behind the reverend up there, and facing the congregation, stood up. A funny-looking dude started giving them hand signals and they all began to sing. Ameer leaned over to me and said, "That's a faggot right there, one hundred percent."

Faggot, that's an American thing, I thought to myself. Or I should say, a European thing. I hear this word used all the time and am still confused by it. I was only sure that we didn't have no "faggots" back home where I come from.

Usually when cats pointed out a "faggot," it was some guy who dressed, walked, or talked and acted like a female. Or, some boy who could not do the same things that other boys did eagerly and naturally, like playing sports, fighting, and fixing things.

My confusion came in when Black American boys called a boy who loves his mother a faggot. Or when the Jamaicans called a "faggot" a "mama man." Or when somebody said a boy who sticks by his mother, helps her out often, and protects her is some kind of "faggot."

To me, there had to be a difference between a boy who acted like or wanted to be a woman, and one who loves his mother a whole lot. For me, loving, standing by, serving, and protecting Umma was like breathing, a strength and not a weakness.

So I just didn't respond to Ameer's comment.

A paper plane came flying from the right side of the room and landed in the lap of the woman seated beside Ameer.

"Excuse me, that's for me," Ameer told the woman. He unfolded the plane and we both read the note at the same time.

"We see you're new to our church. We think you and your friend are cute. We are sitting on your right side, the third and fourth girl in, red dress and long hair and yellow blouse and short hair. Meet us downstairs afterwards." Ameer looked at me and smiled.

"See, I told you, these Christian dudes are faggots. Christian girls want Muslim dick."

Now I knew, based on Ameer's words, that "faggot" also meant a male who wasn't fucking all the girls who wanted to get fucked. I thought to myself, this one word had a whole lot of different meanings. It still meant nothing to me as a Sudanese.

A well-dressed woman, wearing everything brand new, sang a sad song. She looked like she had been to hell, seen the devil, and come back. The tears eased out of her eyes as she sang.

The people stood for what seemed to be the final prayer. I stood too. They bowed their heads. I faced front until the prayer was over.

"C'mon," I told Ameer. "Let's go talk to Chris."

Chris was shocked to see us. He touched the material on both of our dress shirts as if he was impressed. "Get the fuck out of here. You two in church?" he said, then looked around to see if anyone overheard him. He glanced at his father, who was standing at the front receiving people one by one, who seemed to just want to greet him and touch and shake his hand.

"Let's step to the back," Chris told us.

"Is that your mother seated there?" I asked him.

"Oh, yeah, let me introduce you," he said. His mother was polite, but more focused on her husband and his activity at the front of the church. Chris explained, "These are my two best friends from the dojo, who I tell you about all the time."

We also met Chris' younger sister and brother, who were perfectly dressed, well-behaved, faces shining with a thick coat of Vaseline.

As we three walked towards the back of the church, we were intercepted by a young female wearing pretty pumps on her feet, a tight skirt and silk blouse, nipples erect even through her bra. She stuck her foot out as if to trip Chris. He stopped walking. She stood directly in front of him, playfully pushing him and asking, "Aren't you gonna introduce me to your friends?"

He introduced her as his girlfriend, a surprise to both of us. Afterwards she tried to follow us to the back, but Chris told her to go sit down and wait on him. In the back corner of the church, he filled us in about what happened.

"Last night, I almost got away. I was real close. But, the cop who was chasing me tripped and fell and busted his ass. I shouldn'tve laughed, but it was funny watching him down on the pavement, grabbing for his hand radio. I started running again, got about forty feet out of his way, then a police car shot across my path, slammed on the brakes, cut me off. The next thing I knew, 'You Are Under Arrest.'

"They cuffed me and pushed me into the backseat. I was just glad they didn't kill me, 'cause they did clap up some other kid, dead over nothing, some bullshit.

"Another cop car pulled up with three girls riding in the back. The window came down and all three girls were all staring at me. They started speaking among themselves. Then I saw them tell the cop who was driving the police car 'no.' "

"No, what?" Ameer asked.

"No, I wasn't one of the ones who snatched their gold chains. There was like six girls and three dudes whose jewels got swiped at the party. The dumb-ass cops caught all the wrong boys and the real ones got away," Chris said.

"Were you scared?" Ameer asked.

"Hell yeah, I'm not gonna lie. I was hoping y'all would be down there at central booking when I arrived. You know, three is better than one." They laughed.

"How did you get out in less than twenty-four hours?" I asked him on a serious note.

"You must've snitched on them other dudes," Ameer said, only half joking.

"I couldn't snitch on nobody. I never even saw what happened, that shit went down so fast," Chris swore. But Ameer and I both knew it was the Red Hook niggas from the red team that led the whole caper.

"Then how did you get out?" I repeated my question. He answered reluctantly.

"My pops called Mayor Koch, got his ass right out of his bed. The mayor made a couple of calls. Next thing I know, I get released. My pops was waiting right there with the Caddy. I walked out pretending like I was all cool, but I was so happy I didn't have to close my eyes and sleep with all them niggas on the lockup. I almost peed on myself!" We all laughed.

"Does he really have that kind of clout, your father?" I asked.

Yeah, he's head of the Ministers' Conference. The mayor always has to come through him to get anything done in the Black church or the community. So I guess he just owed my pops one," Chris said easily.

"Anyway, the mayor had to do something. His cops clapped a kid; unjustifiable homicide, excessive force," Chris said. I knew he must have heard those phrases getting thrown around last night.

"Unbelievable. What a break, for real," I said. "Me and

Ameer was all worried about you for nothing. You was out there getting the royal treatment."

"Nah, that's cool. I appreciate y'all coming up here. That's alright. I'll always remember how you two looked out," Chris said in a serious tone. "Don't think I got over either. My pops is gonna announce my punishment tonight. I just hope he don't go crazy and lock me in *his jail* for the summer."

When the three of us came out of our huddle and turned around, there were about six girls waiting on us. Me and Ameer didn't know none of them. Chris felt good about this being "his territory" and said, "C'mon let me intro y'all to the church chicks."

As we walked over, I saw the Reverend approaching from the distance. I elbowed Chris to bring it to his attention.

"Young man," the Reverend called to his son.

"Yes, father." Chris tensed up to attention and responded respectfully.

"So you have been joined by your friends," he said dryly. "Well, good for them. Where were you fellas last night when Chris needed you?"

He glanced over at the girls gathered and waiting for us.

"Let's go, gentlemen, step into my chambers." We followed silently. The Reverend pronounced to his secretary, "I need some time with my son, make sure no one disturbs us."

My eyes bounced around the walls of his private office. The images were all foreign to me.

"When you three first met, you were boys. Now you are young men. There is a difference, you know. Boys play. Young men handle their business," the Reverend lectured, no laughter or doubt in his style. He was seated upright in his big black leather chair.

I was listening, but at the same time, I was still looking at the wall over his head. Plastered there was his picture of Jesus. I thought to myself that there is not one Muslim, out of the three billion Muslims in the world, who believes he has a picture of God, or that God could ever be captured in a photograph or painting. In a mosque, we do not have images or pictures or snapshots or symbols or idols on our walls or anywhere else, for that matter.

Muslims acknowledge the great works and life of Jesus. However, we don't believe that Jesus is God, or the son of God. We believe that Jesus was a Prophet, a chosen messenger of God, selected as other prophets were selected by God to carry out and perform incredible and extraordinary works and deeds, like Moses even.

"Boys do things because they want to. Boys respond to impulse. Young men do things because they should. They are in the process of setting up to be responsible, to carry their weight. Are you young men listening? Are you understanding me?"

I looked at Ameer, his arm draped around the chair where he was sitting. He was checking the place out same as I was. I knew when we left here, he would have something sharp to say about all of this.

Chris had his head bowed, listening as though he heard these lessons every day.

"As you grow older, you have to weigh your decisions. Everything you do means something. Your actions all have a value. When you're doing *nothing*, you are losing something valuable, either *time or money* or both. And, they are both the *same thing*." The Reverend was tapping his huge finger on his desktop to emphasize his important words.

"It's easy for you fellas to *lose money*, because *it's not your money*, directly. It's easy to waste your *father's money* and your *father's time*. As a man, it's my job to stop you from wasting money and time, especially *my money, my time*.

"Chris is going to be the first to stop. He's not going to be attending the karate class anymore until he can live a responsible life. He's not going to be playing in any basketball league until he can demonstrate that he understands what is important and what it takes to earn real money. Chris is going to focus on hitting the books, getting top marks in school, and working for his father. *Only* by working with his father will he become careful with his *father's money*."

Ameer waited for the Reverend to take a breath and jumped right in.

"Sir, the party we went to last night only cost five dollars. And when we play ball we earn *our own money*." He was trying to counter the Reverend's assumptions.

"What do you know about money? Do you even have insurance?" he asked Ameer.

Ameer smirked. He probably didn't know what the Rev was talking about, because I sure didn't.

"When you go to apply for insurance, the insurance agent asks several questions about how you live your life every day. They want to know how big of a fool you are, what type of risks and gambles you take with your own life. It's the only way they can figure out how much risk is involved in doing business with you.

"Now you three went to a party, most likely looking for girls, in a neighborhood that is *not your own*, with people who are complete *strangers to you*.

"If I was an insurance agent, on a scale of one to ten, I would say that you three rank a ten as far as fools are concerned," the Reverend said with an angry scowl.

"Who cares that you paid the five-dollar entry fee?" he barked on Ameer.

"I have invested *real money* in Chris, $5,000 on his braces, $20,000 a year for his private schooling, and about $15,000 on his martial arts training, to date. I've sunk a lot of *money* into this one son, and as you know, he has a younger brother and sister." He leaned back now in his big chair.

"Not only is this church a corporation, *his life is a corporation* and *so is yours*, whether you know it or not."

I wasn't mad at the Reverend as I listened. I started to enjoy the way he was throwing the numbers around. I liked any talk about business, setting it up and earning money, as long as the person talking could get around to the point. Then the Reverend continued.

"Last night, before I received the phone call from the police, I was looking through my tax receipts for this year. Counting them up is a big job. I got a couple of crates filled with receipts that have to be sorted out and added up. Every year, every man in business in America has to submit a record of his expenses. Every purchase a man makes matters, has to be documented and reported. You know why?" the Reverend asked. We three sat there silent.

"Chris knows why. A *real friend* doesn't play dumb. Chris, teach these boys what you already know. Share with them what I taught you," he ordered his son.

Chris lifted his head and answered, "Because half of everything a businessman earns in America belongs to the United States government. And every April 15th, that money is due and every businessman has got to pay it." Chris spoke like an automated recording or telephone operator.

"Now tell them what happens to businessmen who don't collect receipts, keep proper records, and pay the government half of their earnings," the Reverend told Chris.

"They pay fines and interest on their debt and they go to jail," Chris answered.

"Straight to jail. Do not pass go, like the Monopoly game. The only thing is, real life is not a game," the Reverend emphasized.

We three spent the rest of Sunday with pencils in our hand and paper at our table, sorting and counting the Reverend's receipts without the help of a calculator. Chris told us that all of it was just busywork, just the start of a string of punishments. He said his father had two expensive accountants, and had actually already filed his taxes, because April 15th had passed more than a week ago and his dad never misses deadlines. He also said that churches don't pay taxes like other corporations do, but his father has other businesses and personal expenses to account for.

There were thousands of receipts. We were just trying to help Chris out, hoping that if we did a good job, his father would respect us enough to let Chris at least continue in the martial arts. We knew the basketball league was out for Chris.

His father did not know that there was a big money prize involved in the game. He did not know it was the Hustler's League. If we told him, we would get the same result, no Chris. Shit is fucked up, I thought to myself. I wish the Reverend and some of his crew had sponsored the league. Then the hustlers wouldn't have to.

When the church cooks brought plates of food back for each of us to eat, I kept thinking, "This church is a corporation." As I looked at the food plate, I saw a separate price tag hanging over each item in my mind. I felt I needed to leave my money on the table for this meal, even for the two glasses of water I drank. The Reverend had convinced me that everything had a price no matter how small.

During our twenty-minute food break, I tried to think about what my father would say about the Reverend's words and opinions.

My father is a deep thinker and planner, and extremely successful in business. When he spoke the truth, it punctured everyone's fantasy bubble.

After a while my father's words came to me, streaming clear-cut across my mind. My father would say, "All men are risks, and all men must take risks. There is no insurance or guarantee. Only Allah can give that, only Allah can take it away."

My father would have his head pressed to the ground, thanking Allah for granting my narrow escape.

45

GROWN

"Half of everything a businessman in America earns belongs to the United States government." "Collect receipts, keep proper records." "If not, go straight to jail." It was eye-opening, new information for me, and mind-blowing.

Sunday night I got more serious. I sat down and got my thoughts organized. Then I began to organize everything else. I pulled out the jewels for Akemi. I sat down with the pen and the pad and wrote out the *agid*. I asked Umma to write out in Arabic the *nikah*, the words Akemi would recite and questions she would be asked during the short and simple ceremony. I would translate the Arabic into English myself. Then I would have the English translated into Japanese for Akemi. Umma was right. Akemi is a jewel and I would have to work very hard to get her and keep her for myself.

I wanted to go by her school and see her. I wanted to make sure she was okay, feeling well and still wanting to be mine. I wanted to see what effect her family was having on her thinking and choices.

I wanted to give her a copy of both the *agid* and the *nikah*, so she could make all of her decisions with a full understanding. I wanted to give her the jewels and other gifts as the *mahr*, or dowry.

After I had everything which concerned Akemi straight, we studied, Umma and I. The citizenship was, after all, a matter of business. Joining the United States of America was not emotional, not a matter of faith or patriotism. It was something I had to study for and pay for and continue paying for in taxes. It was because my life is a corporation and yours is too.

Monday the grind was on. By 10:00 A.M. I was at the lawyer's office with the paperwork for the possible house purchase. The lawyer's secretary wanted five hundred dollars to make a folder with our family name on it, slide my papers inside, and have the attorney look at it and give us a call.

"Is that the total fee?" I asked her.

"That's the total right now," she replied. I left and tried the next lawyer. There was a whole block of them, fifteen in a row. I figured maybe that was a good thing. A professional competition might drive one or two of them to lower their fees.

I found one who would do the closing on the house for two hundred fifty dollars total. She was a "first-year lawyer no experience." She was an African American attorney who at least greeted her potential clients, and not with the standard "fuck you" face.

Monica Abraham, Esq., said she could have the documents reviewed by tomorrow morning. She said she would check the register to verify that Mr. Saul Slerzberg was the actual owner and that there were no outstanding debts and liens against his property. She even bothered to explain some of the concepts to me, which I appreciated a lot.

I agreed to meet her at 10:00 A.M. tomorrow morning but told her I would be in a rush because I had to go to class, referring to Sensei without referring to him.

She said, "I think you're wonderful to carry such big responsibilities on your shoulders, to conduct business for your mom and family, to translate so carefully and cautiously your mother's expectations. You're rare. If you were older I'd introduce you to my younger sister."

I contacted Sensei by phone, asking if it was okay for me to stop by and speak with him for a minute. He said I could, so I headed right over.

"Do you know a place in New York where a Japanese person could take an English language course?" I asked Sensei.

"But of course," he answered.

"Would you be willing to give me their contact information?" I asked. He went into his card file, flipping slowly, his fingers pausing on top of one card. He wrote out the information onto a piece of paper and handed it to me. "You could have asked me this question over the telephone. Is there something else you wanted to say or ask?"

"If I need to get something translated, something written in English translated into Japanese in a hurry?" I asked.

"I can do it," he said.

I paused. "I was not wanting to bother you. I was thinking that if you could recommend someone."

"Someone who doesn't know you, to drop everything they are doing and start translating something for you right then and there while you stand and wait?" he stated out loud to show me how absurd I was to him right now.

"If this is what the person does professionally, I could pay the fee and they could provide the translation for me as soon as possible," I corrected myself.

Sensei seemed disappointed for some reason. He said to me, "The address I have given you, which you are holding in your hand, will serve all of your needs for classes and translations of at least seven different languages. The businesses, as you can see, are all located at Rockefeller Center. There they are used to assisting immigrants and foreigners. There you will find a professional stranger to do as you wish, anything concerning language. If this is good enough, I do have another matter to tend to."

"*Arigato gozamasu,* Senseian," I said, thanking him respectfully. I left.

"Fifty dollars extra for a rush job, no problem," I told the Japanese woman who agreed to translate my documents into Japanese and have them nicely typed and presentable on quality stationery.

"Come back in two hours," she said. The clock read ten minutes past noon.

I agreed.

At 2:00 P.M., I picked up the *agid* and the *nikah* translations.

The woman placed them in an elegant gold textured envelope. I pulled the documents out. The words were neatly and beautifully arranged on thick 8 x 11 gold sheets of textured paper. A real professional job and much more than I expected.

I paid what amounted to twenty-five dollars per page, plus the fifty-dollar rush fee. I made sure to collect their printed business cards *and* my receipt as the reverend recommended I do at all times.

At the jewelers, I paid a small sum to have my jewelry steam blasted and cleaned. Although they tried feverishly to actually buy Umma's high-quality pieces from me, they had to be content with me simply buying their most elegant jewelry cases to put each different piece into.

For only two hundred dollars, I bought two solid gold, twenty-four-karat rings. They were completely plain, no print, no diamonds, no engravings. Fawzi had said that the bangles were the precious pieces and there were no bangles more precious than the ones I had cleaned and glistening in the box.

Two swift deliveries on behalf of Umma Designs were completed. They were the items that the two clients ordered at the tail end of the big wedding, and were patient enough to wait for. I gladly handed them over and accepted the generous tip from one of the clients, which made up for the non-tip from the other.

I picked Umma up at five. We went to the apartment. I showered and dressed all over again. I had never really known what it felt like to be nervous but I was getting a little familiar with the sensation.

She hugged me before I left, saying, "You already have my permission. If it is Allah's will, it will be done." She brushed her hands together to say, "And it is done." We both smiled. I was out.

At Pratt, I waited at her classroom door. This way, there was no way for me to overlook her when she arrived. In fact, I would see her coming down the hall. Her eyes would give away whatever she was feeling, as they always did, and really on just one look, I would have all of my answers.

The closer it got to 7:00 P.M., the more students arrived. At exactly 7:00 P.M. the professor showed up.

"Oh, it's you," she said, smiling. "You're looking quite smart. What's the occasion?" she asked.

"I'm good," I told her, diverting her questions.

"Have you changed your mind?" she asked.

"Excuse me?" I replied.

"About the modeling job," she teased.

"Nah, I'm just waiting for Akemi," I said.

"She probably won't come tonight. She's somewhere preparing for her big show. I'm sure you know all about it," she tested.

"Yes, I know," I told her.

"Okay then, bye-bye. Let me know if you change your mind about the modeling, Akemi or no Akemi." She waved and went in.

I stood against the locker, my heart splitting in half, my body temperature rising, feeling like a fucking fool. I heard her cousin's voice in my ear, and her annoying American accent. "Akemi knows where you are! If she stopped coming around maybe it's because she doesn't want to anymore."

I hopped on the train, thought about not going to the dojo, then thought about going home and facing Umma with no results. I thought about going to Queens instead, to Akemi's studio. Within seconds, I realized that was a wrong move, especially in my state of mind. What kind of a love could she and I have if I had to fight her uncle at his home? I thought about going by the museum where her show was, thinking maybe she was there setting up or rehearsing or whatever.

Then, I just got tight and said, "Fuck it. Should I be chasing her around? If she was my wife, she would be right here with me where I could see her. If my wife wasn't here with me, I better know where she was and it better be a place that I approved of."

If she loved me, how could she just stay away?

Before my heartbreak converted to depression and my depression into rage, I took some deep breaths.

I decided I'd go to the dojo and clear my head. No women to entice or seduce me there. No women to arouse and abandon me there. Nobody with the power to break my heart there. No time or space or possibilities of tears there. I could just choose one of the students there and fuck him up real good to release my disappointment while calling it training.

Later, every student in the dojo was already seated in rows when I arrived. I cut across the back of the room headed for my locker. I needed to change in a flash. Suddenly, they all stood up, the sixteen or so Ninjitsu fighters, and began clapping.

I turned and looked at Ameer like, "What the fuck is going on?" I was surprised to also see Chris. I was so sure he was finished at the dojo.

When I turned to get an answer from Sensei, I saw Akemi standing in his space instead. Her eye was completely healed. When I looked into her eyes, I could see my reflection. I knew then that I had my answer.

She wore a gold tunic dress and Manolo Blahnik sandals, a pair I had seen in that expensive store. Her Fendi python pocketbook was so mean it could be worn without clothes. I had to pull myself back from my fantasy and focus on what was really going on in my dojo.

She looked so good that she had the men on their feet. Even the master of calm, Sensei himself, looked swept away. Now, there were thirty-six eyeballs focused on my reactions. I cut and walked around the men like they were cornstalks in an overcrowded field. As I got closer to her, she stepped up and folded into me.

I embraced her warmly and completely even though I was in shock. I was so used to being a private person. To hold my heart in my hands in front of men who had been with me for years but never really knew me made me feel vulnerable in ways that a fighter should never be vulnerable. If there was ever a time for an enemy to kill me, it would've been right then. I was so open in that moment that I was unlike a ninja, completely defenseless.

She remained there in my embrace. Then I turned her by her shoulders, kept one arm around her, and walked off to move us into a private corner of this large room.

I pulled out the gold envelope and handed it to her. She smiled and pulled the contents out and read them over. Her eyes welled up in tears that remained floating there but never fell.

"Sensei, please continue with the class," I called out. But he didn't and everyone laughed.

Then she turned to Sensei and called out some words in Japanese. Sensei left the room and returned seconds later with a writing pen in his hand. He walked over and handed it to her.

Look how she has him eating out of her hands, I thought to myself. Not to mention I wished I could throw a curtain around her so that no one else could see or stare at her beauty but me.

She started writing on the papers as she walked away. All male eyes positioned on each of her heeled feet moving gracefully across the floor. I wanted to know what she was doing. Although I knew that whatever she was doing, no one could stop her.

She spoke some more to Sensei. He called me over.

"She says that you said all that is needed are two or three witnesses. 'Well, we have seventeen witnesses instead,' " he translated for Akemi.

"It's true that we do have four men here who are at least eighteen years old," Sensei pushed.

Ameer was standing in the back with his hands in the air like, "What the fuck is up with you now?" Chris was mesmerized.

I excused myself to the men's room and performed *wudu*, the washing that each Muslim must do before making a prayer.

I returned and made a prayer at the front of the room facing east.

I recited *Al Fatiha* in Arabic:

In the name of Allah, the Beneficent, the Merciful.
Praise be to Allah, the Lord of the Worlds.
The Beneficent, the Merciful,
Thee do we serve and Thee do we beseech for help.
Guide us on the right path,
The path of those upon whom
Thou has bestowed favors,

Not those upon whom wrath is brought down,
Nor those who go astray.

When I raised up, everyone was standing in complete silence. I pulled the jewels from my inside jacket pocket. I opened the elegant boxes and placed each bangle onto Akemi's wrist. The diamonds on the right, the gold on her left. For me, this was not any type of game.

"Sensei, Akemi may recite her *nikah* now if she chooses," I said. Sensei translated. She chose. She recited her *nikah* in Japanese. Sensei translated her words into English for the seventeen witnesses, four of whom were adults, in addition to Sensei who was somehow representing Akemi and Akemi's understanding as a father, guardian, or family advisor would normally do.

Akemi faced me, and began reading the *nikah* in Japanese from the paper in the gold envelope. She was speaking with no fear, as though no one else was there other than the two of us. Sensei translated the words of the *nikah* into English for everyone to hear and understand. I recited my acceptance of her giving herself to me in marriage. We signed the *aqid* in the presence of everyone.

Sensei placed his signature on our documents, as did two other adult students whom I knew from regular classes.

I opened the box with the simple gold rings and slid one onto her finger. She placed the second ring onto mine.

She held her arms up for everyone to see. She dropped her wrist down to show off her fingers and the ring. Then she bowed over completely before me. These cats went wild with cheer.

Not your average Islamic ceremony, I knew.

Having already signed her name on all of the documents, she handed Sensei the paperwork, plus some papers from her pocketbook, and said some words to him in their language.

The more she spoke to Sensei without my understanding, the more uneasy I became.

She turned to me and folded herself into my embrace. She eased out from me and turned to leave and of course I followed her.

As we exited the dojo, a limousine, double-parked halfway down the block, began driving our way. The driver pulled up and double-parked in front of the dojo. The Asian driver emerged and ran around to open the car door. I told him to get back in the car. I spun her around and looked at her to show my confusion at whatever her plan was.

She placed her hand onto the car door handle. I put my hand over hers; the gold glittered polish on her fingertips looking exquisite against my black skin.

We opened the door and she stepped on the inside of the limo door. Then she turned towards me to show me that she was leaving alone.

She said, "*Aishiteru.*"

In a move that went against all of my beliefs about public intimacy, I kissed her. She leaned against the warm exterior of the limo and her body relaxed. Her mouth was moist and warm. I saw her eyes roll into her head and then close in pleasure. She gave in to the feeling.

Soon, she pushed my body away gently and said, "Sayonara." This is a Japanese word that almost everyone knew, or heard or said before. But since I first met Akemi, it is the one word that I never liked to hear her say.

She got in the limo. I closed her door and went to the other side where her driver was. I leaned in towards him knowing that I was intimidating him. He was a small man. He opened his window only enough to hear me out.

"Where are you supposed to take her?" I asked.

"New Jersey," he answered.

I stood there with my hands on his window, delaying him.

All I could think was that I wanted Akemi to stay here with me. I felt a thousand percent possessive over her, same as I did before we recited the *nikah*, but it was even more pressing to me now.

Instead, I told myself she will be fine and she will make the right choices which are best for both of us. I felt wrong for doubting her in the first place, when it was so completely evident that she is mine, and I am where she wants to be. I pulled away from the driver's window, tapped the top of his hood, nodded to Akemi, and the driver pulled off.

Nobody was fighting in the dojo. Everybody was at the window watching me. Ameer was in the front now, of course. As I approached the building, the curtain that separated the Ninjitsu world from the Brooklyn streets dropped.

When I entered the dojo they were all seated on the floor there staring at me.

"What?" I asked. Sensei was seated in the middle of them on the floor, which I had never seen him do before. With a playful smile he said, "If at your age you can win over such a lovely young wife who will do anything for you and pledge her love with such open loyalty, then perhaps you should be teaching this class, and I should be back here listening and learning from you." The class laughed all together.

I stood there dazed by the whole last hour of my life.

"Loosen up, man, you got the girl!" Ameer said. They all laughed again.

Still thinking of Akemi, I asked Sensei, "What did she tell you?" He smiled.

"Perhaps you'd better get a professional translator to translate the events of this day for you."

"*Sumimasen*, Senseisan," I said, apologizing to him for the disrespect I caused him to feel by getting someone other than him to translate my marriage documents into Japanese.

"Very well," Sensei said. "She said, 'I love you. You are my husband now and I am your wife, nobody can change that.' She also said that neither a beautiful bird, nor a beautiful leopard, is beautiful in a cage; no one can change that either."

"She's deep," Chris said.

"She probably heard that somewhere in a rhyme," Ameer said.

I wasn't saying anything, just thoughts racing through my mind, my heart and my body throbbing equally.

"Do you know the meaning of her name?" Sensei asked, always in the teaching position.

"Her name, Akemi, means, 'Bright Beauty.'"

"Midnight and the Bright Beauty," Chris recited out loud.

Ameer laughed. Some students laughed too, but Sensei did not. I could see he knew now the weight of my heart and the seriousness of this matter.

He continued, "The last thing that your Akemi said was, 'I have to leave now. I have to go back to wipe the tears from my father's eyes.'"

"I don't care if it takes you all night. Now that your under-cover identity has been compromised, I want you to sit here and tell us what the fuck was going on. Don't leave out no details. You might as well sit here and talk to us since you're fourteen, you just got *married*, and *ain't* on your honeymoon," Ameer said, smiling.

Chris seemed speechless with fascination. It was just the three of us now.

"Chris, you wasn't even with us two on Saturday night after the party. I'm telling you, *this man here has two wives and one newborn!* At least, that's all we know about so far," he joked.

Ameer was now standing on his feet animating like he was in a play in front of a packed theatre. "Now, your man did all of this without giving up one word or one shred of evidence. I'm so fucking impressed right now! We all friends here, just give up your secrets," he begged.

"Your ninja wife is the one who blew up your spot by showing up to the dojo. That was your *only* mistake, the *one* thing that you weren't in control of! I'm surprised you even let her know where the dojo was at," Ameer performed. I had to laugh at that one.

"I didn't. She took the paper from my house," I admitted, thinking back to when she was walking around my bedroom, rummaging through my stuff. Then I relaxed a little.

"I'll only tell you two this: Akemi is my girl, my wife, that's it. Bangs, she has love for me, but I can't rock with her. Her daughter is not my daughter. That's all I'm gonna say."

"Akemi, I mean your wife, she's beautiful," Chris said. For the first time, another man commenting on my woman sounded sincere. There was no offense in his compliment. No wrong intention.

"I admire you, man, for real. We been busy playing. You been busy growing up," Chris said so seriously. Then he looked like he went into his own head and began reflecting on something.

"Who is she? Where did you meet her? Is this marriage even legal?" Ameer challenged.

"Our parents have given their permission," I said, holding up the envelope containing all of the signatures including the form signed by Akemi's father. "And our marriage is legal in the eyes of Allah." That silenced him.

"Even the Sudanese bride returns home to her family after the signing of the *agid*. She doesn't go right away to her husband," Umma said, soothing me. She was sitting in the middle of her bed, her bare feet still beautifully painted with

pretty henna patterns. Her lamp lit up her excited eyes as I
recounted the story of my and Akemi's vows.

"The Sudanese wedding takes seven days or more. Do you
know that after the huge ceremony for Fawzi's wedding, the
entire family reconvened two days later for his *walima*?"

"*Walima*?" I asked. I was seated on the floor with my back
up against the wall.

"It is the family breakfast feast where the families celebrate the proof of virginity of the new wife. It is also a prayer
breakfast in hope that Allah will bless the newly married
couple with new life."

"How does the family have proof of the virginity?" I
asked, feeling naive.

"When you go into a new bride, if she is virgin, there will
be blood. It will not be a shower of blood, which occurs in the
woman's monthly flow. Females vary, but there must be
some blood coming from her 'below' on the first night of
intimacy. The husband will know how it feels, how it is and
how it looks. He will take time to see the blood. When the
husband is sure and feels that his bride has not been entered
into by any other man, he is happy. So the families are happy.
No one feels cheated. Everyone celebrates!"

I already knew there would be no *walima* between our
two families. Yet, I felt a heavy Sudanese kind of pride that
there would be blood coming from "below," not a hand-me-
down girl or someone else's leftovers or an abandoned or
passed around piece.

In my bedroom, I kept turning her words over in my head.
"I have to go back to wipe the tears from my father's eyes."

Not back to Japan, my heart pleaded. The driver said
New Jersey. She must be saying that her father has come
here to the U.S. and is keeping up in the New Jersey home
of his brother. Either way, I had to admit to myself, that this
was the first time, since we arrived to America, that I really

trusted any female outside of Umma. Now, after careful thought and observation, I felt within my heart that I trusted Akemi too. Even when I could not see her with my own two eyes standing before me, I trusted that she was good and true, and doing only the right things.

46

THE WHITE ZONE

Early Tuesday morning we made prayer. I took the train ride in with Umma as usual. I asked her if she had known that "Umma Designs" needed to pay taxes to the American government. She looked at me strangely and said, "I go to work every day at the factory. When they pay me, they have already deducted the money for taxes from my paycheck. That's what I pay them."

At 10:00 A.M., I was at the lawyer's office.

"Saul Slerzberg's home is his to sell. He is debt-free as far as liens against his home are concerned. His deed is old, I can update it for you with his consent. Also, I would advise you to spend the money and have the home inspected before your mom agrees to the sale or signs anything," the lawyer said.

"Mr. Slerzberg has already said that if anything's broke, we should just fix it," I informed her. "It's an 'as is' deal."

"Well, usually, if something is not right with the house, and the inspector confirms this fact after his inspection, you can negotiate to have the amount it will cost you for the house repairs deducted from the overall selling price of the house."

"That's not happening here. Eighty thousand for this guy is the magic number. We've looked at a lot of properties. The ones that Umma likes are out of our price range. This place is the only one so far that is in the right location for work and school, at the right price. Mr. Slerzberg is an old guy. He wants to get out of New York quick," I said.

"Yes, maybe too quickly. Maybe you'll sign these papers and hand over your money and he will leave so fast your head spins. Then you find out your house is wired all wrong and is a fire hazard. Or, your air-conditioning doesn't work and it's June! Or God forbid the plumbing is jammed and the plumber wants five thousand to lay new pipes, meanwhile your toilets are backed up and the whole house stinks!"

"Slow down," I told her. "Easy, I understand. We'll get the inspections."

"Sorry," she said, slowing down and content that she seemed to have won her argument and made her point.

"I want to ask you a couple of questions about taxes," I said, leaning forward in my chair on the opposite side of her desk.

"You're wearing a ring today," she observed. "On your married finger . . ."

After completing my business with the lawyer, I headed to the Museum of Modern Art. I wanted to see the place where Akemi would have her exhibit. I wanted to have an idea what she was involved in, and thought just maybe she would be over there too.

The museum was situated in what I refer to as a "White zone." I never take my guns into White zones. I stash 'em before and pick 'em up later. White zones are closed-in areas where it is guaranteed that there will be metal detectors, security, and constant police patrols. White zones are areas where I already know there won't be many Black people, where I will be an obvious standout and automatic suspect. It is very easy to get picked up in a White zone, because the authorities are all the time wondering what the fuck you are doing there and what the fuck do you want?

The museum was a nice-looking, well-kept, oddly shaped facility where it was clear that millions of dollars were being spent to keep the lights on, the thick glass windows shining, the turnstiles and security desk operating, the huge bookstore in the lobby stacked with an inventory of thousands of intriguing items, and the pictures and displays mounted, framed, and lit up.

At the museum entrance, before the security desk, there were seven metal easels on which thick boards were mounted, advertising the upcoming exhibit and exhibitors. "Seven Continents, Seven Geniuses, Seven Youths," the display was titled.

Underneath the board for Asia was a huge black-and-white photograph of my wife, Akemi Nakamura. The caption beneath her photo read, "As Soon As She Sees You, You're Captured."

Looking at her picture, I could see that it was taken before we met. Her ears were not pierced in the photo. I looked at the way her thick black hair, black eyes, and full lips were pulling me. I wondered if they were pulling everyone else also.

Their description of Akemi read:

Sixteen-year-old Akemi Nakamura is the Japanese-born artist who swept our art competition and best represents the artistic talents of the youth of Asia. She has mastered the unique style of combining pencils, markers, and paints together on one surface. Her original artwork also contains numerous creative surprises that make it stand out from the work of her peers.

Her greatest talent, however, is her photographic memory.

*She despises drawing or painting using mounted objects
or models. It is believed that she can look at her subject once,
close her eyes, and then open them and bring it to life on
her canvas in great detail by memory. She is a unique talent unlike any artist the world has known. Her eyes are
more precise than a camera. This is why we say "As soon as
she sees you, you are captured."*

Behind me now were three or four people, also taking a
look, but not a glance, because they didn't leave right away.
They stared instead.

An attendant in matching pants and vest approached the
gathering crowd that was beginning to block the museum
entrance.

"Welcome to the Museum of Modern Art. This exhibit
will be featured on Saturday, May third, here at the MoMA
and will be on display for three months up until August
third. A reception will be held in our auditorium welcoming these seven young artists who have poured their hearts
out onto canvas for your viewing and enjoyment. Will you be
joining us in the museum today?" she asked, pointing towards
the desk where the entrance fees were being collected.

I stepped to the side, away from the group and towards
their attractive bookstore.

I was looking around and not looking all at once. I was
thinking about the phrase, "Seven Geniuses, Seven Continents." I was wondering if I really ever thought of Akemi as
a genius. I thought of how I had lived my life in America
preferring to be anonymous, yet had somehow attracted and
married a female who was selected to represent a continent
of almost four billion people, with India and China having
more than one billion souls each.

I tried to bring it all into perspective, telling myself that
not all of the people on the continent of Asia were young,

so she wasn't really representing all four billion of them. Not everybody on the continent of Asia was an artist, so she wasn't really competing with very many. However, my excellent math skills betrayed me. Because my mind had already calculated that one percent of four billion is four hundred million, if even a half of one percent of four billion teen artists competed in the Asian teen art competition then there still were 200 million contestants.

If the contest sponsors did a lousy job and failed to look at all of the artists' work and just settled on the best out of five thousand teen artists, Akemi still would be considered a phenom, a phenom of international importance and clout.

In falling in love with her honestly, I had not considered her in this way, as a woman who belonged more to the world than to me. As she blew up in significance in my mind, I began to feel local and small, an African boy from thousands of miles away who was just trying to protect and help provide for his mother and sister by building and maintaining a small family business, who also worked in a small fish shop, and fought in a small dojo, and conquered small men like Tafari and Conflict, who were even smaller.

I thought of my father, who was a phenomenon himself, an international phenomenon. I thought of how he saw the whole globe as his backyard and traveled freely around the world with no fear, defeating any circumstances that tried to hold him back and more importantly, propelling himself forward and protecting his interests, his family, and even his culture.

I thought of him as the scientist and builder he was and the great things he built as evidence and testimony to his greatness. I stood trapped in my thoughts, breaking myself down to nothing and then building myself back up again, stronger.

If I am my father's son and he is a phenom, then I should

at least be a small wonder. If she, an artist obsessed with creating and re-creating beautiful finds, found me, then I must at least be beautiful.

If my world is small and hers is so large, then she, who must have seen so very much and traveled so very far, was like a collector of rare jewels, wasn't she? She tossed the rocks to the ground, sold off the rubies, emeralds, and diamonds and held on to one particular gem, the most authentic, purest, shiniest, most valuable one for only herself to keep. Didn't she?

Building further, I told myself that I might operate in a small world, but I am not small-minded and I am not a small man.

I thought of my grandfather from Southern Sudan who when I would be standing still in his village would say, "There is no reason to go anywhere else, you are already in the best place in the world and everything that is actually needed in life is already here."

He would also say that I was "born great," by origin and blood.

Our relationship was pure. It happened between us and never involved the artificial or official or material elements of this world. It was an energy so powerful, words would have only gotten in the way. It was a collage of smiles, glances, and looks along with an incredible effort to read each other's thoughts and convey our feelings. It was a mutual admiration and respect of two young souls in awe of one another.

Lastly, I reminded myself that I was not seeing wrong when I looked into Akemi's eyes. I was not feeling wrong when I was on the other side of her touch, her kiss, our love.

47

RAT

Brooklyn will sober a lover up real quick. I flipped back into focus riding on the subway with the aggressive and weird and wired freaks of New York. I got real clear walking in the Brooklyn streets with the people and prowlers.

I walked over to Bangs' to collect my shit. She, her daughter, grandmother, and two or three other people were all outside sitting on the stoop. She handed her daughter to her grandmother and took off running down the street to meet me.

I seen two male youths on her steps. I figured they must not mean too much to her, because she wasn't hiding the fact that she was sprinting over to see me and wrapped her arms around my neck as soon as she got up close.

"Hey!" she screamed.

"What's happening?" I asked.

"Sorry you can't come in the house today," she said.

"Oh yeah. Why?" I asked.

"There's a rat in there so we all ran outside and locked it in," she said.

"So now the rat's gonna live inside, and y'all are gonna live on the streets?" I asked. She laughed.

"Ha ha! No!" she said, all excited. "I ran down to the exterminator's shop. He wants a hundred dollars to get it out. I got fifty my grandmother got thirty-five but we still fifteen dollars short. And we were gonna use the money to get our power back on."

"What about them two dudes sitting on your steps?" I asked.

"They're just friends, neighbors," she said matter-of-factly.

"Why didn't you tell *them* to get the rat out?" I asked her.

"They're scared of rats. Everybody's scared of rats. You should of seen my grandmother. She was up on top of the counter with the baby when I got home from school."

"Alright, no problem," I told her.

When we got near her stoop, the two cats stood up. One of them gave me the screw face, like he was some kind of tough guy. I figured he probably had a thing for Bangs.

I looked dead at him. Inside I was laughing at these Black American dudes who act all big but *got nothing* and *do nothing*. He might as well be wearing some hot pants and a tube top sitting around afraid and useless with the women, I thought, taking one look at him.

If he couldn't even face down a rat, how could he challenge me? I spent my African summers with my grandfather living in the same realm with the lions.

"Go pay your power bill," I told Bangs.

"Sure," she said, seeming to melt and swoon when I spoke to her forcefully.

I walked past them two and pushed the door open, while they stood to the side and watched. Then I closed the door behind me, 'cause fuck them watching me.

First thing I did was open all the closed bedroom and room doors inside of the house, ending up on the second floor for the first time. The second-floor rooms were same as the ones downstairs—lifeless, dingy, and antique. The last room on the left corner had a bare mattress with a men's pair of pants on top. I stepped in and took a look. There was an empty bottle of Wild Irish Rose turned over on the floor. On the other side of the mattress, in a small space, there was a ripped condom wrapper on the floor. I took a double take.

Everything else in this house was old and dusty as if this place was set back in time, but this scene in here, I knew wasn't from two or five or twenty years ago. It could've been left there twenty minutes ago or two or five *days* back.

I stood quietly in the middle of the hallway up there for fifteen minutes. I didn't hear one sound. Then I walked down to the first floor and stood quietly for fifteen more. I could hear the rat now. It was running around in the grandmother's room.

I pulled out my *kunei* knives, entered her room, shifted some furniture around, and waited. I was excited at having a live target for my practice. I became completely silent and waited some more.

I saw Granny had a box of Fig Newtons on her night table. I pulled one cookie out, crumbled it up, and tossed it around her floor.

I stood in one spot for eighteen more minutes before the rat made his appearance. I saw him. He was big and black like he been living large, an uninvited guest, terrifying the girls and the old lady, with no competition or threat of being shut down.

Now he fucked around and got fat, greedy, sloppy, and slow. He made a run for the cookie crumbs. On my second toss, my *kunei* went right through him and lodged his body up against the dank beige wall. His blood splattered like a small kid's finger painting, adding the only color this room had.

I left him there for a minute while I went to the other room to collect my gun and our shirts. I came across the box of condoms she tossed at me in the alley a couple of weeks ago. Instinctively I counted them again. Thirteen.

In the kitchen I grabbed a brown paper bag. I went back into Granny's and grabbed my *kunei* out of his belly. His tail was frozen stiff in an action pose. I used the brown bag to pick him up. Then I dropped him inside and folded it down. A little bit of his blood soaked through the paper bag but not enough to make it rip open.

In the bathroom, I washed my hands with hot water and soap. The house was still quiet. None of the tough guys had entered to help out or just out of plain boldness or curiosity.

Then I heard someone entering through the front door. The footsteps were heavier than a woman's footsteps. I came out of the bathroom and stood on an angle to see who it was.

He was a grown, older man. I didn't want to move and scare him. I didn't expect him. There was no way he could have expected me to be inside of this house either. But on closer look, he appeared unstable, maybe even drunk.

"Hold up," I called out to him.

"Who the fuck are you?" he asked as though this was his house.

"Exterminator," I answered, holding up the bloody bag.

"Oh shit," he said. "Glad to see you. I hope they don't owe you no money."

"Nah, I did it as a favor."

"C'mon, man, nobody does no favors." He laughed two quick times and then sobered up.

"I don't have no money. Want a quick drink?" He pulled a bottle out his coat pocket.

"Nah, I'm good," I told him.

"Where's Tiffany and the baby?" he asked, looking around.

"Who wants to know?" I reversed it on him.

"Oh, you the exterminator and the security?" He chuckled.

"Something like that." I didn't chuckle.

"This is my mother's house," he said with authority. "Where's she at?" he asked.

"My bad, both of them should be right back."

"Your bad, you right," he said, swigging from his bottle. "Excuse me, you said you didn't want none. So stop staring. You gon' jinx me and make me drop it, staring like that. Then you gon' owe me money. I *don't* do favors," he warned.

"I'm finished. So I'm out," I told him. I kept my eyes on

him while I went back and grabbed me and Ameer's shirts and left.

Outside I called her. "Bangs!" She came running down the street. Her grandmother must've heard me call out too. She came right out of the apartment across the street carrying the baby.

"He's finished," I told them, holding up the bag.

"Boy, you're a godsend. Thank you so much. You the only one of them I know who comes around and does something good. You can come back any time. You're always welcomed in my house," the grandmother said, relieved.

"Where you going?" Bangs asked. I could see the craving in her eyes.

"I gotta go bury this sucker," I said. "Afterwards I got basketball practice."

"When you coming back to check me, *friend*?" She smiled.

"Don't believe a man could only be friends with you, Bangs. It ain't happening."

"So what does that mean?" she asked.

"You asked me not to talk to you about her," I answered sincerely.

"Oh, her again." She rolled her eyes.

"Just take good care of your daughter. She's the best thing you have," I said to her.

"That's right," her grandmother shouted out her agreement. I kissed the baby and told her grandmother and her, "Your son and your uncle is waiting inside of your house." Bangs rolled her eyes and said, "You kissing the baby, but you should be kissing me, Supastar!"

48

NAJA

When I reached back to my area of Brooklyn later that night, the first thing I did was press the voice mail message button. The first voice there was Akemi. She was soft-spoken, expressing musical and very relaxed Japanese so casually, as if I could understand one word.

I smiled, and imagined I got the gist of her talk. "I am still here with you. Everything is as good as could be expected. I'm working hard. I hope to see you soon." She was turning me into a very patient man.

Naja wasn't patient. When I went into her room to check on her, she posted me up. She was awake, sitting in her bed when she should have been lying down asleep.

"You missed family day on Sunday. Will you miss it next Sunday too?" she asked.

"I'm sorry, Naja. It was an emergency. I had to go and check on a friend," I apologized, referring to the trip to Chris' church.

"But you told me that these people are not our friends," she said, puzzled.

"I told you that the people in this building and this neighborhood are not our friends. I said the little girls in your school *are* your friends."

"What about Shayla and Kimmie?" she asked. "They don't go to my school."

"Who?"

"The two who were riding my bike with me the other day," she continued.

"It's hard to tell if they are your friends because you have only played with them once. Besides, you won't really know if they are friends until they get their own bikes."

"Why?" she asked.

"Because sometimes people pretend to be your friend when you have something that they want to use," I told her, feeling bad about poisoning her view of life but knowing that she could not remain naive forever.

"Oh. Well, what was the point of buying me the bike if you don't let me outside to ride it and don't take me outside to ride it 'cause you're never home?" she asked.

"Maybe I'll take you somewhere special soon, where you can ride your bicycle without worrying," I told her.

"Well, if you would have given me my fight training like you said you would, I could ride my bike right here in front of the building," she said, calling me out.

I stood up thinking to myself that the more females a man is related to, and the more females a man knows, the harder it is for him to divide himself up and give them each what they need while protecting them all at the same time.

"What's that smell?" I asked her, looking around her bedroom.

"What smell?" she said casually. "I don't smell anything," she said.

But I knew there was something because my sense of smell is excellent, and Umma's use of fragrance is incredible. There was something in Naja's room alerting my sense of smell and interfering with Umma's fragrances, which was usually the scent that dominated our apartment.

I walked around Naja's room checking. When I slid her closet door open, it was impossible not to see the sparkling eyes of a baby kitten as she sat inside of Naja's house slipper.

I closed the closet door, leaving a small space for air. I turned around and acted like I had not seen the kitten. I wanted to see how Naja would handle this situation.

"Do you keep secrets from your family?" I asked her.

"Do you keep secrets from your family?" she turned the question around on me.

"No," I answered her.

"Are you sure?" she asked.

"We're not talking about me. We are talking about you," I said.

"I don't if you don't," she said, speaking too smart for her seven years.

"Naja, I am your elder brother. It is my job to care for you. It is not your job to take care of me. So quit playing and tell me your secret before it turns into a lie."

"I have not lied to you," she said.

"Have you lied to Umma?" I asked.

"No," she answered. "There is just something I did not say. That's not lying, is it?" she asked, flashing her innocent and childish grin.

"It's not lying *yet*. I'll give you a chance. You can tell me now before your secret turns into a lie," I said calmly.

"I found the kitten outside. I saw it in the bushes in front of Ms. Marcy's window. She likes kittens too. So, she let me run outside and get it. I put it in my book bag and now it's in my closet. I fell in love with the kitten but I knew Umma wouldn't let me keep it because she even told me once before, no pets until we get a new house and a backyard for them to stay in."

"So does that make it okay to bring the kitten here anyway just because you want to, because you feel like it?" I asked her.

"No, but I thought Umma wouldn't understand," she said.

"You thought Umma wouldn't agree," I corrected her.

"You're right," she admitted. "But she's so cute, isn't she? Her name is Wish."

"You should just talk truthfully to Umma. When you hide something, it is the same as saying that you understand that it is wrong. It is the same as lying. The truth is better than a lie," I added almost automatically, repeating the words I heard Umma say to me for so many years.

I also told her, "You should not have given the cat a name until you are sure you can keep it. To give something a name, and to say the name over and over again, is to grow closer to it. That's what our father taught me." I didn't confide to Naja that I learned this lesson when our father was teaching me how to slaughter a sheep. That was the year I stopped naming animals that we intended to eat.

Maybe she felt something from me because as those memories occurred, she begged, "Tell me a new story about our father. Your stories are so good." She smiled and sank down into her bed.

I sat on the floor beside her and spoke quietly.

Umma's sewing machine was humming, still I wanted to be sure not to raise my voice enough for her to hear me telling aloud the stories that would stir emotion inside of her. The stories that she already knew so well.

"Do you want to change your name, because this is the time to do it," the clerk at City Hall told me after Umma and I were granted our citizenship. "A lot of foreigners who become citizens of the United States opt to have simpler names that we can pronounce easily here in America, like Joseph or Robert or Theodore or Benjamin."

"I'll keep my name as it is," I answered him.

Umma smiled politely at the man because he had authority. Like myself, she had learned so much since seven years ago. She knew now how to get the small victories without compromising her beliefs. She wore her thobe today, covered her body, but not the *niqab* which concealed her face, all but her eyes. She pretended that she was saying something so nice. But in Arabic she pointed out to me, "These people are so arrogant and so ugly. They always assume so much."

Looking at Umma's smiling pretty face, the clerk eagerly signed my certificate and said, "Congratulations, you are now a citizen of the United States of America, the greatest country in the world."

I took Umma over to Rockefeller Center. She stood staring at all of the flags they had raised in the open space behind their building and beside their outdoor skate rink.

"I want to show you where the language courses are, Umma. You can sign up for an Arabic to English class. There will be many students there who are just learning at your same pace, from all over North Africa and the Middle East. It will be what's best for business." I tried to convince her. But Umma was still looking up.

"Umma, what are you doing?" I asked her.

"I looked at every flag three times already. There are so many flags. Yet, I still don't see the flag of the Sudan, the largest country in Africa, the land of the Blacks," she said incredulously.

Inside the Rockefeller Center building, I helped Umma to complete her English language course application. We paid the fee and were given the registration and identification cards.

Since I could not escort Umma to class on Monday and Wednesday nights because of basketball and martial arts, I signed her up for the weekly early Saturday morning three-hour workshop. This way, she could ride in with me when I went to work for Cho.

"I'm going to bring Akemi here also," I told Umma. "For

the Japanese to English course. It will be good for her business as well."

"*Inshallah,*" Umma replied.

I dropped Umma at work for the night shift. Since she took the day off to get our citizenship papers, she would have to work from 4:00 P.M. until midnight. Then I headed back over to pick Naja up. She would have to hang out with me once more. I knew already she would like that, especially since she would be sad about having to get rid of her kitten. Umma had been clear this morning that the timing for a pet was all wrong, for our family.

"Pets shed and urinate and tear things apart. I have expensive cloths and pins and needles lying around. I can't afford to have the kitten cause us any setbacks. If we are blessed to get our new home, then, no problem. There will be a place for everything, and everything in its place."

On the train ride to ball practice, the kitten's head popped out of Naja's book bag. She would rub her nose against the kitten's nose and cover its face with her kisses.

"We have to set her free before we pick Umma up from work tonight," I explained to my little sister. "You seem to keep getting closer to this kitten. It's gonna make it real hard on you when you two separate," I cautioned her.

"I have seven hours left." She smiled and placed her face beside the kitten's.

"Saturday night's game is a real one, not a scrimmage. So let's pick up the pace. No home court advantage this time around. We'll have to roll on Brownsville hard and strong. Be prepared to move in, handle our business and move out. And, no partying or celebrating over there when we take it from those boys. You all know what happened last week. The league can't afford for a player to get shot after every game," Vega said, referring to some kid who the cops clapped the night after our first win, which I thought really couldn't be blamed on the league.

"Yo, Coach, I hope when we win, we ain't gotta go out with you again. My girl is complaining that you taking up all my time," Braz said. The team laughed in agreement.

"C'mon, who else is gonna take y'all to see the best movie ever made in the history of film, besides me? I bought you ungrateful crybabies popcorn and soda!" Vega defended.

"I'm not gonna lie, that was a fucked-up movie theatre you took us to. But I hear you because you got the discount. And Tony Montana, he's the motherfucking man," the player named Machete said.

"But he didn't win at the end," Braz said.

"That don't matter," Panama said. "He had so much fucking style when he was doing it. A good ten, fifteen-year run on top of the world, guns, paper, mansions, whips, bitches. I'll take it all."

"Word up," Mateo said.

I just watched and listened. I missed the *Scarface* movie the team went to see that night. Yet what they was saying hung in my head like a riddle. Is it better to have all the best things and a short life, or live average until you're seventy or eighty years old? *What's the value of life?* I thought to myself.

"That's an assignment for you," Vega said pointing me out. "Have you seen the *Scarface* movie?" he asked me.

"Nah," I answered.

"Well, catch up! Go and check it out," Vega said. He glanced in the corner where the bleachers were, where my little sister Naja sat waiting.

"But don't take your little sister, it's no good for her," he said sincerely.

I was skeptical about playing ball with the league and these guys in the beginning. As I looked around the room now, there was Panama, Machete, Braz, Mateo, Jaguar, and the rest. We were all players who originated from some other country outside of the United States.

I wondered if it was set up that way intentionally. I wondered if the reason we all got along so well was because we weren't like the Americans. I thought about Ameer and the crazy-ass red team. I wondered if they was all fucked up because they was all African Americans; they all hated each other and couldn't do anything united, not even play ball. Even their African American coach was a fuckup who didn't show from time to time.

After practice I saw her walking up, still moving swiftly, even with the extra weight in her hands. The team was just letting out so they all saw her coming too. So did Naja.

Bangs came up quietly and sat on the wall with her daughter silently, giving me a chance to play her off and keep on walking past if that's what I wanted to do. I walked over and sat on the wall beside her instead.

"Bangs, this is my sister, Naja," I introduced them.

"Bangs, what does that mean?" Naja asked.

"Ask your brother. He gave me that name," she said, blushing, her pretty dimples showing up for every smile.

"You gave her a name?" Naja repeated, shocked. "Then you must be close to her. You said don't give something a name because you'll grow closer to it, right?" Naja asked me.

"I was talking about your kitten," I said calmly, trying to move her on to the next topic.

"Ooh! I love cats. Can I see it?" Bangs asked.

"If you let me see your baby, I'll let you see my kitten," Naja said. Then they traded. "Put your arm up like this, so the baby's head won't fall back." I demonstrated for Naja.

"Is that what you do when you hold the baby?" Naja asked me.

"That's what I did when I held you," I answered.

"Did you give this baby her name too?" Naja pushed.

"No, I didn't," I said, trying to remain cool. Meanwhile, Bangs was caught up with the kitten.

"Who did?" Naja asked.

"I named her," Bangs answered, finally realizing she was dealing with a clever-speaking little girl who was very protective over her big brother.

"So how long have you known my brother?" Naja asked her.

"You don't have to answer that," I told Bangs.

"About a month and a half or so," she answered.

"Do you know his wife, Akemi? She's very pretty!" Naja told. Bangs' happy-going expression shifted to a look like someone kicked her in a soft space on her body. After she saw that Naja might be getting the exact reaction she wanted, she straightened her face up and responded.

"I haven't met her. But I'm pretty too. Don't you think so?" Bangs asked.

"Not as pretty as Akemi. *Besides*, you *already* have a baby," Naja added. "Where's *your* husband?" Naja handed over the baby and took back her kitten.

"That's enough," I told Naja. Her little body stiffened. Then she settled down some, although her eyes were still rolling around with suspicion.

"Supastar, can I talk to you for one minute?" Bangs asked.

"Superstar?" Naja complained. Bangs and me stepped away a few feet.

"Tell the truth, don't you see that me and you go nice together?" she asked.

"We probably could if I wasn't who I am," I said.

"What?" she asked.

"See, Bangs, you don't even know me. First off, I'm Muslim. I can't mess with no females who I'm not married to." Her eyes widened to twice their size, it seemed.

"I knew some Muslim guys and they wasn't like that," she said.

"They weren't serious," I said.

"So what are you saying then?" she asked stupidly.

"I'm not supposed to even be chilling with you like how we were. I mean, you asked me to tell the truth, right? Look at you. Your body is crazy. How long do you think we could sit around each other and not end up wrapped up into something heavy? And once I went into you, why would I ever stop? And how could that be fair to you, when I know better?"

"I don't see nothing wrong in it," she said.

"That's one of the problems too. *You don't see nothing wrong with it.* And whose pants were thrown across the mattress upstairs in your house?" I asked. She was caught off guard. She paused.

"They must've been my uncle's," she said.

"You told me there were only females living in the whole house, you, Granny, and the baby," I reminded her.

"He doesn't live there. He just shows up sometimes."

"What about the condom?" I asked her.

"What condom?" She was playing dumb.

"The ones that were missing from your box and lying next to the pants and the bottle of Wild Irish Rose," I pushed. She gasped like she was caught in something.

"He must've snuck and did something with somebody up there. He took the condom out my box. He's always taking something without asking," she said.

It sounded true.

"You see, Bangs, I can't do none of this with you. I'd end up killing somebody."

She stepped in close to my body. Instead of getting turned off, she was getting turned on and her nipples were poking through her bra and her T-shirt. Suddenly there was a moist spot spreading. Her milk was leaking.

"I gotta go," I said.

"Please walk me home," she asked. By now she caught on that I thought that was the right thing to do, walk a female home to safety.

"C'mon, Naja, let's go," I said.

"Where are we going?" Naja asked.

"We're gonna walk Bangs home and then we'll go and meet Umma."

"You know where she lives?" Naja started up again.

"Yes, I do," I answered her.

"Did you tell Umma about her?" Naja asked.

"No, I didn't," I answered her.

"Ooh, you lied then," Naja said.

"I didn't lie. I just did not mention it," I defended myself.

"Well, you better hurry up and tell Umma before your secret becomes a lie. The truth is better than a lie every time!" she reminded me.

I saw his dark shadow cast on the stoop in front of Bangs' house. She saw it too. Her entire face changed.

"There go his stupid ass again," she said. "Why don't he go back to his house?" As we approached the stoop, Naja asked Bangs, "Who's he?"

"He's nobody," she said to Naja.

"He's not your father?" Naja questioned.

"Nope, he's my uncle. He's my mother's brother."

"Alright later," I told her when we reached her steps.

"Good night, Uncle Nobody. Good night, Baby," Naja said for anyone to hear.

Bangs walked past her uncle without speaking and entered her home.

I took Naja's hand in mine and picked up our pace to the train station. When we got seated, I asked her, "Why did you act that way towards Bangs?"

"Because I like Akemi," she answered.

"Just because you like Akemi, do you have to make Bangs feel bad?"

"Why should she feel bad? What does she want from you anyway?" Naja asked.

"No female likes to be told that another female looks better than her," I said.

"You're confusing me," my little sister said. "Last night I got in trouble for telling a lie. Tonight I am getting in trouble for telling the truth. Would you rather I did not say anything?" she asked without one bit of sarcasm. "And you said if I hide something, it's because I know it's wrong. Will we tell Umma about my kitten and the girl and her baby?" she asked with innocence.

"Yes. We will tell Umma everything. It's the right thing to do." I felt forced to represent the truth.

When we met up with Umma, my sister immediately revealed that she still had the kitten. Tired, Umma said, "The kitten can stay closed in your room for one more night. In the morning I'll ask your brother to do something with it." Naja was excited and really disappointed at the same time.

Later that night, I thought about how Naja did not say one word to Umma about meeting Bangs or the baby. She looked out for me and held it in, even though things did not turn out the way she wanted them to with the kitten. I appreciated her. I realized she really only wanted to accomplish one thing by acting up in front of Bangs. She wanted to keep her brother away from a situation she knew our mother would not approve of. A situation she felt, even in her young age, was also not right for me.

It was probably unfair to ask my sleepy mother a deep question. Yet I wanted to hear her sincere answer.

"We come from a country where Islam is the law. How can we remain Islamic in a country where almost no one believes as we do?" I asked.

"What is making you ask this question?" she said, looking intensely concerned.

"Islam gives women rules to be modest, to cover, to marry, to be faithful, to pray. I'm surrounded by females who don't do any of that and they keep coming at me all day, all night long," I confessed.

"They are all a test of your faith," she said.

"Many of them will come, but they are not what is best for you, me, your sister, our family, your children to come, *inshallah*. You have chosen a wife, never trade her for a lesser thing," Umma said with a certainty.

"I wouldn't think of trading Akemi," I assured Umma. "But why would anyone want to give a young man such a difficult test of faith?" I asked sincerely.

"Allah is above comprehension," she answered. "Allah is the best knower of all things."

In my room, I sorted out my thoughts and feelings.

I decided I owed it to Bangs to do something special for her. She really looked out for me on the night that the cops were head-hunting. For two days she held on to my gun, and as far as I can see, she didn't fuck with it. Her waiting for me by her window when she heard the police sirens saved me from what could have been a completely different outcome. I couldn't front on any of those facts. Still I couldn't give her what she really wanted either, without frontin' on my beliefs, my family, and my wife.

But I *could* give her something that I *thought* she needed.

Afterwards, I would break it off with her. I already knew from the way I acted at the party that night, and what I saw and felt in her bedroom, that the temptation towards her was too great. The pussy was too easy. The pussy was probably so good, but good pussy is not enough and her pussy is not mine.

• • •

For Naja, I used my charm on Ms. Marcy. It wasn't difficult to convince her to agree to keep the kitten at her place, since I agreed to pay for the cat food, supplies, and maintenance. Ms. Marcy had no one else living in her apartment, which is the only reason we allowed and paid her to care for Naja. Aside from the money, she was very attached to Naja, and Naja was very attached to the kitten. So it worked out.

49

THE KEY

Around 9:00 A.M., I showed up at Bangs' house knowing that she would be in school. I rang the bell. I saw Granny push back her curtain and see who was standing there. Seconds later, she appeared at her front door, still sleepy and sluggish.

"Good morning, Ms. Kelly," I said.

"It sure is a good morning, you coming here and saying 'good morning.' I haven't heard that kind of talk from a youth in a long time," she said, still complaining.

"I have an idea about a surprise for your granddaughter," I told her. She brightened up and listened. She smiled and nodded the entire way through my speaking to her.

Afterwards, she gave me the key to their home. "Take this, just in case I'm asleep when you get back." I took the key.

"Oh, and what's Bangs' favorite color?" I asked.

"Tiffany's favorite color is red."

"Pick something else, her next favorite," I asked.

"Purple," she answered.

At their local hardware store, I picked lilac. I figured Bangs was already too amped up for the color red. It would just excite her more than she already was. And purple seemed too dark. I thought it might sadden her. Lilac was more of a peaceful, girly color. Maybe it would help her to calm down a bit, and mellow.

In Bangs' room, I pushed all of her old furniture to the center. I threw the drop cloth down to protect it. I lined the perimeter of her walls, floors, doors, and doorknobs with masking tape.

I wasn't about to do no dope-ass mural. I am not a painter. But I *was* about to paint her room to make her feel good. I was about to cover up her walls that seemed neglected for at least Bangs' entire lifetime. From what I knew about females, they don't like to live a life without beauty and beautiful colors and surroundings, at least the females who I know and love do not.

Before placing the roller on the first wall, I had to remove the old clippings, pictures, and magazine articles she had taped up. I figured if she was anything similar to me, she probably wouldn't like no one fucking with her stuff, so I tried to take them down easy without ripping them. I placed the clippings into a neat pile on her dresser underneath the plastic drop cloth.

The article on top caught my eye, through the transparent plastic. The title of the article was "CUT SHORT." It read: "The life of Brooklyn teen Darren Sparks was cut short at age 17 yesterday. He was killed by a drunk driver on the evening of . . ."

Right away, I knew this was the baby's father, who Bangs had confided in me was killed by a drunk driver. I thought it was sad. At the same time, it pumped up my determination to do a good job to bring Bangs a little bit of happiness.

The roller made it easy. I was finished by 1:00 in the afternoon. Still, the paint had to dry, and I wanted to be out before Bangs got home, probably around 4:00 P.M.

I knocked at Granny's door, not knowing if either she or the baby were asleep.

"Ya finished?" she asked.

"I finished painting, but it has to dry before I can remove the tape and put the furniture back. I don't know how long that will take."

"Well, take your time. You have the key. The van is gonna come around soon and pick us up, me and the baby," she said matter-of-factly.

"Where are you two going?" I asked. She smiled.

"Well I'm going to take advantage of some of my old lady perks," she said. "The nice people over at the Senior Center have a van that picks us up and takes us on local errands, shopping, and whatnot. Afterwards, they gotta drop me off over at the clinic. Tiffany is gonna meet me over there at 4:00 P.M. The baby gotta get her three-month checkup. I'll be there already waiting on line. You know they give you an appointment but then they still take a hundred hours before they call ya in to see a doctor. They figure if you poor enough to be in the clinic, you shouldn't have nowhere else to go or nothing to do. So they let us just sit and wait."

"Are you expecting anybody to come by your house while you're away?" I asked her, thinking about the situation with Bangs' uncle.

"No, if somebody comes along looking for me, just let 'em ring and knock. They'll figure out that I'm not here. If they know me, they'll know I'm coming back."

"What about the uncle?" I asked.

"My son?" she said. "That fool. He got a key when he hasn't lost it somewhere. When he don't have the key he just tries to knock the door down until we let him in."

"Does he live here?" I asked, double-checking Bangs' story.

"Nope. But he don't live nowhere really. His wife has a house. But that's her house. Every time they fight, she throws him out. He keeps drinking. They keep fighting. He keeps showing up here. I try to keep 'em out because Tiffany doesn't like him."

"Why don't you just change the locks and this time don't give him the key?" I asked her. She looked puzzled for some reason.

"Do you give everybody a key?" I asked her.

"No, of course not," she replied.

But she had given me the key and barely knew me. I wanted her to think about that for Bangs' protection, and the sake of the baby.

"Did you give a key to Darren?" I asked.

"Who?"

"Darren," I said. "Darren Sparks."

"Goodness gracious, who is that?" she asked.

"I am sorry for bringing him up. I know he passed away but I'm just saying, Granny, you can't give everybody the key to your house."

"I thought you were a nice young man. Now you're trying to make me feel senile. Who is Darren Sparks?" she said, her hands now on her hips.

"The baby's father?" I jarred her memory.

Her face darkened, like when someone walks by and steals the light away for a second. Her expression changed and then went blank.

"The baby's father is not dead. Now, I don't believe in that, saying somebody's dead when they ain't. It's like voodoo. You call 'em out dead, then it happens. I got a lot of disagreements with my son. But I don't want him dead either," she said.

"And we don't talk about that in here. The baby was born and that's it. We take it from there. The baby is here. The baby didn't do one thing wrong to nobody," she said, seeming to have no idea that she had exposed the filthy truth.

"Tiffany is your granddaughter, right, Granny?" I asked her to be sure.

"Of course. She is my daughter's daughter, God rest her soul. Now *she's dead*. If I could have it my way—" Then she stopped herself on hearing the baby's soft cry.

I left out when they left, watched them get into the van, and walked back over to the hardware store while the paint continued to dry.

What kind of family is this? I asked myself. The uncle, the one man who was supposed to be protecting the family, was fucking the family instead. The grandmother, old and confused, was welcoming the son, even though she clearly knew that he was fucking her granddaughter. Did she think not discussing it made it okay?

I should've known when I seen her uncle the first time. He was the real rat, not the one I knifed and pinned up against the wall. He had to be about thirty-eight or forty years old. Bangs is fourteen. He had to be fucking her at least since she was thirteen, probably even younger than that.

I felt a fire in my heart.

When I returned, the paint was dry. No one was home and I was glad about it. I placed everything back into its place and removed the masking tape. While I was taking care of all that, I had the locksmith changing their front-door lock.

In her room, I installed a dead bolt lock. This way, when she's in her room, no one could get in unless she wanted them to, unless she turned the metal knob and allowed and invited them in. I even had the locksmith repair the window lock as well.

In the kitchen I emptied and rinsed out a jar. It worked perfectly as a vase for the flowers I brought for her room. I arranged them, filled it with water, and left them on her dresser.

I threw out her dirty old window curtain. For now the blinds would have to do. I thought of how easily Umma could zip through making a proper curtain for Bangs. Then I pulled the thought back. The reality was that this was the last stop for me with her. These gifts made me feel okay about my good-bye.

She ran around to the gym to see me like I knew she would. Basketball practice had just begun. I had just arrived.

"Hey, we're locked out. It's crazy. Granny's key won't work. It won't open our front door," she said with her usual excitement. I could see she was beginning to depend on me as her problem solver.

I gave her Granny's key ring with the new keys to the new locks I had installed attached. "Here, your grandmother gave me her keys to hold," I said.

"Why? When?" she asked. Her questions let me know that Granny didn't spoil the paint surprise.

"I gotta go, Bangs. I can't keep the team waiting." She left reluctantly, as always. But I knew her grandmother and baby were waiting for her as always too.

I also knew she would come back and try to catch me after practice was over. So I left early and headed to the dojo.

50

THE ROPE

"I meant to ask you, Chris, how did you convince your father to let you come back to the dojo?" We were all seated on the floor. The entire class awaited Sensei's arrival from the back room.

"It wasn't me. It was you guys. My mother kept saying how great she thought it was that you guys came to the church. Even my father was impressed that you stayed and helped add up the receipts. To tell you the truth, he thought we were all back there playing and pretending. When he saw the figures matching up with his accountant's calculations, he respected that. He had to," Chris said.

"So are you back in the league? 'Cause you know the blacks play the greens for the season opener. And I wanted to apologize for doing all the dunking I'm gonna be doing on you on May third," I said, laughing.

"You might be dunking. But I ain't gonna be nowhere around," Chris said.

"I'm still on punishment. I can do the martial arts because my father thinks I already put so much training into it and he already put so much money into it. Besides, he thinks that you guys are good and have 'redeeming qualities,'" he said, laughing.

"But I can't play in the league 'cause my father said it's 'high risk.' I can't even go out on weekends until school ends and that's not till June thirtieth." He looked tight about it.

"Well, at least you're here," I told him.

"Who's the red team playing for the opener?" I asked Ameer.

"The orange suckers from Crown Heights. But I took your advice, man. I sat my team down, we smoked some weed and talked about shit. We made plans, big plans. I told them I'll never get used to losing, so we had to get on point," Ameer said. "They took me seriously too. 'Cause if we ain't in the running to get the money, none of this shit makes any c-e-n-t-s." He laughed at his joke. I knew he was serious about that money.

"You got time. The scrimmage didn't count," I reminded him.

"Yeah, it was good we lost. Now that we got real games every week I'll get the gorillas worked up and we'll sweep this thing," he said with a smile.

"Yeah, I'd like to see *that*." I smiled back.

Being four doors down from Akemi's family store had me crazy. It wasn't just a physical thing. I missed her. I missed seeing her. I missed trying to talk to her. I missed her trying to talk to me. I missed watching the unique things she did and ways she went about it. While working, every now and then I'd look out to see if she would breeze by.

I resolved that until she was finished with that art show, I was on a back burner. I just told myself it was the same position she was in, when I was hard at work on the wedding job. She handled it and chilled out with Umma. I could accept and handle it too.

I could tell Cho had been observing me. I guess it was easy for him to see I was a bit anxious. Holding his reliable old knife in his thick swollen working hands, he took a side look at me and said, "Japanese girl make you into nervous wreck."

• • •

Friday evening after Umma and Naja were secured, me and Ameer met up and went over to Chris' house. Since he couldn't get out, we went to him. His family was at church. He was home alone.

We kicked back at first and listened to some music. Ameer had some cassettes of new joints that weren't even released on radio yet. It wasn't so hard to get his hands on them, since all of the rappers coming up were straight out all of our hoods and could even be living in the same building with us even after their joints were banging on the radio.

Chris' refrigerator was stacked, and the cupboards too, with juices, sodas, chips, and cakes. Seemed like they had more shit than the corner store. All of us chose something different than the other to eat and we each made it ourselves.

"Nice house," Ameer said as he made a roast beef sandwich. "You over here living like a king. Don't you know better than to let some project niggas in your place?" He laughed.

"This is my father's house," Chris said. "Don't you remember the speech? Everything in here belongs to the Christian Broadman Corp. That's dad. If I want something, I got to start up my own business and make it happen," Chris said.

"It can't be that bad. You got more than what I got. And your pops pays your expenses too," Ameer said.

"Hold up. Far as I remember, I'm the only one here who has to go to work in the morning. Ameer, your pops pays your expenses too," I joked for true.

"Yeah but I'm living like Hotel Six. Chris is chilling like the Hyatt Regency." We laughed.

Later we played ball on his court. While I shook Ameer to the hoops, I told him, "Now me and you is gonna have to work even harder to win that money. If we get it, we still gotta cut it three ways."

He laughed regular at first then his laugh grew louder and louder.

"What? If me and Chris won in the league, you'd want your cut too!" I told him.

"Yeah, but if he's *not even putting in work* in the league no more, then it's like he's getting *more* free gravy."

"True, but remember you said three is better than two. Two is better than one," I reminded him.

"What the fuck does that have to do with this situation?" Ameer asked.

"We gotta stick together, watch each other's back, keep our word to one another," I said, and sunk the ball in the net at the same time.

"Oh yeah, what's up with you letting us in on what Sensei been teachin' you. You haven't showed us shit."

I turned to Chris. "You got any rope?"

"Yep, in the garage."

"Go get it. I'll show both of y'all something."

51

SIDEWAYS

Late Friday night when I got back on the block, everybody was outside like it wasn't almost 1:00 A.M.

I couldn't miss Heavenly seated sideways on the back of DeQuan's Kawasaki. DeQuan was deep in a conversation with one of his brothers, named DeMon, full grown and twenty-two years old now, but DeQuan was still telling him what to do and how to do it, and how much heart and intensity to put behind it.

"You got something for me?" Heavenly asked softly as I walked by. I didn't answer her or bother looking her way. I acknowledged DeQuan instead.

"Hold up, let me get in your ear," DeQuan said to me.

"I'll be back," I told him as I kept it moving.

When I came back down I handed him the gold chain with the "Heavenly" pendant on it, wiped clean and wrapped in a plastic sandwich bag. I finally had a chance to get it out of my hands without stepping into one of her traps. Since Conflict's only been dead for two weeks or so, she probably had not had enough time to start fucking with DeQuan's head and to cause a rift between me and him who been cool for all these years.

"Take this," I told him. "I found it."

"It's cool, man. *I know her.* She don't give out gold. She collects it," he said with a smile.

"What was it you wanted?" I asked him.

"Oh, sorry I couldn't get up to watch your game. We had to work a lot of shit out at the wake. Some of Conflict's side girls was up there fighting in front of his moms. Superior was tore up about his loss. The shit was fucked up," he said.

"When's your next game?" he asked.

"Next Saturday, May third," I told him. "Brownsville Park, nine P.M."

"A night game in the Ville, huh? A'ight, I'm in there."

"I see you got Conflict's girl on your bike," I said, without looking at Heavenly.

"War booty," he responded and gave me a pound.

I wanted to warn him but I didn't. I knew that he was street-smart and used to dealing with the snakes. But she was a snake with no rattle and no hiss. She strikes, but there's no warning or clues. By the time a man finds out something is wrong, she has already injected too much poison in his system and he can no longer be saved.

There was really no way for me to express it, without it seeming like I had something to do with her.

52

WARMER

"I was speaking to Temirah Auntie last night," Umma said at the breakfast table after *Fajr* prayer early Saturday morning. "She wanted me to come by her house tonight and discuss an idea that her husband had for her and I to offer a culture class for the Sudanese daughters who are growing up here in America. She says that people would pay to have their daughters properly trained and are scared to death of the changes they are seeing in their children who are being raised living in this country. What do you think about a class? Do you think it's good business?"

"I'll come home from work and take you over to their house this evening. Let's sit down and see what they're talking about," I answered.

It was warmer today than it had been any other day this season. No use for a jacket, hoodie, or sweater. The sun took over the sky, flaunting its power.

I knew it was a good day when at around noon, Cho mashed his finger onto his picture on the wall, the one with him standing at the helm of a fishing boat in the middle of the Atlantic Ocean, and asked me, "You coming?"

I smiled and answered, "No doubt."

"Yes or no?" he asked again.

"Most def," I told him.

"What?" he asked.

"Yes, Cho, I would like to come along on your boat. When are you taking it out?"

"On U.S. Memorial Day. The whole day, me, brother Chan, brother Yin, and you," he said.

I was ecstatic. Nine months of dedication and hard work had finally brought forth the invitation I wanted to receive from the start. It was the birth of a real camaraderie between Cho and I, outside of cutting and cleaning fish and hauling boxes.

At quitting time, I was feeling sticky. It was too warm to wear my usual heavy rubber apron and plastics over my clothes. So I rocked today with only a T-shirt and jeans. My welding glasses were dangling from my neck. My gloves were stuffed in my back jeans pocket and I was sweating some.

I washed the guts off of my counter and hosed everything down.

In the bathroom I washed my face, arms, hands and feet just to cool down, feel comfortable, and smell good enough to ride the train. At home I would jump in the shower before taking Umma to Mr. Ghazzali's house.

My gun was stashed and locked in Cho's basement.

Downstairs, Cho's cat must've been feeling the heat. She was giving up a constant purr. Or maybe she was just talking to the other two new cats who were trapped in the cage while she was walking around free. Maybe she was trying to figure out how to get her boyfriend out of the cage so they could make sweet noisy love in the dark corridors of the basement. I laughed at my own imagination.

When I reached down to soothe her by stroking her coat, I plucked a rose petal from her fur. I flicked it off and thought it was a strange find, a flower blossom in a cement cave.

At my locker, I shined my key light to get my combination right. I unlocked the lock, put my glasses back on the top shelf, and checked for my nine. I took off my T-shirt, put my gloves on the top shelf, and reached for a clean tee when I thought I heard something. I stood silently to listen. Maybe the people next door were moving something on their side.

When I got silent, the noise I had heard turned to silence also. I put my nine in my pants and took a short walk around. I ran up on a camper's knapsack, the kind the student tourists used to wear back in the Sudan. Theirs were packed and stacked and looked like they were carrying their whole life in the compartments of the sack held up by two metal bars. They even had rolled-up blankets and thin bedding on those things.

I got serious thinking how I always thought this underground place was a great hideout. If someone were on the run from the police, they would never think to check in the Chinatown underground.

In the winter it would be torture. But now that April was coming to its end, the floors were heated, the air was warm and thick, and the water underground ran hot, producing a steam room effect. There was a toilet. If someone had a grill or a burner, they could really escape from the clutches of the law living down here. The only thing missing was windows that led to the sky, moon, and the stars, and of course the light of the sun.

I decided to walk back upstairs and ask Cho if he knew about the camper's knapsack down here.

When my foot hit the third step on the fifteen-step staircase, I heard the shower water turn on. And that sound was definitely coming from Cho's section.

"What was I bothering Cho for?" I asked myself. I'm the one with the gun and the lethal feet and hands.

I walked down the three steps and moved carefully. I was trying to think like the trespasser. Maybe he turned on the shower to make me think he was still in one area, but had really moved somewhere else. Maybe he wanted me to walk up casually so he could catch me off guard and bang me over my head.

I was up against the wall like a detective. Cho's cat was looking at me like I was an asshole. I figured if the cat would run down the corridor, the trespasser would expose himself out of fear that someone was approaching. But Pussy saw the steam coming from the stall around the corner, which we both could not see into because of the way the stall was positioned.

As I inched down the corridor, making it up to the wall of the shower stall, I checked on the right side of the darkness before turning left into the thick of the steam.

A silhouette was seated in the corner clouded by a full blast of continuous steam. It was too pretty to be an invader. It was Akemi.

She laughed softly, covering her mouth to lessen her voice with her hand. The sound down here multiplied and bounced around the walls. I put my nine away, reached around and turned off the shower water to lessen the steam. I wanted to see her clearly. The water splashed all over my bare chest before it shut off.

As the smoke cleared, she was really there, wearing a paper-thin light beige dress, wet and pressed against her exquisite body. She had no shoes on her feet, her diamond toe ring glistened, her legs were twisted into a simple yoga pose for my pleasure.

She was seated on a fluffy blanket. On top of the blanket was a white linen cloth and a load of rose petals. She had made a bed for us in a hot cave, below the streets of New York, surrounded by steam. I loved it.

"*Mayonaka*," she said, and placed her hand gently on the linen cloth beside herself, asking me to come over without words.

She didn't even have to ask. I approached her, bent down, and laid my gun pointed away from her in the corner.

I could feel her fingers tracing my bare shoulders in the dark. My eyes were adjusted now. She ran her hands slowly over my neck, and both her hands were now exploring my face, like a sculptor. She went down my arms like she wanted to be familiar with each and every muscle and groove in my body. She began caressing my chest, then let her hand be still on my abdomen.

I stood up and removed my pants, my shorts, and my socks.

I lifted her off of the bed and carried her into the shower stall, where I switched on a dim yellow light. I wanted to see her. I wanted to see everything. And I wanted her to see me too, see everything.

In the soft yellow light she leaned against the wall in her paper thin dress, which was held together by only three white strings tied like shoelaces on the side of her body. Pull the string and the dress unravels, incredible.

When the thin cloth fell to the floor, her dark hair lay on both sides of her pretty shoulders. She was the definition of art. As my eyes moved down her body, some delicate and intricate body design was revealed. At first I thought it was an expertly drawn tattoo. Within seconds, though, I realized it was Sudanese henna. She had drawn a henna belly chain, each link life-sized and perfectly situated from her navel leading around her side to her back. The design was so perfect it clung and hung and rode her curves like a real piece of jewelry. I spun her around and the design wrapped around her tiny waistline. Like a real chain, it had a clasp, which was drawn above the split of her ass.

She put her arms up on the wall she was facing, stretching the length of her body so that I could get a rear view. She pulled her hair, which had now spilled down on her back, to the front so that I could see the detail of her second design. It swirled up and around her spine, a vine with tiny leaves.

The design ended with a drawing of two small leaves resting at the nape of her neck. A Japanese spin on a Sudanese tradition, unlike anything I'd ever seen. No henna hands or feet. Henna, for even sexier secret places.

When I looked up amazed from admiring the curve of her back and the wicked canvas her skin made for her artistry, she turned only her face towards me. I leaned in and kissed her. Her body slowly turned to face front, her nipples fully extended and brushing against my chest. She had her eyes locked into mine. "Please," she whispered and smiled. I decided she was the sneakiest feline roaming around down here. And I knew she felt she had waited too long for me to give her what she wanted.

With the palms of my hands pressed against the shower walls, and her tucked in between them leaning, I kissed her mouth gently. Every time I kissed, she sucked. I felt and heard her breath escaping. Suddenly I felt her soft hand feeling the length of my dick, exploring the head with such a light touch and moving down the length of it, not resting until it was beneath my balls. I grew longer and harder on her.

She started that sucking. She sucked my tongue, licked my lips, even licked my face. Her tongue was so nice, not too wet or dry, breath fresh like she was sucking rum candy before sucking me. Now, I was glad I had washed up already. I wanted it to be good for her in every way.

I sucked her neck, feeling like it was mine now. I had one hand softly on her throat. She whined a soft sound. I moved my hand down and felt her shoulders, in awe of Allah's design of women. I felt the soft skin of her arms. Both of my hands held her waist. I worked them back up. I explored her breasts. Touching them lightly first without looking, it felt like they belonged in my hands.

I pushed her back against the wall so I could see them.

In the yellow light, the skin of her titties was beige. The areolas were brown. Her nipples were tan. I licked and sucked them.

She put her small hand over my big hand and pushed my hand down in between her legs. Her leg muscles relaxed and her thighs opened up to welcome me. With my fingers I felt her pussy muscles throbbing on the inside, and I found her clitoris. It was not a little button, it was long and more like a two-and-a-half-inch sliver of flesh shaped like a piece of yarn. I caressed it with my finger and her whole body dropped down to the floor as if she could no longer hold herself up because of the pleasure. She was squatting down with her legs opened and inhaling and exhaling, breathing hard.

I lifted her up and switched places with her. I sat down on the shower stall floor. She stood before me. Her pussy was directly in front of my mouth. I smoothed out the silky bush and used two fingers to open her lips. I put my tongue on her clitoris as I had yearned to do. I sucked it gently. She put her own hand in her mouth and bit down on it to lessen her whine of pleasure. Still I could hear her. I had both of my hands gripping her buttocks so that her clitoris would stay pressed against my mouth. I tickled her with my tongue and she exploded. I released her cheeks and she fell back against the stall wall and collapsed down to the floor where I was. Her head was hanging between her own legs. Her hair was almost dragging on the ground.

I lifted her face and brushed her hair out of my way. I licked her earlobes and stroked the hair on her head. We started kissing once again.

I needed to go into her now. It was urgent. She felt it too, I knew. Without standing up completely, she straddled me. We were both facing one another now, in the sitting position. Then I raised her up, using both of my hands wrapped around her waist, and eased and lowered her body onto mine.

I placed the tip of my dick at the entrance of her pussy. She was so petite.

I didn't have to teach her nothing, instinctively she just began to bounce slightly and softly in a circular sort of motion as her very moist but very tight pussy hole opened up little by little and clung to my dick like a too-tight glove. We rocked back and forth gently like playing on a seesaw. I felt her skin rip open and my dick pushed most of the way inside of her.

With my hands gripping her waist, I pushed her from her hips downward, so I could get the last six inches inside of her where it was meant to be. When I was all the way in and hit her bottom inside, she gasped. I grinded her while she eased up and down, up and down, breathing harder and harder like she was on the ride of her life, the pole controlling all of the motion. Her mouth dropped open and her head was tossed back now. Our hips were doing all of the work.

Me, I felt something that I never had before. It was a sensation so sweet and so strong, like the thrill of being yanked up in the air at an extreme speed and tossed around in the sky with the stars and allowed to fall down to the Earth with no parachute or protection. Her womb was the perfect place, and it gave me the perfect feeling. There were no problems inside of there. It was a hundred percent pleasure, a hundred percent peace. It was impossible to imagine that there was any place better. It was warm and soft and moist. It was tight yet long enough to take it all. And with the friction of each of her inner muscle movements, I felt a higher and higher sensation. I grinded harder, she bounced a little more swiftly. It was skin to skin, flesh to flesh, no condoms or creams or sponges or injections, or pills or plastics or patches or contraptions. When the energy built up so strong that I could not hold it back any longer, I spilled a million warm seeds into her and the rocket ride dropped down as if it was out of fuel. Yet even the drop was a surge of pleasure. I could feel her fluid and mine oozing out as my dick slowly began to relax. She threw her whole body over my shoulders and just lay there trembling on my back.

When she climbed down, she sat beside me in the shower stall. She threw one leg over my leg comfortably. She took one of my hands and put it down there. It seemed like she was ready to go again. But what she wanted to show me, when she pulled my hand back, was the blood on both our fingertips coming from her. Not "a river of blood." Not thick goops of blood. Not stinky or fishy blood. Just slight thin blotches of watery blood. The kind I needed to see, the blood that was not there when I first sucked her clit.

She picked up her white linen cloth and dabbed the blood from herself onto it. She waved it like the Japanese flag, white with a large red dot. She held up her hands like a runner throws their hands up at first place at the finish line. I thought to myself, what a strange girl. But I loved everything weird about her. She was my wife.

She lifted her right leg and used her toes to turn on the shower. We were both standing now, the steam building and rising. The heat was intense. She began to wash my body with her hands and my bar of soap. Seeing her naked, soaked, and wet was erotic to me, so we did it again. I held her up and pressed her back against the shower wall.

I stood and rocked up into her. She bit her lips and climbed the walls. She moaned so much I thought I saw Pussy the cat running up and checking on us. The water poured down heavy onto my face and body. The steam hid us from the no one who was down there.

Making use of the bed she made for us, I lay down like I was in the private room of a fine hotel. My first ever full-out sexual encounter caused me to feel so relaxed and so free and so damn good I wasn't worried or thinking about anything or anyone else.

As she climbed back on top of my naked body, with her naked, soft, and shapely body, I felt my joint stiffen again. I could feel her heart beating in her chest, or maybe it was mine. I could feel her hair brushing against both of my shoulders. I flipped her over and with me back on top, I just grinded her slowly, pushing it all the way in using even the muscles in my toes. Her pussy muscles were throbbing wildly like a second heartbeat, her body lost somewhere below me.

She could not get enough. I thought my weight might be too much for her but she wrapped her legs around me like a frog and just flowed. She bit my shoulders and scratched up my back. But even the abuse felt good. I put my passion prints all over her too, even between her thighs. I was catching on to how to know when she reached her orgasm. She would shake all over, as though it was beyond her control. Her entire body would be trembling. A whining sound came from her belly and rose through her chest, throat, and out of her mouth. If I didn't know it was pleasure, I could've mistaken it for the sound of crying.

When I rolled off of her and onto my back, we were both lying down facing the ceiling. She pulled my hand back between her legs and smiled.

I told her, "No more for you." Somehow she knew what that meant.

I gave her a kiss and when our tongues touched, I started touching her up again, naturally.

I just kept looking into her eyes and kissing her lying there. She just kept licking and kissing me too. It was like a magnetic pull, we couldn't and didn't want to get off of one another. I felt like I couldn't move. Like my limbs weighed a hundred pounds each on their own and my whole body, a ton.

We took another shower eventually. We watched each other dress in fresh clothing.

We packed up our stuff.

We were both leaning on opposite walls staring at one another fully clothed in the dark cave. Our eyes were filled with feelings, and both our lips were wet. We had to calm down the constant throbbing below, hers and mine, before we could raise up to leave.

I got off work at three. Now it was six o'clock.

"C'mon," I told her. She tucked herself under my arm. We walked up the stairs and out through Cho's.

He took his eye off his business for one hot second and watched me leave with the huge camper's knapsack on my back and Akemi's fingers folded into each of mine. We left the bed she made and the rose petals she spread in the down-stairs corner.

"Later, Cho," I said casually. I was too relaxed to think or care.

Outside we walked the other way instead of passing her uncle's shop. I don't know what I expected or what she expected. I stopped and pointed in the direction of her family store. She shook her head no and clung to me.

In the train she was all over me and I liked it. Since we made love it seemed like we could not unglue ourselves. One minute our legs were touching, then our hands, faces, and feet. We were stuck together and could not peel our-selves off.

When we came through our apartment door, Umma looked at me, a long gaze into my eyes. She looked at Akemi, a long gaze into her eyes. Akemi lowered her eyes.

Naja ran out and gave Akemi a princess' welcome.

"Are you ready?" I asked Umma.

"We are both ready," Umma answered in Arabic.

In my bedroom I put down Akemi's camper's knap-sack. When I turned around, she was right there behind me. The energy was so thick between us that I didn't want to go anywhere. I wanted to stay right there locked in my room with her. Even if we didn't touch, the feeling of the love and the energy that swirled around us would have been enough.

But I promised Umma, so we prepared and went by taxi.

53

AFRICA & ASIA

I saw the shift in Sudana's eyes when she saw Akemi walk in. Now Sudana was like a pretty, wide-eyed fawn, looking at a wild cheetah passing by and estimating the danger it might cause. I knew that she liked Akemi, except didn't like seeing her with me.

Seeing now the jewels Akemi wore, the jewels I gave her, including the ring, Sudana's eyes widened even more. She didn't say or ask anything. Her eyes went from the jewels over to me. She gave me one concentrated stare then cast her eyes down and away from me.

We were being separated for a time in Mr. Ghazzali's house, the men from the women.

Then we were all brought back together once again by the call to prayer. Akemi looked uncomfortable but Umma scooped her up and let her watch from behind. I knew what Umma was doing, because we believe there is no compulsion in Islam.

At dinner Mr. Ghazzali, his two sons and three daughters and wife Temirah, myself, Akemi, Umma, and Naja were treated to a Sudanese spread, served not on their main dining room table, but on the floor using the traditional low tables, carpets, and pillows.

Sudana served Akemi with special attention and great hospitality. Her hand was steady holding the steaming kettle of tea and pouring it into Akemi's small teacup. I was grateful for how she was welcoming Akemi. It made me respect and appreciate Sudana even more.

The simple new business deal was brokered, a cultural seminar for Sudanese females. It was good business but really a woman thing. It was the only way for the African women raising children in America to transfer knowledge, power, and common sense to one another. Temirah and Umma would host a class for the daughters of Sudanese families.

The course would include learning our traditions and how to practice them in a foreign land, linking Muslim females together for mutual learning, respect, and support, converting culture into business (as Umma had successfully done), cooking traditional dinners properly because good food keeps the family strong, together, and peaceful and increases the love between them, sewing, making perfumes, crocheting, carpeting, knitting, and even banking funds in a traditional *sonduk*, offering Sudanese females a method of saving, investing in, and financing one another.

These were all things that I had seen Umma do at home naturally in our estate in her building where she met with her female relatives, neighbors, and friends. Back home it was a voluntary gathering, not so organized and defined. But even in my young understanding of life at that time, I could easily tell it was something that the females looked forward to and enjoyed a lot.

Ms. Temirah was the connection to all of the Sudanese families whose daughters would come. After all, she and her sister-in-law had assembled hundreds of Sudanese families for Fawzi's grand Westchester wedding.

The parents would be asked to pay out fifty dollars per session since the information and training was priceless and ultimately each properly trained woman could easily open a competitive business when her course work was done.

Sunday was selected as the best day for the workshops,

above Naja's protest in support of our family day tradition. Once Umma assured her that she would be at her side as part of the feminine class, Naja accepted the time slot.

The location would be Mr. Ghazzali's finished basement at first, since it had a full kitchen and living area as well as separate restrooms. When and if, *inshallah,* the course became a success, they would consider moving into a commercial space, or hotel hall.

Everyone seemed content. I watched Akemi. I thought it must be difficult for her not knowing English or Arabic, having to experience us in silence. Yet she seemed completely at peace and content also.

Before leaving, Mr. Ghazzali said to me, "I see you have taken a wife for yourself. *Alhamdulillah,* please come to the mosque with your family and become part of the *ummah.* It will be difficult to have your Islam privately. We will need to support one another and praise Allah mutually. And, if you haven't registered your marriage with an imam at a mosque, you should. It is your protection of our traditions and beliefs which outsiders and unbelievers will never understand." He embraced me. I embraced him.

"When you marry a non-Muslim woman, you must provide the spiritual leadership and example to her. She will do as you lead. So lead," he finished. I respected his advice. I was one step ahead of it though.

I had so much in mind for Akemi, so much to share and teach and learn also. But I didn't think it required a rush. Weeks ago, after careful thought, I realized that Akemi sees everything. It was Akemi who said, "Like you, your religion is so beautiful." Since she was already beginning to see the beauty and rightness in our way of life, I felt she would move slowly and willingly and relax into the fold of Islam. This way, she would feel like she chose, not like she had lost something, or lost a lot, just to gain a man whom she loved. She had already fallen in love with me. Soon she would fall in love with Allah also, *inshallah*.

Late Saturday night all the females were worn from travel. Everyone took turns washing up in our one-bathroom apartment.

Umma lit the incense and seasoned the fish for Sunday breakfast. She soaked lentils, prepared dough, chopped cheeses, and washed then soaked beans for the *fulu*.

"Tomorrow will be your *walima*." She smiled with knowing contentment. "We will have it for our small family, same as if there were twenty, or fifty of us."

"Akemi looks even more beautiful since you went into her. She's radiant. She's glowing," Umma said softly.

What could I say in response to that? I kissed Umma, went to Naja's room to say my good night, and then returned to my room and closed my door.

Akemi unpacked her clothes and placed them in small stacks. She lined her sneakers, two pairs, and her sandals, two pairs, and her shoes up against the corner wall. Her jewelry was in a neat pile on my desk, even her wedding and toe ring. I figured she was so used to her fingers and hands being free to create and draw and paint, and that maybe this was why she removed all of her jewelry.

On the floor, she stretched as I watched. She was completely flexible, as I had come to know. Within those yoga moves, open leg splits were simple for her. She could even be relaxed in a completely twisted pose.

She loosened her silk robe of a thousand colors and dropped it down but not off completely. She walked towards me and pointed to the side of her waist. I looked to see what she was showing. It was a birthmark.

"I see," was all I said. She lifted her bare leg and turned to show me her foot. She pointed to something. It was a beauty mark on the back of her heel. She smiled.

"I see," was all I said.

She took her pretty foot down and lay down on my floor, dropping her robe all the way open. She pulled her knees up, then opened her legs. She pointed to the inside of her right thigh. Her finger was pointing to the crease that separated her thigh from her pussy. I looked, there was a beauty mark there also, in the softest part of her skin.

I looked at her and said, "You better stop fucking with me, girl." She smiled. Then we made love right there on the floor. I had to turn on some music to drown the sounds of her pleasure.

In the morning I felt a sense of alarm. I felt myself sinking so deep in love it was as though I was drowning but wouldn't do anything to save myself. The love was in my heart, of course. But it was in my limbs too. I could feel it in my arms, legs, and toes, moving in my chest and weighing me, holding me all the way down.

I could hear her breathing and she could hear me too, I'm sure. The first sign that I was awake, she was already moving on top of me. I thought I heard her moaning only to discover it was myself. It was a feeling of complete ecstasy, but for the first time I felt powerless. I was the same man, the same fighter, the same soul, but felt a love so heavy I was surrendered to her.

I was unfamiliar with fear. But now I feared any morning where I had to wake up any other way than this way right here, with this woman right here.

Our *walima* occurred on a Sunday, which was also family day. It was good to see the joy that Akemi brought to everyone. She was like a grown-up daughter to Umma, who she paid such close attention to and showered admiration on, and a big sister to Naja, who had already informed everyone that

Akemi had to learn five words in English every day. She occupied them, which freed me up some. I was grateful for that. Besides, I believed that women needed each other in this way.

As Akemi finished washing dishes after a spectacular meal, Naja appeared with some magazine cut-outs glued to a piece of construction paper.

"Where is Saachi?" she asked Akemi.

"Saachi?" Akemi repeated. "Uncle," Akemi responded.

"Does Saachi have a bike?" Naja continued, pointing to her picture of a bike on the construction paper.

"*Hai!*" Akemi said.

"That means yes," I told Naja.

"Well, say yes then!" she scolded Akemi. "And let's go and get Saachi. I want someone to play with," she insisted, trying to hold Akemi's moist hand.

I looked at Akemi. I didn't know the details of the status of her relationship with her people or my relationship to them either. If she wanted to go see her uncle there was no problem in it for me.

"Saachi, *hai*," Akemi agreed softly.

"Saachi, yes," Naja repeated in English. "*Hai* means yes in English." Naja taught, and then proceeded to say "*Hai!* Yes!" a hundred times until Akemi either understood or gave in. "Yes," Akemi said. Then Naja was satisfied for the moment.

We arrived on Sunday afternoon at her family store. She went inside first. Umma and Naja and I remained outside in the great warm weather.

Akemi returned outside shortly, standing under the canopy with Saachi. Both of them began waving at us to come inside.

Akemi introduced Umma and Naja to her uncle in Japanese. He spoke stiff but polite English, saying, "Hello, pleased to meet you," as he might say to one of his customers.

Umma said in English, "Very nice to see you for the first time, Mr. Nakamura." Her Arabic accent was heavy.

To the Americans, I am told Arabic sounds like an overdose of z's and s's.

I hoped he was satisfied with Umma's greeting because that was as much English as he was going to get out of her that afternoon, or at least for the time being.

Akemi's aunt appeared from the back room of their store. She spoke Japanese to Akemi. Akemi introduced Umma to her aunt. The aunt watched us so closely, it seemed like she had something to say or ask, but she didn't.

I thought it was interesting how they interacted with Umma but not with me, or Naja either.

Akemi touched my hand and then said some words to her uncle in Japanese. He nodded. She spoke some more, standing happily at my side. It felt good seeing her wear her wedding ring and bangles in their presence.

Naja and Saachi were in the background playing and speaking to each other comfortably and easily. Saachi was showing Naja some of the accessories their store sold that she liked. I did hear Naja ask Saachi, "Is that your father? What's wrong with him? Does he have a stomachache?"

"Nope," Saachi answered swiftly. "He doesn't like Black people, but I told him you guys are fun."

Well there it was spelled out and spilled from the mouth of the two seven-year-olds. Only thing was, Umma and Akemi could not understand those English words. But me and the uncle could. I heard them loud and clear. He pretended he did not.

Akemi spoke again to her uncle politely and softly. Finally, he turned to me and asked, "Where are you planning to take Saachi, not far from here, right?"

"To the park, maybe to the bookstore and to dinner. If she has a bike, she can bring it, if you wouldn't mind," I said.

"Saachi has school tomorrow," he said, searching for excuses.

"So does my little sister Naja," I pointed out. His wife spoke to him in Japanese.

"Saachi has to be back here by seven P.M., not one minute later," he cautioned.

Saachi jumped up and down, up and down, up and down. "Thank you, Father." I knew it was only because of his soft spot for his daughter that he allowed her to come. I imagined that she had probably been asking for both Akemi and Naja over and over again, the way little girls tend to press.

Saachi ran in the back and came right out pushing her pink bicycle with the "Hello Kitty" logos all over it.

In the Manhattan park Saachi and Naja zoomed around on their bicycles. They were laughing and smiling. The double burst of energy attracted other little kids who were already there looking bored with their parents or nannies. Soon four or five other children joined them and the race was on, the women who supervised each of them screaming out "Be careful!" in every language and dialect.

Naja was out front, her head covering flying in the wind. Saachi was doing her best to catch up and edge her out. They were playing follow the leader. I had never seen Naja smile so brightly before. Behind the bicycles, kids without bikes began chasing. The whole park was converted into a children's paradise.

When they ran each other crazy and grew tired, they ditched their bikes and climbed up the monkey bars, every child trying to be the head monkey. Umma and Akemi supervised them. I was sitting on the top of the back of a bench reading a book, noticing that I was one of the few young men in the park.

I looked up every now and then, just to be mindful. It was family day, so I had to pay some attention.

In one glance I saw Akemi pushing Umma, who was sitting on a swing. Akemi was excited, repeating something in Japanese. I figured she was telling Umma to kick her feet so her swing would take flight.

When Umma started pushing her legs forward and pulling them back again, and her swing picked up momentum, she smiled brightly also, her head covering on her pale pink thobe falling to her shoulders. She looked young and happy.

Akemi jumped on the swing next to Umma. Naja and Saachi were already swinging beside the two of them. As I watched all four of the females' swings fly higher and higher, their pure joy brought back that feeling of alarm.

Perhaps Mr. Ghazzali was correct. Maybe I should find the right mosque and join in. I would need to be a part of a brotherhood of men with similar beliefs and ideas and complete dedication to protecting their families from all of the definite threats that lingered all day and night every day and night. How else would I be able to secure the three of them, all moving in different directions to schools and jobs all at once? How could I protect Akemi in the same way as I had always protected my mother? How could I be in two places at one time when I had already given my life to Umma, and built my own world in response to what Umma needed and wanted? But then again, how could I not protect my wife also?

My father had been a part of a brotherhood of men, a real one. He didn't have to leave our estate to go to mosque. It was on our property along with my school and everything else that was necessary to have a secure community. But then life wouldn't be life without the intruders, the invaders, men who work overtime to make themselves your enemies, who represent the threats that have to be stopped, eliminated, wiped out.

I pulled my thoughts back and got them under control.

When the girls finally exhausted themselves, pedaling, walking, running, swinging, and crashing into stuff, we went for ice cream. I sent all of them inside the store and stood outside watching the bikes.

I dropped Saachi back at six-thirty, just to maintain a decent amount of respect.

"I have a half hour left," she said to me with a smile after Naja informed her of this fact.

"We'll come and see you again sometime," I promised her.

"Aren't you coming with me?" Saachi asked Akemi. Akemi spoke back to her in Japanese and she and Saachi conducted the rest of their conversation in their language. However, Akemi stayed clung on to my arm.

I felt good to know that her family actually knew that we were together, married, and serious. Before, I was thinking that neither side might really be having the full story.

On the way back to Brooklyn we stopped at The Open Mind bookstore. I wanted to see if Marty had received my order.

He was happy to see me, happier to see Umma, and surprised at the new addition of Akemi. He looked her over in an obvious but harmless way.

When he and I were standing alone, he said, "Who needs to read books? I'm having a great time just watching you live your life."

Akemi came over with a book that caught her interest. It was a picture book on Japan. She flipped through the pages slowly, me looking in with her. She stopped on a map drawing and pointed out a city. She said, "Kyoto, Akemi."

"Oh, yes, Kyoto," Marty said. "It's the ancient capital of Japan. It's got great architecture. It's a really beautiful place. In fact, it is so beautiful, that during World War II when the Americans were going to bomb it, they picked another Japanese location to bomb instead, declaring that Kyoto was too startling and wonderful to destroy."

"That was very nice of the Americans," I told him. "Have you been to Kyoto, Marty?" I asked.

"Only when traveling through the pages of one of my books," he answered with a laugh.

"Do you have my order?" I asked him.

"What's my name?" he said back.

I paid him fifty-nine dollars for a leather-bound Holy Quran written in the Japanese language, a gift I planned to present to Akemi, which was also listed as one of my gifts to her in our *agid*. I would not thrust it on her. I knew she needed and wanted to concentrate on her big show coming up in less than a week's time. In fact, I was surprised that she was spending all of this time with me now. Before, I was all worked up into waiting until after her show to have her all to myself.

Naja also selected two books, while Umma was satisfied with flipping through the pages of an Arabic to English dictionary. I bought it for her. I guessed she was thinking of her English language course set to begin on this upcoming Saturday. Big day, Saturday May 3rd, I thought to myself. Akemi's art show, the start of Umma's classes, my workday at Cho's, and my opening game with the league, different places, different times, one man.

We took turns showering, Umma, Naja, and then me. Akemi showered as we made prayer.

In my room I began organizing the events of my day for tomorrow. I had money on my mind, the possibility of the purchase of the house, which we really needed even more now. I had dropped a lot of cash since I began interacting with females outside of my family, I thought. I pulled out my cash stash box and counted up my savings. I went through all my pants pockets and organized my bills. I threw the stray change into the jars where I kept coins stored. Tomorrow at the bank I would get the paper coin holders. At our apartment I would roll up and count seven years' worth of coins, figure out where I stood, and get more serious.

In the midst of my push-ups, which I had tripled up on since I had neglected working out for the past two days, Akemi came in smelling fresh, new night, new robe. I watched her as she moved around putting her stuff in selected places. I also watched this sneaky feline watching me out of the side of her eyes.

When I hit 360, I stopped. Remaining on the floor, I dragged myself to sit with my back up against my bed. She came over and threw one leg over my shoulder, sitting down behind my neck. Now both of her legs were dangling down. She laid her pretty feet, each one on top of each of my legs.

I put my arm around back and swung her body in front of me, still on my shoulders but facing me. I sucked her pussy, licked that long clitoris. I knew that's what she wanted. I was learning that she liked that right before I went up in her. It doubled and tripled her orgasm.

I knew I was right 'cause now, as I sucked her, she leaned her body all the way back and upside down. The top of her head was on the floor, her hair spread over my feet, the feeling so immense that when she came, she cried real tears.

54

PAYING UP

Naja to the sitter, Umma to her job, Akemi and I to the bank.

Akemi took a seat on a comfortable chair in the bank waiting area.

Same teller, the usual Monday visit. She accepted my deposit, looking only at her own hands counting the small sum of money. She stamped my passbook and slid it through the slot. She glanced over at Akemi and said to me, "Are you serious?"

"Let me get some paper rolls for pennies, nickels, dimes, and quarters," I asked. She rolled her eyes then hesitated. "Please," I added. She gathered them and passed them to me. We left.

Some of these Black American females are funny, I thought to myself. They don't know how to carry themselves or treat a man good, as if fucking is all there is to it. There is no sweetness in them. They stay on attitude all day long, then they get mad when a man treats any other woman special. That teller had been seeing me around and knowing me for at least five years. I barely ever got one sentence or half a smile out of her. So why was she in my business? Why did she care who I loved?

Akemi needed to make a stop in Queens. I took her by her uncle's house. Even though I knew he was not home, and that they were already at their family store, and Saachi was already in school, I still didn't go inside his place.

When Akemi finished up and returned outside where

I was sitting, she pulled a flyer from the MoMA out of her front dress pocket. She pointed at the name of the museum. "Today, eight," she said, having learned a bit from Naja, who had her own way of making her lessons stick.

"Tonight at eight P.M.?" I asked her.

"Tonight eight P.M.," she corrected herself with a smile. I knew that's when I needed to pick her up. I also knew I would have to miss dojo tonight to be on point with Umma, Naja, and her.

After I dropped Akemi off, I headed down to the lawyer's office about the house.

"Well, you look relaxed," the lawyer said. "Did you have a good weekend?"

"I'm good," I smiled and thanked her.

"Okay now, the inspection has been completed. It's an *old house* with a few problems, nothing major, but you knew that already, right?"

"I knew the house was old," I agreed.

"Well the wiring on the house, the plumbing, the structure itself is great. Sometimes these old houses are built much stronger than the new ones. The news ones can easily be all cheap wood, drywall, and sheetrock. Somebody lights a match then 'poof,' the whole place blows up in minutes," she dramatized and laughed at herself.

"The inspection reveals that you may need to replace all of the windows. They suggest especially the ones on the first floor. If this is something you can do in the summertime when you move in, you will end up saving yourself a heap of money on heating for the fall and winter."

"Windows," I repeated aloud, thinking.

"Also, the roof of the house was replaced, um, two and a half years ago. So. That's good.

"This is a relatively simple buy since you want to purchase the home without a loan. You've certainly eliminated the lion's share of the work. No mortgage fees, credit checks, high interest rates . . . great," she said, smiling and folding her hands in front of herself.

"So we have the title search and the inspection completed. We can make our offer and sign the contracts so that Mr. Slerzberg can at least take down his for sale sign, keep the house off the market to other potential buyers. You don't want to get in a bidding war and have some other buyer drive the price up," she said, finally taking a breath.

"As much as I enjoy working together with you, since you are underage, which I find unbelievable, I will need you to come in with your mother. I know you said she has to work. We can set something up for say, six o'clock this Thursday evening?" she asked.

"That's fine," I answered.

"We'll give Mr. Slerzberg a call then. I'll also set up your options for a home insurer. Of course you'll want to insure your house and property, right?" she asked. I thought of Chris' father with the mention of insurance.

"Of course," I responded.

"Would you like me to see if we can push the closing date up some?" she asked.

"Closing?" I responded.

"That's the day you actually pay all of the sums, become the owner, and receive the keys to your new house. The way it stands, I don't see any reason why Mr. Slerzberg has the date pushed all the way back to June first."

"Oh, if you could see all of the junk he has in that house," I said, laughing, "you would know why he has the move-out date pushed all the way back."

"Such nice teeth," she said to me, then looked back down at the paperwork.

"Thank you," I responded. I leaned forward and dropped my head a bit, as I often did to avoid meeting women's eyes.

"If you could get the date pushed up that would be more than perfect. We really want to move as soon as possible," I told her.

Seated on the wall outside of her office, I was thinking numbers. Eighty thousand for the house, another thousand for the "closing costs," including the lawyer's fees, the home insurance cost, the house appraisal cost, the inspection cost, and the title search. Let's say we're at $81,500. Then there would be the actual small house repairs, paints and supply cost and move-in fees. Let's say another $1,000. Now we're at $82,500. We've got $85,300 in our account. Once we buy the house, we'll have only $2,800, left. But the flip side is, there would be no more rent to pay, no mortgage to pay, no bank to seize our house when business got slow or tight, and peace of mind.

I jotted down a note to myself. "Property taxes." I forgot to ask about the amount we needed to pay for our property taxes. I hated that we had to pay them. But I knew that we would have no choice. It seemed like a legalized criminal way for the government to still be collecting some form of rent from a homeowner. They wanted us to pay for our houses twice.

My personal savings, seven years of delivery tips, plus monies set aside from nine months' working at Cho's, and three loose diamonds given to me by my father, that was my total financial value.

I took my assessment and used it as motivation to get my ass up and pursue the stream of new clients who had phoned into Umma Designs over the past week. I jumped on the train and did what I do, make appointments, keep appointments, conversate with clients, make arrangements, and take measurements.

By 5:00 P.M. I picked Umma up. Then we picked up Naja. I secured them and went to ball practice.

55

BUS STOP

Bangs showed up to basketball practice that evening. She arrived earlier than usual, probably because she had figured out that last time I cut out early and avoided her.

I didn't like her sitting around a gym full of sweaty male teens working out. It was not the same as bringing Naja. Bangs was all body. Everything she wore rode her deep curves and highlighted her beauty. Today she wore shorts and a tight tee. Her hair was slicked up and pulled tight, then rubberbanded into a bun. She combed her "baby hair" down and swirled it out onto the smooth skin of her face. Her milky breasts alone were a magnet. She was all smiles and sitting on the top back bleacher against the wall. Her dimples revealed her happiness. I looked up at her face and knew she didn't know that I intended to separate myself from her. I needed her to stop coming for me.

After practice, I met her on the side of the bleachers and slightly underneath.

"Thank you so much for what you did," she said. "Nobody in the whole world ever did anything so nice for me, really." She went to wrap her arms around my neck. I caught her by her wrists.

"Listen, Bangs, you're cool with me. You looked out and I won't forget it. But what you're looking for as far as me and you, that's not happening," I told her.

"Why?" she asked, seeming completely puzzled.

"We already discussed why," I told her.

"Oh that's nothing," she said, referring either to my religion or my relationship with Akemi.

"It's something to me," I told her.

"I didn't mean it like that," she answered, lying, I thought, and now her new lie reminded me of her old lies.

"Who's Darren Sparks?" I asked her, referring to the news article on her wall.

"Who?" She got immediately defensive. "I don't know who that is but if he told you I did something with him, he's lying," she said within half a second.

"Didn't you tell me your daughter's father got hit by a drunk driver?" I reminded her. Her eyes started moving around away from mine.

"He did . . ." she said softly, her voice trailing off and her face revealing her desperate rush to organize her thoughts and her lies. She stood still for the first time since I met her. Her dimples and her smile were gone. Suddenly, she tried to bring them back.

"Did my grandmother say something to you?" she asked, trying to sound pleasant. But I knew what she was attempting to do. She wanted to find out how much I really knew, so she could lie about whatever else remained.

"Is your grandmother your real grandmother?" I asked her.

"Yes!" She looked puzzled again. "She is my mother's mother. Was, I mean."

"And your uncle, is that your mother's real brother?" I asked.

Finally she knew what I was knowing and getting at. "Yes," she answered softly and slowly. She turned away from me slightly and folded her arms across her body. She began fidgeting again, the whites of her eyes becoming cloudy and red as the frustration and stress brought painful tears.

"So is it my fault, Supastar?" she asked with tears falling from both of her eyes. One of her feet started shaking.

I was silent. Of course I didn't think it was her fault that some grown demented man, a blood relative, went into a young member of his own family, his sister's daughter. I thought it was filthy.

In the Holy Quran, it spells out clearly, for all believing men, which women they are allowed to marry and go into and which women are forbidden. It is forbidden for a man to take his siblings' daughters. It is forbidden for men to rape. Still, men who are nonbelievers or fakers don't pause and are capable of great evil. They fuck it up for everybody.

I also thought that *she* couldn't be trusted. She cut out that random newspaper article and put it up on her wall, probably lied about it to every dude she brought up in her bedroom. She probably lied about it with a big smile and her pretty dimples and her skin glowing. And why was she keeping her uncle's dirty secret? Did she like fucking him? And if she hated it, why was she still fucking him? Why were his pants and the condom paper up in the bedroom, same like it would be if two lovers met in a secret rendezvous? And why did she pretend to hate him whenever she saw him? Then in private, what? She would lie down for him and crack open her legs? The whole thing got me heated.

"I thought about killing the baby," she said. "But isn't she pretty?" she asked me in a childlike voice. "I'm glad I kept her. I thought you liked her too. You were the only one who didn't treat me like my baby was my curse."

"I do like the baby. She's innocent," I said.

"I know," she said, smiling. "I'm gonna get her out of that house before she turns five. That's how old I was when he caught me in the corner of my room." She folded her arms back across her chest and crossed one leg over the other and placed one foot on top of the other. She looked closed and uncomfortable or trapped in a bad memory.

"Fuck it!" she said, with a sudden new strength. She

unfolded her arms and untwisted her legs and feet. "You the only one asking me all these goddamned questions, Supastar! I could get any one of those boys on your team to talk to me. Maybe I will. Then we'll see. 'Cause I know why you don't want me around anyway. *You like me too.* I can tell. I felt your big dick up against my leg at that party. When we was in my room, if your friend didn't come along, I could have been all over you. You would've liked it too," she said, smiling now. She started rocking back and forth on the tips of her toes as usual.

"Don't worry, Supastar! I won't bother you no more," she said and ran out the gym suddenly and at full speed.

I left to meet Akemi.

On my way to the subway, I thought about what she had to say to me. Since I never lie to myself, I had to admit, she was right. I do like her. But I don't love her. Bangs is cool, but she's not enough for me. Sure she was fine in addition to Akemi. But if it were just me and Bangs only, it wouldn't work. I would never marry her. I would never rearrange my life to take care of her. I would never introduce her to Umma. Or adorn her with Umma's jewels. Or work hard to get her a place to live. Or expect her to learn my faith, and love and live it. I couldn't protect her honor, because it was already gone. I wouldn't want her to be the mother of my children. I wouldn't give my life for her, or risk my freedom. I couldn't teach her too much, because she was already too slick, and no woman could roll back from knowing too much or being too slick for the wrong reason, to not knowing and not being slick even for good reasons.

I was attracted to her enthusiasm for me and her comical happiness.

Also, ever since I saw her in the daylight at the pharmacy, and in the candlelight in her bedroom, I was definitely attracted to her body. It took everything I ever knew to keep off of her that night. I could feel that I was only seconds away from losing my self-control. And I knew that whatever I wanted to get into, she was wide open and down for it. But was it me getting her open? Or was she just open in general?

I couldn't trust her movements any time I wasn't seeing her standing in front of my face. I knew she might be doing anything. Now, I didn't respect her enough either.

I wanted her to stay away from me because, yes, I believed at the right or wrong moment, like any man, I could easily fuck her. But I already knew I would never fuck her without wearing a condom. If she chased me hard, I *would* allow her to be the first to suck my dick, a thought that had already occurred to me and enticed me once but I wasn't proud of.

I would never suck her pussy, or lick her clitoris. It wasn't a clean place. It wasn't my place. It was a public place, like an outdoor bathroom or bus stop.

So she was right, I needed her to stay away from me for my own good, for my own sake. For the protection of the man I am and want to be.

These were the thoughts that rushed into me. But for some reason, I was still angry even though I didn't know or understand why. Trying to get my head right, I took deep breaths to relax myself.

Bangs said maybe she would talk to someone else on my team. That shit was foul and dangerous. That got me tight. Since I didn't love her, I was asking myself why did the thought of me knowing that she might start fucking with someone else make me feel so heated? When I thought about someone else touching her why did the thought come along with me seeing myself breaking some nigga's neck? If I wouldn't fight for her or risk my freedom, why did I want to merk her uncle? I needed answers from myself.

I was mad at myself for catching feelings for Bangs. It was my fault, I decided. I take responsibility for it. I was mad at Bangs for being what Umma called "a lesser thing." I wanted her to be smarter, stronger, better. I wanted her to be so much more, so I could feel all right about caring for her.

If I had to trade Akemi to get Bangs, I'd throw Bangs out of the picture. But my own father had the greatest woman, Umma, and still had two more wives. I never saw his love for Umma decrease or ease up or change in any way except to grow stronger every day.

It seemed to me that real men are collectors of fine women and the possessions of their hearts and not destroyers or deserters. Only a fool would leave a great thing, when you can always keep it or take it along with you.

There are three kinds of men, I realized. There are the non-believers, the make-believers, and the true believers.

The true believers' feelings are alive and awake. The true believers have hearts that rage. There is no such thing as half-way love for a true believer. When a true believer, a Muslim man, loves a woman, he possesses her completely, guards her with his life. He has high expectations for her, holds her as a treasure, the main ingredient, the spice of life, the wife, the mother.

I had to confess to myself that I do not love Bangs, *but I could love her*. As a true believer, my heart is raging. The more I would have seen her, talked with her, held her baby in my arms, given to her unselfishly, the more she would grow and become a part of my true heart. But then I would be pushed by my same raging heart to murder the man who violated her, to take her as my second wife, to cover up her beauty and charms, to teach her a better way of life, to become the guardian to her daughter.

Once she changed the way she was living, and I went into Bangs, me, this true believer, she would become mine forever, and anyone who tried to hurt her, or seize her from me, I'd sever his head from his neck. And this is my gangster. This is my problem.

I couldn't give a girl who wasn't *steady* that much love or that much power over me.

As in Islam, any woman who is not mine by birth or blood relation or oath of marriage is a woman I need to separate myself from, is a woman whose body I didn't want to see, a woman who I should turn away from and lower my gaze.

Make-believers are men who pretend that they have a belief in life. They lure women with their pretense and trappings. They make-believe that they are Muslims, Christians, Jews, or any other faith. They make-believe that they are strong. They make-believe that they are capable of love. They make-believe that they are part of a family unit. They make-believe that they are protecting you. They make-believe that they are real men.

Non-believers are men and women who don't have to do anything. They have no limits, no boundaries, and no expectations, none for themselves and none for you either. Non-believers are the sons of a painful pair of parents who are either dead in the body, meaning they are absent or deceased, or dead in the mind, meaning they are present, but their ignorance only makes their presence worse. The mothers of the non-believers are prettied-up mindless whores, the uneducated ones and the well-spoken educated ones too. The non-believers have no chance of real love, real family, or real life. Still they are here outnumbering us all.

Meeting Bangs taught me all of that, brought all these thoughts to mind. Umma says every woman who a man allows himself to interact with leaves her trace on him, good or bad. I am grateful to Bangs for these lessons, most of all to know the truth about myself as a man, and to be loyal and true to it.

56

NO GODS ON EARTH

The warm vibe outside of the MoMA and the general feeling of the streets of Manhattan was completely different from the vibe of the Brooklyn hoods. When you are moving in the streets of Midtown Manhattan, there's no bullshit. It's strictly a money-earning thing. Everybody moving in every direction is focused heavily on making money. Every tall building is packed with people making money. Everybody moving in Midtown Manhattan is either making money or delivering messages and packages for people who are making money. Tourists pouring in and out of every groove are spending money, helping Manhattan make more money. Police and security agencies and armored trucks are daring anyone to fuck with the flow of the money.

I met Akemi and we walked in the warm Manhattan air, just enjoying the night.

Back in Brooklyn, the ambulances lit up the night. The police cars prowled, not to serve and protect the people, but to patrol and control them. My block was a crime scene, again.

"First Conflict, then Heavenly," some teenage girl standing outside watching said.

"DeQuan killed her. Dere he go," the girl pointed. I saw the back of DeQuan's head through the rear window of the police cruiser where he was seated, and of course cuffed. It was one of those real bad moments, when your eyes see something, and your mind understands, but your heart won't accept it as true.

It could have easily been me trapped in the back of the police cruiser, about to be hauled off and dumped where they dump young black and Latino men who do anything . . . criminal.

I had Akemi's hand in mine. She was standing behind me pressed against my back. She didn't want to know.

I looked over to the building where my mother and sister were inside. I prayed. I was wondering if it was cool to go inside the building now, or if the police were still in there, roaming.

"They gon' bring out the rest of them too. You watch and see. I heard them when they busted through DeQuan's door. That's my floor, I know," the girl reported.

So I stood still, holding my wife.

DeSean 16, DeRon 17, DeJean 20, and DeMon 22, they all came out in a line, each with a private police escort, hands cuffed tightly behind their backs. Cops came pouring out of the building like excited ants, carrying twenty-four-year-young DeQuan's tagged-up guns, boxes of money, and seized bags of weed. It was enough artillery for him to take over a small country.

A whole company of brothers who stuck together for at least the past seven years that I been here. Actually, it was much longer than that. They were here and organized before I arrived. Now, they are all found out and taken down because of a simple wrong choice of a female with an influential body and a mean-ass walk, I thought to myself.

I took it as a sign. As a rule, I never ignore Allah's signs, I catch them the first time around because who knows if Allah will warn you twice.

Now the power equation in the building would shift, *again*. Now a fucked-up place, that was better off *with*

DeQuan than without him, would become even more fucked up. Now a new nigga would jump in Conflict's spot. A new whore would dress up and pretend to be Heaven, and a new nigga would find a way to get guns to the hood, where cannons stay cocked and loaded, with a thousand reasons to shoot.

I had to get my people out.

57
OUT

Upstairs Umma and Naja were as usual in a different world. Umma was fast at work on the orders I gave her this afternoon when I picked her up from work. Naja was in bed, sleeping.

Akemi sat in the living room watching and fascinated with Umma's fingers moving with precision and speed, with her knitting needles this time. Eventually, she pulled out her sketch pad and began drawing something with her own intensity.

In my room, I packed my coins in the paper coin cases. When I finally finished, my personal savings from years of delivery tips and nine months at Cho's was six thousand dollars and sixty cents.

I don't know why, but behind my closed bedroom door, I started packing up my most valuable personal belongings too. From the back of my closet, I pulled out the one quality suitcase I carried when I arrived in America.

I got it packed and put it back. Then I was on the floor doing my repetitions.

Tuesday I went to see Mr. Slerzberg personally after all my females were straight. On the way to his door, I yanked the FOR SALE sign out of his lawn. I rang the bell.

"Good morning, Mr. Slerzberg. How are you?" I went through the formalities.

"Can we talk business?" I asked him. He came out on the porch this time, instead of inviting me in. He was still dressed in his pajamas and robe.

"I have your money. What do you say we sign contracts on Thursday, and you move out within the next week or so?"

"You have the money?" he asked me as though he needed to hear it twice.

"All of it," I confirmed.

"Two weeks is impossible. This house is filled with a lifetime's worth of stuff," he said passionately. I couldn't tell him what I knew from what I saw inside of his home, that it was all junk. So I tried another approach.

"Mr. Slerzberg, this isn't the only house in the world. But it is the house *my mother* wants. So what can I do to help you get to Florida faster? That is where you want to be, right?" I was trying to entice him with his own dreams and wishes.

"You know it's where I want to be but I was just telling Beth that maybe we should wait because it's warm here in New York right now. It feels nice. It's ninety degrees in Palm Coast, Florida, phew," he said, pulling his robe like he needed air. "And it's ninety-five in Miami!"

"But they have casinos and air-conditioning down there. Listen, I know you love all of the stuff you have packed up in your house. I can get some nice professional guys from a respectable licensed and bonded company to come right away and move all of your stuff wherever you want them to take it." I looked him in his eyes.

"Sounds expensive," he said, catching on. I knew what he required.

"I'll pay it. I'll set it up and pay it. You move out in two weeks. How's that sound?" I asked him through a strained smile.

"Any time you're paying it sounds good to me," he said, laughing. "But I choose the moving company and you pay them," he said.

We shook on it. He agreed to get himself prepared and show up to my lawyer's office this Thursday at 6:00 P.M.

58

THE GIFTS

She got mad when she pulled the Bergdorf Goodman shopping bag from out of the back of the closet in our bedroom. True, the bag was a little bit wrinkled, but the gift that she had given to me was still in there in perfect condition. It was a large box with a thick silver ribbon wrapped around all four sides, topped off with a big silver bow.

She grabbed the bag by mistake when she was reaching for something else. When she realized what it was, she got disappointed and dropped it on the bedroom floor and began softly telling me off in Japanese for not having opened her gift to me.

I laughed at her. It was my first reaction. It was hard for me to get angry at my pretty wife who didn't even know how to scream the right way. She was cute pushing her words out forcefully. Her voice was barely above her usual seductive whispers. It was humorous to me having to guess at what she was saying. Besides, this was our first married argument.

Since she was just going on in Japanese, I started answering her back in English.

"Akemi, I should have opened it, but at the time that you gave it to me, I had too much on my mind. I really wasn't focused on the gift," I said to her calmly. I was sitting on the bed while she was standing up, one hand on her little waist.

She started saying something else emotional. When she finally stopped talking, she poked her lips out and pouted at me. I guess she was frustrated. No Saachi and no cousin here to interpret, no Sensei or anyone familiar, just me and her.

"Bring it to me. I'll open it right now," I told her. But she just stared at me angrily, not knowing what I meant. I just kept smiling at her. I couldn't help it. That's just how she made me feel. Besides, I felt I had the upper hand even though I was wrong for not opening her gift. I knew that my smile alone would melt her slowly. And by now, I knew how to make her feel good deep inside, to give her so much pleasure she would be helpless, to win her over completely. I guess I was growing up more each day, feeling myself and becoming more confident in my power. I think becoming intimate placed another level of strength into my manhood.

"Bring it to me," I gestured this time. She turned her back like she wasn't willing to speak to me. I lay down on my bed and waited. Not even thirty seconds passed before she started to peek back at me to see what I was doing and why I was not reacting to her. When I caught her eye, I said it again and gestured once more, "Bring it to me." I sat up again.

She bent over and picked the gift up. She held it and just stared at me. "C'mon," I called her over. She walked towards me reluctantly. But she was still coming.

When she reached me, I grabbed her by her waist and tossed her down on the bed. She dropped the present on the floor. I pulled her arms up over her head and held them there. She started cursing me again, which got me crazy heated. I tried to kiss her and she turned her face away and used her knee to kick me. With one leg, easily, I pinned both of her legs down. She tried to wiggle herself loose. I just looked at her squirming. "I love you, Akemi. I love you too much." I began sucking her neck. When I took one glance at her, I saw her lips had parted. I knew I was on my way.

I put my hand on her skirt and grabbed at her. She exhaled. I slid my hand under her skirt and into her panties. I used my middle finger, slid it inside of her, and stroked her clitoris gently. She tried to resist me with her words, with whatever she was saying, but her body was already on my side. Her talk turned to moans. They started off softly and grew louder and louder. I bit her nipple and let her express herself. Her moaning was so erotic to me anyway.

When I pulled my hand away, her legs were just beginning to tremble. She pulled my hand and tried to place my finger back where I had it. I turned her around and yanked down her blouse. She purposely rolled herself off of the mattress and onto the floor. She lay there on her back speaking to me in Japanese now so sweetly as I took off my jeans and my shorts.

When I came down on the floor, she began playing at escape. She crawled away from me. I grabbed her by her foot and pulled her leg back. She was face down. I mounted her and entered her pussy from behind. I could feel the pulse inside of her, throbbing and pulling and clutching. The new position got her crazy. She screamed out her pleasure. With both of my hands gripped beneath her body and holding her warm breasts, I humped slow, steady, yet forcefully, until I couldn't hold back any longer. I busted inside of her it seemed like endlessly. When my body eased up she turned herself around. Immediately she squeezed her legs together tightly to stop herself from shaking and then started kissing me all over. There was no more anger. I had conquered her, and in the process I conquered myself.

We played in the shower feeling free. No one was at home. We marked up each other's bodies, which was becoming a habit, because we still couldn't control our passion.

In the living room, all fresh wearing only her panties, she lay on a big pillow and sunk inside like a clam in its shell. Her henna designs made her look continuously royal, exotic, and erotic. She was just lying there staring at me with such love, but more than that. She had awe in her eyes. Or was it amazement?

I was wearing my boxers, about to go to my room and grab my T-shirt. But her stare held me there. "What's up?" I asked her. She broke out in a big-ass smile. I went and sat beside her. She threw her leg into my lap and pulled herself up. She turned in towards me, then straddled me. She just began hugging me, her head lying on my shoulder. We just sat silently like that, no sex, just hugging and rocking. I thought my heart would burst.

In my room her soft hand rubbed a light coat of oil onto my skin: my neck and shoulders, then arms and chest and stomach. She took much longer than I would have taken getting myself ready to get dressed. But it felt a million times better letting her do it. As she finally got down to my calves and ankles, she began rubbing oil onto my feet. Suddenly she just looked up at me from below and smiled.

She lay in my lap so I could do her next. As I touched different parts of her body with the oil, I was watching her subtle reactions, her goose bumps and excited extended nipples, how her toes curled when I oiled the insides of her thighs.

I dropped some tiny droplets of fragrance onto her neck from a small crystal bottle. I pressed my nose to it to see how it mixed with the natural scent of her skin. I got high and found my tongue inside her mouth. We were sliding and climbing and climaxing all over again.

Later, after we were finally fresh and dressed, she came and sat in my lap, holding her gift. I finally unwrapped the ribbon and opened the box and inside of it was another box wrapped in a maroon ribbon with a maroon bow. I just looked at her and she cracked up laughing, so pleased with herself. I unwrapped the maroon ribbon and opened the box and there was another box with a green ribbon and bow. She laughed again. The next box with the blue ribbon and bow had something inside. I opened it and peeled back the tissue paper. It was baby clothing, a tiny little yellow dress and laced socks, all-in-one pajamas and booties and baby shoes, a baby boy's jumper and a matching hat. I held the dress up looking at it curiously. She leaned in and kissed me on the cheek. I looked up at her. She smiled, and said softly, touching herself, "Babies please."

I just looked at her recalling what was happening between us when she first gave me this gift. It was the day after the Coney Island trip, the fight and the black eye. She must have bought these expensive baby clothes, with the price tags still attached, sometime after we had our talk about marriage in the ice cream store. I thought about how she seemed to never have doubted her love for me. She seemed to never have doubted that she wanted to live her life with me, have children for me. The more I thought about it, the more emotional I felt. The feeling began to overpower me.

She reached back in the box again and pulled out a slim box wrapped in a gold ribbon with a miniature gold bow. She handed it to me. I hoped it was not jewelry or anything expensive. I felt the meaning behind the baby clothes, and her intention and loyalty were more than enough and greater than anything else.

But she insisted and her eyes were so eager. I unwrapped and opened the slim box and discovered two season passes to the New York Knicks basketball games at Madison Square Garden for the upcoming season.

59

THE CLOSING

Naja was extra sleepy on Thursday, the morning of our house closing. Akemi and I picked she and Umma up late last night from Temirah Auntie's home. Their women's planning meeting ran overtime. Now we had no choice but to rush along because this was sure to be a long, long day for each of us.

After prayer and breakfast, we four dashed out. Naja was in Ms. Marcy's hands. We escorted Umma to work. Then I took Akemi to her uncle's house where she wanted to go to continue her preparation for her show, which was coming up in only two days. I promised to pick her up in Manhattan at 9:00 P.M. She was going to miss the closing but I was cool with that. It really was Umma's day more than anyone else's, although we would all live in and work to renovate and enjoy the new house, *inshallah*.

Besides, I had never showed or tried to tell Akemi about our new house. I wanted to be sure that Mr. Slerzberg actually showed up and signed the documents. I was already concerned about him possibly disappointing Umma.

Sensei was settled and calm when I arrived for weapons training.

"You seem tired," he said to me after we exchanged greetings. I guessed he was right. When I thought about it for a moment, it was completely different having a wife. I had gained so many new feelings and experiences, but was missing out on a lot of the time I usually spent alone. Instead of reading and thinking or sleeping, I found myself thinking only of the women in my life, their feelings, safety, and security.

"But you also seem peaceful and happy. What an amazing story," Sensei said as though he was considering the thought right that moment. "What story?" I asked. "Your young life," he responded. "You must be careful," he warned. "Enjoy life, but don't let down your guard. You are always a target when you have so much more than other men have. Continue training, conditioning, and keep your mind very alert."

"That's what I am here for, Senseisan. What do you have for me today?"

"There is no rush," he said oddly. "Let's take a walk outside." He was already headed to the door before me. I followed him, thinking how in seven years, I had never stepped outside of the dojo with Sensei. I wondered what was up. He placed the CLOSED sign in the window and closed and locked up the dojo.

Outside the sun was brilliant. The Brooklyn streets were crowded as usual, people going everywhere and nowhere at a fast pace. As we walked the block, it felt good to have Sensei at my side.

"You have to teach me to walk like that," he said, smiling his rare smile.

"Like what?" I asked. But he didn't answer.

"Akemi Nakamura," he said suddenly yet casually. "You know I wondered if she was from the well-known Nakamura family of The Pan Asian Corporation in Japan. When I read her father's name and signature on the document she handed to me, I was certain that I was right.

"What a huge accomplishment," he said, looking for my response. This time, I did not answer.

About seven and a half blocks over he stopped. We were facing a little cement island where a few older Asian men were gathered. We crossed over toward them.

"I want you to meet my father," he said, and began bowing

and speaking to the Japanese elder men. He singled out his father once he had given everyone the greetings. He introduced us. *"Hajime Mashite Boku wa . . ."* I showed him respect and used my greetings in their language. His father seemed surprised. I assumed that was because I was Black or because I was young, I don't know which one.

His father's skin was smooth and his eyes were serene. He was with a male friend playing a game when we interrupted. After our introduction he sat down and resumed his game.

"Do you play chess?" Sensei asked me. "I do," I answered. "Well, this is an ancient game called 'Go.' These men play here every day," he informed me. "The Japanese are the masters of this game.

"People all around the world play it. But most of the young have lost interest. My father and his friend have been playing this game for many years. In fact it never ends until one player gives up. My father never gives up."

I was honored to meet his father. It put a much more personal dimension into our relationship. But I didn't understand his approach to today's weapons class. I had only the scheduled two hours to give my attention and I wanted to spend the time learning not chilling.

I decided to be patient because with Sensei there was always a lesson.

"The board for Go is much bigger than a chessboard," I observed.

"Yes, it's more complicated than chess. It is a war over territory based on life. There are nineteen by nineteen intersecting lines, and three hundred sixty-one spaces. There is much more space to move around in, just like our world. But of course the more freedom we have, the greater our chances of making a mistake.

"The superior Go player is the best thinker," he said focusing on the board game.

"How does anyone know who is the best thinker?" I asked him.

"Great question." He smiled. "The best thinker is the one who can think ahead of the present time and set a strategy in motion that will secure his future. It should be a strategy that his opponent cannot foresee. Because, of course, if your enemy can detect your next move, he will do everything within his power to surround you and capture the territory you thought belonged to you." He paused, giving the words time to soak into my head.

"You see, this game Go is a game about strategy, but it is more about balance."

"Balance," I repeated.

"Sure. Sometimes a new player mistakenly believes that all he has to do is make the most aggressive moves," Sensei said.

"But you do have to be aggressive in life to win," I challenged.

"True, but when you are out of balance and too aggressive in this game, you end up leaving an area uncovered. Your opponent picks up on it and exploits your weakness."

I thought about what he was saying. It sounded true.

"Meanwhile, men who are held back by their own fears play this game too close to the edge of the board just to be safe, but this type of man never gains any territory.

"On the other hand a man who is too eager to control *all* of the territory jumps in the middle of the board and plays too high. He always ends up getting invaded." Sensei was explaining slowly and carefully. I listened and began to understand it was his way of talking to me about real life without getting too personal, which he probably knew was not acceptable to me.

"The thing about this game that is different from chess is that once a player puts his stone on the board in a particular area, it can never be moved, never. This means that before a player makes a move he has to think very hard and very much ahead about the outcome because he will not receive a second chance. He can never move that stone out of that position."

In a café Sensei treated us to lunch, a wedding gift, he said. In the course of us eating, he finally came around to a clear point. "I'm impressed with you, my student, because you have demonstrated the ability to think and do what you believe in, under a tremendous storm of pressure that surrounds each of us every day. So far you seem to have designed a strategy for your life without duplicating what everyone else is doing."

As I thought about his words to me, I wondered what effect his admiring me would have on our future lessons. He was a master and I was his student. Perhaps he thought I had done something great. But maybe I should just get him a Quran, because all that I was doing was trying to follow the strategy that was designed by Allah. Sensei was mistaken in giving me the credit.

I figured he was right about the point of the game of life being to achieve balance. It became clear to me that an excellent thinker and fighter like Sensei could easily be out of balance without the spiritual knowledge that a Muslim has. And the peace that I had achieved at my young age was probably more about setting limits and enjoying more by not trying to have everything.

Monica Abraham, Esq., had one conference room in her Brooklyn office, surrounded by rows of shelved books. Her degrees were displayed at the top of the room close to the ceiling. I guessed that's how highly she thought of them. She probably had to work very hard to earn them, I thought. Her first degree was from Howard University. Her law degree was from Yale.

She took charge of our meeting and handled Mr. Slerzberg and his wife like an expert. Her paperwork stretched across the conference table in short piles, pages opened up to where the signatures needed to be placed.

She treated Umma like an elite client and not a child the way some American professionals tended to treat foreigners who could not speak English well.

After the contract signing, Umma slid the $80,000 bank check across the table and into Monica's hands. Monica handed the check over to Mr. Slerzberg and explained that it deposited as cash and should be available to him the same day as he deposits it in the bank. I paid the other related closing fees with separate checks, which Umma of course signed.

Our attorney looked at me curiously when I handed Mr. Slerzberg fifteen hundred dollars cash of my own money. But that was the side deal I made to get him to move out of the house within two weeks. It was worth it to me and I didn't mind using my own money to make it happen. Mr. Slerzberg counted and recounted the cash. He seemed to like it more than the huge bank check that represented Umma's seven years of careful and exhausting hard work.

Mr. Slerzberg placed copies of the keys to all of the entrances to his house in the trust of our attorney. I joked with myself, thinking there was no risk involved in him turning over his keys before actually moving out. Mr. Slerzberg knew I had been inside of his house and was one hundred percent sure that there was nothing in there worth stealing. In two weeks, we would move in.

In the conference room I embraced Umma. I could feel her breathing a sigh of great relief.

60

GRINDING

I knew we had to keep on pushing because now financially we were next to broke. We still had the minimum one hundred dollars in the bank to keep Umma's account open and active. I still had most of my personal savings, but when you are used to having money, even money that you bank and don't touch, there is a terror that comes when you're down to having none. I'd seen other people walk, sit, and stand around with their pockets flat, worrying but not working and not planning to work. I'd seen enough teens who sat and waited for their parents to toss them a crumb for good or bad behavior. I couldn't do it like that. I couldn't live that way.

Umma and I still had our jobs and the income we earned. And our attendance, work, and reputation were unmatched. Through Umma Designs we would have to stay grinding to replenish our treasure chest. I reminded myself to be positive because it was no small thing that now we owned a home.

I had my eye on that league money now like never before. Vega gave me credit at practice every day for the business approach I took toward my game and of course because of the way my skills, he said, made him look good.

On Thursday night when I met up with my wife at the museum, she had three copies of the Museum of Modern Art program for her art show. It was a fancy pamphlet printed on expensive paper, "a big deal," as her cousin pointed out.

I carried her shopping bags. At our Brooklyn apartment in our bedroom, she opened one of her boxes, peeled back several layers of rice paper, and revealed a beautiful white kimono made of one hundred percent silk. Instead of embroidery, Akemi used a jet black marker and drew the New York City skyline on the bottom part of the kimono. The images were delicate and intricate and accurate. I imagined that she had seen the skyline from the Empire State Building or from the distance in Edgewater, New Jersey, where you can stand right at the Hudson River and look across at the sparkling skyline. She used some type of dye or watercolor to create the brown and grey buildings as well as the colorful skies with the setting sun descending from over New York City.

The sleeves were a wicked cut widened at the wrists. As she draped it over herself and extended her arms, I could see the intricate designs she had drawn. It was awesome to me. Umma would have done the borders with a needle and thread and made it more than exquisite. But Akemi used a marker and paintbrush and made it incredible also.

I called Umma and Naja in to take a look. Umma walked a circle around Akemi. She touched her shoulders and spun Akemi around so that the back of the kimono was now facing me. I could now see how she had painted the rising sun of Japan on the back. I looked at it all once again and put it together in my mind. In front of her was New York City. Behind her was Japan. On her sleeves were the blue waves of the ocean.

With her lovely hand-drawn and hand-painted kimono Akemi had achieved the impossible. She had impressed Umma with designs that Umma had not thought of herself.

My mother lifted the garment off of Akemi and laid it across the bed to get a full view. She stood staring. I knew what she was doing. Probably her mind was flashing a million different patterns and designs of kimonos she could create. Her mind just worked that way naturally. Probably she had already concocted an idea of a kimono she could design and sew from scratch as a gift to Akemi. Her heart worked like that naturally.

"I want to make something too," Naja said, speaking in Arabic. "You guys are just too good. I'll never catch up." Umma hugged her and I did too and Akemi joined in also. "You will learn," Umma promised Naja.

We enjoyed a late-night meal made of Umma's pre-prepared foods. The seasoning soaked in and blended so well it was better than freshly cooked.

After Friday night's ball practice I threw water on my face and hands with a bit of soap, rinsed off, jumped in my jeans and a fresh white tee, and draped a dress shirt over my shoulder. I bounced to meet Akemi on the east side of Midtown Manhattan where she was wrapping up a dinner along with the other teen artists being featured at the MoMA tomorrow.

I didn't know what to expect. Whatever it was, I just wanted my girl with me. We'd race back to Brooklyn, make prayer, eat, and jump in the bed. I needed at least ten hours of rest for the killer schedule I had been keeping this week, and to have the endurance I wanted at the big Brownsville game tomorrow. Akemi needed to rest up for her show also. She had been working and pushing herself hard. They had been working her like crazy too.

When I arrived at the place, the man at the front door asked me to put my dress shirt all the way on. So I did. I weaved in and around the tables. The teen artists and some businesspeople and chaperones were in a reserved section, about twenty-two of them. I could tell they had already eaten. A couple of them were sharing desserts. Many of them had broken up into cliques and were conversating.

Akemi jumped up as soon as she saw me. I walked toward her. She maneuvered toward me. As soon as we reached each other we were holding hands. I pulled her a bit closer and turned to leave out the door.

As we were walking, a woman from the VIP area followed us. She began clearing her throat loudly enough to catch my attention.

"Do you mind if I ask who you are?" she said in her high-pitched voice tone. I introduced myself. She introduced herself. "I'm Linda from the museum. You are?" she asked again after I had already told her my name.

"Akemi's husband," I clarified. She laughed.

"Well, I know that can't be true. I know for a fact that Akemi Nakamura is only sixteen. But I can certainly understand why any young man would admire her, she's quite lovely," Linda said, pausing for my reaction.

Akemi leaned in against me affectionately. While I looked down on this woman, who was at least a foot shorter than myself, I could see that she was nosy and intimidated. But she was more nosy than intimidated.

"Well, I see you certainly are lucky. She seems to admire you too."

"Good night," I told Linda, and we left. Akemi never looked back. In the warm train seats Akemi laid her head against me, half asleep. I thought about how Americans take young love and young family for a joke. I wondered if they thought Akemi and I would be better people if we just made love and used a condom and didn't do anything crazy like get married. Or maybe they would've found us more acceptable if we just fucked without a condom and aborted the babies each time they popped up. Or maybe we would be considered more rational if we both fucked random people for recreation instead of getting "too serious at a young age." I was really understanding Umma's rage with the Americans on this topic.

Back in little Sudan in Brooklyn, we had showers, family prayer, and soup and salad. We kept it light.

Behind my closed door in my overheated bedroom, I could still see the light-blue summer night sky. With my window open, I could hear music streaming in. I lay on my single bed beneath a cool sheet with my wife. I felt her little hand stroking my body lovingly. She began combing through my nappy pubic hairs with her fingertips. Coach said sex would drain us. To be top-notch we needed to leave the females alone until after the game.

But she crawled on top of me nude, her hair brushing on my shoulders, her nipples brushing against my chest, her lips moving on my mouth begging to taste my tongue. I couldn't fucking resist her. I just didn't want to. And what better way to be rocked into a good deep sleep than this?

61

CELEBRATION

Even though it was very early, I felt good in the morning. I got my ten hours' rest and I could feel the difference. I showered before making prayer with Umma in our living room.

After prayer I woke Akemi with a hot cup of tea. I was serving her today. After today she would be serving me. Umma was excited about teaching Akemi to cook Sudanese foods and also to learn some of her Japanese recipes. But she respected the work that Akemi was involved in, especially after seeing her kimono art. She knew what it was like to have too many demanding jobs all at once. So she also served Akemi with care. I could see Umma's pretty fingers moving from the top of Akemi's head to the middle of her back, as she gave her one long beautiful black braid in an instant.

We all rode down to drop Naja with Ms. Marcy.

After a train ride together, I dropped both Umma and Akemi to Rockefeller Center. Both women had full days planned. Akemi had to have her hair and nails done at some Japanese salon where the Tokyo prices were triple the New York rates. She had to meet her translator and kimono team and get prepared for her public performance. I gave her a massive hug, lifting her off her feet. Then I had to push her away as she always had that lingering look in her eyes like she preferred to be with me. I had to smile when she went

from clinging to me to holding Umma's hand in the middle
of Rockefeller Square.

But I had to go to Cho's to make some paper. Everything is real, even when you are in love. I was hoping Umma
would enjoy her first language class. I thought three hours
was a long time to sit in one classroom, but I figured if she
was ever going to learn English, it had to start somewhere.
Even Umma had that mother's look that emerges on their
faces when their children are about to leave their side. I don't
know, women are like magnets, I thought. And as my father
would say, "Women are one hundred percent emotion. Love
them but don't obey them." There was a time when I did not
fully understand these words. But now I did, realizing that if
the women had it their way, they would just remain wrapped
up with their man and their sons and daughters all day and
nothing would get accomplished. Then of course every man
learns that if he doesn't accomplish anything, the same
women who didn't want you to leave their side would lose
their admiration and respect for you.

After work, Umma and I met up and taxied home to
Brooklyn. We scooped up Naja and headed upstairs to
shower and get fresh dressed. Naja wore a very beautiful *hijab*
that matched her up with Umma. Umma wore her *niqab* for
our trip out of our Brooklyn neighborhood, but removed it in
the taxi. I was surprised. Even though her thick beautiful hair
and pretty neck remained covered her face was opened and
exposed. I thought about it a minute, looked in the shopping
bag I was holding for her and soon figured it out. Umma was
still hoping to win over Akemi's aunt and uncle. She believed
she made some progress that day at Akemi's uncle's store
where she met them. I could see now that she had gifts in her
shopping bag again. I just smiled. Of course I believe in family, but in the case of Akemi and I, I believed that after they
were convinced that our love was true, and after a baby was

conceived and born, their connection to us would come about naturally.

Late-afternoon Manhattan was buzzing. The museum was in full use as New Yorkers and people from around the world moved in and out and around the place.

Inside of the museum, I could see the reception area still carved out by the velvet rope. There were tables and empty, used glasses left over. There were trays of mostly eaten finger foods and discarded bottles of wine. There were plenty of trash cans.

"This way if you would like to see the exhibit, sir," a friendly young white woman in uniform pointed.

"I want to have one of those pamphlets over there," I informed her. She went behind the rope and picked it up. I flipped through it.

Akemi Nakamura is a sixteen-year-old artist born and raised in Kyoto, Japan. Her father is Naoko Nakamura, the Chief Executive Officer and owner of the multinational Pan Asian Manufacturing Corporation. Her mother was celebrated North Korean author Joo Eun Lee, who died young of brain cancer.

Akemi is an only child and a student at Kyoto Girls' High School, an affiliate of Kyoto's Women's College, where her father serves on the board.

She is an artistic genius destined to make a tremendous mark on this wide world of art. Please allow her work to speak for itself.

Her exhibit, titled "Asia Celebrates Mother Africa," is incredibly controversial, personal, detailed, and unrivaled. Her decision to present the everyday beauty of African life, as opposed to disease, famine, death, hunger, war, and poverty, places her at the vanguard of forward-thinking youth, a true, rare, and artistic visionary.

We entered the wing of the museum which held Akemi's artwork. We were directed down a particular corridor where her work was carefully mounted on the wall and illuminated. I was amazed.

The first of seven pictures and paintings was mounted behind a glass frame. It was titled **"Mother Africa."** It was a drawing of two female hands, palms facing up. The design of the henna work on the hands was incredibly royal. In fact, it was familiar. I looked at it up close. I stepped back and looked at it again. I went into my memory and saw the exact moment in the lobby of The Palace Hotel, where Akemi flipped my mother's hands open and studied her palms. These are Umma's hands, I told myself.

What kind of a great mind does it take, to take a picture with your eyes and reproduce it without a model or photograph? I began to see even more clearly now the beauty of Akemi's mind and the talent in her hands as I saw the intricate lines she had drawn with her pencil, and the way she worked real Sudanese henna into her creation. I certainly understood the time it must have taken for her to do such incredible drawings. I understood why she needed to shut everybody down and close them out of her studio and go deep.

The second drawing, in which she used pencils, markers, and paints, was titled **"Sacred Modesty."** It was also of Umma, peeking out from behind her veil. The way she drew the decorations on the veil Umma wore that day was precise, accurate, perfect. The way she captured the extreme beauty of Umma's slim face, her big dark, beautiful, soft, concerned eyes and both the feeling and expression that Umma carried made the picture seem like a real live person, a "Mother Africa," a queen. They were right. These pieces of art were unusual. They captured the true beauty of a slice of African life. Like the drawings inside of the African pyramids, which never told a lie, and were never matched or rivaled by any other artistry, Akemi's artwork was the truth.

The third picture was titled **"Humility."** It was a drawing of an Islamic mother and son bowed in prayer to Allah. She captured with her pencil the posture of the prayer, along with the fold of the clothes that the mother and son wore while making the prayer. She saw so much, I said to myself. She was watching, even when we did not know she was watching. Even more, she was using everything in her environment to create her masterpieces. It was ninja-style, I smiled to myself. It was the ability to take what others take for granted or even throw away and make something useful and beautiful with it.

The fourth picture was titled **"Black Beauty."** It was definitely Naja. It was an up-close drawing of my sister wearing her *hijab* proudly. It was the way she caught the look in Naja's eyes, the confidence and inquisitiveness, which made the picture unique. There was no shame or regret in this Muslim girl child. There was no hostage in the *hijab*. There was no hunger or poverty or abandonment. In the drawing, Naja looked like she had the world at her feet and a bright balanced future where her beliefs were an asset, not a curse.

The fifth drawing/painting was titled **"The Young Leopard."** It was me. It threw me back a bit. It was me in the winter the first day that she and I went out on a date. It was my *exact* face. The hair on my head in the drawing was my *exact* hair, which she had collected so quietly in the barber shop that day. I was sure of it. The clothes were drawn exact, my leather jacket and suede Polo shirt. My Lo jeans and even my kicks were the ones I rocked that day. She had poked life-sized holes in the painting and used real laces in the drawing of my Nikes. She even had them tied as I tied them then. This picture was tall, life-sized, about six feet tall and two feet wide.

The sixth drawing/painting was titled **"The Proof."** It was of five beautiful Sudanese women standing sideways in a line wearing beautiful bejeweled garments. They were all looking at something with excited eyes. I wondered what Akemi meant by "The Proof." I thought about it. The familiarity of the art was in the third woman, who resembled Sudana. Yes, it was her. Every set of eyes on each of the young females in the drawing seemed to be focused on something they were all waiting for. It was as though the drawing had energy, even though it was an inanimate object. After staring at it for some time, I figured these were the young Sudanese women Akemi saw at the wedding who, like all of us, were in awe of the bride and the whole feeling of the celebration itself.

The seventh drawing/painting was titled **"Missing You."** It stopped us cold, Umma and I.

"Look, it's our father," Naja whispered. "It is the same as the picture Umma has in her room. I know, because Umma only shows me one picture of Father." Umma and I said nothing.

"And look, it says here that she made this painting using pencil, markers, paint, and cayenne pepper, cumin, turmeric, black cardamom, and coffee beans! That's really nice. Don't you think so?" I heard her, but I didn't respond. I was connected to Umma's feelings and her eyes were welling with tears.

We waited for her from five-thirty until seven when the museum closed. We were supposed to meet her at 6:00 P.M. I was pressed because I had to get to Brownsville, change into my game clothes, and play ball for the league.

"She has probably gone to dinner with her family," I said to Umma and Naja.

I called her Queens apartment and left a message on her voice mail.

I called her cousin and the phone just rang.

I decided that she definitely went out with her family to celebrate. They must have insisted and that was fine.

"We should go home. She'll call," I assured Umma.

In my mind, I was worried about Akemi trying to make her way to our Brooklyn apartment late at night, alone. She is bold like that.

We taxied to our apartment. I made sure Umma and Naja were safely inside. I wanted Akemi inside too while I played ball. I needed that for my comfort zone, and my concentration level.

I arrived exactly at game time, no warm-up, no strategy talks. Vega didn't bark. He just pointed to the hundreds of faces in the overcrowded park, smiled, and said, "Make me look good."

I sank the winning basket. As the crowd cheered and my team celebrated, and the Brownsville fans threw a tantrum and Bangs sat at the top of the bleachers with her girlfriends, I ran off the court. "Vega, I gotta go. I'll check you later."

Sunday it rained and poured, a welcome break from the unusually hot and dry month of April. It was May now and it seemed even the seasons were confused. After prayers, I threw down some tea and left. It was family day, yes. But I was going to get Akemi.

I arrived in Queens at her uncle's house. I knew on a usual Sunday, he would be at work. No one was picking up the telephone there when I called from early this morning. I wanted to check.

I rang the bell, no answer. I walked around and tapped on the rectangular windows, which I knew led to her basement apartment, no answer. I walked into their backyard to the converted garage art studio. I had never been back there. It was impossible to see through the covered windows.

Drenched, I left Queens and headed to Chinatown to their family store. My clothes were dripping rainwater onto their store floor. I apologized, stepped out, wrung my clothes a bit, and stepped back in.

"Excuse me. I am looking for Akemi," I said to her uncle.

He was colder than usual. Saachi emerged.

"Akemi's not here," the uncle said.

"Do you know where she is?" I asked.

"Her father took her back to Japan yesterday. She was crying a lot," Saachi said. The uncle spoke rapid angry Japanese to Saachi, his young daughter. She disappeared behind the curtain.

"Is that true?" I asked him, but I knew it was true. My heart knew it. The uncle did not respond. I left.

I stood still in the open, while cups of pouring rain dropped down from the afternoon black skies. It seemed as if even Allah disapproved of what was happening today.

A police car rolled through, which almost never happened while I had been working on this block in Chinatown. The quick bleep of the siren switched on and then turned immediately off. It shook me to move on. I guessed that the uncle may have called the police because he felt threatened by what he thought I might do stationed outside of his store door.

Instinctively, I walked to Cho's.

He had no customers in the rainstorm. He looked surprised to see me on one of my days off, but wasn't really the smiling type. He walked over and placed his hand on my shoulder.

"Japanese girl leave letter for you," he said.

"Akemi?" I asked.

"Not young pretty one who make bed in my basement, different lady," he said.

"Young?" I asked, trying to know if it was Akemi's cousin.

"Old chicken," he responded. I took the letter, flipped it around, just thinking.

"Japanese girl drive you crazy!" Cho guaranteed me.

"Thanks, Cho. Do you mind if I go to my locker for a moment?" I asked.

"You don't have to ask," he said earnestly.

I put my three-carat diamonds on the jeweler's counter.

"Diamonds are one thing you can count on through the years," my father had said when he dropped them into the palm of my hand. "Use them when you feel trapped."

"Give me a good price for them," I asked.

"Where did you get them?" they asked.

"From Africa," I responded. "How much will you pay for each of them?"

I had this same conversation with twelve jewelers before I accepted the price of fifteen thousand dollars for one of the diamonds. The two remaining ones, I wrapped back up and put away.

In the Manhattan travel agency, I purchased a ticket to Tokyo, Japan. With the ticket in hand, I could get my passport issued in three days. I also purchased a rail pass to Kyoto on the Shinkansen bullet train.

I could carry up to ten thousand dollars cash with me into Japan, without raising any suspicions or tax issues.

At the translator's, I paid a rush fee to translate the letter which Akemi left for me. I wanted to know what it said. But it didn't matter. Either way, I was going to Kyoto to get my wife.

You can get in touch with Sister Souljah:

E-mail: *sistersouljah@sistersouljah.com*

Mailing address: Sister Souljah,
Souljah Story Inc.
208 East 51st Street, Suite 2270
New York, New York 10022

Business and book
speaking events: *souljahbiz@earthlink.net*

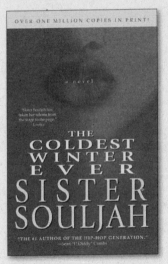